The Accidental Oligarch

A Ukrainian Saga

David Hoffman

Cutting Edge Press

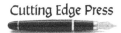

Cutting Edge Press

Part One

Chapter One

Kyiv, Ukraine, 2013

Yavlinsky looked up to see Mykola holding Oksana in his gloved hands. The exotic Royal Python was a favorite in the "Animals Island" exhibit at the Kyiv Zoo. Black with gold and tan blotches, it was coiled in a ball, a little tongue flicking from its small head. The terrarium lay empty.

"What are you doing!" Yuri cried. "Where are you taking Oksana?"

Yuri looked over Mykola's shoulder and saw a silver Land Rover, a man dressed like a chauffeur standing by its open door.

"For him?" asked Yuri, tilting his head towards the car.

"Tak," said Mykola. "The zoo is selling all the animals."

"How much?" asked Yuri.

"For me? Fifty Hryvnia," said Mykola.

"No, I meant how much did the director get? What did he sell Oksana for?"

"I think 3000."

Yuri spit on the ground and kicked at the snow.

"Fucking asshole. We can't do this, Mykola. Oksana's sick, for one thing. You see that white cheesy stuff in her mouth? The animals don't belong to the director. This sucks." Yuri shook his head.

"Look, Yuri, I understand," said Mykola. "But we don't have money to feed all the animals. It's a gift to some oligarch's daughter. They'll take good care of her."

"Fuck that!" Yuri said.

Mykola shrugged. "They're taking one of the brown bear cubs, too—Volodymyr. I know how attached you are to him. But there's nothing we can do."

Yuri threw his cigarette on the ground, crushed it with his boot. Then he turned and walked toward the director's office. Like many of his compatriots, he could profit from better dental care. His skin was too white, and it itched. He wondered if he was lacking in vitamins. He kept his eyes keenly on the path before him as if the zoo were an obstacle course.

He passed by the striped hyenas and several empty cages and turned up the pungent path by the elephants, where a group of students stood gazing. Then he climbed the stairs to the red brick administration building. The smell of dung hung heavy in the air. The dead eyed secretary kept him waiting a long time, but finally she allowed him into the director's office. The room was paneled in fake wood. A crystal chandelier, missing many of its prisms, hung incongruously from a ceiling yellowed with peeling paint. The walls featured photographs of the director shaking hands with a variety of politicians.

Evgeni Khrytor was a large man, overweight, with a pockmarked face and hair dyed the color of ink. He wore a blue serge suit and bright blue tie and held a cigarette in his left hand while offering his right to Yuri. "What can I do for you?" he asked.

"It's about the python, sir. It's sick. I didn't know if you knew," Yuri said.

"All the better," said the director. "We got 1500 for him. If Mr. Melnik had waited a few days, he might have gotten it for free." He took a drag on his cigarette, looking quite pleased with himself. Yuri knew he had pocketed the other 1500 for himself.

"Are all the animals for sale?" asked Yuri, feeling queasy.

Director Khrytor looked suspiciously at him. "Yuri, you know how much I care about each and every animal in the zoo, don't you? But with this recession, the government cut our budget by 85%. I had to do something. I've tried to protect the primates, but frankly, nothing can work. We're at the end of the line. Starting next week, we'll be giving the animals away for free to anyone who can feed them."

The Director tapped the end of his cigarette into a tin ashtray on his desk. He paused before taking another drag. "But I'm glad you came in. I've been wanting to talk with you. I'm afraid we can't meet our payroll again next week. I'm going to have to let everyone go except the vet and those with the most seniority. Yuri, you may be a natural with snakes and elephants, but what can I do? You're young—you're the first to go. I'm sorry." He held out his hand.

Yuri's stomach churned. He was afraid he might throw up on the director's Persian carpet. As he shook the director's hand, he tried not to show his despair. He avoided eye contact, turned and started to walk out.

"Yuri, before you go. The elephants' beds haven't been changed in some time. They really stink. Could you clean that up before you leave?"

Yuri glared grimly at the director and walked out. A cold wind blew dirt and leaves in the air and dark clouds were gathering. The smell of animals pervaded everything. He knew the order to clean the elephant pen was meant to demonstrate the

5

director's superiority. They all acted like that. They not only stole from you, but they also had to humiliate you as well.

He walked towards the shed where his locker was, passing by the baboons. He stopped and watched a female grooming one of her babies and felt a strange desire to trade places with her. He wondered how many of the animals would end up in the private zoos of the rich and powerful. *If we can't take care of the animals, who the hell is going to take care of us?* He wished there were zoos where someone would take care of him.

At the cage with the baby gorillas. Lucy, the smallest, recognized him, scampered up to the bars, and stuck out her hand. "I'm sorry, Lucy," he said. "I don't have anything." He felt himself about to cry but instead he turned and went into the shed and emptied his locker.

After a minute he stopped and put his things back, turned and walked to the elephants. He picked up a shovel and entered through the back of the enclosure. There were only three elephants left. Two had died recently. The paddock was empty. The acrid smell made his eyes water. He took the power hose from the wall and used it to drill a hole through the layers of dung and straw so he'd be able to get his shovel down to the cement floor under the shit. The floor sloped to the rear where drains could carry away the urine and the water when it was cleaned. As he shoveled the putrid waste into a cart, the old bull, Danylo, sauntered in and waved his trunk at Yuri. The elephant's eyes were bloodshot and unfathomably sad.

"Yo, Danylo," said Yuri, looking up. He didn't stop shoveling. He and Danylo were old friends. "What's up? It's getting kind of rank in here, old man." The bull went over to his feed bin, but there were only scraps of hay left. His tail twitched. Yuri had managed to clear half the paddock floor. He took the power washer from the wall again and sprayed the floor down. He heard Mykola calling him and walked out the back.

"Hey, Yuri, how'd it go? Did you see the boss?" Mykola asked.

"Yeah. I guess they've sold off what they can. Next week they're going to give away the rest for free to anyone who can afford to feed them," said Yuri.

"You see, Yuri? I told you; they're really democrats at heart," Mykola joked.

"Look, Mykola. It's over. The boss let me go, said they can't make payroll. We're all out of a job, you too probably." He looked at Mykola and nodded.

Mykola shrugged. "I was expecting it." They stood looking at each other, not saying anything. Finally, Mykola spoke again. "Hey, Yuri, help me give that guy his bear cub. Then let's go get a beer."

They walked past the lions, the zebras and the lone orang-utan, provoking a wave of chattering. It was nearing feeding time. The large brown bears were swaying back and forth as if listening to some inner music while the cubs wrestled with each other. A group of mothers and their children stood watching. Yuri and Mykola entered from the back. The bears were used to them. Stocky, with a muscular hump between their shoulders, they walked with an awkward pigeon-toed gait. Mykola carried a small cage the chauffeur had brought. Yuri threw a little food in a corner, drawing away the two adults and the male cub. Pulling the smallest cub, a female, away from her brother and enticing her into the cage left Yuri feeling hopeless.

Mykola and Yuri carried the cage to the chauffeur waiting by the open trunk. The cub licked Yuri's hand with her pink tongue. The python was already in the back seat in a smaller cage that rested on a white sheet. Yuri and Mykola lifted the cage, gently tilting it to fit under the roof of the trunk, but the chauffeur came from behind and pushed the cage in with a jerk, sending the cub sprawling onto her head. Yuri wanted to hit him. The man slammed the trunk, got in the car and drove off. "Mother fucker!" Yuri shouted after him.

When he turned back around, Yuri saw the director at the top of the drive. He seemed to be pointing at them. A small man in a blue suit and gold wire rim glasses, carrying a leather brief case hanging on a strap across his chest, walked towards him.

"Are you Yuri Yavlinsky?" the man demanded.

Yuri looked at him suspiciously. "I am."

"Were you born on August 14, 1985 in the city of Odessa?"

"I don't understand. Who are you and what is it you want with me?"

"I'll explain in due course, but first I must find out if you are the right Yuri Yavlinsky," the man said.

"I suppose I am," said Yuri.

He wondered whether he should invite the man to meet in the administration building, but the little man in the cheap blue suit was already reaching into his briefcase. He pulled out an official looking document with a seal on it. Yuri wondered whether this might have something to do with some inheritance from his mother's state pension or some insurance policy. He tried to make eye contact, but the bureaucrat would not look up.

"Mister Yavlinsky, you are hereby summoned to the tax inspector's office on Wednesday, October 30, 2013 at 9 a.m., precisely. Do not be late." He thrust the paper into Yuri's hands and took out a pen from inside his jacket. "Sign here."

Yuri scanned the document. He was ordered by the tax court to testify at a preliminary hearing on a default judgment the next morning at the chief prosecutor's office. He was further advised that he could be accompanied by legal counsel, if he so chose. There was some official language he didn't understand and then this final line, "Failure to attend the hearing in person will result in your immediate incarceration."

Yuri felt his heart miss a beat. "What does this mean? I don't make any money to speak of. I don't own anything. You must have made some mistake."

The little man continued to hold his pen out for Yuri to sign. Yuri tried again to make eye contact, to no avail. He took the pen and scribbled his signature at the bottom of the page, then handed the document back to the man. The official reached into his briefcase again and took out an onion skin copy of the summons and handed it to Yuri. "Nine a.m. tomorrow."

Yuri stood for a minute watching the man walk back up the driveway to his small, black government car. The world made no sense.

Chapter Two

A convoy of black Ladas swung into the circular driveway of the Cosmos Club. Sandwiched between them was an armored silver Mercedes-Maybach S600, small flags affixed to its front fenders, in which sat Viktor Raskolnovitch, reportedly the richest man in all of Ukraine.

The cars halted in front of an ornate wrought iron entrance under a canopy supported by marble columns and a row of Grecian statues. A dozen bodyguards in black sports outfits holding Kalashnikovs sprang from the Ladas and took up positions around the entrance. The lead guard inspected the lobby, then spoke into a walkie talkie. Doormen, costumed in red and gold, opened the doors of the Mercedes. Three stunning blond women emerged, covered in furs. Snow flurries and a blustery autumn wind swirled around them. Victor made them wait as he finished a phone call inside the car.

The lead guard dismissed the doormen with a nod of his head and offered a hand to Raskolnovitch as he got out from the back seat. Dressed in a tan cashmere overcoat trimmed in ermine, and a brown fur hat, Raskolnovitch entered the club surrounded by his female escorts.

Inside hung a row of gleaming chandeliers under domed ceilings covered in Italian-inspired frescoes. Twelve-foot gilded mirrors lined the walls, reflecting the splendor of those who entered. Original works by French impressionists reminded guests that they were blessed to be in a temple of wealth. The Cosmos Club served the richest and most powerful men in Ukraine. There were no female members.

Relieved of their coats and hats, Raskolnovitch and his party entered a large atrium under a stained-glass ceiling. All three escorts wore couture cocktail dresses, one in a red silk outfit that showcased her abundant cleavage, another in a blue kimono style dress that was slit almost up to the waist. and the third a purple flapper outfit with cascading ruffles. The three blonds were each considerably taller than Raskolnovitch. The dozen or so lunch guests turned as one to see them.

Raskolnovitch was a short, stocky man in his mid-fifties, wispy-haired, with a nose made crooked from an earlier career as a professional boxer. He was unnaturally tan, dressed in a dark suit with a tie designed like a Miro painting. On his wrist was a gold and diamond encrusted Rolex, a gift from Ukraine's president. It was, he thought, his talisman.

He stopped to tell the women they would be dining alone while he went on to his meeting in a private room off the main dining area. They obediently withdrew to a round table in front of a massive fireplace bookended with enormous bouquets of orchids and roses. Raskolnovitch and his lead bodyguard entered through a door hidden in a quilted silk wall near the fireplace, with two other bodyguards taking up positions on either side of it, their hands folded in front of them like choir boys.

Three men, seated at a polished cherry wood dining table covered in white linen, rose as Raskolnovitch entered. The taller of the men, an American, Ralph Peterson, introduced himself with what Raskolnovitch recognized as a broad New England accent, holding out a large hand to him. He was outfitted in a pin-striped charcoal-grey suit, a blue shirt, and a narrow red club tie with a gold tie clip, his hair dyed chestnut. The two men shook hands. Peterson's grip was firm. His eye contact was a bit competitive, Raskolnovitch thought.

Next to Peterson was his Ukrainian-American interpreter, a former State Department translator, notable for his goatee and oversized black glasses. Raskolnovitch took a seat across from them, next to his accountant, Dmitri Prokofiev, wiry as a weasel.

Before they all sat down, a tall, broad-shouldered man with a shock of brown blow-dried hair and heavy-lidded, aggrieved eyes strode in with studied nonchalance.

"Hi, I'm Paul Manafort," he said to the American.

"Ralph Peterson," the man responded. "We've met before."

Manafort squinted. "Whereabouts?"

"Memphis, 1977, the Young Republicans Convention. I was a member of the Team, one of your whips when you were managing Roger Stone's campaign for chairman. I worked with him throughout the Northeast on the Reagan campaign after that while you were managing the South. You actually gave me a job in the Treasury Department after the election when you ran the White House personnel office. You had quite the mustache then, I recall," he said.

Raskolnovitch regarded this talkative American, who smiled like a Cheshire cat. "Thirty-seven years ago. Seems like yesterday." He rubbed his chin. "Ralph Peterson, Ralph Peterson," Manafort mused. "Yes, I remember now. You went to my alma mater. You were the one who threw up on Roger's shoes the night we partied on that Mississippi paddle boat." They both laughed.

"You know, Paul, I got introduced to this deal by Arthur Cohen, but when I saw you were the one putting it all together, I didn't hesitate," said Peterson. Looking across at the other men who were left standing, he added, "But we can reminisce later. Please excuse us, gentlemen." They all took their seats.

The maître d' entered with an $18,000 bottle of Louis Roederer, Cristal Brut 1990 champagne, which he held for Raskolnovitch's approval, then poured a glass for each of them. Raskolnovitch welcomed them all in Russian and offered a toast for the success of their project. He had invested a lot in this scheme. "You have come a long way. I want you to have every comfort while you're in Kyiv."

Peterson thanked Raskolnovitch in English for hosting him. "May I call you Viktor?" he asked. Raskolnovitch waited for the translation, smiled and raised his glass to him.

"Viktor, I know very little about you," Peterson said. "I did the usual due diligence. I learned you own the finest collection of Faberge Eggs in Ukraine, that you were a helicopter pilot in Afghanistan, and you went from salesclerk to owning the company in two short years. Most impressive. But tell me, in your own words, how'd you make your fortune?" He stopped and took a sip of water.

After the translation, Raskolnovitch leaned forward and said in Russian, "Actually, in this country it's very easy to make money. The difficulty is spending it." He gestured in the direction of Prokofiev. "This is why I have Dima. He's a certified genius. You know, he graduated first in mathematics in all Ukraine, and this in a country well known for mathematicians. We're a good team, Dima and me."

He waited for the translation before continuing. "You asked how I made my fortune. I'll tell you. It was very simple—a matter of basic arbitrage. I worked for a big company, buying and selling tobacco. When Ukraine won independence from Russia, there was little cash and much inflation. The old way, buy cigarettes for cash. The new way, borrow money, buy on credit, and wait while the price of cigarettes goes up and up. I also eliminated middle-men. Today, we control 99% of all cigarettes in the country, also a few steel mills."

Listening to the translation, Peterson nodded. "You make it sound easy," he said. "But please, if you don't mind my asking, with so much cash, how do you protect yourself from all the mafia we read about in the states?"

Raskolnovitch had kept his face implacable as the American spoke, but when he heard the translation, he turned to Dima and burst out laughing. These Americans are so naïve, he thought.

He waited to respond as five waiters came in bearing plates of foie gras garnished with wild pears in a licorice sauce. When they left, Raskolnovitch stood up. "Yes, it's true, much mafia in our country," he nodded, "but they don't bother me."

His expression turned fiercely proud, as if defiant. To the amazement of his guests, he slowly removed his suit jacket and tie and undid the top four buttons of his shirt. The two Americans across from him remained frozen in their seats. Pulling his shirt over his left shoulder, Raskolnovitch exposed a tattooed star and a more intricate tattoo of a domed church, a leaping stag, and a rifle wrapped in chains.

"I am *Vory*," he said in Russian. He tapped the star. "It means I spent time in labor camp, in the north, very cold, very hard. When I was a young man, I killed a policeman who tried to rape my mother. In the gulag I became *Vory*. *Vory* are like brothers. The Mafia won't hurt *Vory*." He put his shirt and jacket back on while the interpreter translated.

When he sat down, the silence was as brittle as frost. "Please, I explain," continued Raskolnovitch. "*Vory* are thieves, like a gang, but a good gang, like family, with its own language and own laws. We helped each other survive in Stalin's gulags and also here; but now thieves are bigger, working with the state, and the *Vory* have grown smaller. There are too many problems in

Ukraine. We need a lot of protection. To survive, one must have a *krysha*, as we call it, a 'roof.' My *krysha* is the president." He tapped his watch. "I helped make the president and he is very grateful."

Paul Manafort smiled, but said nothing. Raskolnovitch saw him as a rival for the president's affection and didn't trust him, but *a deal is a deal*, he thought. They ate their *hors d'oeuvres* in silence as they digested the conversation. The main course arrived: fricassee of lobster with chestnuts and pumpkin in a devil sauce followed by a dessert of pistachio and kumquat with red currants marinated in Arbois wine. Each side spoke among themselves without translation as they ate. Victor was happy to let them ruminate and plan, to have their English waft into the air.

When the dishes were cleared and a Taylor Fladgate Scion Vintage Port was served, they finally turned to the matter at hand, the purchase of the old Drake Hotel on Park Avenue in New York City and the construction of a 65-story luxury skyscraper: "Bulgari Tower," with apartments, a mall, private club and a spa. The project, its partners brought together by the seemingly redoubtable Paul Manafort, would be the largest commercial real estate deal in America. Victor expected a rich spoonful from this dessert.

Manafort spoke up. "Gentlemen, we agreed to put $10 million down and $880 million US upon closing, all in cash. It's a generous offer, we know, but a good one for our partners. So we are very happy," he said.

Peterson stood and raised his glass in toast. They all followed.

When they were seated, Manafort continued standing. "My friends, everything has been agreed," he said. "We will take ownership through a holding company, CMZ Ventures. The parent company is owned by a consortium of New York and offshore companies registered in Panama, the Cayman Islands, and Cyprus. All very legal with little tax exposure. The biggest companies, like Apple, do the same. Besides me, the investors are all Ukrainian, like our host, but the ownership of each company is also held by other companies registered in two dozen countries, like matryoshka dolls folded inside each other."

When he sat down, Ralph Peterson rose and offered another toast in English. The interpreter translated and they all stood and raised their glasses. "Nostrovia," said the Russians. At that, Prokofiev excused himself. "Time visit loo," he said in English. Manafort followed him.

Peterson and his translator spoke quietly to each other. Across from them, Raskolnovitch was bent over his phone.

"Well, Ralph, are you happy?" asked the interpreter.

Peterson smiled. "Like the monkey who peed on the cash register said, 'Pretty soon, this is gonna run into real money.'"

Victor kept his head down as Peterson took a sip of the port and then continued. "It's a good deal," he said. "Our creditors will be very happy. I'm a little nervous about all these offshore shell companies; but, like Paul said, there's nothing illegal about that. But I wonder where all this cash came from and who the unnamed silent partners are. If the source of it is illegal, we could get in deep shit for money laundering."

Raskolnovitch put down his phone and spoke to them in almost flawless English. "My friends, you have nothing to worry about. It's all very legitimate. Maybe some taxes are not paid and some officials got good bonuses, but that is how business is done in Ukraine. In the U.S. you have lobbyists. Bribery is institution-alized in your country. But not to worry. Everything's clean."

Peterson's eyes widened. "You speak English?"

"When I have to," Raskolnovitch said .

Chapter Three

Rabbi Morris Weissgold sat at a window seat in a café across from the bombed out Citizens Against Corruption office on Bankova Street in Kyiv, waiting for Dora to come out. The storefront window was boarded up with plywood. Yellow crime scene tape circled the building like some sick idea of gift wrap. The glass and debris that had littered the street was gone. Halfway through his fourth cappuccino, when a woman in a black raincoat and short blond hair stepped out of the office and locked the door, Morris felt his heart speed up. He recognized her immediately.

He left a large tip, slipped out of the café, and began to follow Dora at a discreet distance from the other side of the street. She walked with a Pilates posture and a chin-up determined stride. Three blocks from her office she got on a number 5 tram. Rabbi Morris texted his driver, who came up quickly. Twenty stops, later they saw her get off before the gate to a complex of white Ukrainian Baroque buildings topped with gold onion shaped domes. Although he had grown up in Ukraine, this was his first visit to the famous monastery of Pechersk Lavra. *Who was Dora meeting in such a holy place?*

Rabbi Morris watched her fall in with crowds of pilgrims, parishioners, and tourists entering the Dormition Cathedral, as if she too was entranced by the heavenly sounds of bells ringing from the Great Bell Tower. He sped up, closing the gap between them. When he entered, he lost sight of her for a moment, her blond hair now hidden under a black scarf. Moving closer, he looked up at the domed ceiling covered with frescoes of angels and martyrs and at the soaring columns. As a line of solemnly chanting monks, swinging incense burners, proceeded to the altar, carrying icons, he mouthed a prayer to himself. Even a devout if unorthodox rabbi could find solace and relief from intrigue in such a place.

He was pressed in just behind her, his chin almost resting on her head. Her hair smelled like lavender. He began to softly chant with the monks, his voice deep and mournful. She tried to turn her head to see whose voice this was so near to her, but the two of them were pressed too closely together. After a few minutes he began to whisper her name, as if a prayer, *Dora Osatinskaya, Dora Osatinskaya, Dora...*

Now she jerked around to face him. "Uncle Morris, oh my God, Uncle Morris!" she said in English.

He took her by the hand, pushing through the crowd into the bright sunlight outside, and led her to a wall in the back of the cathedral that overlooked the Dnieper River and the city of Kyiv below.

She threw her arms around him. "It's so good to see you, Uncle Morris, my favorite uncle!"

"Your only uncle," he remarked.

"Well, you're still my favorite." She looked at him quizzically. "But what are you doing in Kyiv and how'd you know I'd be here?"

"I just wanted to make sure you were in one piece after... you know. And as for locating you, the Company knows everything," he said.

"Don't joke. How'd you find me?"

"I followed you from your office. I wanted to make sure no one else was. They're not. Besides, it's fun being in the field again. I needed to refresh my stalking skills."

She stepped back from him and asked, "Did mom put you up to this?"

He laughed deeply. "No, but she's worried, naturally. I called her when I learned about the bombing, reassured her that you were OK."

"Am I?" she asked.

He smiled. "I told her they only wanted to scare you. They picked a time when no one would likely be at your office."

"How reassuring, Uncle Mo. Thank you. I'll try and remember that."

"Your parents were practically on their way to Newark Airport when I told them I was already coming," he said.

"That's screwed up," she said. "I suppose you promised to bring me back. Get me some desk job at a trading firm in Weehawken."

"Not a chance," he said. "You know me better than that."

He wondered whether this was the time to ask for her help. Her anti-corruption investigations exposed her to danger, as the bombing of her office attested; but what he wanted from her posed an existential threat to the powers that be. He decided to wait a bit longer. He didn't want to push her into it. The dangers were too real. *But hadn't she already chosen this path?*

She looked at him uncertainly. "Are you still a rabbi?" she asked.

"Once a rabbi, always a rabbi. But I'm a freelance rabbi, so to speak. I do a lot of subbing for other rabbis, like a substitute teacher."

She glanced around her. "Still working for Darth Vader? Mom said you were on loan to the White House."

"Not anymore. Couldn't stand all the gossip in the West Wing cafeteria. I'm not much of a desk job kind a guy."

"That's putting it mildly," Dora said.

"Decided to go private," he continued. "I'm a free dog now, a dog who's been let out of the kennel." He cocked his head. "But I put your name on a watch list before I left. The new guy on the Ukraine desk called when the Citizens Against Corruption office got bombed. Who do you think's behind it?" he asked.

"Who knows? Could be almost anyone. We've exposed a shit-load of corrupt officials," she said.

"That investigation you did of the Prosecutor General's office sure got a lot of attention at the White House, by the way."

"Pissed off a lot of people here, too. The PG's at the top of the food chain." She stared at him with cold blue eyes. "So, if mom didn't send you, are you here for work?"

He grinned. "I am," he said, looking around him, "but it's secret." He held his index finger over his mouth. "That's why I came to see you. I think you can help me."

"No way."

An older couple sat on the wall near them. Morris and Dora got up and walked slowly back towards the bell tower. "I just need your help getting some information," he said.

She stopped and turned to face him. "You know I won't do anything with the CIA. I can't. I'm an investigative journalist. My job is to expose corruption. That's our only agenda. If we're seen as agents of a foreign power, we'd lose any credibility."

He smiled. "I would never compromise you, Dora," he said. "But I've got some important information you should know about —and I think we can make a trade."

She looked doubtful. "What's it about?" she asked.

"It's about massive corruption and a threat to the western alliance," he said.

"Don't exaggerate, rabbi."

"I'm not," he said, fixing her with his smile.

"And what would you need from me?" she asked

"I need to get some bank records from a couple offshore shell companies. I think you could probably use some more creative methods to find them that I can't."

She stared at him, and Morris could tell she was deciding whether to trust him. Finally, she relented. "Tell me what you've got."

He exhaled. "OK, you know who Paul Manafort is?" he asked.

"Sure, he's the scumbag political advisor who helped Ukraine's sleazy president return to power."

"Exactly, but he's a lot more than that. He's one of the most significant political operatives of the past forty years." He went on to tell her how Manafort and his partner Roger Stone helped elect Ronald Reagan, then monetized their insider connections with a new kind of lobbying group that also managed political campaigns. If their candidate won, they had access to all the key players in the government, a unique advantage that earned them millions of dollars.

"You're still not telling me what this has to do with Ukraine. It's just politics. It's nothing illegal." They sauntered back to the wall. Dora took out a bag of breadcrumbs and started feeding the pigeons.

"You're right," Morris said. But Manafort, he told her, was brought to Kyiv to help rebrand and rebuild the Party of Regions after the 2004 Orange Revolution toppled the regime. "He succeeded by pandering to Russian speakers and bashing NATO. Six years later, with Manafort's help, the president was re-elected. The oligarch who was the main backer of the party was so happy with Manafort he bought him a \$3.6 million apartment on the 43rd floor of Trump Tower as a thank you gift."

"Nice bonus," said Dora.

"Yeah. But you can imagine how Washington freaked out. Manafort was turning one of our most important allies against us and pushing Ukraine back into Russia's orbit."

"That's seriously fucked up," said Dora. "But I don't see where I come in."

The bells of the Great Bell Tower began ringing again. A crowd of worshippers streamed out from the Cathedral. Morris and Dora moved to the end of the wall, scattering the pigeons.

"We think the president is laundering vast sums of money through some offshore shell companies set up by Viktor Raskolnovitch, an oligarch who's the main backer of the president. We need to find out what's in those shell companies."

"And how am I supposed to do that?" she asked.

"We've managed to identify several of these accounts. The real owner's names are hidden behind a 'nominee director,' some kid whose passport was bought or stolen and used to incorporate the company. He probably has no idea how his identity was used. We want you to find some way to use him to get copies of these accounts."

"OK. Suppose I do this. What does this have to do with Paul Manafort and 'the threat to the Western alliance'?" she asked.

He told her how the FBI was monitoring a deal that Manafort had put together with a *Who's Who* of Ukrainian mobsters to buy the old Drake Hotel in New York. Most of the funds were from Semion Mogilevich, the Don of the Russian Mafia who was on the FBI's Ten Most Wanted list. The other secret investors were Dmytro Firtash and Oleg Deripaska, both considered top associates of organized crime, and that same Viktor Raskolnovitch, who started out selling bootleg cigarettes and now controlled most of the heroin coming out of Afghanistan.

"It was all a massive scheme to launder funds," he explained. "Send 'dirty' money to reputable banks in New York for what appears to be a legitimate real estate deal and then send back 'clean' money from those banks to various accounts in Europe. Then the deal fell apart."

"Elegant," said Dora. She looked at Morris and squinted. A minute passed. She picked at one of her nails. "So, if I understand this, my office got blown up last week and now you want me to investigate the mafia? Am I missing something?"

"Not the mafia, just Raskolnovitch. The FBI is dealing with the Russian mafia. Our interest is with the President of Ukraine. Manafort is his political brains. Raskolnovitch is his main financial backer. We know very little about him. The French are also investigating him for bribes paid to a former French president. It could help us a lot if we could get a look at the accounts of some of his offshore shell companies."

He looked at her intently. "Dora, you're always reminding me to 'follow the money.' Ukraine is in the final stages of negotiating an association agreement with the European Union. The stakes could not be higher for Europe and the U.S. We need to get as much information as we can about the president and his inner circle." He stopped, realizing he was talking too much.

After a bit of silence, Dora spoke. "You know, Uncle Mo, when I was in high school I had two idols, Bruce Springsteen and you. Neither of you has ever disappointed me. I got into this anti-corruption game because I wanted to be like you. I never imagined I'd be sitting here in Kyiv with you like this discussing something this big or this dangerous."

She emptied the last of her breadcrumbs on the ground. "When do we start?"

Chapter Four

By the time Yuri got home, the snow flurries had turned to cascades of white and had begun sticking to the pavement, muffling the sounds of the city. He jumped off the trolley and walked the three blocks to his apartment with his head down against the wind. His flat was in an old stone apartment building on a street that once was lined with trees. The branches on the few that were left were bare. Garbage cans outside the building were overflowing. Ever since the recession, trash collection was intermittent at best. The family flat was on the seventh floor. The elevator worked when there was electricity. Yuri started to climb. The smell of cooked cabbage permeated the stairwell. It was too dark to see his breath. He felt his way along the walls. He was shivering and out of breath when he reached his floor.

He entered with his key. His sister Yana was there in front of him, putting on a coat. He seemed to startle her.

"What are you doing home so early?" she asked.

There was an edge of accusation in her tone. Yuri looked up and down at her. She was wearing knee-high leather boots she couldn't afford, a red mini skirt over black tights, and a white cashmere sweater that accented her breasts. Barely eighteen, Yana had a strong Slavic face and straight long blond hair tied with a red bow that matched her skirt. She wore altogether too much makeup.

She zipped up a coat of fake rabbit fur with a hood and started to walk past him. Yuri took hold of her wrist and stopped her. "Where did you get all that?" he said looking down at her boots and up at her outfit.

"None of your business. Let go of me."

"Did you steal all that?" he asked, still holding her.

"No, it's Christy's. She loaned it to me. Let go of me, I said."

Yuri let go of her wrist.

She faced him. "You didn't answer me. Why are you home so early?"

"I got laid off. The zoo's closing. They're giving away the animals and the workers, too, I suppose. It doesn't matter. They haven't paid us for weeks. I'm broke." He took off his jacket and threw it on a chair, scattering bits of snow on the floor.

A piece of legal-sized paper fell from his pocket.

"What's that?" asked Yana.

Yuri had not wanted to tell her about the strange encounter at the zoo when he was served with a summons. He picked it up and spread it out. There in red ink, he saw again, "Failure to attend the hearing in person will result in your immediate incarceration."

Yana peered over his shoulder to read it. "It's nuts," he said. "They obviously have the wrong guy."

"What are you going to do?" she asked.

"I was going to ignore it."

"Don't be stupid, Yuri. Go there. You have nothing to hide."

"I'm not worried, not about that. I just need a job, but no one's hiring. The whole economy's in freefall." He felt like crying. His baby sister looked like a cheap whore. He had 100 hryvnia to his name, and he had been fired from the best job he ever had.

"It wouldn't be so bad, if your dad hadn't taken mom's pension when she died. Mom's money belongs to us."

Yana shrugged. She reached into her coat pocket and pulled out a bunch of bills, took a hundred note, and held out her hand to her brother. "Here."

He stared at the money, then met her eyes with a look of anger and contempt. "Yana, you're out of your mind. What the fuck are you doing? Do you have any idea what your dad will do to you when he finds out you're out whoring?"

"At least I'm doing something. All you ever do is talk," she said.

"Jesus, I hate what this country is doing to us," Yuri cried out.

"Yeah, I hate it too," she replied. "That's why I'm getting out. Christy and I have been offered jobs in Prague. I'll be gone before dad even realizes I'm not here."

"Jobs? What kind of jobs?" he asked. "Do you have no respect for yourself? Is this how you honor your mother? Are you not ashamed?"

She put the money back in her coat, opened the door, then turned again to face him. "You just stay in your room with Bubbie, Yuri, and draw your little pictures all night and think how virtuous you are. It's not going to put any food on the table. You and your friends can talk all you want about how the oligarchs are robbing the country, but there's nothing you can do about it, but starve. You're pathetic. So, come visit me in Prague when you've had enough."

Yuri thought about hitting her or tearing her clothes off and wiping the lipstick from her mouth. He felt something burning in his stomach, but he just stood there seething. Yana opened the door and walked out.

Yuri closed his eyes but refused to cry. She was right. He was powerless. At least the animals in the zoo would get fed. There was nothing for him here. The future was all in the past. The priests would get paid to keep the masses distracted. The rich would keep plundering the state while people like him would just have to learn to live without dignity. He hated it all.

He went into his room, which he shared with his 90-year-old great-grandmother. She seemed frightened to see him. "Who are you?" she cried out, holding a pillow before her.

"Bubbie, it's me, Yuri, your great-grandson. No need to be alarmed. I live here, right here, in the bed next to you."

She shrank into the corner. Yuri went to the closet and reached up on tiptoes and pulled out a large pen and ink drawing on paper rolled up in an old sheet. He sat on the floor by the foot of the bed and carefully unwrapped it. Just looking at it made him feel better. The painting was half filled with tiny portraits of famous people - Muhammad Ali, Mikhail Gorbachev, Marilyn Monroe and several hundred more. They were exact representations, each figure a half inch or smaller. The pen and ink design represented thousands of hours of meticulous effort. It was, if he said so himself, a work of extraordinary, if eccentric, genius. He was only able to draw at night when Bubbie and his family were all asleep. When he could get his hands on it, he smoked some amphetamine to stay awake. He loved the night. He thought about each of the animals he would never see again, the baby gorilla, the giraffe named Afanasyev, the birds, Danylo the elephant. Oksana.

Just then he heard a commotion, his sister's voice, his stepfather's. He had met Yana on the stairs and had dragged her back into the apartment and, drunk as usual, was yelling at her. Yuri jumped as he felt his stepfather hurl her against the wall. Yuri could hear her moaning in pain, her cries for help, but there was little he could do. His helplessness sickened him. The last time he tried to stop him, six months ago, his step-dad had broken his arm.

He had had to endure the screams of his mother from the time she remarried when Yuri was only eight. It was sad she had died, but also maybe a good thing.

Bubbie remained in the corner with her fingers in her ears. Yuri rolled up his painting again and put it back in the closet. Finally, he went out.

"I'm going for the cops," he said as he snatched his coat and went for the door. But his stepfather grabbed his shoulder, turned him and struck his face with his fist. Yuri crashed hard against the door, his head throbbing. Yana screamed. He could taste blood in his mouth. The big man kicked him once in his ribs. Yuri folded himself into a protective ball on the floor. He could see his father pulling Yana's hair and slapping her.

"If I ever see you looking like that," the man threatened her, "I'll get my friend Tomas to throw acid on your face and you'll be too scarred to ever whore again."

Yuri stood up on wobbly legs, supporting himself against the door, opened it, and left. He would sleep on the street, then turn himself into the prosecutor. There were no other choices left.

Chapter Five

"Dima, come with me to the house," Viktor Raskolnovitch said to his accountant as they were leaving the Cosmos Club. "I'm hosting a reception for the new Spanish Ambassador. We can grab a few private moments together. The girls can ride in your car."

They drove in their convoy east of the city to a small private airfield where a silver and blue Sikorsky S-92 Cougar helicopter sat on a helipad like a diamond tiara in a jewelry box. The Ladas circled the chopper. Bodyguards sprang out from them like toy soldiers. Waiting beside the helicopter was a pilot in a blue uniform with Raskolnovitch's insignia embroidered on a leather jacket . Raskolnovitch's driver jumped from the car and opened the door for him and his accountant.

"It's all warmed up and ready to fly," said the pilot.

"Good," answered Raskolnovitch. "I'll drive."

The three men and five of the bodyguards climbed aboard, followed by the women. Raskolnovitch took the pilot's seat and quickly took off. Visibility was awful, but the Sikorsky had state of the art instruments he could rely on. They flew over pine forests blanketed in snow. All was white, thought Raskolnovitch, in heaven and on earth. Vague outlines of a structure emerged majestically on top of a hill. Sitting before it was a lake, a perfect, unblemished circle of white; and, as they got closer, they could see the contours of a golf course with flags flying above hidden greens. Raskolnovitch felt at peace, like a god approaching his heaven.

The house was a 60-room, seventeenth century mansion where Catherine the Great had resided for a month in 1787 after annexing Ukraine. Four great turrets capped each corner of a chateau topped by gold crosses that shone through the snow. The most prominent feature was a set of enormous wooden doors two stories high with the likenesses of saints carved on them. A pink marble stairway leading up to it was fifty feet wide at its base, framed with walls topped with bronze statues of stags, the symbol on Raskolnovitch's coat of arms, which marked every article of clothing, bedding, cutlery or furniture that belonged to him.

At the top of the chateau's stairs, Raskolnovitch paused and turned to survey his vast estate. If only his mother had lived to see this, he thought. She died while he was still in Afghanistan. He had not been allowed to go home for the funeral. She had worked like a slave for most of her life in a steel mill near Donetsk in Eastern Ukraine, a mill he had recently purchased. Raskolnovitch's father had abandoned her while she was pregnant with Viktor. His father was never heard from again. An icy wind made Raskolnovitch's eyes water and he turned and walked inside.

A few hours later, the main ballroom had filled with the usual diplomatic crowd, an expat fashion opportunity not to be missed.

"Consul General Bertrand, thank you for coming. I know how busy you are. It's always a joy to see you," Raskolnovitch said in English.

"And you, Monsieur Raskolnovitch. I try never to miss your parties. Thank you for inviting me."

Raskolnovitch nodded. "You are most welcome."

Arnaud Bertrand was a regular fixture at the many diplomatic receptions in Kyiv. Viktor thought he must live on other people's *hors d'oeuvres* and champagne. Six foot six and slim, with greying sideburns and abundant, dark-dyed hair, he was somewhat hard of hearing and bowed like a butler to hear any conversation. Next to Bertrand was a stunning brunette with shoulder length hair dressed in a tight-fitting oriental style silk dress patterned in red peonies. Her lipstick matched the color of the flowers. With her stiletto shoes, she stood several inches taller than Raskolnovitch. She had dark almond shaped eyes. He liked her.

"Allow me to present my daughter, Antoinette," Bertrand said in English.

Raskolnovitch nodded. "Most beautiful name, Antoinette."

"Merci. My friends call me Toni."

"I see. I hope I can call you that."

"Absolument," said Antoinette with a practiced smile.

They were standing before a large Matisse collage, doves and shapes like hands in reds and blues, bordered by a huge, gilded frame, that Raskolnovitch had ordered in from Paris. He gestured towards it. "Do you like Matisse?"

"Very much," she said, "though I prefer his paintings and his sculpture." She studied the collage with some care. "I hope I am not being too impertinent," said Antoinette, "but the frame is all wrong. It's a beautiful Baroque frame, but it doesn't go with such a modern work of art."

Raskolnovitch felt a pleasing wave of surprise and amusement. He was not used to anyone saying anything but the most obsequious compliments. "You're right, Toni. I thought contrast would work, but no. You have good taste." He looked up to her and smiled.

A string quartet put down their instruments on the floor below and the room quieted.

"Please excuse me," interrupted the consul general. "My ambassador is about to offer a toast to the new Spanish ambassador and I must join him. I'm sure you will manage quite well without me." He glanced at Toni, bowed, and went down the wide staircase to the diplomatic reception below.

"You must go, too, I assume," said Antoinette.

Raskolnovitch was in no hurry. "There will be enough toasts without me, He smiled. "Officially, the host tonight is the EU representative. He likes to use my house. So I'll not be missed."

As Antoinette Bertrand studied the Matisse, Raskolnovitch studied her. "Tell me, Toni, are you visiting Kyiv for long?"

"No, I have moved here. I found an apartment near the Embassy. I'm studying art with Petro Bevsta. Do you know his work?"

"I heard of him, but not to recognize him," said Raskolnovitch. "Now I will buy something from him. So, you're an artist?"

"I'm learning."

Raskolnovitch felt unusually self-conscious with this woman. "Mademoiselle Toni," he said. "As a good critic of art, can I interest you in seeing my collection of Faberge Eggs? It's quite an important collection, really."

"Ah, I've heard about them," Toni said. "Who among us can resist a Faberge Egg?"

Viktor eyed her, then escorted her through the chandelier-lit hallways until they reached two massive oak doors. A uniformed servant bowed to them, opened the doors and stepped aside as they walked into the East Library, with its twin balconies that ran along three walls and a large walk-in fireplace at the far end.

Raskolnovitch gestured to a wall of glass display cases in

which glittered what had been once the czars' most prized posses-
sions. "They are quite beautiful, are they not?"

"As if God himself had made them," said Toni.

"The Romanovs had good taste in jewelry," he said. "My
Faberge collection is an expensive hobby, I'm afraid. It's getting
almost impossible to add to it." He thought this was an expression
of some humility. He watched to see her reaction.

"This one is my favorite," he said, opening one of the cases
and removing a green, gold and ruby enameled egg sitting on a
gold tripod with lion paw feet. On its surface were twelve panels
with miniature portraits in ivory of the Romanov family painted
in water colors and framed in garlands consisting of one-thou-
sand-four-hundred diamonds. Raskolnovitch saw Toni hold her
breath as he opened the egg to reveal its surprise, a jewelry box
studded in pearls and rubies and thousands more diamonds,
inside of which was a miniature replica of the Romanov crown.

"There are forty-three known Imperial Faberge Eggs left
from the original fifty. Only Viktor Vekselberg owns more. I was
very lucky to get this," he said.

As he turned and placed the egg back in its display case, Toni
said, "They're most extraordinary. You have expensive tastes."

Raskolnovitch laughed. "Yes, I like to collect rare and beautiful things. The more rare and more beautiful, the higher the
costs."

Antoinette looked directly at him. "My dad said you were the
richest man in Ukraine. How does one make so much?"

"It's simple. I have monopoly on cigarettes. Every time
someone buys tobacco, they pay me a little. Is not rocket science."

Antoinette frowned. "That's terrible, if you'll excuse me, but
don't you feel some guilt? You are killing people, and for what, for
your pleasures?" She shook her head. "It's horrible, grotesque, a
crime really."

He remained implacable. "People do what they want. I'm a

big believer in freedom. Personally, I don't smoke. It's a dirty habit. If people want to pay me for cigarettes, that's their problem and their right, too."

"You are too cynical" she said.

"Cynical? You mean I have a low opinion of people? Yes, I suppose I do. When I was in the gulag in Siberia I saw what men could do to one another. We are all animals underneath our fine clothes." He looked her up and down. "We are all capable of the most sadistic crimes. Me, I killed a man once, a policeman who tried to rape my mother. I still remember the smell of cigarettes on his clothes."

He stopped for a moment to see how she reacted. She still was frowning. "But man is also capable of being like angels," he continued. "That's why I collect Faberge Eggs or French art. I am not only cynical, as you say. I prefer the best of man."

"And women?" she asked. "Do you also collect women?"

He smiled. "Ah, you mean the models? Yes, I also collect beautiful women. Is there anything more beautiful?"

"I suppose not," she said. "You have good taste in art and in women, yet I cannot help but wonder, is that enough for someone?"

"Enough?"

"Yes, enough to make one happy. Can one buy happiness?"

"Perhaps not," he said.

At that moment, Dmitri Prokofiev hurried into the room. "Please, most sorry. May I have a word with you, sir?"

"One moment, please," said Raskolnovitch to Antoinette. "Don't leave. It will only be a minute." He stepped aside with Prokofiev. "What is it, Dima? I hope it is important."

"It is. We have a problem, but nothing we can't fix. The American Securities and Exchange Commission, SEC, wants more proof that the money we put down for the Drake Hotel deal is legitimate, clean. They want to see bank records and also tax receipts. Our American friends are very nervous. I told them not to freak out. It's no problem."

Raskolnovitch looked back at Antoinette who was examining some drawings by Cezanne. "Well, we were expecting something like this, were we not, Dima? It's why we bought a small bank. Do what you must." The last thing he wanted was scrutiny from the Americans. Manafort had assured him the deal would sail through under the radar. He should have trusted his instincts. He knew better. Manafort's greed was a liability. They nodded to each other and Raskolnovitch returned to Antoinette.

"My apologies, Toni," he said.

She turned and faced him. "No, it is I who should apologize. I was very rude. I'm sorry. I had no right to criticize." She paused. "I'll share a dirty secret. I love cigarettes as much as I hate them. You are right. It is the smoker who is at fault. Voila. I am guilty and you are innocent." She surveyed her surroundings. "Well, perhaps not innocent," she said. "You know what Balzac said, 'Behind every great fortune lies a great crime.' At least you have good taste."

Raskolnovitch found her most intriguing. "Toni, you don't insult me. About cigarettes, I have no guilt. But am I happy? It's a good question. One can love one's habits, but they're never enough, as you say. At best, they keep me from being bored. But life is more than entertainment, is it not?"

A slow smile spread across Antoinette's face, as if she were discovering an unexpected respect for this man. "Did you know your accountant is a grand nephew of the great composer, Prokofiev?" she asked.

Raskolnovitch looked surprised. Shook his head. "I had no idea," he said. "It's a common name in Russia."

"I asked him if he was related and he is." She glanced behind her at the Matisse collage. "You know, Matisse once drew a famous portrait of Prokofiev," she said.

"No, I didn't know. I must buy it," said Raskolnovitch.

"Monsieur Raskolnovitch—"

"Please, Toni, call me Viktor."

"OK, Viktor—do you always think you can buy anything you want?"

"Yes, anything. Everything has a price."

"Even people?" asked Antoinette.

"Especially people," said Raskolnovitch.

Antoinette observed him. "Viktor, maybe someday you will meet a woman you cannot buy for anything. I think then, maybe you will find it is enough." She smiled and held out her hand to make her exit. He bent and kissed it.

"Perhaps I will." He paused and, making eye contact with her again, said to himself, perhaps I have.

The string quartet began playing again and the sounds of conversations rose from below as Antoinette glided down the sweeping staircase. She could feel him watching her. At the foot of the stairs she passed her father and whispered to him, "It worked."

Chapter Six

The sound of the rain, pounding and relentless, drove all thoughts of his sister from Yuri's mind. He ran toward the intersection holding a discarded pizza box over his head, water dripping down his back. With his other hand he held a package under a tattered military jacket. As he stepped off the curb, a silver Mercedes zoomed through a red light, splattering him with mud. He cursed out loud, but the pelting rain muffled his voice. His one clean pair of jeans was now filthy.

"Hey, Yuri!" he heard someone shout.

He turned and saw Taras waving to him under the canopy in front of Nikolaev's department store, now vacant and forlorn. Yuri ran back to join him. The rain intensified.

Taras laughed at him. "Too bad he didn't hit you. You could've sued him for a million."

"People like that don't lose in court," said Yuri. The silver Mercedes was now far down the boulevard, switching lanes.

"Where're you going in such a hurry?" shouted Taras. The two men had to yell to hear each other over the rain.

"Home. My sister Yana and a girlfriend are leaving for

Warsaw tonight and then to Prague. I may never see her again."
He had not entertained this thought before and the realization
made him choke up. "I thought we'd celebrate with a cake. I can't
remember the last time we had cake," Yuri said. "My step-dad,
her real father, beat the shit out of her yesterday. I tried to stop
him, but I was no match. I think he may have broken some of my
ribs."

One eye was black and swollen. "Yeah, and he messed up
your face. You have a major black eye, man. What a pig!"

"I hate him. He stole my mother's pension from us. He's
stupid drunk all the time. I can't stay home much longer,
either."

"Why don't you leave with your sister?" asked Taras.

"I would, if I still had my damn passport. I sold it last year
when my mom died to pay the costs for her burial. But even if I
had a passport, I don't know who would look after my Bubbie."
Yuri mourned selling his passport. Ever since he was a kid, he had
longed to travel, to see the outside world that flickered on the television screens. He'd studied English every year in school, prac-
ticing along with music videos, so that he would have the words
he needed to make his way. But now his English was as useless as
a business suit.

From under his jacket, Yuri produced a pink box and,
opening the lid slightly, revealed a round frosted holiday cake
inside.

"Where'd you steal that?" shouted Taras, laughing.

Yuri cupped his hand by Taras's ear. "I traded for it. You
know Natalia, Oleg's sister? She works at Wolkonsky's, the
bakery on Khreschatyk. I drew her portrait. I hate doing those,
but what the hell. Took me just half an hour."

"You should do that on the Maidan," Taras shouted. "The
tourists pay good money for those caricatures and no one's better
at it than you."

"Thanks, but no thanks. If I start doing that, I'll never finish my real painting."

"Yeah, but you need to eat, too," said Taras.

"I'll eat cake," said Yuri. "Then I don't know what I'll eat."

"I thought you were working at the zoo," said Taras, lowering his voice.

"Not any more. they're laying everyone off. I haven't been paid in weeks and now they're planning to give away the animals to anyone who can feed them. You need an orangutan, by any chance?"

"My girlfriend would love it. But our apartment's a closet. So, what are you gonna do? What about the mill where your step-dad worked?" asked Taras. "Are they going to reopen it anytime soon?"

The rain had started to let up. "I doubt it," said Yuri. They stepped out from under the roof and looked up at the sky.

"Here, Yuri," said Taras. He reached into his pants pocket and pulled out a small plastic bag. "Why don't I trade you? You can draw my portrait."

"No, fucking way," said Yuri, shaking his head.

"What about the cake?" asked Taras.

Yuri looked down at the open box and hesitated. He looked up at Taras and smiled.

"Oh, shit, man."

He wanted more of that rock candy, a light amphetamine. It was a ticket out of the gloom and despair that defined his life. It put him in the zone. Painting, he believed, was his salvation. But living in a tiny apartment with his Bubbie, his stepfather and sister, he found it impossible to paint during the day. Given rock candy, though, he could paint all night like a madman. With no further thought, he thrust the cake into Taras's hands and took the baggie from him. His sister would never know. The rain stopped.

They bumped fists and he took off again for his house, feeling like a real loser.

He hated this panicky feeling that never seemed to leave him anymore. It was better with the animals, but now even that was gone. His sister was smart to leave. There was no future here in Ukraine. But it sickened him to think of Yana prostituting herself. She was still a child. If Bubbie died, there'd be nothing keeping him here in Kyiv anymore, he knew.

He climbed the smelly stairs to his flat. Yana opened the door as he was putting in his key, took one look at his battered face, and threw her arms around him. "My Yuri, you were so brave to try and save me. Look at you!" She held him at arms' length and examined his bruises. Her own face was heavy with makeup, but Yuri could see the signs of the beating she had taken.

"I hate him," he said.

"Me, too," said Yana. "But today we must celebrate. I bought a cake and some cheap champagne," she said.

Yuri felt as empty as a sieve. He stared at the cake and faked a smile.

"How kind of you, sis. I should have brought something. Please, excuse me."

Bubbie was asleep in her rocking chair. Sunlight came like a surprise guest, brightening the living room. Yana opened the champagne, spraying their faces. It felt so good to laugh again. They shared old stories about their childhoods: the time Yuri fell through the ice, the day Yana threw up on Svyatyy Mykolay, St. Nicholas Day, and, always, their mom's thwarted ride in a hot air balloon.

"Yuri, you must visit me in Prague. I'll have a nice apartment. I'll cook for you. You will meet all my friends," she said.

"As soon as Bubbie dies," he said. "I'm ready for a big change."

Chapter Seven

The sun was just setting over the Aegean Sea, turning the low clouds pink and gold as Raskolnovitch banked the helicopter for a landing. The man sitting next to him, Jacques Gavi, a former French president, caught sight of the sleek 80-meter tri-deck superyacht lying just outside the blue green waters of the Kos marina. With its all-white fluid lines and slender hull, the yacht had a classically elegant look. Interior lights were just coming on as the helicopter approached a helipad on the upper deck by the bow. At the stern end of the ship, a second helipad had been retracted to reveal a heated infinity swimming pool. A dozen young women in bikinis were swimming or lounging about it.

When the rotors stopped, Raskolnovitch and his guest disembarked. Yet another young woman awaited them with glasses of champagne.

"Welcome, Mr. President, to my home away from home," Raskolnovitch said to him in English, taking him by the arm. "After we freshen up a bit, my business partners will be eager to meet you. There are also several lovely young ladies who would enjoy the honor of your company. I think you will find them most accommodating. But first, allow me give you quick tour of my little ship."

"Viktor Ivanovitch, *c'est eblouissement,* dazzling," said the Frenchman. "I have never seen anything more beautiful."

Raskolnovitch smiled. "It is very fast, it can go 19 knots and 10,000 kilometers," he said.

He led them to his own stateroom suite, past a large jacuzzi, protected by a plexiglass wall. The suite consisted of a bedroom with an enormous round bed covered in a gold bedspread, a separate living room paneled in dark cherry wood, with a massive gas fireplace, and a bathroom that included a steam sauna and open shower area with nine shower heads. The walls of the bedroom were decorated with elaborate depictions of erotic poses from the Kama Sutra. There were sizeable port holes on the port and starboard sides. Floor to ceiling curtains circled the entire suite at the touch of a button.

"*Whaou! C'est genial!,*" said the Frenchman shaking his head in disbelief.

A hidden door in the living room opened to a glass elevator that took them to the cabin deck two stories below. It stopped by an interior dance floor with a large disco ball and colored lights. It was empty then and there was no music. Raskolnovitch pointed to a door that led to the crew's quarters. The boat could accommodate 24 crew members, but there were only 14 today plus eight security guards. On the other side were six double guest suites. They passed through a fitness area and a large pine wood sauna and then entered onto the outdoor deck.

Before them was the heated Infinity pool where a few of the women were still splashing about and others, topless, were catching the last rays of sun on lounge chairs. They waved to Raskolnovitch and his guest. Guards in black uniforms and sunglasses strolled back and forth along the deck. A waiter in white was picking up empty glasses. A group of sea gulls followed off the stern, squawking loudly. Behind them lay the blue green sea, the yachts in the marina, the beach with its green and yellow umbrellas and the white houses of the Greek island of Kos.

"*C'est magnifique,*" said the Frenchman.

Raskolnovitch loved to impress powerful men like this, especially ones taller and better educated. He walked over and whispered to three of the girls, then continued with his tour. He explained that a garage underneath held an armored limousine, a speedboat and launch ramp and an assortment of water toys. They walked past the lifeboats to a pair of staircases that swept up to the main deck which featured a billiard room, movie theater, hairdressing salon, library, piano bar, and Raskolnovitch's pride and joy: a round rotating dining room with full-length windows port and starboard. The dining room was decorated in super-white leather and marble, glossy black lacquer, and Makassar wood.

"I'm not known for being speechless, monsieur Raskolnovitch, but I'm afraid I am at this moment. You must be very proud," said the former French president.

"When I divorced, my wife was so angry to lose this, she tried to hire someone to blow it up. Luckily, I discovered the plot," said Raskolnovitch.

"Ah, when my wife and I divorced, she set fire to our bed. French women can be very liberal about our lovers outside of marriage, but don't ever divorce one."

They laughed. Raskolnovitch held the Frenchman by his arm and showed the former president to his VIP room. "We have much important business to discuss at dinner this evening. Maybe my friends will help you with the investments you mentioned. You and I maybe can find ways to help support your upcoming presidential campaign, and perhaps you would return the favor by helping me become a citizen of your great country. If it all works, maybe I would loan you this boat, have a great celebration."

That night after much wine and champagne, Raskolnovitch retired to his suite. He felt a little sad and disgusted by this business, by the ease with which he bought what he needed from this pretentious politician. Deals were much cleaner with the *Vory*, in the old days, after his time in the gulags. These French politicians were like peacocks strutting around pretending to be so righteous, but could be bought like anyone else. It was all theater: one had only to wait patiently for the last act.

The three escorts he chose earlier were waiting for him. Phaedra, a slender redhead with large, enhanced breasts, introduced herself, kissing him chastely on both cheeks. She was wearing a see-through cotton blouse that barely reached her hips.

"I'm Zoe," said a brunette with a coy curtsy. She pulled a string on her blouse, revealing her breasts, and took his hand and held it to them.

When she stepped aside, the third escort came up to Raskolnovitch and kissed him passionately on the mouth, her tongue caressing his own. "They call me Athena. We are all from Athens and we are very happy to be here with you."

Then she kissed him again and lifted his suit jacket off his shoulders and let it fall to the floor. She untied his tie and began unbuttoning his shirt.

Zoe, the brunette, moved behind him, pressing herself against him, reached around and undid his belt and loosened his fly. The pants fell around his feet. Phaedra was on one side of Raskolnovitch kissing his neck and moving her hands all over him. She reached for Zoe and led her to the great round bed, threw off the gold cover and lay down with her. They began to make out and turn each other on. Raskolnovitch watched them as Alexandros bent down to remove his pants, shoes, and socks. He was already getting hard. She helped him take off his briefs and put her mouth on him.

Raskolnovitch was delirious with pleasure. Beauty moved him like nothing else. It was the closest he could come to God, he believed. These young Greek girls were gorgeous and as delicate as Faberge Eggs. He wished he weren't so drunk on good wine and wondered whether he had the capacity for so much joy. He couldn't believe how lucky he was, but he knew he didn't deserve it and that thought nagged at him.

He could satisfy any carnal desire he wished, but there was a kind of diminishing return to that. His mind flashed again to his days in the gulag with the *Vory*. Then, he would, quite literally, have given a finger for one kiss. Now his any fantasy could be fulfilled with a casual command. But fantasies met soon lose their power to excite. Still, these indulgences always put him in the moment, took him out of his head.

Alexandros led him to the bed where Zoe was lying with her head between Phaedra's legs. The three women were inventive and responsive, and even if they faked their orgasms, the sound of their pleasures pleased him. When he finally came, he lay panting in a wave of sadness. It left him terrified.

Chapter Eight

At precisely 9 a.m. on Wednesday, Yuri Yavlinsky arrived at the Chief Prosecutor's office of the State Tax Service. The hallways were dimly lit and there was a heavy musty odor. He pushed open the massive, lacquered door. There was a cute young receptionist at a desk painting her nails. Several young men carrying stacks of papers and files moved about as if they had important tasks. A large ceiling fan whirled above. The wooden floors creaked underneath him.

"Excuse me, I was told to be here at nine. My name is Yuri Yavlinsky."

The receptionist scowled at him and pointed to a door across from her. He turned and knocked on it. "No need to knock," he heard her say from behind him, "just go in."

Behind the door was another, more private, wood-paneled reception area. There were three men in dark suits seated on couches. They all turned to stare at him. A tall woman in a blue tailored outfit holding a clipboard came out from an inner office. "Your name?" she asked.

"Yuri Yavlinsky," he said, conscious of his worn dress pants, his only pair, and the frayed collar of his shirt.

"Please follow me," she said, turning back to the office she had come from. Yuri followed. They entered into a large, tall-ceilinged room, adorned with frescoes. There were framed pictures on the walls and on a mantle, above a working gas fireplace. The room was warm. Seated in a high leather chair behind a massive mahogany desk with a half dozen phones and stacks of folders was a heavy-set man holding a telephone receiver in one hand while he dictated something to a stenographer sitting in a chair next to him. The man had heavy eyebrows and large bags under his eyes. Yuri noticed he was missing two fingers on one hand. The woman who led him in gestured for Yuri to take one of the two wooden chairs in front of the desk. She sat next to him in another.

The man stopped dictating, said a few words on the phone, hung up, and turned to peer at Yuri. The stenographer left.

"Mr. Chief Prosecutor, this is Yuri Yavlinsky," said the woman sitting next to him, "the one with Global Opportunities Fund."

Confused and nervous, Yuri stood up and offered his hand. The man behind the desk stayed put, looking up at him with a malicious, penetrating glare. Yuri sat down again.

"Mr. Yavlinsky," the prosecutor said finally, "you are charged with tax evasion, a violation of Section 7031.204 of the Tax Code." He pushed an open folder across his desk to Yuri. "According to our records, you owe a total of eight-hundred and thirty-three million, nine-hundred and twenty-three thousand, one hundred and twenty-one hryvnias—approximately 30 million US dollars, give or take a few hryvnias."

A chill ran through Yuri. His heart raced, his leg shook, and his head throbbed. And then, without a thought, he felt himself smile and, though he tried to suppress it, he began to laugh. He looked back and forth from the prosecutor to the woman in blue, who both remained stone-faced.

"Please excuse me, Mr. Prosecutor," said Yuri. "You obviously have the wrong Yuri Yavlinsky. The most money I've ever had in my life was perhaps five thousand hryvnias. I'm unemployed now." Again, he laughed, his nervousness escaping like air from a balloon.

"Mr. Yavlinsky, I'm afraid this is no laughing matter," he said. "This is one of the largest money laundering and tax evasion schemes we have ever investigated. Official articles of incorporation list you as the director of ten companies which together are worth more than one billion US dollars. Can you account for how this might be?"

Yuri looked back and forth between the prosecutor and the woman next to him and shook his head. "I have absolutely no idea," he said. He reached in his pocket and took out a hundred hryvnia note, worth about four US dollars. "This is all I have in the world."

The prosecutor reached into a folder on his desk and took out a page. "Here is a photocopy of the passport used to register a corporation, Global Opportunities Fund. Is that your signature? And this," he took out another page. "Is this not your signature on these articles of incorporation?"

Yuri felt a surge of adrenaline. He recognized his signature and, suddenly, the memory of what had happened left him terrified. It was Kafkaesque, but all too real. In a flash he realized the gravity of his situation. He forced himself not to cry.

"Mr. Prosecutor, I had no idea what I was signing. My mother died around Easter and I had no money to bury her. She wanted to be buried next to her family in Odessa. My step-dad took the burial expenses she received as a state employee. I was desperate. A man offered to buy my passport from me for three thousand hryvnias. I didn't think there was any chance I would need it, so I sold it."

Yuri began breathing heavily. The truth was so innocent and yet so damning. He was distracted by a high-pitched buzzing sound, then realized it was in his head. He tried to calculate what his actual jeopardy might be. Could he be a scapegoat for whoever bought his passport? Was ignorance a legal defense?

"Mr. Yavlinsky," said the prosecutor, his hands folded under his chin. "Looking at you, I can tell that you aren't the real director of this shell company, but you are undoubtedly complicit in a crime. You received something of value in a scheme to defraud the government. If everyone sold passports as you did, these travel documents would lose their legitimacy. No country would honor them. There are consequences for conspiring in a crime, even if you are just a bit player. Do you have a lawyer? I can appoint one for you, if you don't."

Yuri shook his head. The buzzing sound got louder. His leg started shaking again. His breathing increased. He became fixated on the prosecutor's missing fingers.

"Sir," Yuri started, "I'm very sorry for what I've done. I meant no harm. I wanted only to give my mother the burial she wanted." He somehow managed not to cry. "The crime is that my stepfather stole her pension! I had to do what I could to bury her. He paused for a moment. "I can't afford a lawyer. If you can provide me with one, I would be very grateful."

When he finished, the woman in blue got up, walked behind the desk and whispered something in the prosecutor's ear. He didn't take his eyes off Yuri, but nodded his agreement.

She stood up and addressed Yuri. "Mr. Yavlinsky, with your permission, I would like to ask a Ms. Osatinskaya to represent you. She is a lawyer, a very good one, I might add. She runs a small non-governmental organization that works to expose corruption. I think she may be able to help you."

Yuri nodded with some enthusiasm. The noise in his head subsided slightly. "Thank you," he said.

The woman picked up one of the phones on the prosecutor's desk and spoke rapidly to someone. Yuri was able to follow most of it. "She'll come right over," the woman said. "Please have a seat over there." She pointed to a green couch on the opposite wall. "Her office is just across the street. She'll be here in a few minutes."

Yuri was glad to get some space from the prosecutor's persistent glare. He sat on the couch and waited while the prosecutor and the woman in blue dealt with other business, ignoring him. After about ten minutes, the woman led Yuri out of the office to a small empty room down in the basement. It had a table, two chairs and a lamp.

"Ms. Osatinskaya will be here shortly," said the woman. She left him there and locked the door behind her as she went out.

Alone, Yuri finally allowed himself to cry. He hated his poverty, his depression, his tears. He missed his mother. When he stopped, he wiped his nose on his shirt sleeve and wiped his eyes. The noise in his head continued, but lower now. He got out of his chair and paced around the small room. What would jail be like? Would he have a cell to himself? He had heard horrible stories about conditions in the jails in Ukraine. Soon he was more afraid than he had ever been before.

There was a knock at the door. Yuri wasn't sure what to do. Finally, he said, softly, "Come in."

He heard a key turn. The door opened and there was a woman about Yuri's age holding a leather briefcase.

"Mr. Yavlinsky? I'm Dora Osatinskaya. I'm a lawyer. I'm here to help you, if I can."

She was dressed conservatively in a red pant suit with a

white blouse and white scarf, about Yuri's height. She had on a pair of black flats. She was fairly pretty. Her hair was blond and short, one side longer than the other. Best of all, she looked like she knew what she was doing. But what stunned Yuri, what removed all other thoughts from his mind, were her eyes. They were the most beautiful, penetrating blue eyes he had ever seen.

Chapter Nine

"Viktor Ivanovitch, how glad I am to see you." The Ukrainian president, suntanned and overweight, but well-groomed in a grey Italian suit and perfectly coiffed hair, greeted Raskolnovitch in the usual bear hug.

"And good to see you, Mr. President," Raskolnovitch replied.

"May I offer you some brandy?" asked the president.

"Yes, thank you."

The president's personalized brandy with his picture on the label was a feature of any visit to the dacha. They sat next to each other in one of several gold couches in a cavernous reception room carpeted with exquisite inlaid wooden floors before a large fireplace. On the other side of the room was a limited-edition all-white Steinway grand piano signed by John Lennon, the "Imagine" model featured in the iconic video for the peace song.

The sprawling mansion, on the banks of the Dnieper River, had originally been a monastery and later a guest house for visiting Communist officials. In each room there were canaries in gilded cages that served as early warning systems for a poison gas attack, reassuring the notoriously paranoid president. The house had been retrofitted with an elaborate double filtration climate control system to prevent any noxious attacks. Raskolnovitch found the incessant bird sounds distracting and felt only contempt for the president's fears. But the man was his *krysha*, his protector, and, therefore, commanded his respect.

"Viktor Ivanovich, I trust you've got this TV licensing business under control. Under any circumstance, we must own this national channel."

"Mr. President, the bids won't be unsealed for another two weeks, but we were able to get an early look and adjust accordingly."

"Good. I know I can count on you. I assume you have seen the attacks on me in *Ukrayinska Pravda*?" asked the president. "This journalist is a danger. He has tried to make this television licensing thing into some kind of scandal."

He leaned forward. "I want you to do me a very important favor," he said, staring intently at Raskolnovitch. "I want him eliminated. His head has grown too big for his body. It needs to be removed. I think you understand. If you help me with this, I assure you, there will be no end to my appreciation. But you must be very careful. This reporter has many friends in the West," warned the president.

"Mr. President, your wish is always my command," said Raskolnovitch. "Consider it done."

He wished his *krysha* had more confidence. *Ukrayinska Pravda* was an insignificant online publication. Kidnapping and killing one of their journalists would only make matters worse. But he would do the president's bidding, regardless. It gave him some leverage over him.

The president stood up, handed Raskolnovitch a slip of paper, smiled, filled their glasses again, and offered a toast. "To our partnership."

Afterwards, the president led Raskolnovitch past the sweeping staircase, through a hallway of gilded mirrors and chandeliers and out the front door. They walked toward the stables and stopped outside the kennels where the huntsman was gathering his hounds. "Beautiful beasts, these dogs, aren't they?" noted the president. "And obedient, too." The kennel huntsman held up a plate loaded with freshly cut steaks. The president tossed them to the barking hounds, which spurred a frenzy of excitement. "They love me!" shouted the president above the din.

"Just like your constituents," Raskolnovitch remarked.

Just then, Paul Manafort, the president's American political advisor, emerged from behind several barrels of oats. His hair and outfit were exactly like the president's, Raskolnovitch noted. They all shook hands. Raskolnovitch didn't trust the man. He was too slick, too American. No one doubted he was responsible foir the president's remarkable return to power, but the shadow government he built with supporters in every ministry was loyal only to him. The president himself seemed under his spell.

Manafort nodded to the president, then turned to Raskolnovitch. "Viktor Ivanovitch ," he said. "Thank you for the Cosmos Club lunch. Peterson was impressed. The deposit for the Drake deal cleared overnight and is in escrow. It all looks good." He did not mention the SEC investigation, which caused Raskolnovitch to wonder what else he might be hiding. They shook hands again and the president and his advisor returned to the house.

Raskolnovitch turned and walked up to his helicopter on a landing pad by the shooting range. His bodyguards, who had been smoking in a circle warming themselves around a firepit, snapped to attention. He took the lead guard by the arm and led him to a small hunting lodge and pushed open the heavy oak door with its great iron hinges. It was dark inside. With his lighter he lit some lanterns that hung in the hallway. The lodge was essentially a trophy room with a fireplace opposite the door. The walls were covered by the excesses of an overemployed taxidermist. There were framed displays of cartridges in every size and caliber and long rows of antique pistols and muskets. Standing under an enormous boar's head, Raskolnovitch faced the chief of his security detail.

"Kostya, I have an important assignment for you. It must be done with absolute care and discretion," Raskolnovitch said gravely.

"I understand, sir."

"There is a certain journalist who has disturbed our president and must be disposed of." He handed the guard a sheet of paper folded twice that the president had given him. "Here are details. I want you to follow this man, from a distance of course, and learn the patterns of his movements over a few days. Do not carry a cell phone with you. Wear a hat or something to disguise your features from surveillance cameras. You will want to discover some place where this man is alone and could be kidnapped without witnesses. Once you have determined this, I want you to meet in person with an old friend from the *Vory*, Konstantin Kniezinsky. Tell him that I want this man eliminated and decapitated. You will pay him 30,000 in U.S. currency, which Prokofiev will give you. There must be nothing in writing or on the phone. Understood?"

"Understood, of course," said the guard, nodding.

"You are to tell no one about this, ever."

The guard nodded again.

This was distasteful business. Raskolnovitch had killed men before. The memory of looking through the scope of his rifle in a firefight along the Kabul-Jalalabad Road when a wounded Mujahadeen fighter made eye contact with him, begging for mercy, had often haunted him. That was his first face-to-face kill.

Rockets from his helicopter didn't count. Now, as he looked into his guard's impassive face, he felt like the matter was in competent hands. Kniezinsky was *Vory*, a pro's pro, he knew. There would be no surprises.

Chapter Ten

Dora Osatinskaya noticed how Yuri averted his eyes from her gaze. Poor guy, she thought, another bedraggled young Ukrainian with no prospects and now no passport. Young men like him in Ukraine were caught in a downward spiral with few ways out other than drugs, crime or the army. The streets were full of them, so often preyed upon by the more powerful. He offered his hand. "It's good to meet you, Ms. Osatinskaya. "Please, have a seat."

"Please, call me Dora," she spoke in fluent Ukrainian. She was impressed at his manners, as if this situation were a social one and his predicament not dire. They sat across from each other. She tried to reassure him with a smile. Placing her briefcase on the wooden table, she took out a manila folder, and set the briefcase on the floor. She could see his nervous apprehension, but behind his veneer of shyness, she also sensed a reserve of strength. It surprised her how poised he was under the circumstances. "I suppose they explained what I do," she continued. "I'm a lawyer and, if you and I agree, I'll be authorized to repre-

sent you. For free, I should add. I work for a non-profit organization that is fighting corruption, so there is no cost to you."

She studied him carefully. His features were familiar: high
cheekbones, prominent eyebrows, dark brown narrow eyes. He
reminded her of her cousin Izzy. Though he was thin on his
frame, he had the posture of an athlete or soldier. There was
something disarmingly intelligent and generous in his eyes.

"You're American. I can hear it in your voice," said Yuri. "I
mean, your Ukrainian is fine, but still I can tell. What are you
doing here?"

"I'm Ukrainian too. I was born here. I lived in the US, but I'm
working here now."

"Why? Everyone I know dreams of living in America."

"There are things I can get done here. Good things. Good
things for you, possibly."

Yuri perked up at that. "What kind of things?" he asked.

Their eyes met. "Our country is suffocating from corruption,
from the top to the bottom. The Orange Revolution inspired me
to do something. I came back here because I thought everything
would change after that, but it hasn't. The oligarchs still control
everything and the only way to get ahead here is to bribe your
way up. I believed if I could expose the worst of this corruption, it
might help."

Yuri shrugged. "You're a dreamer," he said. "Everyone
already knows the government steals."

She wished she could tell him about Morris's plan, how Yuri
could help them prevent one of the most corrupt deals yet. But
she'd have to admit that she was deceiving him, entrapping him
in her scheme. She needed to turn the conversation back to him.

"We can debate this another time, Yuri. But for right now, let
me make sure I understand the situation you're in. I take it this is
all a surprise to you?"

Yuri nodded and let out a long sigh.

"So, you knew nothing about these companies or taxes or any of this until they charged you? Is that right?"

"Yes. Correct."

"But you remember selling your passport to someone?"

Yuri nodded.

"And did you also sign other papers then?"

Yuri bit his lower lip. "Yes."

"And the only reason for this was to pay for your mother's funeral?"

Again, he nodded. "She died. If I didn't have the money to bury her, she wouldn't get buried."

Dora could hear the ache in his voice, but also a tinge of anger at the dilemma he had been in.

"Had you ever met this man before, the man who paid for these signatures and your passport?"

"No, never."

"Have you ever seen him again?"

"No."

"How did he find you?"

Yuri let out another breath. "He mentioned something about a friend of his at the State Employees Credit Union who had given him my name. I had gone to them the day before to see if I could get a loan to pay for the funeral. I thought I might use her pension as collateral. Someone at this office must have told the man who bought my passport how desperate I was."

Dora now studied him carefully, her arms crossed in front of her. He had a certain natural confidence. With a little bit of work, she thought, he might be perfect for the role she and Uncle Morris had devised. "Tell me about yourself," she said.

"There's not much to say," he began, switching to English, which surprised her. "I'm unemployed. Just got laid off from the zoo, a couple of days ago. I live with my sister, great-grandmother, and step-dad. Actually, my sister left two nights ago for Prague. My mother died around Easter, my father when I was just an infant. I never knew him. Mom remarried about eighteen years ago."

He shook his head. "I can't imagine why she did. He's a real lout." He pointed to his eye, which was still purplish and swollen. "He lost his job last year when they closed the steel mill."

"Tell me about your mother and your birth dad, if you don't mind," Dora said.

Yuri looked like he was beginning to enjoy this. Dora wondered whether anybody had ever before asked him about himself.

"Mom was a translator and a simultaneous interpreter. She finished in the top one percent in the national exams and dreamed of being an interpreter for the president, but she hadn't attended the right Party schools and was forced to get what jobs she could. She worked for some oligarchs and local politicians but got disgusted by the corruption she witnessed. Everything was about money, she said."

Dora sat back in her chair. "I suppose your mother's language talent explains how you speak such perfect English," she said.

Yuri smiled. "Yes, she raised us speaking English, Russian and Ukrainian at home. Plus, my sister and I grew up on Sesame Street. Later, I got hooked on American movies and rock and roll."

"What about your dad, your birth dad?" asked Dora.

He paused collecting his thoughts. "My dad, my real dad, worked in a foundry at a steel mill in Donetsk. He was a real rabble rouser, I've been told. His friends nicknamed him 'Lech' after Lech Walesa. I guess he got beat up pretty bad trying to organize an independent union. He died from a disease of the kidney, but my mom thought it started from the beating he took."

Yuri winced, as if he'd let forth too many words. "What about you? You speak Ukrainian better than most people I know in Kyiv."

"Thank you. I grew up in Ukraine. My parents tried to speak English in the house when we moved to the States, but usually we all just switched back and forth." She was surprised how comfortable it was to talk to him. He would be perfect.

It had become easier to make eye contact with him. She spoke again. "If I'm going to represent you, we'll need to get to know each other. So, if you don't mind, tell me something more personal about yourself. What makes you tick? What do you get excited about? What would you like to be doing?"

Yuri smiled. She smiled back.

"I loved working with the animals at the zoo. I could have done that the rest of my life. But I'm also an artist."

"What kind of art?"

"I draw hyper-realistic miniature caricatures. Pen and ink. I've been working on a single painting for the past four years. It's a kind of time capsule, all the important people in our generation —sports figures, movie stars, politicians, famous people of all kinds. You'd recognize most of them," he said.

"What are all those miniature characters of yours doing?" she asked.

Yuri laughed. "Everything imaginable. Some are eating at a restaurant, some are figure skating, some are engaged in erotic acts."

She kept her expression sympathetic.

"It's a kind of gigantic cartoon."

"I can't wait to see it," she said. "What are you going to do with it?"

"Nothing probably. It's just for me. My mother always wanted me to become an architect. I got accepted into the National Academy of Fine Arts and Architecture, but we would have had to pay a huge bribe. Mom was willing to do anything to get the money, but I wouldn't let her. She wanted to borrow it from one of the oligarchs she worked for, but he wanted certain favors. I just didn't want any part of this rotten system."

He sat up straighter. "So now you know everything about me," Yuri smiled. "What about you? Tell me something personal. What makes Dora tick?"

"Me? I'm kind of a health nut, a vegetarian, really into yoga."

"Duzhe dobre, very good," said Yuri.

"I was born in Lviv, but my parents emigrated to Israel in 1991 after independence. My mother's Jewish."

Yuri raised his head, meeting her eyes. "My mother, too."

"I was twelve when we arrived in Tel Aviv. Everyone was very nice to us, but we hated it. They wanted us to be real Jews, not some secular socialists. Sharansky? You've heard of him?" Yuri nodded.

"He expected us to conform, not to complain, to become good little Israelis. My parents and I, I think we felt more comfortable around gentiles." Yuri nodded.

"So, we emigrated again, to America, to New Jersey. Bruce Springsteen and all. At first the boys thought I was kind of exotic coming from Ukraine. But when they learned I was Jewish, I was just another Jew in New Jersey. I got a scholarship to NYU and then to UC Berkeley for law school. I came here two years ago to start a local NGO to help expose corruption." She was surprised how much she talked about herself.

"You must be very busy," said Yuri.

"I am. The state is very weak. The oligarchs are very strong. We are just a small NGO, but we think we can make a difference," she said.

"Is your family here with you?" asked Yuri. "Do you have a husband?"

She blushed. "No. I live alone."

There was an awkward silence for a moment. Then Dora

said, "Yuri, tell me, can you think of anything else that might help us identify the man who bought your passport?"

"I'm sorry I don't have more information about this man. What can we do?"

She heard his initial panic return to his voice. "Look, Yuri. I know the prosecutor. He's a good man, honest, one of the very few who aren't corrupt. He has no interest in charging you for tax evasion. Selling your passport is a different matter, but I'm sure he'll drop that, too, if you fully cooperate." Yuri's eyes brightened. "I'd like to ask him if he'll release you to me, if you agree to work with me on this case. You could be very helpful. If we ever find who's behind this shell company, you may need to be called as a witness. But in the meantime, you'd work with me to uncover the fraud. Would you like that?"

"There's nothing in the world I'd like more," he said.

Chapter Eleven

He had never worn a suit before. Yuri, standing on a small stool, stared at himself in the mirrors. He straightened, held his shoulders back. This feeling was something new and unexpectedly pleasurable. He no longer felt like a little bug in his apartment hiding in the dark. He blushed at himself.

"You look very handsome, Mr. Yavlinsky," said Dora, making him blush even more.

An older man, thin and mostly bald with tufts of hair around his crown and a blue chalk behind one ear, eyed him with care. "Yes, this dark blue suit looks good on him. I just have to take it in a little here and here," said the tailor, pinching the suit in places. He bent down and took his chalk to mark where the pants needed hemming.

Leon Kaminsky, Yuri had learned, was a distant cousin of Dora's who had taken her into his family when she first came to Ukraine as a student one summer. It seemed like she knew more people in Kyiv than he did. They were all standing in the back of Kaminsky's little shop in the Solomyonsky district.

"So, Mr. Yuri Yavlinsky, I will now tell you what this is all about." She took a paper from a large purse and waved it in front of them. "The prosecutor will consider suspending all charges, as long as you continue to be a cooperating witness and actively assist in the investigation of the fraud associated with the sale of your passport."

Yuri stepped off the stool he was on and bowed to her. "Thank you. I will do whatever you need."

"Wait, there is more," said Dora. "At my suggestion, the prosecutor has managed to have your passport restored. It was necessary to try our new strategy." She reached into her purse again and took out the familiar blue Ukrainian passport and handed it to him. It was like being reunited with an old friend that he didn't know he had missed.

"On various articles of incorporation, you are listed as the director of ten offshore shell companies scattered around the world. These companies don't actually do anything. They just hold money that the real owners want to hide, often to shield them from tax authorities or because the funds were the fruits of crimes, like extortion, drug money, things like that. The system is designed to be totally opaque, but perhaps you hold a key that could shed some light on this operation. How would you like to go with me to Cyprus to look at one of your accounts?"

Yuri felt the same unsteadiness he had felt a moment before standing on the little stool. The world he had inhabited in the tiny apartment living with his Bubbie had suddenly changed scenes. He was dressed in an expensive suit, somehow involved in a billion dollar scam he knew nothing about, being asked by a woman with sapphire eyes to travel with her to Cyprus. What was he getting himself into? This was not like shoveling elephant shit.

Dora could see the questions on his face. "Yuri, this must all be a bit confusing," she said. "There is a risk. Whoever is behind this shell company does not play by the rules. All we're doing is searching for documents. But these documents could pose a mortal threat to whatever criminal syndicate this is. We'll have to be very careful. These people play for keeps."

Yuri glanced at the images of himself in the tri-fold mirror. He had always considered himself a stoic, able to adapt to the hardships of life that were his lot. Somehow, though, he had stepped into a parallel universe for which he was totally unprepared. Something told him he would be killed in this adventure. And yet, compared to the life he was leading—stuck with a brutal stepfather and sharing a room with his senile great-grandmother, poor, unemployed, without even his whore of a sister— what did he have to lose?

"When do we leave?" he asked.

"Tomorrow morning, 10:15."

Chapter Twelve

Yuri had never flown before. He didn't sleep at all that night, more from excitement than nervousness. While he listened to a symphony of snores, wheezes and heavy breathing from his beloved Bubbie, he drew like someone possessed. He dressed Christopher Reeve up as Superman in drag walking down the aisle in a cross-dressed wedding with a female Humphrey Bogart. Presidents Reagan and Gorbachev were toddlers holding rattles, sitting on a wall, while Fred Astaire and Ginger Rogers were seated as judges at a pie eating contest. When his alarm went off, just as he had started to place a naked Che Guevara on a toilet seat, his heart jumped. He would have sworn it had only been a half hour since he started.

Dora was waiting in a taxi for him when he came out from his apartment building in the early morning light. He was dressed in his new blue suit, but hadn't been able to figure out how to tie the striped tie that Leon Kaminsky had chosen for him. He carried a change of clothes and his toiletries in a gym bag. In the back seat with him, Dora helped him with his tie. He liked the light touch of her fingers on his neck and how deftly she pulled down the collar of his shirt. She smelled like narcissus. When he asked her what he should expect at the Bank of Cyprus, which she had told him was their ultimate destination, she held a finger to her mouth.

At Larnaca, he followed her to the check-in counter and through security. It amazed him that everyone else seemed so fluent with the routine. The racks of whiskey, perfume, and jewelry glittering under neon lights surprised him by their sheer quantity; otherwise, the airport experience was quite familiar from all the films he had seen. They settled in their seats for the two-hour and fifty-minute Ukraine International flight to Cyprus. Dora declined the sandwich that was offered. Yuri asked if he could have hers as well as his own. "I missed breakfast this morning." The truth was he had missed breakfast most mornings, and other meals too.

"Just don't spill anything on your clothes. You've only got one set," she said.

There was no one in the seat next to them. Whispering, she explained what to expect when they got there. "We'll go through customs first. They'll ask you whether you're there for pleasure or business. Just say pleasure. We're there for the beach, even though it's cold outside. If they ask where you're saying, it's the Grand Hotel. That's the nicest one in Cyprus. You won't have any problems with Customs. After that, we'll take a taxi to our hotels. I'll be staying down the street from you at a cheap hotel, the Hotel Strovolos."

"Why do I get the Grand Hotel and you get the cheap one?"

"Because you're an oligarch and I'm just a poor investigative reporter," she said. "We all have our roles to play."

Yuri listened. "This afternoon we'll go over to the main branch of the Bank of Cyprus" she continued. "You'll ask to see the manager. You'll present yourself as the director of the Global Opportunities Fund and show them your passport. Ask for a copy of the registration papers and the last three statements of account. It should all be routine."

"What if something happens?" Yuri asked.

"I don't anticipate that. The worst that can happen now is they'll have some excuse not to give you these documents."

"Have you done this before?"

Dora shook her head. "This is an experiment," she said. "We've never tried this before. The closest we've come was when I took a job as a secretary in a bank that was believed to be laundering money for the Russian mafia. Before I could learn very much, I got fired for refusing to have sex with the bank manager."

"Oh, that sucks. I'm glad you refused," Yuri said.

"Thank you. But I did process a large cash deposit one day that gave us an important new lead. Mostly, we work in the office analyzing massive amounts of data, most of it publicly available."

"Is it dangerous?" asked Yuri. "I would think the mafia would want to stop you at any cost."

"It can be dangerous. Our office got firebombed after we documented how the prosecutor general took bribes from a construction company for a contract to build a highway. If I hadn't gone out to walk a neighbor's dog, I might have been killed."

"But you kept at it," said Yuri. "Couldn't you just be a lawyer living in Springsteen, New Jersey?"

"I think the greatest thing one can do in a life is to work for a cause that's bigger than ourselves," she said.

"You should've been a rabbi," Yuri told her.

"That's what my uncle Morris always says. He's a rabbi, a real one, though you'd hardly believe it. Maybe you'll meet him someday."

The captain announced that they had started their initial descent into Larnaca Airport, the flight attendants collected the trash and told Yuri to put his seat into an upright and locked position. He peered out the window. The sea below seemed to rush up at them and then he saw the beach coming closer and a runway miraculously appeared as the plane landed with a slight bump.

"Wow! That was better than in the movies," he said and they both laughed.

During a long lunch in the chandeliered restaurant of the Grand Hotel, they talked about Obama and the new pope, Taylor Swift and Lady Gaga. "Have you seen *Sluha Narodu, Servant of the People?*" asked Yuri. Dora shook her head. Yuri couldn't believe it. "How can you work against corruption in Ukraine and not have seen that? It's the most popular show on television. I never miss an episode. It's a satire. Volodymyr Zelensky plays a history teacher who rants against corruption. His students shoot a video of him that goes viral and he is unexpectedly elected President. It's hilarious."

Afterwards, they walked in the afternoon sun to the imposing red brick façade of the Bank of Cyprus. It felt good to be in a foreign country. Yuri had been having the best time since he was a kid, but as they walked up to the bank, his heart began to race.

"It's showtime, Yuri," said Dora. "Do you feel ready?"

"I suppose so. I'm a little nervous, but I'll be all right," he said. He was a lot nervous, and he didn't know if he would be all right.

"Remember, you're actually the official director of this company. Keep telling yourself that," she said. Just be yourself. I'll meet you outside. Good luck."

It had all seemed unreal until this moment. But there was nothing as real as a bank, he thought, as he climbed the stairs and pushed open the heavy glass door. There was a long line of tellers and people bustling about. He spotted a small office behind glass walls with a man at a desk. The sign read "Assistant Bank Manager." He tapped on his door and stuck his head in. The man looked up.

"How may I help you?" the man said.

"I'd like to see the bank manager," said Yuri in his most authoritative voice.

"I'm afraid he's busy right now. Can I be of help?" said the assistant manager.

"It's about the Global Opportunities Fund. I'm the director. I need some copies of documents," spoke Yuri.

The man looked him up and down, then came around his desk and offered his hand.

"Yes, of course, the manager will be most happy to meet you, sir. We were not expecting you. Can I get you something, some coffee or water?"

"No, thanks," said Yuri.

"If you don't mind," said the man with an obsequious tilt of his head, "I'm required to get a copy of your passport. I'm sure you understand."

Yuri handed it to him.

"Please follow me, Mr. Yavlinsky." He led Yuri to the other end of the bank and knocked on a door with a brass plaque that said, "Stephan Kreutzman, Manager."

"Come in," said a gruff voice from within.

"Mr. Kreutzman, I have a gentleman here from the Global Opportunities Fund. He'd like to have a word with you."

With that, the manager's face lit up. He stood and walked over to Yuri as if an old friend. "Please, welcome. I'm Stephan Kreutzman, the bank manager. How can I be of service? And with whom do I have the pleasure of speaking?"

Yuri kept his expression implacable. He was beginning to feel comfortable in his role. The man had a firm handshake, but Yuri gripped harder. He looked confidently into the man's gray eyes. "My name is Yuri Yavlinsky. I'm the Director of the Global Opportunities Fund. Something has come up and I need to get authenticated copies of our last three statements and our registration."

Yuri could not have anticipated what came next. The manager's expression changed to one of surprise. "But I have already Fed Ex'd these to you this morning, as Mr. Prokofiev requested," he said. "For the SEC, yes?"

Yuri was taken aback, unsure how to respond. He nodded his head slowly, trying to understand what he had just heard. He looked over the manager's shoulder at the photos on the wall of the man posing with other silver-haired men in suits and noticed his own reflection in a window in his new outfit. For a second, he flashed on his meeting with the zoo director, on the photos that hung in his office, and then heard himself say, "Yes, thank you. It was much appreciated. I'm afraid this matter is of such importance that we need hard copies immediately."

The manager smiled, rubbing his hands together. "Of course. I quite understand." He stepped from his office and whispered something to the man Yuri first spoke with, who had waited just outside. Yuri had never had an experience like this. No one had ever been deferential to him before. He felt oddly euphoric. *I could get used to this*, he thought.

The manager returned and said it would be but a minute, as they had already prepared these documents just hours before.

"How long will you be staying in Larnaca, Mr. Yavlinsky?" he asked.

Yuri had rarely heard his last name spoken. "I am just here to collect these documents, I'm afraid."

"I hope you can at least spend a night here. We have wonderful restaurants in Larnaca, excellent fresh seafood. You must try La Maison Fleurie."

"Thank you. I will," said Yuri. "I'm staying at the Grand Hotel. I had a superb lunch there this afternoon."

The assistant manager returned with a folder and handed it

to Yuri. There were handshakes all around and the two men walked him back out through the bank. Yuri felt powerful, in control. It was only when he painted in his room at night that he ever felt such authority in his own life, but never outside of that, never with other people. With each step his confidence grew. As he approached the front door, an outlandish thought entered his mind. Before he could reflect on it, he stopped and said, "Mr. Kreutzman, I realize I have no local currency. Do I have sufficient funds for a small withdrawal, perhaps just 3000 Euros worth?"

The manager smiled. "I believe you have enough to cover that." They walked over to one of the tellers. Yuri signed a withdrawal slip and the teller handed him 5000 Lira. He shook hands with the managers.

"I hope we see you again Mr. Yavlinsky," said Kreutzman.

"I think you might," said Yuri, and walked out into the sunshine.

Chapter Thirteen

"Hello, Toni?"

"Tak." Antoinette Bertrand recognized the voice immediately. She was actually expecting this call.

"It's Viktor, Viktor Raskolnovitch."

Toni waited three beats. "Viktor, how did you get my number?"

"Is easy. How are you?"

"I'm good. I just finished creating a painting and am enjoying a glass of wine and a cigarette that made you even richer, I suppose," she said.

"Duzhe dobre. Very good. So, now I am in your debt. May I take you to Kanapa's for dinner tonight? Have you been? Has your father the consul general not taken you? It's best restaurant in Kyiv," said Viktor.

Toni laughed. "Maybe I have plans tonight, Viktor Ivanovitch."

"Perhaps another time, then."

"Viktor, I am playing with you," she said. "I would love to have dinner with you tonight, but not at Kanapa's." She thought for a moment. "There's a small Vietnamese restaurant on my street, very simple, very intimate. Do you like Vietnamese food?"

"I think so," he said.

She could tell he was caught a little off balance. "It's very casual," she said. "Perhaps you could borrow a pair of jeans."

It was his turn to laugh. "Tak, I have jeans, real American jeans. Shall I make reservations?"

"I don't think this restaurant takes them," she said.

"No problem. When may I pick you up?"

"I think it will be better if we meet there. It's called Hue." She spelled it for him. "Let me look a second... It's on Fastofsky Street, 2213. Your driver can find it. How about eight?"

"Perfect. Fastofsky 2213 at 8 p.m. I'll be there," said Raskol-novitch.

"And Viktor."

"Yes?"

"Please, no bodyguards."

"You won't see them, my dear Antoinette," he said.

She arrived late, on purpose. Three black SUV's were double parked at one end of the street and three on the other. Viktor was at a small table in the back. He stood as she walked in the door.

"I was afraid you weren't coming," he said.

"It takes a girl a while to get ready." She looked around the room. Three of the dozen tables in the restaurant were occupied by burly men in black with gold chain necklaces, looking notice-ably uncomfortable. Gesturing towards them, she asked, "Do they like Vietnamese cuisine?"

Viktor smiled. He was dressed in a Chicago Bulls sweatshirt and blue jeans. Toni had on a pair of black corduroy pants and a pink cashmere turtleneck.

"I hope I'm not overdressed," he said.

"No, not at all. You look very handsome in that. Much younger," she said.

A Vietnamese woman with a deeply wrinkled face placed two menus on the table and two glasses of water. Besides the obvious bodyguards, three other tables were occupied by older Vietnamese couples and two others by young white women. The restaurant was furnished with wood chairs and metal tables covered with white-and-red-checkered oil cloth. Chinese paper lanterns hung from a ceiling with exposed pipes and heating ducts casting a soft red light.

Raskolnovitch looked up at the waitress. "Thank you," he said, but she did not appear to hear him.

"So, Toni, do you come here often? Is very charming," said Raskolnovitch.

"It is, isn't it? The Pho is excellent. The real thing," she told him.

"Pho?" asked Raskolnovitch.

"Yes, a traditional Vietnamese soup. You should try it with chicken or beef."

Raskolnovitch smiled. "Duzhe dobre, Very good."

She sensed he enjoyed being out of his glass bubble. Toni asked, "Viktor, why do you have so many bodyguards. Do you have many enemies?"

"Yes, many, too many," he said. "Ukraine is very dangerous. Many scores to settle. Many gangs. There are powerful crime families. Some control ports, shipping, cars. Some liquor. Some prostitutes. Everyone wants to control politics. There are Georgians, Chechens, Uzbeks, many, many Russians. Everyone wants a piece of the pie, but the pie's not very big. Me, I'm lucky. The president likes me. Putin likes me. But I'm forced to keep a small army to protect me or someone will steal my pie. You understand?"

"But Viktor, this is no way to live. How can you ever relax?

You must always be looking over your shoulder. Do you ever wish you could be anonymous? Go around by yourself, not worry that someone is going to kill you? Be like a normal person?"

"Tak. Of course," he said. "Sometimes I fantasize that I'll give it all up. But you can't have everything, can you? I enjoy playing this game. Maybe I'd be bored without some danger, I think. I like my toys, my yacht, my estate, my helicopter. I could give it all up, but for what? To work in an office, to have a nice boss, maybe be a street cleaner?"

The waitress came back for their order. Toni smiled. "We'd like some Pho, please." She turned to Viktor. "Chicken or steak or brisket?"

"You choose," he said.

"We'll have steak, please," said Toni.

"To drink?"

"Water will be fine. Thank you." The waitress gathered their menus and left.

"Maybe I could be a waiter or a cook," said Viktor, watching her return to the kitchen.

"I think you would make a good fireman or policeman," she said.

"No, policemen. They're too corrupt," he said. Then, "What about you, Toni? You're a painter. Is it enough? Do you want to be famous like Matisse? Or something else, maybe?"

She smiled, sat back in her chair and thought a moment. "I used to think I would be an actress, later a politician or a diplomat like my father. It's funny how we try to be like our parents or how our parents wanted to be, isn't it? My mother wanted to be an actress, but instead she taught literature at a lycée in Dijon. They divorced when I was little. I had no memory of my father, growing up. But then my mother was killed in a car accident when I was twelve and my father came back to take care of me. I travelled all over the world with him. It was a good life, a good education. I tried acting school, but I realized I wasn't ambitious enough. It wasn't the real me."

She paused, breaking eye contact, then looked up again. "Then I had a love affair with an artist in Paris. We were married for a while. I fell in love with painting. I eventually left the artist, but part of the artist, I guess, never left me."

He gazed at her, lost in thought. "So, is painting enough? Does it make you happy?"

"Oh, yes. *Sans doute*. I am happiest when I paint. I don't need anything else."

"But you must also make a living. Is a problem, yes?" asked Viktor.

"Not really. I never worry about money. It seems to come when I need it."

"You are lucky. For me back then, money always disappeared when I needed it."

"I understand. But Viktor, tell me, was there ever anything you wanted to be before you became the tobacco tycoon?"

He nodded. "Yes, I always wanted to be an airline pilot. When the war started in Afghanistan I had a chance. Someday, maybe I'll take you to the Pamir Mountains in Kyrgyzstan, by helicopter. Would you like that?"

"It sounds wonderful."

The waitress brought two large steaming bowls of soup plus smaller bowls of bean sprouts and basil leaves and placed them before Viktor and Toni.

"Thank you," said Toni. She watched Viktor as he suspiciously sipped his soup, bent over the bowl.

He raised his eyes with a look of surprise. "It's very good, very, very good, maybe the best soup I ever tasted."

Toni laughed. "There is a lot to experience down here on earth," she said. "You seem to have anything you've ever wanted. Is there anything you can't have?" she asked.

"Of course." He took two more spoonfuls of soup before answering. "There is always love."

"Have you not found that before?" asked Toni.

"I was married once before the war. We were very young. She ran off with a Georgian guy while I was in Kabul. She asked for a divorce. No problem. She was the wrong girl for me. Then I got married again, to the president's niece. We were very happy for ten years, maybe more, but nothing could ever satisfy her. She yelled at everyone. Me, I never yell. I treat all people the same."

"How sad," said Toni. "You deserve better."

His face brightened. "And what about you, Toni. The artist in Paris, is he the only husband?"

"It's complicated," she said, looking away. "I was never officially married to the man in Paris. We told everyone we were man and wife, but neither of us believed in marriage. Five years ago, I met a banker in Bern and we got married. Legally, I'm still married, though we haven't talked in two years. We had a good life, lots of money, lots of superficial friends. I prefer a simpler life."

Raskolnovitch nodded. "My life is not simple, I'm afraid. Is very complicated. Many people to manage. Many people try to hurt me. Too many business deals. Always politics."

They ate in silence. Finally, his soup finished, Viktor looked up and said, "Toni, maybe you want a simple life, but sometimes it's good to enjoy yourself. It's cold in Kyiv. I have a beautiful yacht on a Greek island. Maybe one day you'll come, go sailing, get tan."

Toni smiled. "I've heard of your yacht, even before I had heard of you. I was at a cocktail party in Geneva with my father. Jacques Gavi, the former president of France, was bragging to someone about being on some fantastic boat and all the beautiful women that were there."

Viktor tilted back in his chair and laughed with great amusement. "He is bragging now, but if ever I threaten to show the video I took of him, he'll deny he ever saw such a boat."

Toni shut her eyes and rolled her head to indicate she was not impressed.

"What about skiing? You like skiing?" he asked, hoping to change the subject.

"I like it, but my real passion is ice skating," she said.

"In a few weeks, I'm going to Davos. You must have heard of Davos, the World Economic Forum. There's great skiing, but also there is the biggest ice-skating rink I ever saw, like football fields. Maybe you should come with me." He looked so innocent in his Chicago Bulls sweatshirt. *"Duzhe dobre,"* Toni said. "You may have found my weak spot, Viktor."

Chapter Fourteen

When Dora saw Yuri come bouncing down the stairs by the bank entrance, he looked taller than she remembered. An irrepressible, goofy smile lit up his face. He held a file in one hand above his head like a trophy. Dora's eyes widened It actually had worked. "Oh, my God, you got it?"

"All of it," responded Yuri. "They could not have been kinder."

He moved to embrace her, but she held up a finger to stop him. "Not now, not here. We mustn't attract attention." They walked along the boulevard away from the bank. A tall, handsome man with salt and pepper hair and wearing a yarmulke smiled as he passed them, Dora, blocking Yuri's view of him, nodded back.

"How about I take you to dinner at La Maison Fleurie? I hear the seafood is excellent," said Yuri.

"You should have been an actor, Yuri. You're very believable in your new suit," said Dora, looking him up and down.

He put his hand on her shoulder, stopped and turned to face

her. "I'm quite serious," he said, pulling out the roll of liras from his pocket.

She froze as the realization of what must have happened hit her like poison. "What the fuck! Yuri, tell me it's not true. Oh, my God. No. Please no. You'll get us killed."

Yuri's smile vanished. "No, Dora, listen. It's nothing. It's only 3000 Euros. They'll never notice such a small withdrawal. It was easy, normal. The bank manager didn't hesitate at all. Really, there's nothing to worry about. Let's go celebrate."

She grabbed both of his arms in her fists. "Yuri, listen to me. This is serious. These oligarchs will stop at nothing. They'll kill you as easily as swatting a fly. It's one thing to get documents on behalf of law enforcement. But this is something personal. They can't overlook that. You stole from them. If they find out, and they will eventually, they'll come after you. They'll shoot you or blow up your car or poison you, probably torture you."

Yuri looked in her eyes. "I don't own a car. I have nothing to lose. I'm not afraid of them."

"Well, you should be," said Dora.

She tensed as she saw a thin, devious smile spread across his face. "No, I'm not afraid. It is they who should be afraid. I feel strong and free for the first time in my life. I will not crawl back into my cave. These people, they steal from everyone. Maybe they need to know what it feels like to have someone steal from them."

He looked around him. The sun was low in the sky sinking towards the sea, illuminating the clouds from below. The noise of the street threatened to drown out their conversation. "Come, let's get a drink. I have a plan, but let's get someplace where we can sit and discuss it in private." Yuri looked up and immediately hailed a taxi.

"La Maison Fleurie, please," he told the driver.

Chapter Fifteen

Yuri didn't actually have a plan, but one was forming in his mind as they rode in the taxi to La Maison Fleurie. His newfound confidence matched his suit. But he saw how frightened Dora was. They rode in silence.

The restaurant was just opening when they arrived and the dining room was empty. It was too dark to sit at the bar on such a beautiful evening. He asked to be seated outside on the patio under the glass canopy where they could watch the sky turn pink and red. They sat alone at a table with a white tablecloth and a bouquet of yellow flowers. He ordered a bottle of champagne. Dora appeared terrified, unable to speak.

"Look, relax," he said. "I'm on your side. We want the same thing. You can fight corruption in the courts, but they own the judges. This is not America. This is Ukraine and Russia, real mafia states. The oligarchs control the government. People like us can't win. I'm happy to help you with these documents. Maybe something good will happen. But I have a plan, a way to really hurt them. I'll need your help, but I don't want to put you in danger. Just point me in the right direction. I'm not concerned with my own safety, only yours."

A waiter in a tuxedo arrived and placed a pedestal with an ice bucket next to them. They watched a ribbon of light form on the sea in the distance.

Dora stared at Yuri with a look of fear and wonder. "I can't let you do this, Yuri. I got you into this. Your death will be on my conscience forever. Please don't do this to me, for my sake," she said.

Another waiter arrived with the champagne and two crystal glass flutes. He showed the label to Yuri. Yuri had never tasted champagne before but had watched this scene unfold in movies a hundred times. He nodded. The waiter nonchalantly twisted the cork off in a white napkin while looking at the sunset. The sound of the cork popping buoyed Yuri's spirits. The waiter poured them both a glass, bowed, and disappeared.

"Dora, I understand, but you must let me make my own decisions. You are not at all responsible for what I'm going to do now. Go back to Kyiv with your documents. I'll testify, if you need me to. But for the first time, I feel like I have a purpose to my life. I can do some good. These bandits are destroying my country and my family. If it were a war, I would enlist. Why not fight now? You've given me a chance, that's all. You're not responsible for what I do next."

She lifted her head. Her deep blue eyes, which had intimidated him before, were soft and wet. He could read the fear, but there was something else, attraction?

"Someday, I'll explain why I'm so afraid for you," she said. "I can see now that I can't stop you. Go ahead and tell me your goddamn plan."

He wondered what she meant by 'Someday, I'll explain why I'm so afraid for you.' But he saw something else that attracted her that was as strong as her fear, something unspoken. She had given in too quickly. He could tell she knew he was right. Exposes and lawsuits might slow down the corruption that was eating away the rule of law, but the oligarchs' grip on society would continue undeterred. Her inner Joan of Arc was biting at the bit, he saw. First a toast," he said. "To our success getting these documents." They each took a sip, their eyes still on each other. The champagne had a sharp, dry taste that brought back memories to Yuri of eating fruit peels when his mother baked pies. The tiny bubbles made him want to laugh.

"OK, Dora. If the bank gives me company documents and even lets me withdrawal a little cash, why wouldn't they let me transfer larger amounts? If I withdraw some serious funds, maybe I could do some good, pay the back taxes, for example. It's perfectly legal. What could they say?"

Dora looked at him as if he were mad. "You are fucking crazy!" she said, but her face betrayed a hint of admiration. "Do you really think it can be that easy?"

Yuri took a much bigger swig of champagne. "Maybe I take small amounts at first, so the bank gets used to me, small enough that it doesn't arouse suspicion, either here or with whoever it is that watches these accounts in Ukraine. Then, one day, we transfer funds to the tax authorities in Kyiv. The burden would be on the bank to explain why it wasn't honoring a payment to the legitimate authorities of Ukraine on an order from the director of the account." He leaned in closer to her. These bastards used me to steal from the state. It's the least I can do to pay the state back."

He watched as she considered what he was proposing. "Or, better yet," he said. "We transfer ownership of the company to another shell company like they did. They won't be able to find the new owners any better than we could."

"They will definitely kill you," she said.

95

They sat in silence after that. That cold truth sat between them like a ghost.

"Let's drink to my health, then," said Yuri, taking large gulps of champagne.

A few people had begun to wander onto the patio, a man in a fedora who sat and opened a newspaper and, closer to them, an older woman dressed in a white silk pants suit holding a white poodle in her arms. The waiter soon brought the woman a plate filled with slices of steak, which she proceeded to feed to her dog. Yuri stared at her. The champagne had gone to his head, fueling a sense of power and resentment.

He turned back to Dora and gestured with his eyes over to the woman. "My family hasn't eaten meat in a month. That dog —" he stopped, unable to finish the sentence. "I'm going to do this, Dora, even if it means my life. These gangsters won't play by your rules. We need to fight them the only way they'll understand. Go back to Kyiv with your papers. I'm going to hang out here a little longer and see what can happen next."

Dora finished her glass and studied him. A waiter came over and filled their glasses again. The woman in white put the poodle down by her feet and opened a menu. In the distance, the sun was vanishing below the sea.

Yuri smiled at Dora. She smiled back and began to laugh.

"You crazy motherfucker," she said. "Here's to you."

He bowed his head to her. The champagne was making him giddy. "Did you ever see *Thelma and Louise*?" he asked.

"Of course."

"This feels like a *Thelma and Louise* moment. Maybe I'll drive off a cliff, but maybe I'll get to the other side," he said.

She reached over and held his arm. Her eyes were wet. "I'm half tempted to join you. But it's sheer suicide."

"I can't let you, Dora. You've given me my freedom, but I

can't take you down with me. You can help me, guide me with information, but I need to do this by myself."

She didn't let go of his arm. A tear fell down her cheek. "I have an idea," she said. "This Global Opportunities Fund is just one of your many holdings. They're incorporated in a half dozen countries. Why don't we see, if we can get all their registrations and accounts? We could go after all of them. With that information we could expose their criminal conspiracy. Maybe your plan can work, but let's do our research first."

"Will you go with me?" he asked.

She let out a deep breath and shook her head. "I can't Yuri, I —" she paused for a long moment, looking at him with a frown. Finally, a smile broke across her face, "What the fuck! Why not? If it worked once, it may work again. We only live once."

He lifted his glass, "Here's to Thelma and Louise and to Dora and her health."

Chapter Sixteen

Two days after they returned to Kyiv, Dora and Yuri went together to the tax office. The receptionist told them to go in. The prosecutor was expecting them, she said. They knocked on the inner door. "Please, come in," they heard a voice say.

Yuri held the door open for Dora. The prosecutor stood up and shook hands with Yuri who was still dressed in his new suit. It felt quite different than when he was here as a potential felon wearing his frayed shirt and only good pants. "Please sit down," he said, motioning for them to take the two seats in front of the desk. Dora thanked the prosecutor for meeting with them.

"It is me who must thank you," he said. "What you've done is extraordinary, a big breakthrough. The documents you brought are the first real opening we've had in this case. We are very grateful. Corruption is sucking the blood out of our country, but it is very hard to prove. Now we have some evidence we can use to go after these oligarchs. Thank you."

Yuri nodded. He felt a sense of pride, something he hadn't felt since he was a kid.

The prosecutor continued. "I have good news for you, Mr.

Yavlinsky. We have formally dropped all charges against you. You have done a great service for the nation." He handed him a paper with an official seal on the bottom and then turned to Dora. Yuri let out a breath.

"And you, Dora, I must admit I was very doubtful you would succeed. I will never underestimate you again. It was a crazy strategy, but you somehow managed to pull it off. Bravo."

"Thank you," said Dora. "But Yuri should get all the credit. He's a born actor. He's earned his reward. Neither of us, though, are ready to quit, sir. You've got what you need for a case of tax evasion, but to prove corruption, you'll need more. The real owner of this shell company will claim that all the deposits made to it came from other corporations, other shell companies. Without being able to see their books as well, we can't claim that this is ill begotten income." She paused to make sure he could follow her. "I'd like to propose—we'd like to propose, I should say—that we try the same gambit for one of the other companies. If it worked once in Cyprus, it might work again in Panama or else-where. What do you think?"

The prosecutor shut his eyes and shook his head. "I think it's extremely dangerous," he said, "for Yuri especially. The 'benefi-cial owner,' as we so euphemistically call it, will take this as an existential attack, which it most certainly is. He will stop at nothing to protect his wealth. Yuri would be in grave danger, Dora. I said I'll never underestimate you again, but I can't just let you put yourselves in harm's way."

Yuri again noticed the two missing fingers on the prosecutor's hand. "Sir, if I may," interrupted Yuri. "It's really not as difficult as it may look from here. I'm not worried. I'd like to do this."

The Prosecutor stared at Yuri and said nothing. Then, he stared at Dora, but neither of them showed any sign of backing down. He sat back in his chair, tapping his fingertips together, thinking.

Finally, he spoke. "I want you to know who you're up against. The name you gave us, Prokofiev, which the bank manager in Cyprus mentioned, was the clue we needed to identify the true owner of that account."

He picked up his phone and in a minute an assistant came in with a projector, a laptop and a screen.

"Might this be the man who bought your passport?" the Prosecutor asked.

Yuri looked at the image on the screen. "It is," he said. He felt again how foolish and naïve he had been.

"His name is Dmitri Prokofiev. He's the financial brains behind this benefactor of society and humankind."

Soon a mug shot appeared of a young man of eighteen, with brown hair and a pugilist's nose, obviously broken several times before. Another photo followed that appeared to be of the same man as an Air Force cadet and finally a third photo of him, now in his mid-fifties, dressed in a tuxedo.

"This is Viktor Ivanovitch Raskolnovitch, purported to be one of the richest men in Ukraine. He's sometimes referred to as the 'Tobacco King.' He owns the state cigarette concession, controlling 99% of all cigarettes sold in the country." Yuri recognized the photograph from an article he had read in some magazine left on a bus. He imagined drawing him standing on a pile of corpses. He also has a majority share of a steel mill in the Donbas. But these are not the main sources of his wealth. In addition, he also controls most of the opium coming out of Afghanistan with labs in Tajikistan that process the raw paste into heroin. We estimate he brings in thirty million dollars a month, all in cash. He launders all that through a series of offshore companies, most of which are in your name, Mr. Yavlinsky." He smiled ironically at Yuri. "These shell companies then invest in legitimate businesses, washing the money clean of its corrupt origins.

"Raskolnovitch is thought to be a cold-blooded killer, having eliminated two rival gangs in the mid-eighties with a veritable army of Chechen and Afghan veterans. He is the principal backer of our esteemed president. If anyone epitomizes the corruption of our country, it is this man, Viktor Raskolnovitch."

He looked long and hard at Yuri. "You may not be worried, Mr. Yavlinsky, but you should know who you are playing with."

Yuri realized he should be afraid, but what he felt was very different. He felt pride. He felt powerful. He was David against Goliath. He made eye contact with Dora. Did he read something similar in her expression? He knew how serious this was. They were in the tiger's cage and he had learned in his previous incarnation to keep a respectful distance from any such beast. Everything told him to back off, not to press his luck. But something else in him refused to turn away.

"With all due respect, sir, I'd like to try this one more time," Yuri said. He looked at Dora and, this time, he felt sure he saw a smile in her sapphire blue eyes.

Chapter Seventeen

Viktor Raskolnovitch piloted his Gulfstream G650 jet as they neared Davos and invited Toni to sit next to him in the cockpit. He felt most in control when he was flying. It was a crystal-clear day. The indomitable Alps spread out below them, snow dust blowing off the peaks. Raskolnovitch tipped the nose down and started its descent from heaven back to earth, gracefully returning to reality.

"C'est éblouissant!" exclaimed Toni.

Every civilian and military airfield within a hundred miles of Davos, Switzerland, had been deployed to accommodate the thousands of private jets that were descending on the World Economic Forum. The event was the ultimate summit of the elites: the bankers, politicians, CEOs, media moguls, philanthropists and celebrities at the top of the food chain of money and power, and the journalists, pundits and non-profit leaders who sought to meet and be seen with them. Raskolnovitch was proud to be among them. After all, he was, in his way, a banker, a politician, a CEO, a mogul, a philanthropist, and a celebrity. They landed about twelve miles from Davos Village. Two black

SUVs drove up the runway to meet them. Viktor turned off the engines, removed his earphones, and turned to Toni. "It's very cold outside, Toni, minus 5 degrees. I brought something to keep you warm, if you'd like." He unzipped a garment bag and took out a full-length black sable coat that looked like it was still alive.

"It's very kind of you Viktor, but I brought my own mink. It belonged to my Swiss grandmother, Agnes Bertrand, who was something of a renowned artist in her time. She was said to be part of an occult circle in Zurich with Carl Jung, possibly his lover. I am told I resemble her, but she died when I was too young to remember," Toni said.

Viktor thought she was being a little pretentious. He had never heard of Carl Jung. He felt disappointed that she rejected his gift, and such a beautiful and expensive one at that.

"That's too bad," said Viktor. "So, you are Swiss, not French."

"On my father's side. My mother was French."

She unfastened her shoulder straps and walked back to the passenger cabin to put on boots and her fur coat and hat. A white muffler hung from her neck.

"You look very beautiful," said Raskolnovitch as he emerged from the cockpit. "Probably best we go skating first before we get caught in the madness. Did you bring your skates?"

"No, I left my skates in Paris. I'll just rent some," said Toni.

"No problem," Raskolnovitch said. "I brought some for you." He unwrapped a shoe box covered in brown paper, inside of which was a pair of white leather figure skates. "Please, try them on," he said.

"How did you know my size?" Toni asked, surprised. "This is so kind of you." She took off her fur coat, sat on one of the armchairs, and pulled the skates from the box.

"I made a guess. It's like Cinderella? No?"

Toni laughed. She pulled the sides apart and inserted her

foot. *"Incroyable!"* she said. "It's perfect. But, honestly, how did you know?"

Raskolnovitch smiled. "It was truly a guess. But I have other sizes, just in case."

They drove in one of the SUV's to the edge of town where security guards checked their vehicle. The Davos Promenade was hard packed with snow. They got out and walked a short distance in their boots to the Congress Hall where they received their badges, white ones with a little gold dot, which was the highest designation, reserved for those who gave a quarter of a million dollars or more. In general, the whole village was an "entourage-free zone," but Raskolnovitch was allowed to have two of his bodyguards accompany him.

German Chancellor Angela Merkel was speaking in the main auditorium when they arrived, a much anticipated address after Edward Snowden's revelation that the NSA had tapped her cell phone for the past ten years; but Viktor suggested they head, instead, to the ice-skating rink while it was still light. Several people came up to say hello or introduce themselves to him. Jamie Dimon, the head of JPMorgan Chase, stopped to shake his hand. The CEO of Deutsche Bank waved to him as he walked past. This was the ultimate in corporate speed dating. If someone could take time lapse photography and map all the movements of people at Davos, they'd have a perfect diagram of the pecking order of the world's elite.

They continued down the length of the Promenade, arm in arm. "Thank you for bringing me here," she said.

"It's my pleasure," he nodded.

"What's your plan for this evening after ice-skating?" she asked.

"We'll take the funicular to our chalet and you can change for dinner. Paul Manafort is hosting an event to honor Ukraine's president. It's important I be there. Many celebrities. I think maybe Elton John is coming. It should be very interesting," said Raskolnovitch.

"And good food, I suspect," said Toni.

"Indeed. After dinner we'll go to the Wine Forum and taste great wine. It's the best party at Davos. We may see your friend, former president Gavi, there for a short meeting, if possible. Is it OK?" he asked.

Toni laughed. "Monsieur Gavi is not my friend. I never actually met him. I overheard him once at a diplomatic reception in Geneva. He doesn't know me. But I would enjoy meeting him."

At the other end of the Promenade they came to a nondescript residential area with a sports complex that housed Europe's largest outdoor skating rink, two and a half square kilometers of perfectly manicured ice. Surprisingly, there was no one skating, only a lonely Zamboni, driving in lazy circles, resurfacing the ice. Raskolnovitch could see Toni's heart drop when it appeared that this ultimate skating fantasy was closed, but it was not. On this most perfect day, with the Alps towering in the distance, she had the rink to herself. She hurriedly laced her skates, goose-walked over to Raskolnovitch and kissed him on the cheek. "Merci Viktor, c'est une reve, a dream, thank you." And then she headed out onto the ice.

Raskolnovitch stood by the railing and watched her glide across the immense expanse of ice as graceful as a swan in her mink coat and hat. She held her arms wide as if about to fly. She was clearly in her element, skating backwards and forwards without a glance of caution. She spun in place, in centrifugal grace, bringing her arms up next to her body and stretching them above her, as if in prayer, then went tearing across the ice bent over on one skate, arms outstretched.

Raskolnovitch retreated to the stands lost on his cell phone, looking up from time to time to watch his beautiful Antoinette pirouette across the ice. He was envious of her prowess but knew how clumsy he would look on the rink, forced to hold onto the railing like a child. He'd rather indulge himself in the spectacle of her beauty and joy.

A mother and two little girls came on the ice, staying near the perimeter. Viktor looked up and saw a man in a puffy quilted jacket and black knit cap skate nonchalantly in a large figure eight, passing close to Toni, almost colliding with her.

Startled, the man fell just as he passed her. Toni went over to offer her hand and steadied him as he got swiftly to his feet. They exchanged a few words. Toni made sure Raskolnovitch could not see the man pass her something.

Rabbi Morris Weissgold got up, brushed the ice off his jacket and skated away from her.

After a half hour, she came up to Viktor, breathless, face flushed. "Oh, Viktor," she exclaimed, "That was perfection. I have never experienced anything so ecstatic and yet so sublime. Thank you. I did something I have only dreamed about, skating with my eyes closed. It was pure bliss, like a religious experience. I am very grateful. Thank you."

"I got to watch an angel. It was also a great experience for me," he said.

They walked back towards the village center in a kind of rapture. Raskolnovitch was tempted to take her in his arms and kiss her, but he would not let himself. She was his Faberge Egg, he thought. He must hold her with absolute care, not soil her with his vanities. Perhaps someday, but for now he felt something entirely new, something righteous. He would not spoil it with his greed.

They took a four-minute ride on the 110-year-old blue and yellow funicular up to the Grand Époque-style Schatzelp Hotel, a mile above Davos Village. The sun had already begun to set below the ragged crests of the Alps casting the alpine plateau in shadows. They were met at the top by Raskolnovitch's two body-guards. He realized that she had been unaware of their presence and was surprised to see them. The guards directed them to the Villa Guarda, set in the pines discreetly near the hotel.

Raskolnovitch showed her to her room. When she opened the door, she was greeted with a fantastical display of colors. Roses filled every conceivable space, their fragrance intoxicating. There was a fireplace going in one corner, a king-size four poster bed and south-facing windows with a spectacular panorama of majestic snow-covered peaks. "Viktor," she asked, "how can I ever thank you?"

Chapter Eighteen

The shimmering glass and steel skyscrapers of Panama City converged and glittered like a disco ball as they rode in a taxi to the American Trade Hotel in the city's historic old town. Yuri felt a surge of excitement. He had not slept at all on the plane and he was anxious to get to the bank in the morning. Dora had dozed most of the way, but jet lag weighed her down. "This is going to be different than sleepy Cyprus," she said, as they strained to look up at the tall buildings.

Rather than show up unannounced the way they had in Larnaca, they decided to call from the hotel first to set up an appointment with the bank manager. The receptionist spoke little English and it took several conversations with two different people before someone understood that they needed to meet with the bank manager himself. An assistant recognized the name Advanced Holdings International, the shell company that Yuri Yavlinsky nominally owned, and suggested that he meet with the manager over lunch.

"That's very kind," said Yuri, "but I'm afraid I won't have

time for that." He arranged to meet in an hour. Dora would go with him, then wait out of sight outside.

They agreed he should walk out if he felt the slightest thing wrong. But Yuri didn't anticipate any trouble.

As he strode into the lobby of the HSBC Bank, Yuri felt himself take on the posture and gait of a man at the top of his game. He had a slim new leather briefcase, which he had bought in Kyiv. As he passed a window, he caught a glimpse of himself and thought he looked especially good in his suit and his brand new short haircut. But then his eye caught the reflection of a security guard watching him from across the atrium. The man, bald and bearded, dressed in a dark suit, appeared to be talking into a mic clipped on his lapel as he followed Yuri's movements.

It could be nothing, Yuri thought. The man might just be admiring him. But who was the man talking to? In a moment, the barometric pressure of his emotions dropped as if he were in a sudden summer storm. What was he walking into? Was he so naïve as to think this Raskolnovitch character wouldn't have noticed an unauthorized $3,000 withdrawal from his Cyprus account?

Yuri scanned the atrium to see if anyone else was following his movements. Alarm bells rang in his head. He felt himself start to sweat. His heart beat faster. Wouldn't Raskolnovitch have warned them to be on the alert for someone posing as the director of his shell company? Yuri stopped by another window to look at the reflection to see if he was being followed. It wasn't too late to turn around and exit. He hadn't announced himself yet. Dora was waiting in the HSBC Plaza. Shouldn't he warn her? But he didn't see anything else out of the ordinary.

You mustn't panic, he told himself. *The Cyprus scam worked because you were calm and confident. You need to pull it together.* He looked back at the bank guard who was now laughing as he spoke into his mic and no longer seemed to be paying attention to him. *It's nothing*, he thought. He took a deep breath and exhaled. A heavyset woman with round glasses, dressed in a black skirt and white blouse, came up and asked if she could help him. He told her he had an appointment with a Mr. Michaels, the bank manager. She accompanied him to a rear office.

Michaels was a tall thin White man with a dark mustache and a deep tan. He looked up through thick glasses as the woman announced Yavlinsky's arrival. The manager stood and walked around his desk to greet him. "It's good to meet you, Mr. Yavlinsky," said Michaels. "Is it your first time here in Panama City?"

"No," Yuri said. "I often come to visit the toucans at the Soberanía zoo."

They chatted for a few minutes. The manager apologized but asked to see his passport to verify his identity. "It's getting more difficult to conduct business from overseas since our government tightened the rules. Now, owners, like yourself, are required to appear here in person. I'm sorry you had to come all the way from Ukraine just to get some papers. Normally, I would fax them to you, but I understand you need original documents that are apostilled."

Yuri nodded and thanked him. Ten minutes later the woman with round glasses reappeared holding a stack of documents. There was a copy of the Articles of Incorporation, a certificate of public registration, a notarized copy of the latest financial statement, and a letter of reference from the manager himself, which he signed with a gold fountain pen. Yuri noticed the bottom line in the financial statement indicated a balance of two hundred and thirty million dollars. He didn't blanch. They shook hands and Mr. Michaels offered to accommodate any future banking needs he might have.

"If you ever have reason to create another corporation, I would suggest you see my colleague, Mr. Rodriguez, at Mossack Fonseca." He handed Yuri a business card with the man's contact information. "He is very capable and very discreet. We often work together on matters like this." Yuri felt like a door was opening before him.

He thanked the manager and the woman who assisted him and strode back out of the bank lobby. The guard he'd noticed earlier was preoccupied watching a shapely blonde woman. Yuri headed to the front door, his heart no longer racing with fear but pulsing with a sense of triumph.

Dora was waiting for him on a bench, enjoying the sun. Her face turned fearful when she saw his unbounded exuberance. "My God,Yuri. You promised me you wouldn't withdraw any more funds. Tell me you didn't."

"I didn't," he said grinning. "I've decided to take the whole thing."

Part Two

Chapter 19

Dora could barely keep up with Yuri as they practically danced back to their hotel, giddy with excitement. It was hot and muggy outside, and they were glad to escape into the cool air conditioning of the American Trade Hotel. They took the elevator up to the third floor and went to Yuri's room to examine their loot. Dora watched, hardly breathing, as Yuri spread the statement of accounts over the bed. There were deposits from a half dozen offshore shell companies and payments to six others. Hundreds of millions of dollars had passed through these accounts in the last six months and there remained a balance of two hundred and thirty million, two hundred and sixty-two thousand, eight hundred and seven dollars and change. They looked at each other in shocked disbelief.

"Holy shit!" Dora said.

Yuri swallowed hard. "My God!"

Dora felt the cold claw of vertigo closing in on her, sucking the air out of the room. She could see the same fear engulfing him.

They stared at each other, unable to speak. Finally, Yuri said, "The bank manager told me that if I had need to register any other corporations, I should see this man." He held out the business card he had been given.

Dora looked at it. 'Felix Rodriguez, Senior Accounts Manager, Attorney-at-Law, Mossack Fonseca.' "What are you thinking?" she asked.

"I'm thinking we may only have a short window of opportunity here before this Raskolnovitch character moves this money out of our reach." He paused for a moment and Dora girded for what would come next. "I'm thinking we should open our own shell company and transfer these assets to it."

Dora had a bitter taste of panic in her mouth. "Yuri, this is war. This guy's a killer. We're out of our league here."

"It is war," he answered her. "I had a great uncle, Uncle Kurt, my Bubbie's brother, who organized a band of Jewish partisans to fight against the Nazi invaders. They were all betrayed by Stalin and ended up killed at Babi Yar. Why is this any different? Wouldn't it be better to die for a good cause than to let these bastards steal our country?" Courage rose in him, visceral like fear, but its opposite.

"I'm going to fucking do this, Dora," he declared. "It feels like the time I rode the zip line roller coaster at Bukovel, in the Carpathian Mountains. I was scared but excited." He leaned toward her. "There's a chance, even if it's a very small chance, that I can hit this oligarch where it would hurt the most. It's worth the risk. They're going to come after me anyway. They have my name. They know who took their documents and their three thousand euros. At least this way, the playing field's a bit more even." Dora sat frozen on the edge of the bed. She, too, had an Uncle Kurt who was executed at Babi Yar. But her thoughts were of something more recent. There was pressure building in her head that threatened to explode. She tried to speak but was afraid she'd start to cry.

Finally, she composed herself and said, "When I was fourteen, my brother drowned right in front of me," stopping to let her words sink in, not taking her eyes from his. "We were in South Orange, in New Jersey. We had gone out to walk our dog. We walked across a frozen pond where some of my friends went skating. Bobby, my brother, started running with our dog Alfie on its leash. When he stopped suddenly, Alfie skidded on the ice. It was funny. But the second time he ran, the ice broke under them and both Bobby and Alfie fell in. I ran to the hole, laid on the ice and put my arm in. The water was black, and I couldn't see anything. I screamed for help and some of the boys rushed over, but there was nothing any of us could do."

She looked away and didn't say anything for some time. She struggled to contain herself. "I was helpless," she said to Yuri. "I couldn't save him. I felt responsible for his death. I should have known better. I was older. It was my idea to walk on the ice. But it was all because I wanted to be seen by the boys there." She paused. "My parents tried to forgive me, but I couldn't forgive myself. I grieved for years, stopped seeing any friends after that. I didn't date until my third year at Berkeley. Now, the grief and the guilt I felt then, I'm feeling again now."

Yuri looked at her as if the floor had opened under him. He didn't seem to know how to respond. They remained silent for a few minutes, processing their feelings.

"I'm sorry," said Yuri. "But it was no more your fault than it was the river's."

"I don't believe that; but, in any case, this plan of yours is different than that. This is something I can prevent. You don't have to do this," she said.

"You're right, Dora. But sometimes in life you make choices with risks you think are worth taking. I could spend the rest of my life regretting not taking it. The life I'd go back to would be dreary and meaningless. It's the right thing to do. You know it is. I'm sick of watching all these mafia guys get richer than God while I shovel shit and my little sister has to run off to Prague to become a prostitute to survive."

Dora could see there was no stopping him. He was already sliding on ice. She had set this all in motion and now it was too late to turn back. She wanted to tell him that she and her Uncle Morris had tricked him into all this, but she was afraid she'd lose any influence over him, if she did. He'd have every right to hate her. She realized in that moment that she cared about that, maybe even more than what Morris wanted from her.

"So, what's your plan, Yuri? You gonna set up another corporation and transfer the money in this account to it?"

Yuri nodded, smiled. "Fucking right."

"I guess there's no stopping you, is there?" she said.

"No. It's game on, Dora."

She shook her head. "I don't want you to do this, Yuri. You're just asking for trouble. It's suicide."

"Look, Dora," he said. "I care a lot about you. You're the strongest woman I've ever known. I believe in you and what you're trying to do. That's one of the reasons why I'm doing this. But I can pull this off by myself. There's no reason to involve you anymore."

She smiled at him through wet eyes. "Fuck that, Yuri. If I can't stop you, I need to join you. No way I'm letting you fight this alone. I got you into this. I can't quit now."

The struggle inside her was a familiar one. Danger drew her to it like forbidden love. Her training as a lawyer was a bridle she never fully took to. Being a "good girl" was a suit that never quite fit. She had always wanted to be more like Uncle Morris. This was her chance.

They called Mossack Fonseca for an appointment, said they

were only in Panama City for a short time, and were told to come right over. They walked out of the hotel into the thick warm air of Panama and waited two minutes for an Uber.

"Edificio Arango Orillac," Yuri confirmed with the driver.

"Si, si señor."

Chapter 20

They were still setting up when Toni arrived early with Viktor at the Grand Hotel and walked up the stairs to the second floor for the Wine Forum tasting. The host greeted them warmly.

"You are early, Viktor Ivanovitch. Were you worried we would run out of La Romanee?" the man joked.

"Please, allow me to introduce my fiancée Antoinette Bertrand," replied Raskolnovitch. "Toni, this is Vidhi Tambiah, the founder of the Wine Forum. He used to be the director of strategy for the World Economic Forum, before he discovered that love of expensive wine was the greatest common denominator among the guests here. Now he pairs wine with philanthropy and everyone loves him."

"It's an honor and pleasure, Mademoiselle," said Vidhi, taking her hand and kissing it. He turned to Raskolnovitch. "I believe your president and Mr. Manafort are waiting for you in the blue room down the hall. He just arrived. You'll excuse me, please. I must attend to a few things before the crowd arrives."

The host turned and walked into one of the great rooms

where Toni could see tables of Grand Cru burgundy being displayed.

Toni smiled at Raskolnovitch, feeling herself almost blushing. "Fiancée?" she asked. "I don't recall your proposing. Perhaps I forgot."

Raskolnovitch laughed, shrugged. "I liked how it sounded. I trust you were not offended."

"Not at all," said Toni.

Raskolnovitch laughed. "Well, it's the first time I've seen Vidhi Tambiah kiss a woman's hand," he said. "It is sure to provoke some rumors here."

Toni noticed him glance past her and she turned to see the only other early arrival standing alone with a plate of *hors d'oeuvres* in the back of the Napa room. "Toni, darling, would you be so kind as to entertain that gentleman over there while I have a short talk with the president. I'm quite sure you'll enjoy it. I believe you'll recognize him from the birthmark on his scalp." With that, he turned and walked down the hallway.

Toni walked into the room that was showcasing California vintage wines from Napa Valley and went up to the man standing alone at the back of the room.

"President Gorbachev, how delightful to have this opportunity to meet you," she said, extending her hand. "My name is Antoinette Bertrand."

When he smiled, she recognized the magnetic confidence that she had seen thousands of times before on television. But alone in this large empty room, he seemed diminished. He was shorter than Toni and his suit looked rumpled.

He took her hand with a politician's firm grip. His eye contact was intense. "I'm very glad to meet you. I was lonely here by myself. I seem to have had the time wrong for this event," he explained. "But the *hors d'oeuvres* are excellent and now I get to speak with a beautiful woman without all the distractions."

He had not lost his charm. They spoke about Russia, about the loss of his wife Raisa, and whether Ukraine would join the EU. Gradually, guests began to arrive, and the room soon filled with the sounds of conversation and laughter. By the time Raskolnovitch came back to her, people were pressed all around them. She introduced Raskolnovitch to the former Russian president, who seemed to know who he was, but didn't return his smile. All around them people were tasting and comparing wines. There were recognizable faces, outfits to admire, and endless waiters carrying plates of *hors d'oeuvres*.

"This must be heaven on earth for wine lovers," Toni remarked.

"It is," said Raskolnovitch, "Your old friend President Gavi is looking forward to seeing you again, Toni. I took the liberty of inviting you. I thought it would amuse you."

Toni smiled at Viktor as they kept snaking their way through the crowd, with Raskolnovitch shaking hands with various men they encountered. She reached into her purse and felt for the lipstick case that Rabbi Morris had handed her at the ice-skating rink and pressed the top of it three times.

Raskolnovitch led Toni out of the noisy room into the hallway and up the stairs. The wine tasting had begun to go to his head. He needed to be sober for this meeting with Gavi. There was much riding on it. Having Toni beside him would impress the former French president. Raskolnovitch's bodyguards were standing like statues by the door to a hotel suite. They nodded as the couple approached and opened the door for them. Inside, Jacques Gavi and an aide were seated at a coffee table looking over some papers. They rose as Toni and Raskolnovitch entered. The smell of cigars and Roquefort overcame the orchids that were on the table.

"Mister Prime Minister, allow me to present my fiancée Antoinette Bertrand. Toni, my dear friend, Jacques Gavi," Raskolnovitch began. They shook hands. The president poured them each a glass of champagne. The aide introduced himself.

"Mademoiselle, je suis enchantè," said the former president to Toni. "I presume you speak English." She nodded. "Good, then we are all at the same disadvantage," he said.

They went through the obligatory small talk and noted the celebrities they had spoken to downstairs. "It is truly a magnificent event, is it not?" said Gavi. "An event I look forward to each year. I attend so many of these wine tastings, as you might imagine, but this is by far the best." Up close, the former president looked tired. There were deep lines around his eyes. His dyed black hair and bushy eyebrows gave him a distinguished look in photographs, but he had an unfortunate habit of sniffing after every couple sentences.

"I agree," said Raskolnovitch. He realized that the conversation was entirely between him and the former president. The aide and Antoinette were invisible, but this was an important meeting. Toni, he thought, would just have to settle for being a spectator. He was sure to hear about this later.

Turning to business, Gavi said, "Thank you again for the introduction to your friends. It looks like they will make substantial investments in the venture I proposed. We agreed that they will cover the finder's fee for you. Again, my thanks."

Raskolnovitch nodded and smiled. "And the other matter?" he asked.

Jacques Gavi turned to look at Toni. Raskolnovitch saw that the Frenchman was clearly uncomfortable with her presence for this discussion. Viktor saw that Toni realized this, too. Obligingly, she stood and excused herself, leaving her purse on her chair as she exited for the bathroom.

"Yes," said Gavi, clearing his throat, I have spent considerable time looking into this. It can be accomplished, but..." He stopped and took a sip of champagne. "Normally, this would require an edict approved by the parliament, but that is not an option. We must proceed very discreetly. There are ways around these citizenship prerequisites, but there are at least four levels of review and the Ministry of Foreign Affairs must finally sign off on any exceptions. In sum, for you to obtain French citizenship, a great deal of political capital must be expended. I believe I have obtained tacit approval from the Deputy Foreign Minister and other officials in the chain of approval, but the cost, I'm afraid, will be quite high, ten million euros, to be exact."

He waited to see Raskolnovitch's reaction, but Raskolnovitch just looked him in the eyes until the former president finally looked away.

"There's no problem," said Raskolnovitch. "I can get that."

Gavi's face relaxed and he smiled. "Bravo! France will welcome you as a son, monsieur. Of course, we must be very careful how this is handled. We can stay under the radar for now, but eventually, especially if you purchase property, as I assume you will, there will be questions. It is a political decision and will be explained as such. Despite certain allegations about your businesses, we'll consider it an advantage to offer you citizenship. Many will want to welcome your investments in our country. In any case, we can handle any noise that this might eventually generate most easily when I move back into the Elysée Palace. In that regard, my aide will explain how we'll handle the delicate logistics of this transfer to my campaign."

The aide handed Raskolnovitch a manila folder just as Toni returned to her seat. The talk pivoted to wine. "Frankly, I thought the Rousseau Chambertin was superior," Gavi remarked, wiping his brow with his handkerchief. Raskolnovitch laughed, turned to Toni and kissed her on her cheek.

Chapter 21

Mossack Fonseca occupied the first two floors of a large all-glass modern cube of a building. The architecture suggested transparency, but this law firm specialized in anything but. "This is the belly of the beast," Dora whispered to Yuri, "where the biggest players hide their money. If we could ever expose the secrets that live here, the whole house of cards might come tumbling down."

Yuri and Dora waited in plush leather chairs with shiny metal frames. A receptionist offered them coffee or water. Yuri declined; he was feeling a creepy calm that he didn't want to upset with caffeine. After about ten minutes, a secretary in a blue suit came out and escorted them to an inner office. A man, not much older than they, with short, curly black hair and wire-rim glasses, greeted them at the door. His suit jacket was hanging on the inside of the door and he had his sleeves rolled up.

"Mr. Yavlinsky? I'm Felix Rodriguez," he said shaking hands with Yuri.

"Good to meet you," said Yuri. "Thank you for seeing us on such short notice. This is my associate, Carol Glasner."

Dora fixed her eyes on him, smiled, and shook his hand.

Rodriguez gestured for them to take seats on a couch while he sat in a chair facing them.

"What can I do for you, Mr. Yavlinsky?

"Yes. I have some reason to believe that certain persons may have an interest in a corporation I have registered here in Panama, Advanced Holdings International, and I think it may be prudent to shield its assets in another entity. I understand you have some experience in these matters."

Rodriguez smiled. "That's pretty much all we do. Since you're here in Panama in person, I can facilitate this quite easily, if you have the necessary documentation."

"That shouldn't be a problem." Yuri took out the papers he had received that morning from Mr. Michaels and handed them to Mr. Rodriguez along with his passport and even a recent utility bill, which he had brought with him after researching Panamanian registration laws before they left Kyiv. He hoped Rodriguez wouldn't realize that he lived in a dump of an apartment block. Dora and Yuri traded glances as the lawyer looked through the papers.

"You have all the documents I need," he said. "However, as a 'nominee director' you would not have the authority to withdraw or move these assets, I'm afraid."

Rodriguez peered down at one of the documents more carefully. Yuri held his finger to his head as if shooting himself. He saw Dora deflate. Rodriguez laughed. "Whoever drafted these articles of incorporation must have cut and pasted sections from some template. It seems this *does* give the 'nominee director' a power of attorney from the beneficial owner with signatory privileges. Normally, ultimate beneficial owners build a lot of safeguards to prevent this. If it's an error, it's one whopper of a mistake," Rodriguez exclaimed.

He showed them the paragraph in question. Yuri felt himself relax.

"Now, do you intend to take ownership under your name or do you have a nominee director I should use? If not, that is something we often do for clients," said Mr. Rodriguez.

"For the moment, let's keep it in my name. That would be easiest," Yuri said in as casual a voice as he could muster.

But Dora interjected. "No, Yuri, I think it makes more sense to use a nominee director," she said, looking at him hard.

Yuri got what she was saying: registering it in another name would make it more difficult for Raskolnovitch or anyone else to find it. "Yes, of course." He felt more confident with Dora beside him.

"Fine, I understand," said Rodriguez. "This is a fairly simple transaction. Now, how much of the assets in Advanced Holdings do you intend to flow into the new corporation?"

"All of it," said Yuri.

"Normally, we charge a flat $5,000 fee to register a new company, but I would suggest that with such a large amount as this, you opt for our premium service, which will give you the additional protection you will need to secure the privacy of these assets. I would personally manage your account. The fee would be $25,000 plus any associated legal costs that might be required, as, for example, if the new corporation were sued or documents subpoenaed."

Yuri waved his hand. "Yes, of course."

"I assume you'd like to set up an account at HSBC with Mr. Michaels?" Rodriguez asked.

Before Yuri could answer, Dora spoke up. "No," she said. "Use another bank. In fact, when the funds are transferred, do it in such a way that Mr. Michaels doesn't know its destination. Can you do that?"

Yuri got it: Dora was protecting Michaels. When Raskolnovitch found out that his account in Panama had been emptied, he would surely force Michaels to reveal whatever he knew, and the less he knew the better. "Yes, the funds will pass through us. No one but you and I will know where it resides," he said.

Rodriguez stood up. "There are several forms to be signed and notarized," he said. "It will take just a few minutes to produce these. Can I get you some coffee or something stronger while you wait?"

They smiled, nodding their heads. Yuri felt he could use coffee or something stronger, or maybe both.

"Then, I'll be back very shortly." Rodriguez looked at his watch. "We can file the necessary paperwork today, but it won't be until tomorrow afternoon when all this is complete and you'll have access to the funds. Are you able to stay another day in Panama City?"

"We can," said Yuri. He reached into his leather briefcase and removed a red manila folder. "Here are papers for an offshore company I've registered in Cyprus. I'd like you to arrange to transfer those assets as well into the new corporation, if you can."

Rodriguez smiled. "Yes, of course. We can prepare all the paperwork and have you sign them before you leave Panama.

When they left Mossack Fonseca a half hour later, Yuri kept himself stone-faced as they walked down the humid boulevard. He half expected someone to grab them from behind. He felt as if they had just stolen the keys to the kingdom.

Finally, Dora stopped and looked behind her. There was no one tailing them. Yuri turned and looked at her. She closed her eyes and covered her mouth with her hands. "Oh, my God," she said, "I think we did it."

"I need a drink," said Yuri.

"I thought you didn't drink," she said.

"Only champagne. Only when I'm with you."

Chapter 22

They sat alone at a table in front of a wall of books at the Café Varenye in Kyiv on Petlyury Symona near the Botanical Gardens, having taken the flights home in exhausted silence. Outside, the weather had turned unseasonably warm and there were puffs of white clouds floating in a blue sky. Dora looked around her, but there was no one near them. "What now?" she asked.

Yuri took a sip of his cappuccino

She held his gaze. "They'll come after you, you know."

"Yeah. I guess I need to disappear for a while. Want to go with me to California?" he asked. "I've always dreamed of renting a convertible and driving down the coast."

She smiled. "I wish I could, Yuri. I love hanging out with you." She reached over and put her hand around his. "But I can't. I've got an organization to run and I'm going to be very busy trying to explain to the authorities what you've done." She poured some milk into her coffee, looking around her again. "Besides, I think you'll be safer travelling alone," she continued. "We'll need some way to communicate, something encrypted.

You'll need to get a new identity I know someone who can help us." She was thinking of Uncle Morris. He'd surely know what to do. "This guy Raskolnovitch will employ an army of private investigators, Russian SVR, Israelis too. You'll have to go deep underground."

"I downloaded a new app called Signal," she said. "It's an encrypted messaging service. Install the app and then we can talk, and you can set it to disappear your messages after you read them.

He turned over his hand and she placed hers in his palm. She felt drawn to him. "I wish it were different," he said. "I wish I hadn't gotten you into this mess. I'd give anything to take you with me, but I can't put you in such danger. Maybe someday things'll settle down and I'll come back for you."

Her eyes teared up. She squeezed his hand. Their silence acknowledged some line they had crossed. She had wanted to avoid this, hoping to keep a professional relationship. But the truth was she had been attracted to him from the moment they met, drawn to his boyish innocence and vulnerability and his unassuming masculinity. They were in this fight together now and it was hard for her to hold back her feelings.

But she knew what really constrained her. She had deceived him from the beginning. Instigated by Uncle Morris, she had arranged the whole charade to have him served with a summons and threatened with arrest, had recruited the Chief Prosecutor and his assistant and set Yuri up for the role he was to play. She was afraid she'd lose him now, if he learned how she had manipulated him. But if they were to come out of this whole, she had to reveal herself.

"Yuri, there's something I need to tell you." She let go of his hand and looked down at her cup. "I haven't been completely honest with you." She paused, took several breaths before continuing. "I set you up for this, the whole thing. It was wrong of me to do this, but I guess I thought we could get away with this without you or anyone being hurt. She felt herself about to cry. You didn't get me into this mess. It was me. I got you into it."

She could tell he didn't understand. "My Uncle Morris put me up to this. It was his idea. The government, the American government, was worried that Ukraine was moving back to Russia and away from Europe and the West. The FBI was investigating a massive money laundering scheme in New York that involved the president and his political advisor, this American dealmaker Paul Manafort, and the Russian mafia. They were using Raskolnovitch's shell companies to launder hundreds of millions of dollars. Uncle Morris wanted me to get the nominee director to ask for the accounts, which could prove..."

She stopped talking. His face was full of confusion and anger.

"I thought he was a rabbi," said Yuri.

"He was. I mean, he is. But he was also the head of the Ukraine Desk at the White House," Dora said.

"CIA?"

"He used to be," said Dora.

"When did your uncle suggest this plan?" asked Yuri in a scarily even voice.

Dora's heart was racing now. "A couple of weeks before we met."

He stared hard at her. She was afraid he'd run out or start screaming.

"Are you telling me this whole thing was a set up? The summons, the deal with the Prosecutor, you posing as my lawyer?"

She nodded. She would give anything to take it all back. She wanted to speak but nothing came out. She felt a tear roll down her cheek. "I'm sorry Yuri. I shouldn't have done any of this. I didn't mean to hurt anyone. I just..."

She stopped, meeting his gaze. She reached for his hand, but he pulled it away. "You have every reason to hate me."

He said nothing. Finally, he reached over and took her hand in his. "And this," he asked, looking at their hands, "Is this, too, part of the charade?"

Her throat contracted. She felt like she couldn't breathe. She shook her head.

She felt his hand soften. "I'm sorry, Yuri."

She knew what he had to be thinking: She had betrayed him. How could he ever trust her again? She had used him. Dora and her uncle had turned his life upside down. How cynical, how superior they must feel themselves.

"It was immoral to treat anyone like that," he said. "You think you're better than everyone?"

She realized he was still holding her hand. He paused, and Dora saw a look of surprise cross his face. "You should have just asked me," he said.

Then he let go of her hand. The space between them suddenly grew large. He stood, turned, and left.

Chapter 23

He took a taxi home. The hole left by Dora felt like a fatality. He had known loneliness his whole life but had never felt this alone before.

As he approached his apartment, he saw two men in black track suits standing by an SUV, smoking cigarettes across from the building entrance. He told the driver not to stop at the end of the block. There was an alley behind the building and a rear basement door by some dumpsters. He went in and climbed the seven flights, expecting to meet killer thugs at each turn. He opened his apartment with trepidation. Inside, there was blood on the walls and pooled on the floor. His stepfather was covered with it, tied to a chair, his throat cut, his chin resting on his chest, like a rag doll. In his lap was a sign written in blood, "This is no game."

Yuri couldn't breathe. He felt as if the door to his life had slammed in his face. He vomited on the floor, tip-toed around the blood, and walked into his bedroom, knowing what he would find. Bubbie was sitting propped up on the bed, a round bullet hole neatly in the center of her forehead. A thin stream of blood had trickled down her nose and onto the white cover. She had the same confused look on her face that had always greeted him.

He sat on the edge of the bed and began to cry. This was all his fault. Thank God his sister had left. He wished they had killed him instead of his bastard stepfather and his beloved Bubbie.

When he stopped heaving, he noticed bits of parchment on the floor, the drawing he had worked on for four years torn to pieces. He slowly picked them up, shreds of Mickey Mouse fucking Snow White from behind, John Glen on the flying trapeze, Brigid Bardot dressed as a nun. They no longer seemed so amusing. The drawings taunted him with his careless guilt. He caught a glimpse of himself in the mirror and was appalled by his business clothes, a damning reflection of his responsibility for these crimes. There was no ambiguity about it. He stuffed the torn drawings into a paper bag and made his way out of the bedroom.

He stood in the center of the living room as if waiting for something to happen. The smell of blood and vomit nauseated him. He half expected his mother to walk in. His eye caught sight of a pile of scrapbooks in a bookcase against a wall, scraps of a family's life. Gone forever was the little boy pictured in those books. His old life had ended and a new, harder, deadlier life had begun. He was a stranger to himself, as guilty as he was innocent.

He walked out of the apartment for the last time and closed the door behind him.

"This is no game," kept repeating in his mind as he descended the stairs to the basement, clutching the paper bag with his torn drawing, ready to run for his life. His self-loathing began to harden into something else, a core of hatred petrified into a crucible of revenge. He would destroy these fucking killers and this drug lord oligarch that fed on people's addictions. He had the money now to fight back. There would be nothing that could stop him. He had nothing more to lose.

Chapter 24

It was late when Yuri reached Prague. He took a taxi to the city center and sat at a café across from the Old Town Hall Tower that had free wi-fi, frantically scrolling through web pages of escorts on his phone. There were hundreds of profiles. He began to despair he'd ever find her. After an hour of fruitless searches, he ordered a steak and frites. He hadn't eaten all day. He went back to scroll again through endless pictures of young prostitutes: Amy, Angel, Angelina, Antonia, Ariana, Ariela. The faces on this site had been blurred. He turned back to Ariana and stared. He had never seen his sister naked. The longer he looked, the more he was convinced it was her.

Price 200 Euros. Age 18. Location Prague. Height 157 cm. Eyes brown. Bust size 36C, Bust type natural. Ethnicity white. Weight 52 kg. Hair blonde. Orientation bisexual. Smoker yes. Nationality Ukrainian. Languages English, Russian, Ukrainian. Services Gfe, threesome, classic, role play, duo, HDJ, BJC, COB, foot fetish, spanking, golden shower, CIF. Available for outcall. Meeting with man+woman. He was certain it was her. She had dyed her hair blond. He didn't know what half the services even meant, but one thing more than any other disturbed him: she smoked.

He called the contact number. A man answered. Yuri said he wanted to book two hours with Ariana. She could meet him in an hour, the voice replied. Yuri gave a false name, said he was staying at the Frimi Boutique Hotel. He would meet her there. 200 Euros plus cab fare. It was that simple.

He walked to the hotel and booked a room, paying with cash. He said he had forgotten his passport, handed the receptionist an extra 100 Euros, and registered under a false name. He waited in the lobby. The walls were red and crystal chandeliers sparkled from the ceiling. He watched the clock on the wall above the receptionist. Yana was half an hour late. He thought of what he would say, what he would do.

When she finally walked in, he hardly recognized her. She had heavy makeup around her eyes and bright red lipstick. She was wearing a leather mini-skirt with tall boots and a short-waisted leather jacket. He stood up and walked towards her. She didn't seem to recognize him.

"Hello, Yana."

She froze, looked around her. "What the fuck are you doing here, Yuri?"

"Something's happened," he said. "Let's go to my room where we can talk."

She looked at his suit clothes suspiciously. He took her arm and guided her to the elevators. They were both silent and nervous. He opened the door and entered his room. It was sparse but had two comfortable chairs.

"What's going on, Yuri? Why are you here and what's with the outfit?" she said.

"Your dad's dead. So is Bubbie."

She looked at him like he was crazy, as if squinting would somehow bring everything into focus.

"I'm sorry," he said.

She shook her head, not knowing how to react. "Bubbie, too. How? What happened?"

"It's a long story, sis. They were murdered by some thugs that were out to kill me. It was all my fault. Remember that summons from the tax authorities I showed you the night you were leaving? Well, they arrested me for selling my passport that time when I paid for mom's funeral. Some oligarch used my ID to register some offshore shell companies to launder drug money. The prosecutor let me off when I managed to get some documents they needed from a bank in Cyprus. Now that oligarch is after me." He didn't tell her about the 3,000 Euros.

"How were they killed?" she asked. Her face was distorted with fear.

"They were both shot," he lied.

She put her face in her hands and began to cry. Her body heaved. "He fucking deserved to die," she said. "But Bubbie?"

"I think she was killed while she was asleep," he lied again. "She probably never felt anything."

After her breathing slowed, he told her the rest, told her about taking control of one of the shell companies, told her that they'd be coming after him and might threaten her to get to him.

He went over and held her. "Listen carefully, Yana. We're both in great danger. But I've got plenty of money. You don't have to ever work again." He paused, waited to see her reaction. "We'll get new identities somehow and disappear for a while." He thought of Dora and the prosecutor. "I got this double room for us. We can stay here for a couple days while I get us new papers and passports. You shouldn't go back to your place for anything, no matter what. Can you do that?" She nodded she could.

"We'll fly to London," he said. "I'll buy us a flat and set up some bank accounts. I'm going to find a way to go after these guys, but I'll need to hire some protection and some lawyers first.

I know this must all be too much for you to take in. We'll just have to take it one step at a time." He lifted her chin and looked in her mascara-smeared eyes. "I'm really sorry I got us into this mess, sis. I promise I'll do everything I can to protect you."

She tried to smile but started to cry again. She threw her arms around him and sobbed.

Chapter 25

Viktor sat alone, wrapped in a towel, feeling apprehensive, though he couldn't figure out why. It was hot in the sauna, 90 degrees Celsius. It was always a point of pride with the *Vory* to endure saunas at a heat most mortals couldn't stand. In former years he and his *Vory* comrades would plunge into icy waters at Epiphany to prove their mettle, but he had not done so for some time. Was he getting soft? Wealth could do that to a man.

The door to the sauna opened and Kostya, his chief of security, came in, still dressed in his black track suit.

"Kostya, what's up? Did you find the boy?"

"No, he wasn't home, but we left him a message he won't mistake. His father put up quite a struggle before he lost his head, so to speak. An old lady was an inconvenience, but no more. I posted a couple of lookouts. If the boy turns up, we'll show him the scene in his apartment and then take him," said Kostya.

"Good," said Raskolnovitch. "The only reason someone would go to Cyprus for those documents would be to investigate us. It must be the Americans and the SEC, but why would the kid take 3000 Euros?"

"Maybe he just got greedy," said Kostya.

"Maybe. Something doesn't smell right to me, though," replied Raskolnovitch.

Kostya wiped the sweat from his brow. The front of his shirt stuck to his chest. "Anything else?" he asked.

"What's happening with that other matter I gave you, the one with the journalist?" Raskolnovitch asked him.

"I did what you asked, sir, followed him for several days. He walks his dog every night, even picks up his poop," said Kostya. "There's an alley on one side of a church cemetery, where there're no street lights and no houses. I doubt there are any surveillance cameras, but I was careful scoping it out in any case. I gave all this to your *Vory* friend along with the money. He'll let me know when he's done."

"Duzhe dobre, very good," said Raskolnovitch.

There was a knock on the sauna door and Dmitri Prokofiev poked his head in.

"Viktor, can I speak with you, urgently?" said Dmitry.

The tone in Dmitry's voice made Raskolnovitch's heart rate speed up. It had been a long time since his unflappable CFO displayed such tension. "Put a towel on, Dima, and come sit by me." He turned to Kostya and nodded. His security chief bowed and exited the way he came in, without turning his back to him. In a minute Dmitry entered and stood next to his boss. His hands shook.

"It's worse than we thought. We're under attack," said Dmitri. "I tried to get the records the SEC wanted from our offshore company in Panama, International Property Developments, and I was told the account had been closed."

"Closed?" shouted Raskolnovitch. "What do they mean, 'closed?'"

"I was told that the funds and all the stocks, all of them, had been transferred to another company. I haven't been able to find out which yet, but I will. I learned it's being handled through Mossack Fonseca. We used to use them. I'm reaching out to my contacts there right now to find out what's going on."

"Is the boy involved in this?" asked Raskolnovitch.

"I think so," said Dmitry. "I spoke with the bank manager and he dealt with someone who matched his description."

"Get the surveillance video from both banks. I'm going to turn this yid into sausage."

"Maybe you shouldn't, not yet anyway," said Dmitry. "We may need him to recover our money. He's still the nominal director. If we kill him, we may never be able to transfer the funds back to us."

Raskolnovitch fumed as he considered his options. "This Jewish kid, Yavlinsky, couldn't be doing this by himself. We need to find out who's behind him—and, Dima, we should find out what he's afraid of losing, even more than his own life." He paused for a moment. "How much was in that account, Dima?" Raskolnovitch asked.

"Two hundred and thirty million and change," said Dmitry.

His words hung in the air like icicles in a cave. Raskolnovitch looked up at Prokofiev through heavy lidded eyes, and Dimitry shivered.

"Tell Kostya I want him to tear down everything this Yavlinsky cares about and then bring him to me," said Raskolnovitch, spitting out his words. "You are right, Dima, we must not kill him right away. There will be time for that. But let's find out everything we can about him. Is he still in Kyiv? Where has he travelled? Who are his friends, his relatives? Most of all, who is he working for? And get me a meeting with Don Semion. Firtash can set it up. I'll go to Moscow, if need be. Mogilevich and the Bratva have people in almost every country. This boy will not be able to hide for long."

Raskolnovitch stood up, pulled off his towel, and threw it on the floor. He walked out of the sauna without another word. He showered and shaved and dressed for his dinner date at Kanapa's with Antoinette.

Chapter 26

Yuri and Yana came back to their hotel room the next morning with pre-paid "burner" phones and some food. He took one of the untraceable cell phones out of its box, connected to wi-fi, and downloaded the Signal app, praying that Dora had already installed it as well. It rang several times before she answered.

"Dora?"

"Yuri, is that you? Where are you?"

"Dora, Thank God I got you. Something horrible has happened," he told her.

"I know. It's all over the news," she said. "I'm so sorry Yuri. It's my fault. I knew this would happen." She began to cry. "I'm sorry! I'm sorry!"

"Dora, listen, please," said Yuri. "If anybody's to blame, it's me. I should never have taken those 3,000 Euros. It's my fault. It's not a game." The phrase rebounded in his head, as he vividly recalled the scene of carnage in his apartment. He waited for her crying to stop. In their silence, the distance between them was unnerving.

"Anyway, it doesn't matter whose fault it is or how this whole business started," he added. "We're in this together now. I want to make this work." He glanced across the room at his sister, sitting in a chair biting her nails.

"You've got to get out of there, Dora. They'll find out who you are and come after you, too," he told her. "We'll need to go someplace where they can't find us. I've got my sister with me. We're holed up in a hotel in the old city for now; but we're planning to go to London, if we can get new passports and visas. Can your prosecutor friend help us with that? I don't have a clue how to go about it," he admitted.

Dora's breathing slowed, and her voice returned, more composed. "I'm working on that."

"Look, I think we're OK as long as we don't leave the hotel, but I'm nervous," said Yuri. "I called that attorney at Mossack Fonseca, Felix Rodriguez, and he's wiring money to my sister's account here."

"Be careful, Yuri. They know your sister's name. It's all over the papers. Yours, too. There's all kinds of speculation. They know you both lived at that apartment and disappeared just when these murders happened. Now you've got journalists looking for you, too. The sooner you can get out of Prague, the better."

"And what about you, Dora? Can you join us in London? It's only a matter of time before these killers connect the dots," said Yuri.

"I can't leave just now," she replied. "I caused all this. It's just like with my brother." Her voice trembled again. "I'll get out of here as soon as I can, but I have to stay here a while to help the investigation." As soon as he hung up, the landline phone in his room rang. "Mr. Kurtz. Hi, it's Stephan from the front desk. I just want to warn you. There were some freaky looking men asking about you. They had a photo of you and said they were looking for a runaway girl and her boyfriend. They offered a ten thousand koruna reward. I thought you might want to know."

"Thank you. I owe you one," said Yuri.

He could feel things closing in. It would get worse, he knew. They needed to stay off the streets, but he would need more money to get to London.

"C'mon, sis. We'd better move fast before anyone finds out about the money that was wired to us," he said.

"I'm scared," said Yana. She looked like a little girl sitting in the oversized armchair.

They walked separately down cobblestone streets in the shadows of medieval walls on a dark cloudy day. The bank was in a former armory on a side street close to the main square where tourists had gathered to watch the astronomical clock. Yuri looked around him for any suspicious characters as he walked through the front doors behind Yana. The bank lobby was empty. A young female teller with red hair and bright purple streaks greeted them warmly. But when Yana asked to withdraw half a million korunas in cash, almost 22,000 dollars, the teller's face froze.

"I'm sorry, ma'am. We can't give out that amount of cash, I don't think. Let me check."

She left and spoke with a man in a blue suit, both of them looking back at Yuri and Yana suspiciously. Yuri could barely sit still. When she returned, she said, "We can only give out up to two hundred thousand. If you need more, we can order that, but it will take a day."

Yana looked at Yuri.

"That's fine," he said. "We'll take the two hundred thousand now. Can you give us a cashier's check for the rest?"

The girl with the purple and red hair looked at him wide eyed and smiled. "Yes, I think so," she said, then walked in back and returned a couple minutes later with a check and a metal drawer from which she counted out two hundred thousand korunas. Yuri glanced around him to see if anyone else were watching. Next to him, Yana stood biting her nails, transfixed by the growing stack. The teller put the cash into two large manila envelopes and handed them to Yuri.

"Good luck, sir," she said with a look of expectation, as if he were about to parachute out of a plane, which was what he was feeling. He smiled back. He and Yana turned and left together. The wind was blowing debris in the gutters down the street when they came out. They walked with studied indifference, their hearts running ahead of them.

"Yana, we're probably less likely to be spotted if we separate," Yuri said, handing her one of the envelopes. They headed back to their hotel on opposite sides of the street. On a corner by Mikulasska Street, a man in an orange sports outfit eyed him, then looked at his phone and began to follow him. Yuri pretended not to notice, ducked into a department store, and hurried up an escalator before the man could enter. He ran by the men's clothing section, grabbed a pair of pants from a rack and quickly slipped into the dressing rooms. He texted Yana, "Meet at the hotel."

Yuri waited in the dressing room, heart thudding, for fifteen minutes, which felt like an eternity. He couldn't stay there all day, he knew. The pants he had taken were not far off from his size, so he put them on. He poked his head out and didn't see the man or any others that might be searching for him. A saleswoman with long blonde hair stood by a desk picking at her nails. He called to her. She was wearing a name tag, Anastasia. He spoke to her in Russian.

"Miss, can you do me a big favor?" He handed her two thousand korunas. "There're some people looking for me I don't want to meet. Could you possibly pick out a raincoat and a hat for me and keep the change?" He made eye contact with her.

She looked him up and down. "Maybe better pants, too," she

said, and smiled at him wryly. In a few minutes she returned with a gray wool hat, a pair of jeans, and a black raincoat and handed him the change. He gave it back to her with another two thousand koruna note.

"Thanks," she said, passing him a piece of paper with her phone number on it. "Maybe you need a friend."

He smiled back at her, looked over her shoulder, and went back into his dressing room to change. He put his suit into a bag she gave him and stepped back among the racks of clothes. There was an elevator by the men's room and he took it to the basement. But there was a man holding a walkie talkie standing by the fire exit, so he went back up to the floor where he started, his heart racing. Anastasia was helping another customer. When the man left, Yuri went up to her.

"It seems I could use a friend," he said. "Would you mind walking out with me?"

She looked around. "Sure, why not?"

They went down the escalator, close together, chatting like lovers. She put her arm through his. There were two men at the front entrance looking for him, but they paid no attention to the couple as they walked out. At the end of the block, Yuri stopped and looked behind them. There was no one following. He kissed her on her cheek.

"Thanks, I owe you," he said.

He stayed off the main streets as he navigated his way back to his hotel. Yana was in the room.

"Thank God, you're all right," she said. "I was so worried about you."

Banknotes were spread out on the bed. Her eyes were smeared. She looked like she had been crying. "Nice disguise," she said. But she was shaking. "I'm so fucking scared."

When he reached Dora, she was at the French Embassy in

Kyiv. "Hold on a minute," she said. "I have someone you need to talk to."

"Allo, Mr. Yavlinsky?" The man had a deep, distinguished voice and a slight French accent. "I am Arnaud Bertrand, the Consul General of France. Let me first say how very sorry I am about the loss of your stepfather and great-grandmother," he began.

"Thank you," said Yuri.

"What you've done is very daring and creative, but, regrettably, very dangerous. I admire your courage. We here at the French Embassy and beyond will do what we can to protect you and, where we can, provide information to the police to help bring the killers of your family to justice."

"Thank you," said Yuri again.

"Mr. Yavlinsky, I am issuing you and your sister travel documents you can use to go anywhere in the E.U.—French passports and European Union visas in someone else's name. I would suggest you meet with a colleague of mine, a Mr. Matthew Palmer, when you get to London. He will make sure you are safe. He is, let us say, close to British intelligence. You can trust him."

Yuri flashed a thumbs up to Yana. He saw the fear in her face begin to turn to cautious excitement. A gust of air blew through the open window fluttering the curtains.

"Thank you. How do I find Mr. Palmer?" asked Yuri.

"He will find you at the airport when you arrive. He will have a place for you both to stay. The Brits are very experienced at protecting fugitives, political dissidents, and Russian oligarchs out of favor with the Kremlin. Mr. Palmer is especially knowledgeable about these matters. You will be in good hands."

"Good. We need to get out of Prague fast. There seems to be a whole menagerie of people looking for us here," said Yuri.

"I understand. Get over to our embassy. Ask to see the Consul General. He's expecting you. He'll have your travel documents and tickets. Your flight is at 5:10pm on Ryan Air, one way."

"Monsieur Bertrand, I think you may have saved our lives. I don't know how to properly thank you," said Yuri.

After a long pause, the Consul General spoke again, his voice steady but grave. "Yuri, you are in a war now. Stealing those funds was very brave, but impulsive, and frankly very naive. From now on, you will need to stay a few steps ahead of Raskolnovitch to survive. I appreciate how much you want to bring him down, even more so after what he did to your family. We do, too. But courage will not be enough. To fight this oligarch, you will need to think like an oligarch. To win, you will need to be an oligarch."

"Yuri"—it was Dora's voice now— "I'm staying with Leon Kaminsky, your tailor. I'll be safe. I have a few things to finish up with here with the tax inspectors, but then I'll take the evening British Air flight to London to join you." The phone was silent for a long five seconds. "I miss you terribly."

Yuri felt a longing for her like nothing he had ever felt before. The phone connection was a tease, a fragile thread that tied them together. He wanted to tell her he loved her, but that seemed trite. It felt bigger than that. "Please be careful, Dora."

"I will. Yuri, I've had a few minutes to examine the documents we got in Panama. We looked at the bank balance but buried in the small print of the financial statements we found majority shares that the company held in six other offshore accounts," she told him. "The total worth of your holdings may be closer to a billion dollars."

Chapter 27

Raskolnovitch landed the helicopter with a jolt, like throwing a bag of cement, and he jumped from the cockpit before the rotors had stopped turning. His guards hurried behind him as he swept around the giant statue of Lybid to the front of his mansion and rapidly climbed the pink marble stairs. His butler was waiting for him outside the ornate two-story wooden doors, holding a sheaf of notes in his hands. But as he tried to read him his messages, Raskolnovitch strode past with his head down and walked quickly to the library.

No one was there when he walked in. He paced around the elaborate parquet floor, deep in thought. Taking a key from his pocket, he opened one of the display cases and removed a revered Faberge Egg that had belonged to Tsar Alexander III. It was royal blue, encrusted with tiny diamonds, rubies, and pearls, and interlaced with gold threads. He had paid almost 40 million dollars for it at Sotheby's to celebrate the purchase of a steel mill where his mother had given the best years of her life. An urge to smash the delicate egg seized him.

What does all this wealth mean, just sitting there in these

display cases? he asked himself. Had he gotten forty million dollars' worth of happiness? Was there anything he could buy that would take away the pain he felt from the loss of things? He thought of all that Toni had told him about his pursuit of money, how much more there was to life. But thinking about this just got him angrier. He could not let someone take what he had spent a lifetime building. He might lack certain graces, but above all else he was a fighter.

He recalled the young boy sex slaves that some of the mujahideen kept with them in the Panjir Valley. He would die before he'd let himself be used like that. He had fought with his fists when he was in the gulag to keep from being abused by some of the older prisoners and had become a pretty good professional boxer after he got out. Sometimes, though, he feared he was getting soft as he aged. Would some young kid have dared to rob him a decade ago? Not a chance. There would be hell to pay.

At that moment, there was a knock and Prokofiev, Kostya, his chief of security, and Nikolai Lazovsky, a former head of Russian counterintelligence who now worked for Semion Mogilevich, the godfather of the Russian mafia, assembled in the room. Raskolnovitch was embarrassed to let Don Semion's man see him this agitated. In his world, any sign of weakness was scorned and invited attacks. But Mogilevich had the foot soldiers he needed.

Raskolnovitch carefully replaced the Faberge Egg in its case and motioned for his guests to take seats in the leather chairs in front of the fireplace.

"What do we know?" he asked.

Kostya spoke first. "The boy is in Prague. His sister hasn't returned to her apartment there. We presume they are together. We have a hundred soldiers on the ground. It's only a matter of time before we find him."

"Remember," said Raskolnovitch, "we are not to harm them, not yet. This boy must think he's Superman trying to fuck with me. But he will soon learn who's Superman. What else do we know?"

Lazovsky took out an iPad and clicked on a video for Raskolnovitch. "We got the surveillance footage from the banks in Cyprus and Panama," he explained. "The boy seemed to be acting alone. Then we convinced the police to let us see what they had outside the bank and this woman, Dora Osatinskaya, as you can see, is clearly in on the job."

"Girlfriend?" asked Raskolnovitch.

"Doesn't look like it," said Lazovsky. "But she knows what she's doing. She's on a mission."

"The worst kind," said Raskolnovitch, "a bitch with a mission."

"Yeah, she runs a little non-profit here in Kyiv dedicated to uncovering corruption, said Lazovsky. "Up until this caper, all they did was expose government officials who took bribes. It was all about shaming dirty cops, politicians and bureaucrats. They never did anything like this direct attack on anyone before."

"You think she put him up to this?" asked Raskolnovitch.

"Probably," said Lazovsky. "The boy hasn't ever done nothing like this, far as we can tell."

"What about the American SEC or some other government agency?" asked Raskolnovitch. "Have they abetted him?"

"Not a chance," said Lazovsky. "They're too law abiding. I think we're dealing with somebody wanting to take over your turf, somebody gunning for you."

Raskolnovitch shook his head. "Nobody's that stupid."

Lazovsky shrugged. "Somebody's stupid."

Raskolnovitch was beginning to dislike this Russian. "So, what do we know about the girl?" Raskolnovitch continued.

Kostya was well prepared. He took out a small spiral notebook. "The girl is 27, born in Ukraine but raised in Israel. Her father was a refusenik."

"A Yid?" asked Raskolnovitch, "like the boy?"

"Hey, be careful with your language," said Lazovsky. "You know Don Semion is a Ukrainian Jew. He don't like people talking bad about Jews."

Raskolnovitch was now seriously irritated by this man. He needed Semion Mogilevich and his Russian Mafia. No one else could muster a hundred men in a night. But he made a mental note to distance himself from Don Semion when this was over. He'd have a big bill to pay, but he didn't want to be in his debt after this.

"What else?" asked Raskolnovitch.

Kostya continued. "Both parents were Trotskyists. The girl, Dora Osatinskaya, went to New York University and then the University of California at Berkeley to become a lawyer."

"A lawyer?" asked Raskolnovitch.

"Yeah. A lawyer and a radical feminist, a bad combination," said Kostya.

"Imagine being married to a bitch like that," Lazovsky remarked.

Raskolnovitch was in no mood for jokes.

"Continue," he said to Kostya.

"It seems she joined every left movement at NYU. She got in trouble for organizing a hunger strike and a sit-in to protest the university's investments in bio-tech companies that used animals for research. At Berkeley, she wrote an article in the law review about how corruption was weakening the new government of Ukraine."

"What new government?" asked Raskolnovitch.

"This one," said Kostya. He flipped through his notebook. "The article helped land her a job at the World Bank, but she soon left for Transparency International. She became a so-called expert on corruption. She started an anti-corruption NGO here with funding from the Ford Foundation."

"Not Renaissance Foundation? Not Soros?" Raskolnovitch asked.

"Not that I can discover. But her NGO is like a research institute. They analyze data and then publicize results, try to shame people to make them stop. They never did anything like steal from someone."

"I'll teach her what shame means. Worst shame is when you watch yourself being skinned alive. It's a terrible way to die. I knew Afghans who were expert at this. Maybe I'll bring them here for her." Raskolnovitch was working himself into a fury. "So, where is she? What are we doing to find her?"

Kostya sat back in his chair, as if to avoid being singed by his boss's anger. "We are watching her apartment and her office. I am getting names of clients, friends or colleagues. Also watching bus, trains and airport. By this evening I'll know everyone she ever talked to."

"What about her phone?" asked Lazovsky.

"We are monitoring it. She is using good encryption on Signal app. Can your friends break that?" Kostya asked Lazovsky.

"No, not yet."

"Credit cards?" asked Lazovsky.

"Nyet. Nothing,"

Raskolnovitch stood up. He felt rage rising to his chest. He was a fighter, not a shadow boxer, he reminded himself. He needed to do something, not sit around like this doing nothing. He made eye contact with Dmitry, who had remained silent during the meeting.

"Listen carefully, boys," said Raskolnovitch. "Either you bring that girl to me by tonight or you will know what it feels like to be shamed."

Chapter 28

The color of the light faded as dark purple clouds settled above them and gusts of wind scattered dirt around the horses' hooves. A groom held the reins as Toni stepped up on the mounting block and threw her leg over the chestnut mare. Raskolnovitch was already on the black stallion. He felt his world was in order with such a beautiful companion. They trotted around the racecourse. Toni had ridden before as a child, but it had been many years since she had been on a saddle. She was in an exultant mood. The fall foliage surrounding his mansion was at its height of glory, spreading a blanket of colors across the forest's floor. But Viktor seemed irritable and preoccupied.

"What's wrong, my lord? Where are you?" she asked.

He laughed when she mocked him like that. "I'm OK. But there are many big troubles. I think maybe you are right and being a lord is not worth the price."

They began to pick up the pace trotting side by side. "And you, my princess, how are you this morning?" he asked.

"*En exstaze*, as we say in French, ecstatic. I have not been on a horse since I was a young girl. This is thrilling for me. Thank you."

The trot became a canter. She felt like she was gliding on air. They circled the track once and then headed to a path into the surrounding forest. A stream cut across the trail and their horses leaped together without breaking stride. Toni laughed out loud and began to sing the chorus to a French nursery rhyme, *Nous n'irons plus au bois*, "we will not go to the woods."

Entrez dans la danse,
Voyez comme on danse,
Sautez, dansez, Embrassez qui vous voudrez.
She translated for him:
Join the dance
See how we dance,
Jump, dance,
Kiss whomever you want.

Just then a golf cart emerged from around a curve, forcing them to stop. Nikolai Lazovsky, Kostya, and another guard stood up and Kostya yelled up to his boss, "Sorry to interrupt you, sir. We think we've located the girl. I thought you'd want to know immediately. We've traced her phone. I sent Mykola and a dozen men. They'll be there in..."

Raskolnovitch held up his hand to stop him. Dismounting, he asked Toni to excuse him for a moment as he walked over to the men.

"It's OK," she said. She reached into her pocket and pulled out her phone. "It's my dad calling. Please take your time."

Raskolnovitch listened, striking the air with his fist. After a minute, he returned to Toni and apologized.

"Antoinette, my dear, I'm very sorry, but I must leave immediately with the helicopter to Kyiv. Please, no need for you to stop riding. I'll have my guard accompany you, from a distance. I'll be back before you know it. I'm very, very, sorry," he said.

"Viktor, what is it?" she asked. "Will you be all right? Please, don't worry about me. I'll be fine."

"Everything's good. Not to worry. I'll fix my big problem now. It's good," he said.

He drove off in the golf cart with Kostya and Lazovsky while the guard, riding Raskolnovitch's stallion, followed Toni on the trail at a discreet distance.

In Kyiv, in the Lukyanivka neighborhood, not far from Babi Yar, the ring of an old-fashioned telephone interrupted a story Leon Kaminsky was telling Dora about her father. There was something ominous in its tone. The old tailor picked up the receiver and held it to his ear.

"Tak. Tak. One moment, please."

He handed the phone to Dora.

"It's for you. A Mister Bertrand?"

Dora took the phone, not breaking eye contact with her cousin.

"Dora, you must listen carefully and do exactly what I tell you," commanded the consul general. "I've just learned this moment that Raskolnovitch has discovered where you are by tracking your phone. You're in imminent danger. His thugs are on their way to you now. Get out of there immediately, but leave your phone where it is. Don't take it with you. Run quickly."

Viktor Raskolnovitch's helicopter was heading for a small neighborhood park a hundred meters from Leon Kaminsky's apartment. He had ordered his men to secure a place where he could land. A dozen of his black-clad guards were rushing to the apartment with orders to seize the girl and block any escape routes in the neighborhood.

"Don't harm the girl," barked Raskolnovitch into his Bose headset. "I want to interview her myself. I'll take her back with me. Keep the tourists away. No photos. This has to be done quickly."

Sitting next to him, Kostya tracked his men's progress on an iPod in real time. Viktor looked down into Kostya's lap and followed along. Three black Ladas turned the corner by Kaminsky's apartment building and stopped abruptly next to the park. Four men in black track suits, their faces hidden behind balaclavas, jumped out of the lead car and chased away a group of parents and children, clearing an area for Raskolnovitch's helicopter to land. Four other guards rushed to the apartment building. The last group took up positions behind the building and at either end of the street.

"The area's secure," said Kostya. They were only a minute away. On the ground, terrified neighbors heard the sound of the approaching helicopter and got off the street. The silver and blue Sikorsky landed in a vortex of noise and wind.

Raskolnovitch followed the men into the apartment building. One of the guards pounded on Leon Kaminsky's door. When there was no answer, he smashed the door open with the butt of a semi-automatic rifle and burst in. Raskolnovitch entered behind them. In the middle of the room stood a table with Dora's cell phone.

A tea kettle on the stove was still hot and dishes were strewn around.

"Someone warned them," he said to himself. "Someone I must kill."

Chapter 29

Yuri and Yana ran through the hotel lobby like thieves. A gray Volvo was parked outside, an Uber sign affixed to the passenger side window. The driver, wearing a yarmulke and a black turtleneck, opened the door from the inside.

"Are you Mr. Kurtz?" he asked.

Yuri nodded and they got in.

"French Embassy?" the driver asked.

They rode through Prague with Yuri imagining every other man on the street was looking for them. Yana held tight to Yuri's arm, shaking with fright. At the French Embassy they were calmly escorted to the second-floor office of the Consul General, Monsieur Guillaume, a short, trim man in a gray suit and green and purple silk scarf.

"Please be seated. May I get you anything, some coffee or water?" asked Guillaume. Their hearts gradually slowed to normal. The Consul General reassured them they were out of any immediate danger.

"It was very fortunate that your friend, Miss Osatinskaya, went to see my colleague, Monsieur Bertrand, yesterday. We have been following this oligarch, Raskolnovitch, for some time and the information you've provided us may be crucial in bringing him to justice. I'm very sorry it has cost you so much, though. I offer you my deepest condolences."

He went on to explain that British intelligence was cooperating in their investigation. "We each have our own interests in Monsieur Raskolnovitch," he explained.

MI6 would do all in its power to protect them in London. They would be met by Matthew Palmer at the airport and taken to a safe house. He handed them plane tickets and French passports in the names of Jean and Sophie Gremion.

Yuri began to feel like a cog in a machine far bigger than he could grasp. British intelligence, French diplomats, Ukrainian prosecutors, and a major drug lord—it was all too much. How long had it been since he was shoveling elephant shit at the zoo? He hadn't had time even to grieve the murders of his family or confront his guilt, and now things were accelerating even faster beyond his control. His main worry was Dora's safety.

They rode to the airport in a black Citroen sedan with diplomatic plates, accompanied by two officials from the Embassy. Yuri's heart skipped a beat when he recognized the driver was the same man who had picked them up at the hotel, though no longer wearing a yarmulke. When the man winked at him, Yuri felt a surge of relief.

Entering the terminal, Yuri saw two tall, blond men in black
T-shirts who were obviously surveilling the incoming passengers. The driver suddenly pushed Yuri, Yana and their diplomatic escorts towards the security gate, but the other two men got there first.

"Halt! Federal police," shouted one of them, holding an identity card in his hand. "Please, follow me," he demanded, grabbing Yuri's arm.

The driver pulled Yuri away. "Back off," he said. "These two have diplomatic immunity. You have no jurisdiction."

Several security guards surrounded them. A Czech soldier in camouflage and beret with a semi-automatic rifle and bullet-proof vest strode up to the group and demanded to know what the problem was. His gun commanded authority. Yuri was sweating and trembling.

"These two are wanted for questioning in a murder investigation. We have orders to take them in," said the taller of the blond men.

As the consular officials showed the soldier their diplomatic passports, the driver spoke up. "These two are under our protection. If these men are policemen, I'm Mickey Mouse. You should arrest them."

The soldier looked hard at the blond men. "Let me see your papers," he said.

The two thugs spit on the floor, turned, and walked away.

"You'll be safe now," the driver told Yuri and Yana, as they prepared to pass through security. "Someone will meet you on the other end."

"Thank you," Yuri said to the driver as the two of them shook hands good-bye.

Chapter 30

Yana hardly spoke a word to him on the flight to Gatwick. He felt unmoored without Dora. His desire for her felt like a matter of life or death.

They walked through the line reserved for EU citizens, past baggage claim and through the big green doors that read , "Nothing to Declare." Just in front of them was a short, solidly built man in a three-piece suit, bowler hat, and umbrella who strode right up to them and introduced himself. He looked like the star of a Visit Britain tourist commercial.

"Welcome to England. I'm Matthew Palmer at your service, terribly glad you've arrived safely. I heard you had a bit of a row at the Prague airport. Well, all's well that ends well." He offered his arm to Yana and guided them through the crowd of passengers out of the airport and into a waiting black cab. He folded down the seat behind the driver and faced them. They pulled into traffic on the left side of the road.

"Well, I do say, you look very well considering the adventure you've been through. We'll head over to your apartment now where you can rest and freshen up a bit. I've got to run off to

Heathrow in a few hours to fetch your associate, Ms. Osatin-skaya, and then will bring her to meet you at the apartment," said Palmer. "There's plenty of food there, if you're hungry."

Yuri and Yana hadn't said a word yet. Yuri spoke up. "I'd like to go with you to the airport."

"Oh, yes, of course. By all means," said Palmer. "My job is to make you as comfortable as I can." He moved on to other business. You'll find the apartment fine and proper, but you'll want a place of your own. Tomorrow I'll take you to a real estate agent who can suggest the kind of housing that would be appropriate for a person of your means. There's no rush about any of this, of course. There's also the matter of finances. I understand you've suddenly come into quite a fortune. You'll want to be able to access your accounts and hire someone to help you manage them. I've taken the liberty of arranging an appointment tomorrow with a Richard McEwan, a wealth management expert, at Berenberg Bank, the second oldest bank in the world, since 1590 or something. You'll be in good hands."

He paused while Yuri and Yana absorbed all this. "Most important is your security. I dare say we have a great deal of experience in this. You can feel very safe here in London. There are many billionaires living here, precisely because we can guarantee them peace of mind. We have some excellent private security firms we rely on. You'll be in good hands, I can assure you."

Palmer smiled like a Cheshire cat, not a worry in the world. The effect was infectious and Yuri, to his surprise, found himself smiling back. They rode past stately row houses with tall pillars and marble stairs, and through a leafy neighborhood to a quiet *cul de sac*. Yana was asleep on Yuri's shoulder when the cab stopped in front of a three-story manor house at the end of the block. He woke her gently, "We're here, sis."

Palmer handed them each a set of keys as they walked up to the grand entrance of 23 Pimperton Street. When Yuri pushed open the large black lacquered door with its round brass knob, he found himself face-to-face with a muscular young man in a green sweatsuit, an automatic pistol in a shoulder holster across his chest. Yuri glanced at the three monitors on a table next to him showing various angles of the entrance and the streets around the house. A semi-automatic rifle leaned against a wall. There appeared to be at least one other guard at the far end of a hallway. The young man in green held out his hand.

"Mr. Yavlinsky? I'm Peter Brooks, Empire Security. Welcome home. We'll be providing you twenty-four-hour security," he said. He pointed to a stairway behind him. "Your quarters are on the second and third floors. You'll be very private up there. May I help you with your things?"

Yuri glanced down at the plastic shopping bag he carried. "I think I'll manage," he said. "But thank you."

The entry was paneled in dark oak, carpeted in Persian rugs and decorated with Victorian furniture. Yuri, Yana, and Palmer mounted a wide circular staircase to a set of large double doors. The guard downstairs called up to them.

"There's a code, 7521, on a pad next to the doors," he said.

The décor of the second and third floors were like the first, with Victorian lamp shades, large gilded-framed mirrors and blue-grey wall-to-wall carpeting. A kitchen and dining room were off to one side. There were two bedrooms on the second floor and a large master bedroom and guest room on the third with windows overlooking a small park. Yana was stunned into silence by the opulence. Palmer suggested it would be best "for now at least" to keep the shades drawn for security reasons.

Tea somehow appeared in the dining room with a plate of cold cuts and a bowl of fruit.

"I've arranged for a cook for the time being," explained Palmer. "There's a pad and pencil in the kitchen where you can jot down anything you might want. I'm sure you'd like to change out of these clothes sometime. We can stop at Harrods first thing tomorrow."

Yuri had never eaten with sterling silver. He had never been in an apartment like this. Being protected and served by others was completely foreign to him. He didn't know whether he'd ever get used to it. The sense of power he had felt when he first went to Cyprus with Dora had disappeared. He longed for the time when he could return to that and go after Raskolnovitch. But he was lost without Dora. Everything would fall into place when they were together, he told himself.

Yana stayed at the apartment while Yuri drove with Palmer to Heathrow. He felt excited but nervous as he watched the arrivals board and saw her plane had landed. They waited outside the Customs door as passengers from that flight began to stream out. Yuri's heart skipped a beat every time the doors swung open and more people emerged. The line of passengers thinned until only a straggler or two came through. They waited in silence for a few more minutes, but Dora did not appear.

Chapter 31

Yuri stared at the Arrivals door. Dora's absence was becoming an indisputable fact. He tried to remain hopeful. It could be anything: she was unavoidably delayed, her taxi had been caught up in traffic, she had been bumped from the flight for some reason. But why hadn't she called? Maybe she lost her phone. Maybe it ran out of battery power before she could call. He pictured her running to catch the plane, missing it and then discovering her phone was dead.

But surely something bad had happened. She would have found some way to call, if she could. The fear that Yuri had felt the last seventy-two hours rested on a brittle scaffolding of hope. Without that, there was nothing to support him. Fear had begun to reify into grief. He struggled against this, refused to allow himself to think of Dora in the past tense.

He was left with an unfathomable sense of guilt and power-lessness. He realized now, too late, how much he really loved Dora. She was his Joan of Arc. Where he was careless and impulsive, she was strong and principled. She acted with strategic vision and discipline. He was just playing at this game. And he found himself now overcome with grief and desire. He would gladly die to hold her in his arms, to kiss her, to lose himself in her sapphire eyes.

He felt Palmer pull him away. "Come on, we need to see a former colleague of mine who's chief of security here at Heathrow. There'll be some simple explanation, always is. He'll put the pieces back together again, I'm sure."

They walked through dark hallways behind the façade of the usual passenger areas, as if in an alternate reality. Palmer displayed an ID to a guard that allowed them to pass into a secure area. They walked through a room filled with dozens of TV monitors and stopped in front of a large metal door with a red and white sign that read "Director Airport Security." Palmer knocked and, after a moment, a male voice told them to come in.

The man sitting behind a large oak desk looked up with surprise. "Well, I'll be buggered!" he said. "Look what the cat drug in." He stood, stretching out his hand to Palmer. "Matthew, it's been too long. How are you and what brings you back here to the dungeon?"

He was a large, serious looking man with reddish hair and ruddy cheeks. He wore black suspenders over a blue dress shirt with sleeves rolled to the elbow.

"Randolph Hastings, meet Yuri Yavlinsky," said Palmer. "Hasty and I worked for years together at MI6 until he lost an eye to a sniper in Basra and got the golden chariot ride out of the service. Smart lad, he was."

Yuri noticed the unsettled eye that didn't track like the other.

"Yuri just arrived today from Prague. Kind of a harrowing trip, I'm afraid, Russian mafia tried hard to stop him. Bit of a row at the airport," said Palmer.

"Yes, I think I heard something about that. Some French consular chaps were involved, I recall," said Hastings. "We monitored your arrival, I believe."

Yuri looked surprised. "Thank you. I had no idea."

"We like to work unseen when we can. Isn't that so, Matthew?" he asked, apparently referring to some inside joke.

"We were hoping you might help us track Mr. Yavlinsky 's partner, a Ukrainian-American with a US passport, Dora Osatin-skaya, who was supposed to be on the British Airways flight that just arrived. She didn't get off and Yuri hasn't heard from her," said Palmer.

"Let's have a look." Hastings turned to a desktop computer. "Osatinskaya, you said? O-S-A-T?" Palmer nodded. "Oh, yes, here it is. You'd best hurry. She's on an Air France flight from Frankfurt that just landed."

The news struck like a kiss. Yuri felt blood rush to his head. His heart accelerated. He could hardly believe what he was hearing. He had an urge to throw his arms around Hastings.

"If she's got no luggage she'll be out in a jiffy," said the one-eyed man.

They quickly thanked him, then Yuri and Palmer retraced their steps at a trot. Passengers were already streaming out of the customs area. Yuri scanned the crowd frantically searching for blonds. No Dora. But people were still coming through the large opening doors. Twice he thought he saw her. Then, finally, there she was, looking a little confused at all the people lined up holding signs. He rushed to her, held her in his arms, and then, for the first time, kissed her. They looked into each other's eyes. She seemed in a state of shock. He looked exultant.

"Thank God, you're safe!" he exclaimed. "We were so worried when you didn't get off the British Air flight."

Dora felt bewildered. Everything was moving too fast. Her mind was still sorting out what had happened to her and now she was in the care of a British intelligence officer in a foreign country and had just kissed the young man whose fate had become bound with her own. She needed to get back some semblance of control.

Yuri stepped back. "This is Mr. Palmer. He's been our guardian angel. I can't imagine what we'd have done without him."

"Where's your sister?" asked Dora.

"She's back in our apartment. We're all exhausted," said Yuri. "What happened? Why didn't you call?"

"Raskolnovitch tracked my phone. Bertrand warned me. My cousin Leon and I barely escaped. We left the phone in his apartment and ran for it. He's gone into hiding in Odessa with my uncle Morris. He'll be safe."

She paused while she tried to compose herself. "It was frightening. There were men with automatic weapons running around looking for us and a helicopter landing on the playground next to the apartment, but we managed to jump on a bus. I figured they'd get my itinerary off the phone. When I got to the airport, there was an Air France flight leaving for Frankfurt. I just made it. The same plane continued on to London. I couldn't call you because I had left my phone and I wasn't able to leave the plane in Frankfurt. But you're here and I can't tell you how glad I am to see you."

Yuri realized how tied he was to her; their fates had become one. He wanted to tell her how beautiful she was, how much she meant to him, how she was the bravest person he'd ever met. But all that would have to wait till they were alone. While Palmer went over the arrangements with her and told her what she might expect, Yuri was thinking that he'd never want to be apart from her again.

With Dora next to him, he felt his confidence slowly returning, like a basketball being pumped with air. Mostly, he felt relief. They were safe, for the time being. MI6 seemed quite willing and able to protect them. He was excited, too, to explore London with

Dora, to flex the new muscles of his improbable fortune. The wave events he had precipitated with the sale of his passport and his assaults on Raskolnovitch had turned into a riptide from which Dora and he could not escape. A righteous anger began to rise in him, and he began to plot their next moves.

Chapter 32

Raskolnovitch was dreaming of the time he plunged a kitchen knife into the back of a policeman who was lying on top of his mother. The man's pants were pulled down around his knees and he reeked of alcohol and tobacco. In the dream, the cop was laughing at him. What startled him awake, though, was something seemingly unrelated, an insight that he had been betrayed by Nikolai Lazovsky and his boss Semion Mogilevich, the godfather of the Russian mafia.

Who else knew about the tracking of the girl's cellphone? He asked himself. Someone had tipped off this Dora Osatinskaya.

Raskolnovitch slowly began to see some patterns emerging like film developing in a darkroom. Mogilevich was making a play for his territory, without even firing a shot.

Mogilevich was Jewish, and so were the boy and girl. Raskolnovitch disliked Jews. They always stuck with their own. They'd stab you in the back if you gave them a chance. Who was it that had suggested we hire Mogilevich—was it Prokofiev or me? Wasn't his uncle, the composer, rumored to be Jewish? But if I can't trust Dima, who can I trust?

The sheets were wet. He tried to calm his heart. He had suffered a heart attack once and the doctors told him the next one would kill him. For a while he stayed off alcohol and fatty meats, but lately he had started indulging again. He was being lazy. The people around him would sense that, like wolves smelling blood. The *Vory* would always protect their own, like Jews did. But he had gone outside that circle, had gone off on his own. What about his *krysha*, the president? Would Mogilevich dare make a move on him without his consent? He needed to deliver that journalist's head quickly.

He sat up. The beating of his heart slowed. There was no doubt someone had tipped off the girl. She was either in hiding somewhere or had made it to London with her yid boyfriend. It would be hard to get to her there. He felt sure she would be the only leverage that might force the boy to give back his money. But who warned her? It had to be Lazovsky. There was something about that arrogant rat he never liked. It couldn't be Kostya. Kostya was like a son to him. Kostya would fall on a grenade to protect him. And he chastised himself for doubting Dima's loyalty even for a second. Had to be Lazovsky, he repeated to himself.

His mind drifted back to his dream and his mother. He had been thinking about her a lot recently. He missed her. How he wished he could show her his Faberge Eggs or take her on a cruise on his yacht. She would have been so proud of him. Or would she? She was very devout, went to church as often as she could. He could imagine her scolding him for his lifestyle and the source of his wealth.

He threw the sheets off him, swung his legs from the bed. He needed to clear his head. He walked into the shower and stood under cold water for several minutes, thinking what to do. The *Vory* had a thing about enduring cold water. But it had been years since he had joined his comrades in the ritualized ice water plunge for Epiphany. The cold shower refreshed him. He'd have to figure some way to lure the girl back to Kyiv. But that could wait. His immediate problem was figuring out who had betrayed him. Slowly, he began to devise a plan.

A few minutes later, Raskolnovitch saw Lazovsky being led through the bedroom suite, joining him on the balcony, bowing as he stepped through the open French doors. Prokofiev followed and nodded. A table was set on white linen with silver platters and pitchers that reflected the early morning sun. Below them a dozen thoroughbreds grazed on the sloping pasture.

Raskolnovitch looked up from his paper. "How'd you sleep?"

"Very poorly," replied Lazovsky. "The boy and the girl got away. I should fall on my sword."

Not a bad idea. He looked at Lazovsky but didn't say a word.

"There's something big going on we don't understand," Lazovsky continued. "They're getting help from the French government. The girl was accompanied by two French consular officials and we traced the last call made to her phone to a land-line at the Embassy. Our friends in the Kremlin are looking into it. It shouldn't be long before we get more information. In the meantime, we should assume the girl made it out and is in London."

Raskolnovitch raised his eyebrows, looked up at Prokofiev.

"There's more bad news," added Prokofiev. "The bank in New York filed a suspicious transaction report, after the SEC received some official complaint. Maybe nothing will come of it, but when I spoke with Ralph Peterson he was literally crying on the phone. They are close to defaulting on their own mortgage. He needs more proof of the origins of our funds."

Raskolnovitch laughed. "The origins? I'm more worried about where the fuck they went and how to come up with the rest of what we owe. Without the Panama funds we don't have the liquidity we need to complete the sale. We need to stall them. In the meantime,"—he shifted his gaze back to Lazovsky—"we have to find out who the rat is. The girl was tipped off. She and her cousin left in a hurry right after they received that call from the Embassy. How did they find out?" The question hung like a cloud in the silence.

Finally, Lazovsky spoke up. "That's what kept me up all night. It has to be someone in your organization. No one else knew. Could've been him," he said, nodding at Dima, "or your pilot or your security. Did you tell anyone else?"

Raskolnovitch continued to gaze at Lazovsky. *I mustn't show anger or suspicion. Not to act would be a sign of weakness,* he reminded himself. *He's taller than me, got a longer reach. I'd have to get in close, pound him in his kidneys.*

But Dima stepped in. "Or it could be that your Godfather wants to *khoche trakhnuty nas.*"

"What's that mean?" asked an exasperated Lazovsky.

"It's Ukrainian for 'fuck us up,'" said Dima, smiling.

Lazovsky's face reddened. His eyes narrowed like a serpent's. "Semion Mogilevich boils his enemies and eats their entrails, but he is faithful as Job to his friends. Don't ever accuse him again or he'll put you in the first category. The only thing he might 'fuck up,' as you say, is your mother."

Prokofiev was unflappable. "We must ask ourselves 'who profits from this adventure?' Who put these kids up to this? They didn't dream this up by themselves and then get the French government to protect them. Someone's moving on us and this is not the last attack. We must prepare for war," Prokofiev said.

Raskolnovitch looked from Dima to Lazovsky and back to Dima. He would bet his life on Dima, he thought. It had to be Lazovsky. He would lay a trap.

"Look, we've got multiple problems, but I don't think they're connected," said Raskolnovitch. "We'll have to be careful who we tell what to. First, we've got to find the rat. In the meantime, we'll need money to complete our Drake Hotel deal, but also to fight a war, if we have to. I'm emptying our warehouses in Afghanistan of all our inventory. It's a risk, a big one; but I've got to have this cash soon."

"How much?" asked Prokofiev.

"Ten thousand kilos more or less," answered Raskolnovitch. "It's coming by train from Mazar-i-Sharif to Hairatan in Balkh province and then on Uzeb Railways. We've done this before, but never on such a scale, maybe 500 million dollars."

"You'll make much less, I'm afraid," interrupted Prokofiev. "You'll flood the market for months, maybe a year or more. We'll be lucky to get 25 a kilo."

Raskolnovitch kept his eyes on Lazovsky. "Yes, we'll lose a lot, but it can't be helped." The bait had been laid. If Mogilevich was really moving on him, he couldn't ignore such a sum. He put down his fork, wiped his mouth, and dismissed them with a flick of his hand. He thought of Toni. *Les jeux sont fait,* he said to himself.

Chapter 33

"Get some sleep," Matthew Palmer said with a wink, one hand on the doorknob. "Tomorrow will be a big day: financial advisers, security services, and if you've the energy, some rather sizable shopping. Bits and bobs, plenty of decisions."

Yuri smiled, nodded, then closed the front door behind him. Dora was upstairs in the master bedroom talking with Yana, sitting on the bed with their backs against the dark Tudor headboard, as Yuri walked in.

Dora looked up at him and smiled. "I have so much to tell you guys, but I wanted us all together and alone," she said.

"You can trust Matthew," Yuri said, seating himself cross-legged facing them.

"I'm sure we can," replied Dora, "but I wanted to debrief you first."

They all looked at each other, as though about to board a roller coaster. "So, here's what I learned," she began. "It's all very hush hush. It seems the French are investigating their former president for bribery, corruption and violations of campaign finance laws. It's an explosive development, especially as he is expected to be a leading contender for president in the next election. Raskolnovitch is suspected of illegally financing the campaign. It seems the French have a mole inside Raskolnovitch's operation. I owe my life to this mole. Whoever it is warned the consul general, Bertrand, and helped me escape."

Their eyes darted back and forth from each other.

"Bertrand confided in us because we provided him a key piece of evidence in the documents we brought out of Cyprus and Panama. I guess it confirmed payments made to this former president."

Yuri stared at his sister. Yana looked as though she had just heard from a group of extraterrestrials. The last three days had pulled the rug out from her world. Her face was ashen white.

"Are you OK, sis?" asked Yuri.

"This is all so out of our control. I'm scared."

"Me too," said Dora. "I'm real scared. I just had to run for my life from a bunch of guys in black wearing balaclavas and carrying machine guns. We're just pawns in a game that is so much bigger than us. I want out. I think if we offer to return all of Raskolnovitch's money, he'll be happy to call off his dogs. If we don't, he won't stop until we're dead."

Yuri understood the trauma she had just gone through, but he couldn't agree with her. "It's not as simple as that," said Yuri. "They need us alive to get their money back. And, besides, I don't want to let these thugs win. It's worse than a foreign invasion." He turned to Dora. "You came back to Ukraine to fight this. Now you've got something to fight with and you're going to give it back? I don't get it."

Dora looked hard at him, as if calculating how to protect her queen. "Just because I chose to fight corruption doesn't mean I have to sacrifice my life for the cause. It's already cost two lives. Haven't we done enough? We got the documents to prove he's bribing public officials and moving large sums of drug money around. My mission was to expose corruption. It's the government's job to do something about it. We've already succeeded. The shell companies are something extra. We can give that back to him and the British, the French and the Americans can go after him in their courts. We don't need this money to win."

"But we do," Yuri replied. "We've just done more damage to Raskolnovitch than all the court cases in the world combined. Your friend Bertrand said it clearly. 'If you want to fight, you need to think like an oligarch. If you want to win, you need to be one.' I'm in this to win and not just because he killed Yana's dad and our great-grandmother. I'm doing it for my country and for my own self. All my life I've felt like a loser. I don't feel like that anymore."

Yana said, "But Yuri, that's all fine and good for you. But what about us? What about dad and Bubbie?"

"I guess you have to make your own choice. I've made mine. If I can believe what we're being told, we have as much money as we could ever spend. We can set you up with your own place, your own security. It's me they're after," he said.

"That's not true," said Dora. "Those guys in balaclavas were after me. We're in this together, whether we like it or not. There's only one way to get over this safely and that's return the money."

"Yuri, please listen to her," cried Yana.

There was a long silence, like tiptoeing through the room of someone sleeping. Yuri wanted to release them from their fears. He was responsible for this situation. He mustn't let his pride put them at greater risk. He should declare victory and do what Dora said. She would love him all the more for that. He didn't need to be her knight in shining armor. He just needed to protect her. He started to say that, but Dora spoke first.

"Yuri, I understand how you feel. I admire your courage. But I don't even get what you plan to do with this money to fight him," said Dora, her blue eyes wide and open.

Yuri's voice softened. "I'm not sure. I'm not sure what a rival oligarch would do. I guess it would be to hurt him where it counts, attack his finances. That's why what we've done has freaked him out so. I'd use the courts, too. Tie him up with lawsuits, put him on defense. I'd hire private investigators to find out what he's hiding, where he's vulnerable. And I'd seek out his rivals and offer to join forces."

As he spoke he began to feel the advantage of his position, as a boxer might who senses his opponent weakening. The momentum was his. Why would he let go now? He was anxious to start using Raskolnovitch's fortune against him.

"I'm sick of this," Yana said. "I don't understand why you got us into this in the first place. All it's done is get people killed. I'm going to bed. You guys can figure it out."

She slid from the bed and went downstairs, leaving Dora and Yuri alone for the first time since she arrived. He reached for Dora's hand and they looked at each other without speaking.

She had never appeared more beautiful to him. The memory of kissing her at the airport lingered on his lips. He wanted to tell her that he loved her and would do everything he could to protect her, but before he could form the words, he heard himself say, "Dora, I'll give it back. You're more important to me than all this. I"—he stopped for a moment, letting his thoughts catch up to his words—"I, I think I've fallen in love with you."

He saw her face, tense with worry, dissolve into a smile. Her eyes took in the full measure of him. She leaned forward, parting her lips. Their mouths met, warm and moist. She threw her arms around his neck. He pulled her in to him. Their eyes never closed. Their tongues, first tentatively, read the pulse of their desires. An irresistible surge of energy woke a sleeping giant in his loins. She pulled back, though, her eyes moist.

"Yuri, I love you, too. I have since the moment I saw you. I can't bear the thought of putting you in danger. But if I don't let you play this out, you'll always resent me. You'll always feel like I took away your manhood. We're in this together," she declared.

He wanted her. He would do anything for her. But the hero in him would protect her above all else. He didn't need money or justice; he just needed her.

"No, Dora. You were right. We'll do what we have to do to settle this thing. My manhood means nothing. You're the only thing that matters to me," he said.

"Let's decide this tomorrow," she said and her eyes, those irrepressible blue eyes shone coyly, as she began to unbutton her blouse.

Chapter 34

Yuri felt unsteady on his feet. The view from the 8th floor conference room of the towering glass and steel skyscrapers that surrounded Berenson Bank on 60 Threadneedle Street reflected the unfathomable financial power of the City of London.

When he turned he saw Richard McEwan enter with a million dollar smile. McEwan's casual self-confidence reflected generations of good breeding. Yuri felt at ease. He and Dora sat in soft leather swivel chairs. Yana had decided to sleep in at home.

Matthew Palmer introduced McEwan to them. "I can assure you that there are no better hands to manage your finances than Richard's. He handles some of the greatest fortunes in Europe, including several that belong to rather prominent Russian emigres, so he is quite familiar with your situation."

McEwan smiled as though hiding some secret. With his good-natured nonchalance, he explained the role he could play as custodian of Yuri's newfound wealth: overseeing his investments and advising on any and all financial decisions. "You could think of me as a kind of personal valet for anything having to do with money, everything from shopping for clothes to acquiring assets with eight zeros in the price tag." He paused for a moment, watching their reactions.

"Your 'situation,' as Matthew called it, is actually quite unique," McEwan went on. Palmer had a chance to look over your balance sheet, which Dora shared with the French Consul in Prague, and has spoken with your attorney, Mr. Rodriguez at Mossack Fonseca. It seems you have an unusual amount of cash. We don't often see such massive liquidity. I suspect the former owner of these assets was preparing to launder these funds somehow. At the moment they are just sitting in your accounts, not earning anything, costing you, in effect, a loss of some $130,000 a day. So, this is one of the first things we should discuss, I would think," said McEwan with his devilish smile. "We'll want to know how aggressive you'd like to be and whether you have particular preferences for your investments."

Yuri sat up straighter in his chair and leaned forward, his forearms resting on the table. He cleared his throat, glanced at Dora, and then said to McEwan, "We've come to a very difficult decision. We don't think we'll be needing your services." He looked at Palmer and back to McEwan. "We've decided it would be best to return the funds to Raskolnovitch."

There was a moment of frozen silence, as if the two men were caught in the flash of an old-fashioned camera, faces grim with shock and dismay. After several seconds in which no one moved, Yuri continued. "This oligarch won't stop until we're killed. The only way to protect Dora and my sister and me is to give him what he wants. We'll trade him our lives for his money."

Palmer raised his eyebrows at Richard McEwan. Then McEwan spoke, his generous smile crumbled into an expression of implacable resolve. "You are out of your depth, Mr. Yavlinsky. You don't know what you're talking about." He leaned towards Yuri. "Giving this oligarch his money will merely insure your death. The only thing stopping him from killing you now is that he needs you alive to transfer the funds. Give the money to him and he won't need you anymore. Men like Raskolnovitch don't keep promises. You've shamed him, made him look weak and vulnerable to his enemies. He'll never stop because you say you're sorry."

He put his head back, shaking it from side to side as though he couldn't believe what he was hearing, then leaned forward again. "Raskolnovitch understands one thing, and that's force. You're a very naïve young man, Yuri. You're going to have to toughen up quickly to protect Dora and your sister. You can be safe here in London, but it will cost you a small fortune. You can only afford that because you have these millions." He stopped and looked at Palmer. "Besides," he said, "you have a debt to pay. This fucker put a bullet through your great-grandmother's head. You've come this far. Don't clutch now."

Dora spoke up. "You're being unfair, Mr. McEwan." Her sapphire eyes blazed. He sat back in his chair. "Yuri only agreed to this whole operation because I forced him into it, and then he insisted he had to take it all the way. He wanted to use this wealth to attack Raskolnovitch, even if it was a suicide mission. He agreed to give everything back to protect me. I was the one who was scared. But I can see now how naïve I was."

She turned to Palmer. "You're the one who's supposed to know these things. Is he right?" She shrugged toward McEwan.

"I'm afraid so," Palmer said. "We can protect you here in London. We've had a lot of experience with dissidents and oligarchs who are on the outs with powerful enemies, but it costs a lot. If you give back these funds, we won't be able to help anymore. I suppose you could try and hide somewhere, but that would be bloody bonkers. Better to stay and fight."

"Let's say you're right," said Yuri. "How can this end? How can we use this money to fight him?"

"A very good question," Palmer answered. "I think you know

some of the things that are about to befall Mr. Raskolnovitch on various legal fronts. There's even more that you don't know. But there are ways in which law enforcement agencies are limited in what we can do. We could never have stolen from his wealth as you did, for example. We are restricted from exposing some of the connections we know he has to the president of your country. Take a look at *Ukrayinska Pravda*'s series of investigative reports on the president's attempts to rig the bidding for a new national TV license. The oligarch behind this television venture is your friend Raskolnovitch. It appears the journalist who wrote these articles is missing. I would start there."

Yuri and Dora looked at each other. Dora spoke up. "I trust you have our best interests at heart. You and your colleagues helped save our lives in Kyiv and Prague. We at least owe you our confidence. Yuri wants to do battle with these pricks and so do I. We're in. We'll stay and fight."

The relief in the air was palpable, as if a storm had passed. Richard McEwan laughed. "I love the way you Americans talk. I feel like I'm in a Western at the OK Corral."

"Quite so," added Palmer. "Let's get these pricks. But first, let's get you settled. The sooner you have your security in place, a house to live in, car and a driver and the other necessities of life, the sooner we can get to work."

Yuri admired how Dora's presence commanded the room. None of them could look away from those irrepressible eyes. He realized how dependent he had become on her good judgment. They complemented each other. He took in the whole of her and admired her, as one might a great painting.

"And your funds?" asked McEwan, startling Yuri out of his revelry. "How would you like us to invest them?"

"Do what you think is best," said Yuri, sitting back in his chair. "We'll be spending a lot in the coming weeks, I suspect, so keep enough liquid."

McEwan chuckled. He seemed to be enjoying himself. "It will undoubtedly take a while before you comprehend just how much money you have now. I think you'll find it rather difficult to make a dent in it, no matter how much you spend. But let's try, shall we?" His smile was disarming. He paused, rubbing his hands together. "Pace yourselves. It's going to be a very long day."

Chapter 35

A liveried butler led Raskolnovitch to a sitting room near the entrance to the president's palace. The walls were hung with floor to ceiling gilded Baroque mirrors. He sank uncomfortably into a silk upholstered chair and studied his reflections. He felt old and tired. He hadn't slept well since this whole affair with the boy and his girlfriend started. But what really bothered him this morning was to be sitting here in this antechamber waiting to be summoned. That had never happened before. Normally, the president greeted him by the front door with his usual bearhug and an offer of his signature brandy. He couldn't remember the last time he had been asked to wait for anyone.

On his lap he held a square box wrapped in red velvet with a gold ribbon. He wasn't happy with this sordid business, he thought, but it had to be done. He looked at his watch. Had his *krysha* abandoned him? It made no sense. He was the president's principal source of funds. They were partners in the steady spigot of cash that flowed through the tobacco monopoly and the armored trafficking of drugs across the Hindu Kush. It would be suicide for the president to forsake him.

Through a leaded glass window, he saw the president on the walkway by the front door shaking hands with a man in a black overcoat and fur hat. The man looked familiar to Raskolnovitch, but he could not recall why. A moment later there was a knock on the door. The butler reappeared and led him to an office off the president's bedroom.

The president was seated in a high-backed leather chair reading a stack of papers on his desk. When he saw Raskolnovitch, he put down his reading glasses and came around the desk to greet him, his face grim. They shook hands and the president motioned for them to sit next to each other in the two leather recliners in one corner of the office under a bust of Peter the Great.

"What's wrong, my *krysha*, no hug this morning?" said Raskolnovitch. "You look like you've just seen a ghost." Raskolnovitch's heart was beating fast, but he tried to project an air of confidence and good humor.

"My own ghost," replied the president. "That was Bortnikov who just left, Putin's guard dog. He came here secretly. I had no warning. He just showed up, unannounced."

The president held his head in his hands, looking down between his legs. "I've been bullied before, but never like this. Our sovereignty and my own life are at stake."

He stopped and looked up to meet Raskolnovitch's gaze. He had the look of someone condemned. "I've been caught between two immovable forces, Viktor. Whichever way I turn, I lose. The Europeans have offered us 18 billion US, if we sign the association agreement with the EU and the IMF another 14. Putin gives a little less, but Bortnikov made it clear they would not allow Ukraine to join the EU or NATO under any circumstances. You know what that means. They can shut off our gas, seize Crimea and the Donbas and maybe invade, like they did in Abkhazia and Ossetia in Georgia. I'm stuck. Either way we lose."

Raskolnovitch had never seen his *krysha* so worried. The man seemed to have aged overnight. He had been a master at playing one side against another, always keeping his opponents off balance by exploiting their internal divisions. But the tragic misfortune of sitting between Russia and the West could only be finessed so far. Geography is destiny, he knew.

"I thought you had already decided. Everyone expects you to sign the Association Agreement with the European Union any day now. Even the Prime Minister said so, just yesterday," replied Raskolnovitch.

"I thought so, too. But now I've received an ultimatum. To be honest with you, Viktor, I've never liked this IMF bailout and the EU thing. We didn't have much of a choice, though. The state's bankrupt. But now we are forced to choose."

He wiped the sweat from his brow. Clearly, the head of Russia's federal security service had unnerved him.

"You and I are Russians, Viktor. We grew up that way. It's our mother tongue. We are Russian Orthodox. Of course, our people want to be like the rich Europeans they watch on television. But we don't speak their language. We pray in a different church. Our history has been forged with Russia since the very beginning. If we side with Europe, we'll have to live with their rules. You and I, Viktor, will not be able to do business as we have and our country will be overrun with homosexuals and Mercedes. Do we really want that?" asked the president.

"Of course not. You are certainly right," said Raskolnovitch, keeping his eyes on the man.

The president sat up straight in his chair. "And yet, Viktor, I'm told you are making plans to move to France, to get French citizenship, to escape."

Raskolnovitch forced a wry smile. "We all have to hedge our bets, don't we? But it's merely a wish. We dream of Paris, but our fortunes and our fates are here." He paused for a moment.

"Still, I admire your intelligence operation. How did you learn this?"

"There is little I don't know," answered the president. "Frankly, I was a bit hurt that you did not choose to tell me you were engaged, and to a French girl, the daughter of the French Consul General, a man I don't trust. I have reason to suspect she is not his daughter at all. You should be careful, Viktor."

Raskolnovitch's face hardened. "No, my *krysha*. You would be the first to know, if I were truly engaged. I have enjoyed this woman's company, but I have so far not even invited her to my bed. You have nothing to worry about. Like my fantasy of French citizenship, this is just a mere indulgence, a way to appear respectable."

The president laughed. He slapped Raskolnovitch on his leg.

They heard a knock at the door and the president's American political advisor, Paul Manafort, entered. Raskolnovitch noticed he came in unannounced, a privilege that even he, Raskolnovitch, didn't have. Manafort was dressed in a royal blue suit and gold tie, his abundant brown hair fluffed low over his brow. There was a noticeable change in the emotional atmosphere. Manafort was his usual buoyant self, smiling as if he knew something they didn't. He shook hands with Raskolnovitch, who didn't bother to stand.

"Viktor Ivanovich, I'm so glad you are here," said Manafort, his heavy jowls fixed in a devious grin.

When Raskolnovitch said nothing, the president spoke up. "Paul, Viktor and I were just discussing how one can buy an appearance of respectability in France, a topic you and I talked about just this morning before Bortnikov so rudely interrupted us."

"Precisely what I wanted to talk with him about." He turned to Raskolnovitch. "We understand you managed to buy quite a bit of respectability with Jacques Gavi. He is likely to make a comeback and be the next president of France. Ten million dollars can buy one a considerable amount of respectability, I presume," the American commented.

Raskolnovitch wondered how the president and Manafort knew so much. "All my indulgences are expensive," he remarked. "As are mine," replied Manafort. "We share that trait, so to speak." He waved his hand and a garish green cufflink flared at his wrist. "But we also need something from Monsieur Gavi. If we break off our negotiations with the EU, we need a voice of moderation who can understand our point of view. A sympathetic European leader, especially one as popular as Jacques Gavi, could be very persuasive in blunting any sanctions or negative repercussions."

"I understand," said Raskolnovitch.

"Europe is like a fickle woman," Manafort continued. "She wants to be admired and sees herself as virtuous. She will hate being rejected by a new suitor. But Ukraine is an expensive taste and a person such as Gavi might well make the case that any further expansion of the EU might be a mistake and might provoke the Russian bear. He has already said some things along these lines. Perhaps you should suggest a new quid pro quo."

Raskolnovitch was growing more and more irritated with this man. He had a way of making everyone around him feel small, even the president, while he puffed himself up. He hid his arrogance behind an obsequious smile, but Raskolnovitch could see through that. He could smell his arrogance even through his expensive cologne.

"Indeed," said the president. "Maybe you should double your investment in France. It might serve us all well."

At that, the president's advisor nodded his concurrence, shook hands with Raskolnovitch, turned, and left.

The president took time examining Raskolnovitch's face as though searching for some hidden message. "You know, Viktor,

I've been worried about you. There's talk that someone's made a move on you, that some of your offshore accounts have been compromised. I heard you hired a hundred of Mogilevich's crew, but your fish got away. There's also a rumor that the American SEC is investigating you. It looks like you might need a friend."

Raskolnovitch looked back at the president and held his gaze. "I'm doing everything I can to resolve this problem," he said. "We'll soon have things under control, but I can assure you there is nothing to worry about. As for friends, I already have the best one money can buy." This little impertinence amused the president.

"We are partners, you and me," continued Raskolnovitch. "Partners watch each other's back. I brought you a little present, that would remind you of that and might even cheer you up."

He reached down and lifted the red box by his feet and handed it to the president.

"Should I open it now?"

"By all means."

The president untied the gold ribbon and spread apart the velvet wrapping like a surgeon. Inside was a box made of polished curly maple. The president opened the lid and looked in, his expression changing from one of shock and horror to grim satisfaction. A smile spread across his face.

"You've done well, Viktor Ivanovich," said the president, as he lifted the severed head of the young journalist.

Chapter 36

"Hey," Viktor heard a voice say.

"Hey," he said, turning to see her. Toni was dressed in a full-length fur coat and hat, the ones she had worn in Davos. The sight of her lifted him from his ruminations. It was as though she were the only object in color; all else was black and white.

Raskolnovitch greeted her with a kiss on each cheek. They sat across from each other at a small round table.

"It's so nice and warm in here," she said. "It's freezing outside."

They were at Salon Mrozyvo, a popular ice-cream parlor, its walls painted in red and white candy stripes. The air was heavy with the smell of waffle cones baking. None of his security guards were visible.

"Perfect weather to meet for ice cream, *n'est pas?*" said Raskolnovitch.

"*N'est pas?*" repeated Toni. "You are becoming more French by the day, Monsieur."

She wrestled out of her coat. Underneath, she was wearing skinny legged jeans with a soft pink cashmere sweater.

She removed her fur hat and spoke again. "It's said of Churchill that at the start of World War II when he saw lines of people in Moscow waiting in sub-zero weather for ice cream cones, he realized the Russians could never be defeated."

"He was right," Raskolnovitch said "but what he didn't realize was people queued for ice cream because it was the only thing available."

Toni ordered a hot fudge sundae and Raskolnovitch a butter scotch.

"Here, I have something for you," Toni said. She handed him a shopping bag. Inside was a framed charcoal sketch wrapped in newsprint. "I had an assignment to draw someone's face from memory. You were easy to remember."

He held the drawing up as though catching the light and studied it. The face looked sad to him. There was something menacing about it, the broken nose in the center like a lunar landing site, the eyes downcast and sad.

"It's amazingly like me. Am I really that sad, though?"

"Not today. In fact, when I saw you as I walked in here, I thought how happy you looked. But I think the drawing captures something essential about you, the feral and frightened look of a little boy lost in the woods, searching for a way home."

Raskolnovitch smiled. "Perhaps you are right, my dear. I am still looking for home."

He reached down and lifted a brown leather briefcase from which he took out a large manila envelope. "Speaking of that, your friend Gavi sent me these."

She took the envelope and pulled out several glossy photographs of a sprawling stone chateau with its own moat and drawbridge in the middle of an ancient woods just twenty kilometers from Aix-en-Provence.

"This is incredible, Viktor. Does this mean that your citizenship has been granted?"

"No, not yet. But it's telling me to expect progress. He thinks I should buy this property. It's very beautiful, *n'est pas?*"

Toni laughed. "Yes, it's very beautiful. How much?"

"Twenty-two million Euros," he said. "But Gavi thinks I can get it for much less."

"Downsizing when you retire is smart, Viktor. You want to age in place. A small castle is easier to keep clean," she said.

"Yes, much cheaper too. Easy to heat.".

"Is getting citizenship what you're trying to accomplish with Monsieur Gavi?" she asked.

Viktor smiled. "Indeed. It's very expensive, French citizenship. Maybe easier to marry a French woman," he said.

She looked at him sharply. "Now it is you who are playing with me, *n'est pas?*"

For a moment it felt like he was in a movie. "Could you imagine yourself living in such a place?" he asked.

She caught her breath and smiled. "Are you proposing to me?"

"Perhaps," he responded. "Everything in its time."

"I don't understand you, Viktor. You intrigue me. I've enjoyed your company; you've treated me like a queen and yet you've made no attempt to go further than that. Most suitors would not be so restrained. You are not generally a cautious man. And now you dangle a castle before me. I may be able to draw your face, but I don't have a clue what's inside your head."

Raskolnovitch smiled. A waitress interrupted them with silver bowls.

"Toni, you are very precious to me. Maybe I give up everything for you." He paused, thinking. "In my life, I have anything I want. I am a free dog. It's true I can have beautiful women, food, drink, palaces, anything, like a magician, just snap my fingers. But you, maybe I can't have you. It's what makes you so attractive to me. I don't want to own you like everything else in my life.

Maybe someday you will ask me. I am a patient man, believe it or not. You are worth waiting for."

Toni looked as if she might cry. He could see her struggling. She said nothing but reached over and held his hand. The silence was like a great weight on his heart. He wanted so badly to kiss her. She might let him at that moment, he thought, but what would it mean? Better to wait.

A minute passed. Finally, she spoke. "We should eat before our ice cream melts." She looked down, averting his eyes. Then she asked, "Why is your French citizenship so important to you, Viktor? When Ukraine signs the Association Agreement with the European Union, you will be on the road to European citizenship. You won't have to be a French citizen to buy your chateau. You could come and go as you please."

Raskolnovitch felt the muscles in his face begin to twitch. "We'll never sign, Toni."

He could see her expression drop. He thought back to his conversation that morning with the president. It was true he was hedging his bets. It was not just a fantasy or a mere indulgence. He wanted to have his cake and eat it, too. He wanted to keep all his riches and enjoy them in a land of freedom, pleasure and beauty like France. But at that very moment, what he really wanted was her, Antoinette. His mind recalled the president questioning whether she was actually Bertrand's daughter. What had he meant by that? He made a mental note to follow up the next time he spoke with his *krysha*.

"I met with the president this morning. Bortnikov was there, the head of the Russian FSB. He gave Ukraine an ultimatum. The president will choose Russia. He has no choice." He knew he should not have shared this with her, but he hardly cared. He had much bigger problems to worry about.

She stopped holding his hand and started in on her sundae. "This is delicious, *n'est pas?*" she said, and added, "Spa-sibo."

Raskolnovitch laughed. "How do you say, 'you're welcome,' in French?"

"*Je vous en prie*," she answered.

He felt himself swimming against the current. "Toni, I have to leave for London tomorrow. Is there any way I can convince you to come with me?"

"I wish I could, Viktor, but I must finish a big project for my class," she said. "How long will you be gone?"

"I don't know," he said. "Not too long, I hope."

"I also hope not," she said. "It's too cold here to be eating ice cream alone." She looked away from him for a moment and he thought he saw a small crack in her usual confidence, as if she had conceded something to him.

Chapter 37

London spooled past the tinted glass windows of their new Land Rover SUV, as if they were watching a BBC travelogue. The monuments, the roundabouts, the black cabs and white marble steps evoked a nostalgia for an imagined past that Yuri had never known, solid and unchangeable. Their own lives, turned inside out, were anything but. They rode in silence, holding hands, each processing the morning's events.

She squeezed his fingers, then leaned over and kissed him.

"It's all going to be all right," she said.

"God, I hope so," said Yuri.

Sometimes he felt like he was drowning and was clinging to Dora for life. But another thought intruded into his mind, which he tried to deny, a realization that he enjoyed this new role. It was fun being rich and powerful. There were risks, but nothing great ever happens without risk, he thought.

"Yuri, why are you smiling?" she asked.

"It's my birthday today. Did you know that?" he asked. "I was just thinking how much I liked being rich. It's embarrassing for me to admit that. It seems very funny to me."

"Well, happy birthday," said Dora. "I learn more about you every day, it seems. Quite a birthday you're having. You just bought two expensive cars with drivers and we're on our way to see a home that costs seven million pounds. Except for the fact that the Russian mafia is out to kill you, you should be pretty happy."

"I am," he said, "but mainly because of you. It feels like we've been thrown into a lifeboat together.'" He looked at the driver in the rearview mirror and was glad there was a glass separating the front seat, giving them their privacy.

Dora laughed. "I once wrote a report at school about people who had won the lottery. It didn't work out so well for most of them. They just switched one set of problems they were used to for another for which they were totally unprepared."

"Sounds familiar," said Yuri. "But best we enjoy this while we can."

They passed in front of Buckingham Palace and a minute later turned down a cobblestoned lane lined with imposing Tudor mansions and onto a narrow mews that ended in a *cul-de-sac* where a solitary lamppost held sentry. There were four former stables, now garages, covered in ivy and painted in soft pastels behind which rose a three-story, five-bedroom, six-bath white brick house with large, divided glass windows and a tall cupola high enough to get a view of St, *James's Park.*

Matthew Palmer and Richard McEwan were just getting out of the other Land Rover, greeted by a tall elderly woman in a feathered hat, apparently the real estate agent. Two of Yuri's recently hired security guards stood discreetly on the opposite side of the mew. Yuri's driver opened the car door. They stepped out into a blustery London afternoon and shook hands all around. They entered through a tunnel of rose arbors down a stone path leading to a set of wide French doors that opened to an interior courtyard surrounded by stone walls with windows and balconies, iron gas lamps and cascading pink bougainvillea.

At the rear of the courtyard was a large entryway, but they walked through another set of French doors to their right into the most beautiful kitchen Yuri had ever seen. Inspired by Monet's kitchen at Giverny, according to the feathered-hat lady, the floors were an orange terracotta and the walls were made of large blue and white tiles edged in tiny floral designs. One wall was covered with copper pots and pans arranged in ascending sizes. Another held shelves of fine china and crystal glasses. There was a large stone fireplace on one end of the kitchen and on the other a ten-burner stainless steel stove encased in small, hand-painted tiles. A massive butcher block table ran the length of the room.

Light poured into every corner of the house. There was a large chandelier in the dining room above a long oak hunter's table, a wood-paneled living room with two large fireplaces side-by-side and an elevator hidden behind ordinary doors in the adjacent hallway. The upstairs bedrooms each had their own balconies facing the courtyard and large windows looking out on St. James's Park.

Yuri thought to himself, *I wish Taras or Mykola could see me now.* The image made him laugh out loud. *I should bring them here,* he considered. *I'll need people I can trust.*

It took Yuri and Dora less than a minute to say yes. They were each smitten. The security guards were delighted with the set-up, which had only one point of access and windows situated far from the street. Palmer and McEwan smiled like contented parents. The agent did her best to hide her excitement as Yuri signed various papers. They could move in as soon as escrow closed, she said.

"Happy birthday," Dora said to Yuri.

"It's your birthday?" asked Matthew Palmer. "Smashing, I'd say, well done. A day of gifts. I think you'll be quite happy here, and safe, too." They walked out through the overhanging arbors on the path covered in rose pedals. "Is there anything else we can do for you before you go back to your flat?"

Yuri stopped, put his hands in his pockets and thought for a second. "Yes, there is." He turned to Richard McEwan. "I'd like you to arrange a gift of 5 million Euros to the Kyiv Zoo on the condition that they rehire all the staff that had been let go. And, could you locate someone who does art restoration? I have something badly in need of repair. I'm sure I'll think of other things, but this will be a good start. Thank you."

"I know just the chap," said McEwan.

"Also," he said, making a spur of the moment decision, "Dora told me the FBI is investigating a money laundering scheme to buy the Drake Hotel in New York, which Raskolnovitch and that American blowhard Paul Manafort are developing. The account we got hold of in Panama was used as collateral. I'd like to make a formal complaint to the American SEC, letting them know that this offshore corporation's under new management now and we want to withdraw from the deal."

Palmer's eyes lit up. "There's already some SEC investigation, but this ought to put a wrench in their gears," he replied.

They said their good-byes. Palmer and McEwan would be dropped off and the second Land Rover taken to Yuri and Dora's flat. The security detail followed them out into the traffic. In the rear seat Yuri and Dora looked at each other in disbelief. She held a hand over her mouth suppressing a laugh.

"Who stole the cookies from the cookie jar?" she sang.

"What's that?" asked Yuri.

"It's an American children's song," Dora explained.

They arrived at their flat and found Yana downstairs talking with one of the young, lean security guards whose tattooed forearms filled out a tight-fitting T shirt.

"You're awake," said Yuri.

"It's almost six. I've been up all day."

They walked upstairs. Tea had been set out on the dining room table.

"How'd it go?" asked Yana. "Did you give all the money back? When do we leave? Where do we go?"

Yuri looked at Dora.

"No," Dora said. "They convinced us that giving the money back was not a real option. It wouldn't stop them from hunting us. The only way we could guarantee our safety was to use the funds to get the best security money could buy."

Yana's face dropped. Her hand shook as she poured them hot water. "But I thought we had all agreed."

"We had, but I think we were being very naïve. These Brits have had a ton of experience guarding people like us," said Dora.

"*People like us?*" repeated Yana. "You mean people who steal a billion dollars from a drug lord?"

"Yeah, something like that," said Yuri. "Look, Sis, a lot's happened today. I think you're going to like it. It's my birthday, you know. I got us all some gifts. We bought two new cars, Land Rover SUVs, and we got drivers to take us around. You'll always have a car at your disposal. More importantly, we hired the top security company in London that will give us round the clock, 24/7 security. They protect some of the richest people in the world here. And we just bought a house, just a stone's throw from Buckingham Palace, that you're going to fall in love with."

But Yana's face went in the opposite direction. She held her head in her hands like she was about to scream. She was shaking with fear and anger.

"I've been on the run since you showed up in Prague! I've never been so scared in my life. Every second I'm afraid someone will kill me like they murdered dad and Bubbie! I'm terrified. I finally got a little sleep when you agreed to give back the money—and now you want me to live with surveillance cameras and 24-

hour guards and you think I'm going to feel safe. Are you fucking serious?"

"It's just temporary, Yana," said Yuri. "This will all pass over in a few months, really, it will. In the meantime, you'll be as safe as anyone could be. You'll love the house, and you could do anything with your life that you want. Anything you've ever dreamed of. You talked about going to fashion school or getting your cosmetology license. You could do anything."

"You treat me like I'm your *child*," said Yana. "You buy a house without even asking my opinion. You think you can just buy my happiness? I managed to run away from home and now it's worse. Who the fuck do you think you are? You're both so high and mighty on your white horses. But you're no better than this Raskolnovitch creep. At least he worked for his money! You just stole it, like common thieves. You pretend to be doing this to fight corruption or something, but nobody asked you to do this."

"Yana—"

"You're big fucking hypocrites. You can try and justify anything, but the truth is you're selfish. If you hadn't robbed this guy Dad and Bubbie would be alive and I would not be on the run."

"Your dad beat you raw, and you had to run off to become a prostitute in Prague."

"But he shouldn't had been killed. Or *our* Bubbie!",.

"Sis, I'm sorry about the house. I should have asked you," said Yuri.

"There's no fucking way I'm living in that house. I might have been a prostitute, but I have too much self-respect to live off drug money."

Yuri pushed back his chair and stood up. "I understand what you're feeling. A lot of it's true. I'm the one responsible for dad and Bubbie. But we're in this now and we need to protect ourselves. And whether you care to admit it or not, we *are* in a war. You, me, every Ukrainian. Our government's been taken over by mobsters. I'm not just talking about your usual shitty corporate corruption. I'm talking about gangsters taking over the state. We should all be up in arms."

Yuri was almost shouting now, looming over her. Yana shrank back from him. "The Orange Revolution didn't go far enough. Somehow, we've accidentally hurt the biggest gangster of them all more than law enforcement agencies around the world have managed to do. If we were to pull back now, we'd be accomplices to his crimes. We've got to fight with everything we've got."

Yana stood up, too. "You self-righteous prick. I don't need your money. I know how to live on my own. You go enjoy your new home and your fancy cars. Your blood money. I'm out of here."

Yana walked out of the room, down the stairs and out the front door into a cold and darkening London evening.

Chapter 38

Viktor Raskolnovitch woke up at the Connaught Hotel in Mayfair feeling hung over, although he hadn't had a thing to drink the night before. In truth, he never felt comfortable in London. The city took itself too seriously, he thought. It lacked a sense of humor. He lifted the silver cover off a chafing dish on a cart by his bed, under which sat a just-delivered plate of over-cooked fried eggs, undercooked bacon, sausages, tomatoes, mush-rooms, and a slice of black pudding. The sight made his stomach turn. He wanted a cigarette but remembered that he had given up the habit years ago.

Taking a few bites of toast to absorb the coffee he drank like medicine, he shuffled off into the bathroom. A hot shower soon soothed him. He tried to play with himself to get his mojo moving, but he remained as flaccid as an eel. His mind drifted to the conversation in the ice cream parlor with Antoinette the day before. He had almost proposed to her, but he was not sure whether to feel disrespected or encouraged by her reaction. Still, he was glad he explained his reticence to make any sexual advance. It would only work, he knew, if she were the one to initiate it. Would that disappear, if he had her? Or maybe it was just too real, too intimate. Maybe he was afraid of being rejected. As always, he finished with a cold shower and stepped out feeling revived, though a slight headache lingered.

He got back in bed and picked up one of the newspapers that had come with his breakfast. The headline in the *Daily Telegraph* read *Putin Ultimatum to Ukraine*. The news rekindled his headache.

"Alexander Bortnikov, Director of the Russian FSB, met secretly yesterday with the president of Ukraine to deliver a blunt ultimatum to reject the Association Agreement with the European Union and join a Russian-sponsored bloc instead. According to informed sources, the meeting, which took place at the president's palatial home, warned of immediate economic, social and military consequences should Ukraine move closer to the EU."

There was widespread condemnation of the report throughout the Western Alliance. The newly elected president of the EU, Jean Claude-Junker, told the European Parliament, "Blackmail has no place in the modern world. The European Union stands in solidarity with Ukraine and the right of its people to self-determination."

The headline in the *Financial Times* read *Ukraine at the Crossroads*.

He threw down the papers and began to pace across the hotel suite. He shouldn't have told Toni what he knew. Of course, it could have been anyone around the president who leaked the news. It could even have been Bortnikov. Maybe Putin wanted the threat to be known. But still, he should never have told her. The news reports were unsettling in their own right. He feared the public would not stand for this. Ten years earlier, the president's election was reversed in a popular uprising. Another Orange Revolution, as it was named then, was a real possibility.

The phone rang. The front desk announced his visitors and a minute later there was a knock at the door. Still in his bathrobe, Raskolnovitch greeted his guests, a very tall Semitic-looking man with curly red hair and a shadow of a beard who looked like he could be a basketball player, and a shorter, stubbier, middle-aged man whose bald head was partially covered by a yarmulke. Neither of them looked the part, though what that might be, Raskolnovitch wasn't sure. His sometimes-partner Moskowitz had told him that there were no better black bag operators anywhere than these two. Former Mossad, these two men were reputed to be the ones who tracked down Colonel Kaddafi in 2011, two years earlier, and played some important, but undefined role, in the capture of Osama Bin Laden a few months before that. Their company, SKB International, offered a full range of services from surveillance to kidnapping. He poured them coffee and they got down to business.

"Mr. Raskolnovitch, it's a pleasure to meet you. We've heard a lot about you from your business associate, Ilan Moskowitz," the short bald man began. "I'm Harry Beinfeld and this is my partner Chaim Kurtz. We appreciate the urgency of your situation and are prepared to take whatever steps you require to eliminate the problem." Their English had a slight British accent. Raskolnovitch wondered if they had grown up or gone to schools in England, but said nothing. Although he had a visceral loathing of Jews, he admired their intelligence and their cunning.

"We've made enquiries," said the redhead, as if this were some euphemism. "We were surprised how sensitive your case is. I'm afraid you're caught up in something that's much bigger than this specific drama. The mention of your name caused all our usual sources to slam the door." Raskolnovitch lifted his head. "But we were still able to piece together enough of the puzzle to get a picture of what you're facing. We located the young man and his sister and the girlfriend you hired us to find with a stroke of some luck."

Raskolnovitch's face brightened. "What kind of luck?".

"We keep a few of the drivers at MI6 on a kind of retainer," said the shorter man. "It's paid off for us many times over. You'd be amazed at what information they pick up. By chance, one of our usual informants drove your three friends from the airport. They were accompanied by an intelligence officer named Matthew Palmer. We thought that was curious. Palmer's quite high up the chain. He wouldn't be involved if this were just a case of bank fraud or money laundering,"

"Go on, please," nodded Raskolnovitch.

"Palmer deals with matters of state actors. He's more involved in politics than anything to do with financial crimes," the short man continued. "There appears to be some formal task force involving the French foreign office and MI6 and possibly the Americans. We don't believe you're the target of this investigation, per se, but, frankly, your name is radioactive. We believe you are under surveillance."

Raskolnovitch looked around the room, as if expecting to see cameras. He clenched his fists as if in fight mode.

"Don't worry, Mr. Raskolnovitch. We've already scrubbed this room just before you arrived in London. We take every precaution with our clients. You're clean," said the tall one.

"What could be behind all this?" asked Raskolnovitch, pouring himself another coffee from the silver pitcher. Holding up the *Financial Times*, he questioned, "Is it related to this?"

"Perhaps," said the redhead again, "but we don't see how. The French are less involved in this Ukraine EU business than the Germans or the Poles or even the Americans, for that matter. It seems the French are the ones driving this case of yours."

"And the kids?" asked Raskolnovitch. "Yavlinsky and that young woman, Osatinskaya, how could they relate to this?"

The two ex-Mossad agents both shrugged. "It makes no sense," said the short squat one. "The boy has no history whatsoever. He worked at the fucking zoo. He's just a kid with no history, no prospects. The girl more so, but she's just a bit player, not the sort of person to have friends in high places. She was mostly an investigative journalist, never did more than march in a demonstration. We think, maybe, it was an accident. Maybe they found something in your bank records that was incriminating and the powers that be are protecting them as witnesses. Or it could be some personal connection, perhaps with this Consul General in Kyiv, Monsieur Bertrand, who seems directly involved."

Raskolnovitch looked up. His eyes narrowed. "I have a good contact in that office. Perhaps I can learn something."

The short man spoke. "We've dealt with this man Bertrand before. He has never been a very active agent. He's mostly been an informer. He was helpful to us when we worked for the Mossad. He's queer, you know, and single. We could put some pressure on him, if we need to."

This information rattled around Raskolnovitch's brain like billiard balls. He wanted to correct them but said nothing. He would deal with all this later. It was too much to process all at once. He pulled back his chair, stood up and paced back and forth before his guests.

"So, gentlemen, tell me what we should do. It seems pretty complicated," said Raskolnovitch, sitting down again.

The two men looked at each other. The short man gestured to the redhead, Kurtz, to answer. "You must understand, it's very difficult to do anything kinetic here in London. Your three friends are under the protection of MI6. If anything were to happen to them, we'd have the whole of Scotland Yard after us. Nothing is easy here. But that doesn't mean we do nothing." Kurtz leaned forward, speaking with a strangely sympathetic earnestness. "We understand you need this young man, Yavlinsky, to return your money. We can threaten him, but that's about all." He leaned back. "But perhaps we can make this threat more credible."

Raskolnovitch's face lightened. The headache that had been building in his skull disappeared. He heard once again the sound of the bell that signaled it was time to get off his stool and get back in the ring. "The boy may not fear for his life, but maybe he cares for this girl or his sister more. Maybe," he paused, thinking, "maybe like *The Godfather*, we make him an offer he can't refuse."

Chapter 39

Yuri woke up dreaming about animals escaping from the zoo, but he couldn't quite hold onto it, as he struggled to remember which city he was in. He felt Dora's warm body next to him. The reality of his present whereabouts slowly came into focus. He stealthily pulled the sheets off and slid from the bed. He walked to Yana's room to see if she had come back during the night, but, as he expected, the room was empty. A sense of foreboding left an acidy taste in his mouth. He went downstairs and made himself some coffee.

The papers were filled with stories warning that Ukraine might not follow through with plans to sign the Association Agreement with Europe. The conflict between Putin and the West was coming to a head. Dora startled him when she came up behind him and put her arms around him. He hadn't heard her tiptoeing down the stairs. She read over his shoulder. There were calls, apparently, for people to congregate on the Maidan. It seemed that another large-scale protest, like the Orange Revolution, was in the offing.

"How'd you sleep?" asked Dora.

"Fair. How about you?"

"Stressful," said Dora. "I kept worrying about Yana."

"Yeah, me too," said Yuri. "I checked her room. She's still out somewhere."

"We need to find out if Palmer has learned anything," Dora said.

Yuri nodded.

Dora made a pot of tea and some toast with jam. They read next to each other in silence. Dora scanned the article in the *Ukrayinska Pravda* that Palmer had given them, exposing corruption in the award of a national television license.

"Can I read you something?" she asked?

"Sure."

"Police fear foul play with missing journalist,'" Dora read. "An investigative reporter for *Ukrayinska Pravda* has been missing since Thursday night when he was last seen walking his dog. The journalist, Georgiy Goritzky, had recently published a 5,000 word expose of the president's manipulation of an auction for a national independent satellite news channel. Viktor Raskolnovitch, Ukraine's richest oligarch, who built a fortune from his control of the tobacco market, is bidding for the channel, though he has no previous experience in the media industry."

Dora lowered the paper and looked at Yuri. "I met that reporter at a party just a couple months ago."

"Shit," said Yuri, not looking up. "That sucks. I wonder why Palmer thought we should start there."

Dora skimmed further through the article, "According to this," she said, "the fix is already in for Raskolnovitch to get the license. Goritzky argues that the license should rightfully go to a group of local independent stations, not to foreigners or to the president, but they don't have the resources to compete with these big players."

"Maybe that's what Palmer had in mind. Is the bidding over?" Yuri asked.

"Not according to the *Financial Times*," said Dora.

"It would be poetic justice to beat Raskolnovitch with his own money, wouldn't it?" said Yuri, looking up at her.

He saw Dora's face brighten. This battle with Raskolnovitch was the storyline of their relationship. It's what bound them together. Yuri would not admit this to her, but he enjoyed playing the hero for Dora. Without this drama, she would never have been attracted to him, he told himself. This unemployed young man, someone who drew caricatures at night in a room he shared with his great-grandmother, was no great catch. But this audacious figure in a bespoke suit, someone who stole a billion dollars from a drug lord, walked with a swagger. The combination of power and righteousness, he decided, had to be an aphrodisiac.

"You know, a lot of what Yana said I agree with," said Dora. "I'll feel much better the sooner we start using these funds to bring him down." She paused. "I know someone involved with one of these independent broadcasters. Should I call him?"

"For sure," answered Yuri. "Tell him there's a good oligarch who's ready to back their bid with all the resources they could want."

"What else?" she asked.

"What do you mean?"

"How else should we spend all this money we've got?" she asked.

He thought for a moment. "Dora, in those accounts from Panama, weren't there monthly mortgage payments for some mansion outside Kyiv? Raskolnovitch must have borrowed that money for some reason."

"A lot of these oligarchs like to use other people's money when they can, even while they struggle to launder cash," said Dora. "He bought his mansion, a plane, and a helicopter that way. Monthly cash payments look more legit than huge amounts of cash. What are you thinking?"

"Maybe Palmer or McEwan can figure out how we can purchase that debt and foreclose on him," Yuri said.

"I suppose you could make a generous offer to the bank to sell these debts," Dora mused. "It's a small bank, I believe."

"Or, maybe we buy the whole bank with these debts and all," said Yuri.

Dora's face bloomed into a grin. "Good idea. Thinking like an oligarch. What else?"

They made a list of all the charities and institutions they would support. It was fun, but a dread hung over them. They didn't know how much time they had. It felt as though they were playing a game of Russian roulette. Sooner or later there would be a cost to their play.

"Before anything, we need to find Yana. Before Raskol- novitch does," said Dora.

Yuri jumped as they heard a knock at the door. It was steel- reinforced and the knock rang like a bell. He glanced up at the clock above the refrigerator. It was 7:20 a.m.

"It's John," said a voice. "One of the night guards."

They opened the door and a tall, broad shouldered man with a crew cut, sporting a holster strapped across his tee shirt, handed them a letter with the seal broken.

"A delivery man just gave us this. We always open any pack- ages to make sure there're no explosives or poisons. You never can be too cautious."

"Thanks for the letter and reminder." He pulled it out of its envelope.

Dear Mr. Yavlinsky,

I believe you have something that belongs to me. We need to meet to work out how you will return this to its proper owner. I am in London and can meet anywhere you wish. Your safety is guaranteed. You can contact me at the Connaught Hotel in Mayfair. I will remain here as long as necessary.

Please give my best regards to your friend, Miss Osatinskaya and your sister Yana.

Sincerely.
Viktor Raskolnovitch

"Oh fuck, Yuri, he knows we're here!" Dora cried out.

Yuri held her. He tried to reassure her, "They wouldn't have asked for a meeting if they could touch us here. They're just trying to frighten us."

"Well, it worked," said Dora.

"We're safe here, for now at least," said Yuri. But he was scared too.

"We can't keep living like this," said Dora. "Maybe we can negotiate some kind of deal, or maybe we simply hide somewhere. I know of a commune in Northern California near a remote mountain town called Forks of Salmon where Abbie Hoffman hid out. He'd never find us there."

Yuri was silent, thinking hard. Living on a commune in Northern California sounded very attractive, but he had to stop running. He heard himself speak before he knew what he was going to say.

"Dora, listen, I know you're scared. So am I. We can't keep running and I don't want to spend my life in hiding with some new identity. We'd always be afraid." Then, surprising himself with what came next, he said, "I think we're looking at this all wrong. This invitation to meet could be our opportunity. Rather than worrying how to protect ourselves, we should use a meeting as a way to go after him. Isn't what a real oligarch would do?"

Dora was about to say something, but Yuri continued. "I want to kill him. I really mean it. I want to avenge what he did to Bubbie and my step-dad. Think of all the people he's killed from heroin and tobacco. I'd have no qualms doing it. We just need to figure out how."

Yuri felt his fear melt away, felt his confidence return.

"You're not serious, are you?" asked Dora.

"Fucking right I am. I'd kill him with my bare hands, if he were here now."

"Viktor Raskolnovitch was a professional boxer, a soldier and a killer. You're an artist. I don't want to hurt your feelings, Yuri, but I don't think your anger would be enough to overpower him. We need to be real here," Dora Said.

"I am real. We can hire some professional assassins. We've got the money. That's what an oligarch would do. He's sitting there at the Connaught Hotel. We could poison his food or shoot him. How hard could it be for some killer to take him out?" Yuri said. He pumped his fists. "Think about it. We'd be free and clear."

Dora reached over and held his wrists tight. "I won't do this, Yuri. That's not who we are. If we end up killing anyone, we've lost the fight. We've become one of them. We can't let their money or our hunger for revenge corrupt us. I won't have any part in it. I'll leave."

Another rapping at the door made Yuri tense.

"It's John again. Gentleman here to see you. He's on our cleared list. Just wanted to make sure before I let him up."

Yuri felt a jolt of fear before he pulled open the door. Looking past the guard he saw the broad shoulders of Rabbi Morris Weissgold bounding up from the landing. Dora rushed past Yuri and threw her arms around him. Morris thrust a hand over her shoulder to shake Yuri's.

"Hi, I'm Morris Weissgold," he said.

"Yuri Yavlinsky. We've met before, I believe, in a taxi in Prague. But it's good to meet you officially, finally." Yuri stepped back and looked at him more closely. "I never got a chance to thank you for what you did at the airport. And I owe you a tip, I suppose. I'm glad we get to be properly introduced at last. Dora's talked endlessly about you," said Yuri. "Come in." He closed the door behind them.

"It's a bit of an obsession we have for each other, I'll admit," said Morris.

"Uncle Morris, why are you here?" asked Dora.

"I have an appointment with Prime Minister Cameron to discuss this *meshuggah* Brexit business. Thought I'd stop by."

"Stop teasing," said Dora.

"I promised your mom I'd look out for you. I was 'counter-casing' this joint, watching to see who else might be watching. Just before that courier showed up, there were two men in overcoats standing by a parked limo smoking and looking up at your apartment. It was obvious they wanted you to see them, to frighten you. It's an old trick. I think I might have broken one of their knees, before I managed to persuade them to leave." He turned to face Yuri. "So, what was in the letter?"

Yuri and Dora exchanged looks and shrugged. Yuri handed him the letter.

After reading it, he looked up and smiled. "Frankly, this letter tells me he's run out of options. He can't do you any harm here in London. He knows that. You've got his money and you're well protected. The fact that he's here in person shows how weak his hand is." He folded the letter and slid it back in its envelope. "This Raskolnovitch—he might be a thug, but he's also a realist.

He'll want to cut his loses, make you some deal." Rabbi Morris met their eyes. "And he doesn't know that Yana's left. He wouldn't have said 'give her my regards.'"

"How'd you know about Yana?" asked Yuri.

"Matthew Palmer. He and I once shared a prison cell in Tripoli. We've been working closely together since you arrived here."

"Did Palmer say anything about Yana?" asked Dora.

"Scotland Yard found her registered at a small hotel in Soho, but she checked out early this morning before they could contact her. I'm sure they'll find her again very soon."

"Should we be calling Palmer to let him know Raskolnovitch's here?" asked Yuri.

In a perfect imitation of Palmer's voice, Morris said, "Not to worry, old chap. We've been tracking him since he arrived."

"Have they?" asked Dora.

"Yes, but Palmer will be surprised how quickly he found your safe house. Raskolnovitch obviously has some real time intelligence."

"Why didn't Palmer tell us Raskolnovitch was in London?" Dora asked.

"He was coming here to brief you this morning around eight. I didn't want to upstage him, but when I saw those two muscle heads outside, I thought you might need to hear this right away," said Morris.

"I was just planning to hire a professional assassin when you showed up," Yuri remarked

Dora started to object, but Morris interrupted her. "That's not such a crazy idea, Yuri, but only as a last resort, and not here in London. The Brits solve 93% of their homicide cases and, besides, you're guests of MI6. They wouldn't take kindly to your killing an oligarch just a kilometer from Pall Mall. They pride themselves on protecting them."

Dora picked up the note. "What do you think we should do?" she asked Morris. "Should we meet him?"

"What on earth for? What could he possibly give you? You've already taken everything. There's nothing more for you to gain. You won't be able to buy your safety, no matter what he might promise you. I would advise you not to answer this note at all." He paused for a moment before continuing. "The French passed on some information they intercepted from wiretaps. It seems Raskolnovitch has more important things to worry about right now. He's about to go to war with the Russian mafia. He thinks Mogilevich put you up to this. There's bad blood on both sides."

"Maybe we should encourage that," said Yuri.

Morris held Yuri's gaze, then paused to look at his watch. "I've got to get going. I've got a plane to catch. I'll be in DC, but I'll come back as soon as I can." He turned to shake Yuri's hand. "It's a pleasure to meet you. Take good care of my favorite niece." He walked to the door, turned and said, "There's one other thing I know that I'm not at liberty to share with anyone. Raskolnovitch doesn't know this yet, but I can assure you that he will be leaving London before tea time."

Chapter 40

Viktor Raskolnovitch lay on the massage table in his hotel room at the Ritz after the masseuse had left, hoping to fall asleep. But his heart refused to settle down. He couldn't get Toni out of his mind. He had tried calling her a dozen times since he arrived in London, but she never answered. Just before his massage, though, she had emailed to say she would be in Paris on some business and shopping at secondhand stores. 'Was there anything he needed?'

Reluctantly, he peeled off from the table, showered, and dressed. Not surprisingly, he had no response to his note from the Yavlinsky kid, but the warning had been delivered. He needed to get outside and breathe some fresh air; but first he would meet with the two guys from SKB International.

Precisely on time, Harry Beinfeld and Chaim Kurtz knocked on the door and entered. They took the same seats from the day before.

"Any news?" asked Raskolnovitch.

"Too much," said Kurtz, the tall one, "but not what you were looking for."

Raskolnovitch felt his face flush. He didn't like their expressions. He nodded for them to continue.

"We discovered you're being wiretapped," said Beinfeld, the short bald man. "The order seemed to have been issued by an examining magistrate of the French Assize Court and upheld by the Court of Cassation, France's supreme court. We believe that it's connected to a case against the former French president Jacques Gavi, who as you may know is running for president again. The papers are full of rumors that he will be charged with embezzlement, misuse of public funds, corruption, influence peddling, and money laundering."

Beinfeld told Raskolnovitch there were allegations that Gavi had met with an unnamed foreign oligarch on a yacht and at a private meeting in Davos during the World Economic Forum, where arrangements were made to finance his upcoming election campaign.

"They claim to have witnesses with direct knowledge of these transactions, plus tape recordings and wiretaps," added Kurtz, the tall red head.

Raskolnovitch felt as though he had put his finger into an electrical outlet. His heart beat out of control. It could only be Toni, he realized. He tried not to show any reaction. He rose from his chair and walked over to the bedside table where he had left the nitroglycerine tablets his doctor had given him to prevent another heart attack. He placed one under his tongue and another between his cheek and gum, closed his eyes for a moment, and then returned to the table.

"Was my name mentioned?" he asked.

"No," said Beinfeld.

"What do you advise?" asked Raskolnovitch in a small voice, his palms resting on his knees.

"We spoke with your lawyer," Kurtz answered. "He agrees with us that it is not safe for you to remain in London. Scotland

Yard could detain you. Just minutes ago, he was served with an 'assignation pour le témoin,' a subpoena for all documents, recordings, and videotapes of your interactions with Monsieur Gavi. We believe it would be best for you to return to Kyiv immediately."

Raskolnovitch was not used to taking instructions, but he felt he had no choice. He called in one of his guards and told him to pack up everything and meet him at the plane. Then he walked out of the hotel into the cold and threatening air and ducked into a limousine the two men had summoned. Kurtz handed him a phone he could use and took the two he was carrying. On his way to Farnborough, Europe's most exclusive business aviation airport, he called his lawyer who confirmed what he had just learned. Then he called Prokofiev.

"Dima, it's me. Call me right back at this number on a different phone, one you've never used," he said and hung up.

A minute later, his phone rang.

"The news is not good," said Prokofiev.

"I'm on my way back. Meet me at my Kyiv house. Listen, Dima, I need to see Antoinette Bertrand. Have Kostya find her, whatever it takes," said Raskolnovitch.

There was a sudden clap of thunder that made his phone crackle and then a burst of rain.

"Kostya can't do it," said Prokofiev through the static. "He's downtown being interrogated about that missing journalist. Apparently, they discovered the torso, but not his head. The police noticed Kostya's Lada when they looked at video from the week before in the neighborhood where the kidnapping took place. Kostya was advised to say nothing, but eventually he'll have to explain what he was doing there. I sent one of our lawyers with him."

"Fuck, fuck, fuck. What an idiot!" Raskolnikov said. "I told him to watch for street cameras. At least he won't break. I'm sure.

But Dima, I must find that girl, Antoinette. Do whatever is necessary to bring her to the house. Use force, if you have to, but don't harm her."

Three hours later, as he was flying over Poland, his new phone rang again.

"Viktor, it's Dima. We found her, Ms. Bertrand. She was waiting outside her apartment with two suitcases for a car to take her to the airport. There was no need to use force. She got in, thinking the car was the one she had ordered. Oleg told her you wanted to see her. She insisted he take her to the airport or she'd miss her flight, but she did not put up any struggle when we brought her to the villa."

"Duzhe dobre, very good," said Raskolnikov. "Please, make her comfortable, but don't let her out of your sight. I should be there in hour and half, I think."

He landed in snow flurries at an airstrip thirty kilometers from Kyiv and took the helicopter to the villa. An overly built three-story stone structure constructed in the Stalinist period, it had been a guesthouse for visiting Communist Party nomenklatura. It had few windows and rooms that were cavernous and cold. The president had essentially given the home to Raskolnovitch after it was confiscated in 1994.

He set the helicopter down on the rooftop heliport. The young woman, he was told, was in the living room with Dima. Not waiting for the rotors to stop, he hurried across the roof in a swirl of snow and noise and entered through a metal door. He took the elevator down to the first floor. Two guards standing outside the living room saluted and opened the twelve-foot high doors. Dima and Toni rose when he entered. She was wearing a grey kimono-like silk outfit like the one he met her in. Her elegance and grace were apparent in the simple act of standing.

"Viktor, what is the meaning of this?" she said, her voice

diamond hard, more a statement than a question. "Why have you forced me to miss my plane?"

He felt his rage begin to wilt at the sight of her and steeled himself for what would come next.

"Dima, would you kindly leave us?" he asked. When the door closed, he motioned for her to sit. There was a bottle of wine opened. He poured himself a glass and sat across from her, their knees nearly touching. Their eyes wrestled with each other. She seemed for a moment like one of his Faberge Eggs, her beauty enhanced by the fragility of her captivity. For a moment, he imagined tearing off her dress and forcing himself on her.

"You are going to Paris to testify?" he asked. He had considered feigning ignorance of the Gavi case, but there was no reason to play that game now.

"What are you talking about?" Toni said.

He laughed, took a large swig of wine, and put down his glass. "I wondered why you took such interest in Monsieur Gavi."

"I don't understand. What does he have to do with anything?" she said.

"You knew about him on the yacht. You were at the meeting in Davos," he spoke.

"Viktor, what's wrong with you. What is this about?"

"And the girl. It was you who warned her about her cell phone," he said.

He could see a sliver of panic in her eyes. She started to reach for her glass. Her hand was shaking slightly. She put her hand back in her lap. From his days in the Gulag he knew the smell of fear. She said nothing. It was useless to lie anymore.

"You would have made a great actress, Toni, too bad. You fooled me. You understood my vanity too well. What a fool I've been. I believed you." He was surprised how calm he remained. But his calmness only frightened her more, he saw. He took another gulp of wine and felt the heat rush to his head. He had not decided what he would do with her.

"And that fag Bertrand, posing as your father. What audacity you have. You must think I'm an idiot. Tell me, my dear Antoinette, what is your real name?" he asked, pouring himself another glass.

Her chest rose and fell. She gathered up her strength and stared fiercely at him.

"My name is Antoinette," she said, and, after a pause, "Antoinette Schwab. I am an officer of the DGS, the General Directorate for External Security. My mission was to discover any foreign influence in Gavi's campaign. My efforts were not directed at you."

The anger he had tamed rose again in him. "You betrayed me," he said.

"It's not as simple as that, Viktor. I did my job, very well, it seems. But it was not all an act. I had become very fond of you. I saw through the big, bad oligarch routine. I saw someone with grace and caring as much as courage, a man searching for meaning in his life. When you showed me the chateau in France and practically proposed to me, I felt I had to act on my feelings." Her voice was growing firmer, more confident. "They were going to charge you as a co-conspirator, but I convinced them to give you a chance to turn state's evidence and testify against Gavi. I was on my way to Paris to speak to the prosecutors about that. The truth, Viktor," and here she stood up over him, "is that I found myself falling in love with you."

Her words stung. "That's worse!" he shouted. "You knew I loved you and you still betrayed me." He stood up next to her. Her height intimidated him. He couldn't be sure what to believe. She had fooled him for so long. How could he believe her now? The conflict between his heart and his head made him nauseous. He wanted to cry.

"So, it was you who put Yavlinsky and his girlfriend up to it, to steal all my money?" he said.

"No. I had nothing to do with them. Viktor, you don't need all that money. You have enough to buy that castle in France. We could be happy there."

"We?' he asked.

"Yes, you and me," she said.

He did not believe her. She was playing him. She had betrayed him and now she was lying to save her life.

Toni put her arms around him and bent to kiss him, but he pushed her hard and she fell backwards against the chair and onto the floor. He pulled out a silver-plated gun and fired three times.

Chapter 41

The sound of gunshots reverberated in her head for what seemed an eternity. She waited for the pain to hit. Time stopped. Her mother and the childhood nanny she called Aimee appeared to her. Still, the explosions rang in her ears. She thought to move but seemed unable to send a signal to her body.

When her eyes opened, she saw him standing over her. He appeared to be screaming, but she could hear nothing except the echo of the gunshots. Slowly, the realization that she had not been hit rose to the surface.

He grabbed her by the arm and lifted her up, then swung her over his shoulder and carried her out the door. Dima Prokofiev was waiting in the hallway.

"Is she dead?" he asked.

"Not yet," said Raskolnovitch. "I fired next to her head. Perhaps we can use her somehow. Take her to a safe room downstairs and make sure she can't escape."

He let her slide off his shoulder and slump to the floor. Her head was bursting with a searing pain. She still felt the roar of the blasts pulse inside her. Dima took her under her arms, a guard lifted her feet and they carried her to the elevator. The basement was dark and dank. They deposited her on the cold cement floor of an empty room without any windows. It all seemed unreal to her, as if she were a detached witness to these events. When she was alone, she began to take account of what had happened to her.

He had fired three shots close to her ear. She had lost much of her hearing, probably permanently, she deduced. The absence of emotions surprised her. She felt none of the elation she expected at being alive, nor any fears either. As the minutes passed, the sound of the explosions slowly faded, and she could hear or sense her heart beating. She began to shake. The floor was cold. She struggled to her feet. It's just shock, she told herself. Once she was upright, her brain began to function again. The training she had received at the General Directorate for External Security clicked in. Stay calm, focus on what you want, not what you fear, pay attention to details, and no matter what is done to you, keep repeating to yourself that you are a soldier and a patriot. Help will come.

Upstairs, Raskolnovitch sat alone on the couch and stared at the three round burn marks on the white carpet. He felt empty inside, angry at Toni's betrayal and angry at himself for continuing to hold on to a shred of hope that she might have been telling the truth. In a corner of his mind he saw himself happy living with her in the chateau in Provence. But that was out of the question now with the Gavi investigation. His fantasy of French citizenship seemed a ridiculous, naïve delusion. He should have killed her and put an end to the whole affair. She had used him, lied to him. She deserved to die. Had he hesitated because he was too weak? Had she been able to take advantage of him because he had let down his guard? It was the same with the Yavlinsky kid.

Prokofiev walked in, saw him sitting with his head bent over his knees, and sat next to him. "You OK?"

Raskolnovitch continued to look down as he spoke. "I suppose so," he said.

"Well, at least we have a little more clarity," Prokofiev said. "Between what the two Israelis discovered and what Ms. Toni told you, it does seem like the French are after Gavi, not you. We're just roadkill."

Raskolnovitch sat up. "I think we can assume that Toni is the one who warned the girl Osatinskaya. She must have overheard Kostya and me when she and I were horseback riding and called the girl."

"Or, called her handler at the French Embassy," Prokofiev noted. "The last call to the girl's cellphone came from there."

"Toni claimed she was trying to arrange a deal to get me immunity in exchange for testifying against Gavi."

"Could be," said Dima.

"Our *krysha* wouldn't like that, though. He and that scumbag Manafort want us to double down on Gavi and get him to support our turn away from the EU."

"That can't happen now," said Prokofiev.

Raskolnovitch stared at the three round burn marks in the white rug and rubbed his head in thought. "There's got to be a way to turn this to our advantage.".

"We should be able to trade her for something," suggested Prokofiev.

"But only after we force her to tell us what she knows," Raskolnovitch replied. "No doubt she and that fag Bertrand will know who's behind the Yavlinsky kid and his girlfriend. I doubt the French would try something as audacious as what they did. The French don't have the balls, but clearly, they're helping."

Prokofiev stretched out his legs and folded his hands behind his head and said, "If Miss Bertrand was the one that warned the

Osatinskaya girl, then I guess we can assume Mogilevich isn't making a move on us. That's a relief."

"We'll see. Our train should arrive in Uzbekistan tomorrow. The trap's been set. It was probably a waste of time, but it will help to clear things up. In the meantime, our biggest problem remains the Yavlinsky kid and our money. Our little nightingale downstairs ought to help us shed some light on that," said Raskolnovitch. "Maybe you should try to persuade her, Dima. Do what you must."

Prokofiev stood up and started to walk to the door.

"On second thought, Dima, let's try and do this in a civilized way. We don't want to burn any bridges." He wondered if he were just being soft again. "I'll call Bertrand. You may be right about a trade."

"Be careful," noted Dima. "The call's sure to be recorded."

Raskolnovitch called on his encrypted cell phone while standing on the rug where Toni had lain as Prokofiev watched. Bertrand answered on the second ring. "Allo?"

"Mr. Consul General? This is Viktor Ivanovich Raskolnovitch. I'm worried about your daughter, Antoinette. She called me on her way to the airport and sounded hysterical, as if someone had kidnapped her. We were cut off and I haven't been able to reach her again. I think we need to talk as soon as possible. Perhaps if we work together, we can find her. I suggest you come to my house immediately. I presume you understand my meaning," he said with a slight laugh.

"Of course," replied Bertrand. "I'll be right there."

A moment later Toni's cell phone rang in Prokofiev's hand. They let it ring until it stopped. Thirty minutes later Raskolnovitch watched from the window as a white Citroen C6 with a French flag on its hood pulled in front of the house. A security guard asked him to empty his pockets and patted him down with expert care. A butler escorted him to an office on the second floor where Raskolnovitch and Prokofiev were waiting, seated on a blue couch. There were no handshakes. Raskolnovitch pointed to a chair and the tall weary diplomat folded himself into it.

"May I offer you a drink?" said Raskolnovitch, holding a decanter of scotch in his hand. Bertrand nodded and was handed a glass. "How is she?" asked the Consul General.

Raskolnovitch laughed. "Quite well, I assure you, for the time being." He paused to let Bertrand's discomfort rise. "She was kind enough to tell me her real name and rank in the DGS. The ruse you played was quite convincing, I must admit. Though I'm surprised you thought a homosexual could play the part of her father. I always assumed that being gay was a security risk in the French diplomatic corps. It would seem your career could be hurt, if that fact were made public." He let the threat hang in the air. "But let us move on to Toni. This is not really about you," he said.

Maintaining eye contact, Bertrand took a sip of scotch.

"You may be wondering why I brought you here," Raskolnovitch continued. "As an experienced diplomat, you know the value of a peaceful negotiated settlement. You strike me as a reasonable man. You may not be Antoinette's real father, but I'm sure you would not like any harm to come to her, *n'est pas?*" he said.

Bertrand nodded.

"So, let me make you a proposition. First, you tell me your interest in me regarding Monsieur Gavi or anything else—and what you know about the Yavlinsky caper and Miss Osatinskaya. It appears they are under your protection, if not your direction." He paused again, then added, "I'll only ask you this once and you will answer truthfully or Miss Antoinette Schwab will suffer a most creative end."

Bertrand cleared his throat and gulped down the rest of his drink. He rubbed his brow and then spoke. "It was a stupid ruse,

I admit. As you've undoubtedly discovered, former president Gavi is under active investigation for corruption and various violations of our election laws. We had reason to believe that he had financed his campaigns with illegal foreign contributions from Libya's Colonel Gaddafi and, after the Colonel was deposed, by certain Russian and Ukrainian oligarchs, you among them. Ms. Schwab was able to record certain conversations with you and Gavi that directly implicated the former Prime Minister. You were to be named as a co-conspirator, but Toni, Ms. Schwab, was convinced that she could persuade you to turn state's evidence against Gavi. Frankly, the prosecutors were not persuaded. Given the evidence in hand, they did not see what your testimony would add to the case. But Toni persisted. At my urging, she was returning to Paris to make the case in person that you should be granted immunity in return for your full cooperation."

"And what was your position?" asked Raskolnovitch, considering his options.

"I supported her. She believed you possessed certain compromising videotapes taken on your boat of Monsieur Gavi engaged with prostitutes that could be used to exact his cooperation. The French state has little interest in charging you, Mr. Raskolnovitch, and little chance of enforcing any prosecution. There is more to gain by offering you immunity," said Bertrand.

Raskolnovitch stared at the Consul General and exchanged looks with Prokofiev. Finally, he asked, "And what is the connection with the Yavlinsky kid and Miss Osatinskaya?"

Bertrand's eyes brightened until it seemed he was almost smiling. "We had nothing to do with them at first. Apparently, it was Ms. Osatinskaya's idea to use the fact that Yavlinsky was a nominee director of one of your shell companies to try and pry financial records that would prove corruption. Yavlinsky took it a step further, withdrew some funds for himself, and somehow managed to take it all and transfer your assets to a new shell company. Voila!"

"I still don't understand why you got involved," said Raskolnovitch, finishing his own glass of scotch.

"The tax authorities contacted us. It appears the financial records could be used to prove transfers of funds to Monsieur Gavi's election campaign and might also be useful in, shall I say, pressuring you to cooperate," said Bertrand.

Raskolnovitch laughed out loud. "You operate exactly as I do. Do unto others so they don't fuck with you." He rubbed his hands together, thinking. "So, maybe, we make a deal. I give you Toni and testify against Gavi and you drop all charges against me and guarantee me citizenship."

"And the videotape?" asked Bertrand.

"Why not? If it will convince Paris to grant me immunity, of course," said Raskolnovitch.

Bertrand suddenly stood up and began pacing in front of Raskolnovitch and Prokofiev, his index finger against his lips. "And what about Yavlinsky and Osatinskaya? I could help you there, too," he said.

Raskolnovitch and Prokofiev looked at each other. Prokofiev then asked, "Can you deliver them to us?"

"Perhaps," replied Bertrand. "They trust me, you know."

"And what in return?" asked Prokofiev.

"How much is it worth to you, if I can deliver them to you?" Bertrand asked.

Raskolnovitch stood up and moved close to Bertrand. Tall men had a great reach, and it worked best to move in close to them, his instincts recalled. "A great deal," he said. "Perhaps a million."

Bertrand was now beaming. "And if I can get you all your money back, all that remains, how much would that be worth to you, a finder's fee, so to speak?"

Raskolnovitch and Prokofiev looked at each other again and Raskolnovitch nodded to Prokofiev to answer. "One percent would be quite reasonable."

"Two," said Bertrand.

Raskolnovitch smiled and offered his hand.

Chapter 42

It had been two days since Yana had disappeared. Dora felt driven down by the relentless rain and their anxious waiting. Messages of reassurance from Palmer and Scotland Yard sounded patronizing and hollow. There was nothing they could do, despite having all the money in the world, and this, more than anything, fed their despair. Exasperated, Dora told Yuri they had to get out of the house.

They made reservations at a three-star French restaurant nearby and got dressed in their new clothes, which improved their mood a bit. At least they were doing something, not just sitting around as if they were in the waiting room of a hospital. Their driver escorted them one at a time under an umbrella to their black Land Rover. A second car with two security guards followed close behind. Yuri's phone rang. Dora overheard Palmer confirming yesterday's news that Raskolnovitch had indeed left London and was back in Kyiv. But still no sign of Yana.

The restaurant was opulent, sparkling with candles, exuding nostalgia for a colonial past that at once felt seductive but made Dora's eyes roll. They ate Orkney scallops, sautéed foie gras, and native lobster, along with the finest champagne and wine. Dora was surprised she had an appetite. Yuri handed the tuxedoed waiter a credit card without even looking at the bill. This new life they were living felt to Dora like a sour, opulent dream.

They returned to the house, relieved to get out of the pounding rain and into the quiet and security of their temporary home. They settled onto a couch in their matching silk pajamas to check their email. Dora saw it first.

"It's Yana, an email from Yana!" she yelled. She read it out loud.

"Don't worry. I'm fine. I'm in Kyiv. I feel safe here, the first time since this insanity started. I took a train from London to Vienna and then flew home. I had a lot of time to think. I'm with friends. No one you know. I assume you saw the news. Prime Minister Azarov announced Ukraine is not going to join Europe. They are going back to Russia. It's like we're returning to the time of Stalin. No one will stand for it. Did you see Mustafa Nayyem's Facebook post? In case you didn't, here it is:

'Let's meet at 10:30 pm at the Independence Monument. Dress Warm. Bring umbrellas, tea, coffee, a good attitude, and friends. Repost highly appreciated.'

We all went there. At first there were only a few hundred people. We couldn't believe it. But thousands of people began to arrive from every direction and soon the Maidan was filled with a sea of young people in the rain all chanting 'shame, shame' and 'Ukraine part of Europe.' I couldn't stop crying with joy. It was like 2004 and the Orange Revolution. I was too young then to understand. But now I feel the power of the people united.

Nothing can stop us. My generation won't allow it. The police have done nothing yet, but we are expecting an attack. For the first time in my life, I think, I feel really, really happy. There's a reason to be alive. I will write more soon. I'm sorry if I freaked you out, but I am good, happy but very cold. I love you. Yana.

Dora's heart was pounding. She held her hands over her mouth, then hugged Yuri.

"She's safe, thank God," said Dora.

"Yes, but for how long?" asked Yuri. "It's only a matter of time before Raskolnovitch finds her. We've got to get to her before he does. She's using an encrypted phone. At least we can communicate with her."

Dora got up and turned on a switch on the wall that said TV. It was the first time she had tried it. A hidden projector screen descended from the ceiling and the sound surrounded them. She flipped through a dozen channels until he saw coverage of the Maidan demonstration on Euronews. There was a mass of mostly young people, tens of thousands of them, with yellow and blue Ukrainian flags and the thirteen-starred EU flag unfurled in the frigid air, a pulsing exuberance of people chanting together, "Ukraine Part of Europe" and "Sign, Sign." All of them—with Yana somewhere in their midst—were massed around the gold-topped, white Corinthian column that was Independence Monument at the center of the Maidan. They were pumping their fists in unison and chanting as one, the same passion, the same demand, one voice. Surrounding them, a phalanx of black-helmeted police in riot gear was beginning to mass. Dora felt excited and scared just watching then.

The television footage showed one of the leaders of the opposition, Vitali Klitschko, trying to speak to the crowd with a megaphone atop a flatbed truck emblazoned with his party's posters—but demonstrators demanded he leave. There was no room for partisan politics. Everyone was equal and united, said one of the demonstrators. Dora could feel their unyielding defiance, even as the the mood was joyous and uplifting. Yuri watched the coverage, rapt. She tried to imagine the protest through his native Ukrainian eyes. The sleeping giant of his country's nationalism seemed to be rising again for the second time in a decade. "We want to be a normal democratic country like Europe and the West," said a blond teenager in a red knit cap, her breath turning to smoke as she spoke.

Dora opened her laptop when the news coverage ended and Yuri turned off the TV. There was another email. "My friend Pavlo wrote," she said. "He says he's incredibly excited by our offer to help with the TV bid, but he can't leave Kyiv right now because of the Maidan demonstrations. They're doing their best to cover it day and night. But he's asking if we could meet in Kyiv instead?"

Yuri paced back and forth in front of the TV. "Maybe we should," he said. "That may be the only way we can get Yana out."

"Would we be safe there?" asked Dora. The idea of returning unnerved her.

"If we keep moving around, I don't see how Raskolnovitch and his thugs could find us. Besides, I'm not sure I could stay here watching television while everyone else is out in the streets risking their lives."

"Me, too," said Dora. "Palmer will freak out, but, hey, this is a free country. I think we should go. We could help."

Chapter 43

The blue and white boxcar at the rear of a train from Mazar-i-Sharif rumbled across the Afghanistan-Uzbekistan Friendship Bridge in the border town of Hairatan. It stopped for unloading on the Uzbek side next to an endless line of railway cars hauling weapons and provisions for NATO troops headed in the opposite direction. With a clattering of metal on metal, the railcar was uncoupled from the main train, which continued further towards the port.

The day was grey, the air dry and full of dust. It smelled of grease and oil. The rail line disappeared at an infinite point on the flat landscape. A truck pulled up alongside the boxcar and four Uzbek guards toting AK47 assault rifles leaped from the cab and took up positions around it. Two customs officers wearing identical cheap blue suits arrived in an official looking car to remove the seals and inspect the cargo. They had been well paid for their efforts. The heavy doors grudgingly gave way to slide open. Inside, the floor was covered with burlap bags of wheat, but otherwise the boxcar was empty.

The customs officers made their way to the far-left corner, removed a few of the bags, and ran their hands along the wood floor until they discovered a loose board that covered a lever which unlocked a hidden compartment underneath. The secret space ran under the full length of the carriage. One of the men pulled open the large trap door and shined his flashlight in the cavity. Instead of the ten thousand kilos of heroin he was expecting, there was nothing.

At that same moment there was a screech of cars outside and a sudden commotion. Ten white vans formed a circle around the railcars. The Uzbek guards raised their rifles, but they were badly outmanned by about two dozen soldiers in camouflage uniforms armed with Kalashnikovs. The custom officials emerged blinking into the cold sunlight and held their hands up as the Uzbek guards were ordered to drop their weapons onto the ground.

"No fire! No reason fire," yelled one of them. "There's nothing here."

Later, it was reported that the two dozen soldiers spoke Russian. After examining the boxcar and its secret compartment, they left in a cloud of dust. Immediately, one of the four guards used an encrypted satellite phone and called a number in Ukraine.

Viktor Raskolnovitch's new cellphone rang with an unfamiliar tone.

"Da," he answered.

He listened for a minute without speaking and then hung up. For a moment, he felt confused. The information seemed to confirm that Semion Mogilevich's Russian mafia had attacked him. Raskolnovitch had fed the false information about a massive shipment of heroin to the Don's man, Lazovsky, to test his loyalty. No one else had been told. But now Raskolnovitch had convinced himself that Toni was the source of leaks, that it was

Toni who had warned the Osatinskaya girl. So he was expecting that the bait would not be taken and there would be no attack on the train. But now he had to confront the fact that Mogilevich was moving against him. He would have to hit them back somehow.

His head hurt. He couldn't get Toni out of his mind. She had not lied to him about going to Paris to plead for immunity for him; but had she been sincere about love? He poured himself a drink. It was not his custom to have any alcohol during the day, but he needed this. He asked Dima to come up to his room.

"Our little trap worked," Raskolnovitch told him, pouring himself another drink. "The Don tried to help himself to our stash. A trainload of heroin, apparently, was too much for him to ignore."

"He wouldn't have stopped there," Prokofiev said. "He wanted to take over the whole business. With all that's going on in the streets, they think your *krysha* is too weak or distracted to protect you."

"What do we do now then?"

"They're smart enough to figure out that this was a trap, that we know what they're up to," said Prokofiev. "If they had succeeded in hijacking a real shipment, surely we'd know it was them. Either way, they were willing to risk being found out. It's like an act of war. Don Semion controls most of the sex trade in Ukraine. We can ask our *krysha* to order the police to shut it down for a while, till Mogilevich backs off."

"The police are too busy chasing kids on the Maidan right now," Raskolnovitch said. "I think it's best we let things lie the way they are. We can act anytime on our own schedule. Maybe it's wrong to tempt them like we did. Sometimes you get what you fear."

Dima nodded. "Agreed," he said. "We've got too much on our plate to take on the mafia right now. The TV sale has been frozen, and they've asked for new bids after that journalist went missing. We haven't heard yet from Bertrand whether the French would agree to a deal for your immunity and whether you'll have to testify against Gavi. The Drake deal is dead and the money we put up has been frozen. It's all costing a lot of cash. Without the Cyprus and Panama accounts, our cash flow has become critical. We may have to sell something."

"Like one of the Faberge Eggs?" asked Raskolnovitch.

"Perhaps. I'm nervous about trying to ship large amounts of our inventory from Afghanistan right now. There're too many eyes and ears on us. But we've got to do something. The tobacco money isn't covering our expenses," Prokofiev said.

"What about Kostya?" asked Raskolnovitch.

"They released him after eight hours," said Prokofiev. "He didn't give them anything, but I told him to disappear for a while."

This cascade of bad news was draining the color out of the room. Raskolnovitch felt weary. He hadn't slept well for three nights. When he was a boxer, he could come back harder whenever he was knocked down. He prided himself on that. But now he could not summon the energy. The thing with Toni had taken the fight out of him. He was tempted to confront her again but was afraid she might weaken his resolve.

He had never questioned his actions before. There were no moral imperatives inhibiting him in the past. Had he acted too rashly? Surely, she was lying to save her life when she talked of living together.

Raskolnovitch finished his glass of whisky and stood up. "Dima, I've got some girls waiting down the hall for me," he said. "Let's meet again this afternoon. In the meantime, keep pushing the Israelis."

He walked down the hallway and stopped as he reached for the door. Perversely, he wished he could talk to Toni about all this. Her betrayal felt like an act of God, a test he had failed. But he was no Job. He would not take this insult laying down. It was those damn kids, those yids. Everything started to go to hell with those kikes. He couldn't understand why it was taking so long to find them.

Chapter 44

The next morning Yuri connected with Yana over encrypted email and told her they would come to Kyiv to meet her on the Maidan. The news coverage the night before had inspired him. He felt a surge of optimism. It was all one fight against corruption and the abuse of power by criminal oligarchs who had captured control of the government. Maybe in Kyiv, they could use their sudden wealth in support of the protesters. It was time to go on offense.

He called Richard McEwan.

"Richard? It's Yuri Yavlinsky. You offered to help me use my funds to fight back against Viktor Raskolnovitch. I'm ready now. I have a few ideas."

"I'm all ears, Yuri," said McEwan. "Nothing would please me more."

Yuri took a deep breath. "I'd like you to hire a solicitor to initiate a lawsuit in Ukraine to challenge Raskolnovitch's bid for a TV license on whatever grounds can be found—anything to slow this down." He paced as far as the cord would stretch. "Also, we should petition the Council of Europe and the European Broadcasting Union to prevent it." He knew of Ukraine's membership in the EBU from the time the country won the EBU's song contest in 2004 in one of the most popular prime time broadcasts in Europe, east and west. "And Richard, one other thing. Can you do whatever you can to identify any banks or financial institutions that may have loaned money to Raskolnovitch?"

"What are you thinking?" McEwan asked. "Sounds devious."

Yuri smiled. "I'm thinking we should buy these loans or the banks that hold them. It's not enough to take his funds away. I want to find a way to own him."

McEwan sounded pleased to hear Yuri fight back. The phone call with Palmer, however, was predictably difficult. Yuri understood the risks Palmer laid out, but he persisted. In the end, Palmer offered to assist them with their plans. Five minutes later he called back to say that two security guards would accompany them on their trip. A car would come by to pick them up and take them to St. Pancras Station, where they'd board a Eurostar train to Paris and from there a private jet to Kyiv. This way there was little chance they'd be discovered.

They were mostly silent on the ride to St. Pancras, constrained as they were by the two guards who accompanied them. Alone with his thoughts, Yuri worked out a strategy for how they'd avoid detection. They would use their false passports to register in different hotels each night. He'd have one of his guards meet Yana somewhere and bring her to them. Beyond that, it was hard to anticipate what the situation would present, but he was in a hurry to get to the demonstration and join with his generation in what had started to look like the beginning of another color revolution.

He was only eighteen in 2004 when the Orange Revolution overthrew the man who, once again, was president. He couldn't understand how his countrymen had elected him again. Yuri had taken to the streets with his friends back then, but the failure of the new government to root out corruption and prevent rule by oligarchs caused many young people to give up on politics. Now they were back in the streets again determined to join the West and forge a real democracy once and for all. But how could he help them? They would need funds to sustain their demonstration, if it lasted for more than a few days. He could buy ads on social media, in newspapers, maybe even on television and radio supporting their cause. Dora could help expose the regime's corruption. If there were arrests, he could provide legal defense teams.

Standing amidst the crowd queuing for the Eurostar track, he looked around and marveled at the diversity of nationalities waiting with him. It astonished him that he could get on a train in London and walk out of it in Paris in just over two hours, never showing a passport. For Yuri, as for the young demonstrators, this was the future, their future. They refused to go back to Stalinist times. Europe meant freedom and modernity. It was something worth fighting for, the right to travel, to work or study abroad, to speak or write without fear of arrest.

Dora was on the phone with her friend Pavlo from the TV consortium and agreed to meet him in Kyiv tomorrow. She, too, seemed eager to join the fray.

At the Gare du Nord, they were met by a driver and car. Someone from the French Embassy accompanied them to a private airport near Orly, where their car drove on the tarmac right up to the stairs of a six-seater silver Cessna. Riding in a private jet almost made him laugh out loud. The rain glistened on the runway and on the wings of the plane as Yuri and Dora mounted the steps and settled into leather chairs. Yuri felt like he was Marshal Earp in the gunfight at the O.K. Corral was dark and clouded. Yuri reached Yana on her encrypted phone and arranged to have one of his guards meet her at a cross-street just a couple of blocks from Independence Square.

The ride into Kyiv brought back grisly memories for Yuri of entering his apartment and finding his step-dad and Bubbie murdered. The rain came down like bullets and traffic slowed as they got closer to the center. On the radio they learned that the Berkut, the special riot police, had cleared Independence Square of demonstrators and demolished their tents during the night, ostensibly to prepare for a Christmas Fair; but thousands of young demonstrators had reoccupied the Maidan in the morning despite the freezing rain.

They parked a block from the rendezvous point with Yana. Over the sound of rain on the roof, they could hear the chants of the crowd a few blocks away. Yana wouldn't be coming for an hour, so they walked towards the demonstration. Dora, Yuri, and the two guards were dressed in hooded sweatshirts and rain jackets and fit in with the largely student demonstrators. Chants of "Shame, Shame" grew louder as they approached. A drum kept up a martial beat. Yuri felt an optimism he hadn't known since he was at the restaurant in Cyprus. The space around the Independence Monument was packed with people. All the buildings and monuments surrounding the square were lit and giant video screens flashed advertisements casting a surreal blue neon light on the crowd.

There was a makeshift stage and sound equipment where Svatoslav Vakarchuk, a famous pop singer, exhorted the crowd. Reminded that the president had once been convicted of rape, they took up a chant, "Convict out! Convict out!" Shouting with them, Yuri felt a surge of power and pride as if all the pent up emotions of the past weeks were released by his voice. He was buoyed by the sea of Ukrainian and European Union flags that fluttered above the thousands of umbrellas and sheets of plastic. People gathered around bonfires in metal trash bins to keep themselves warm. The mood of the demonstrators was exultant, as if at a festival. Yuri remembered the feelings of empowerment he felt as a student in the Orange Revolution on the same spot ten years earlier. There was an expectation that the government would be forced to sign the Association agreement in the face of such massive protests. Students in Lviv had called for a national strike and thousands of protesters were streaming to Kyiv in what seemed an irresistible show of opposition. To rhythmic chants of "Do What We Want, Do What We Want," the demonstrators jumped up and down as if on springs, their energy boiling over.

Yuri turned to Dora. "I haven't seen you smile like this since Panama." They held hands and jumped together with the crowd, laughing out loud.

But Yuri felt a cloud come over his euphoria when he noticed thousands of black-clad riot police wearing body armor and black helmets and carrying shields and batons begin to surround the demonstrators. The crowd took up a chant, "The Police With the People," their voices rising as tension built to a crescendo. Suddenly a contingent of "Ultras," the nationalist soccer clubs that often fought against rival fans, appeared wearing yellow construction helmets, raising the prospect of violence. But it soon became apparent that the Ultras had come to protect the demonstrators, not attack them. Word quickly spread that they had signed a truce with the other clubs to join together in defense of the Euromaidan protest. Demonstrators applauded as they let them pass to the front of their lines like gladiators going to battle.

"We need to go," said one of the guards to Yuri and Dora, grabbing them by the arm.

"Wait," said Yuri.

But suddenly things got crazy. There were explosions of tear gas grenades and the police, dressed like storm troopers, charged into the peaceful crowd savagely beating the demonstrators with their clubs. Everywhere people started screaming, trying to escape. Yuri grabbed Dora's arm, holding her close to him. His nose and throat burned like hot peppers. Girls standing on the

stage began singing the national anthem. Yuri searched frantically, but there was no room to run. The Berkut were ferocious,
clubbing everyone in their path. Instead of ordinary plastic or
rubber clubs, he noticed, they swung metal batons. Scores of
people just dozens of yards from them were soon covered in
blood. Tear gas, shouts, sirens, crying, the singing of the national
anthem, and screams of fear and pain filled the air.

The two guards quickly led Yuri and Dora back the way they
had come, away from the advancing Berkut. Along the way Yuri
almost collided with one of the Ultras whose face and head were
covered in blood. He looked dazed. It took Yuri a moment to
realize he knew the young man.

"Taras," shouted Yuri, "It's me, Yuri."

The young man looked up through blood-caked eyes at him.

"Yuri, is it really you?"

Yuri and Dora helped steady him. Yuri was elated to see
Taras, but he was freaked out by all the blood. He worried now
that Yana might have been hurt by the Berkut.

"We've got to get you to a hospital. Your eyes are swollen
shut. Can you see?" asked Yuri, shouting urgently over the
roaring crowd.

"Yes, yes. I'll be all right. What about you? I read about the
massacre at your place—your step-dad, your bubbie. The papers
said it was you who did it. Everyone was searching for you. But
then they said you were out of the country when it happened.
What's going on?" asked Taras.

"It's a long story," said Yuri. "Let's get you in our car and see
how badly you've been injured first."

Yuri, Taras, and Dora hurried down another block, the two
guards shadowing their every step. In the trunk there was a first
aid kit and they cleaned Taras's head wounds and bandaged the
cuts on his brow, neck, and hands in gauze. Yuri quickly introduced Dora and the guards and gave a rushed recounting from

the aftermath of his firing at the zoo to his last battles in the war they were fighting with Viktor Raskolnovitch. Taras knew Raskolnovitch as the oligarch behind the president. A wry smile spread across Taras's face as he heard the story.

"You are one crazy motherfucker," he said. His laughter rang out against the shouts and the pop-pop-pop of explosions three blocks away. "So, what? You're rich now?" he asked. "You want some rock candy?"

Yuri laughed. "Thanks, but I think I'll stay straight for now." Yuri had begun to imagine himself doling out lots of cash to help sustain this movement. Taras, he knew, may have lots of faults, but he was the most loyal friend he knew. He would trust him with his life. To fight Raskolnovitch meant also to fight this corrupt regime and the mafia culture that underwrote it. Even with all his money, he and Dora could not do it alone. Taras offered him a trusted lieutenant who had an amazing assortment of contacts.

"Listen, Taras, I have a proposition for you. I need someone to help me here, someone I can trust. I'll pay you well, I promise."

Taras went to hug him, but stopped when he looked down at his bloody jacket.

"It'll be dangerous," added Yuri.

Taras pointed to his head. "I love danger. I feast on danger. When can we start?"

It was now time for one of the guards to meet Yana at the end of the block.

"Be careful," said Dora.

Yuri turned back to Taras. "We may need your Ultra friends to help us, too." He reached into his pocket and pulled out a wad of hundred Euro notes. He counted out thirty of them and handed them to Taras.

"Here's a down payment. We'll need a lot of protection," said Yuri. "Raskolnovitch has some scary dudes around him.

When we have our showdown, we're gonna need our own army."

They hi-fived each other. The life had come back to Taras's face.

Yuri looked over Taras's shoulder to see Yana walking towards them with the guards at her side. She broke into a run. Dora and Yuri jumped out of the car and embraced her. She was shaking uncontrollably. "I'm so sorry, so sorry," she cried.

At that moment, the bang of a stun grenade exploded just twenty meters from them, a bright incandescent flash. The guards hustled Yuri, Dora and Yana into the back seat next to Taras and the car peeled away from the Maidan. Yuri saw the look of recognition on Yana's face. She knew Taras. She'd long had a crush on her older brother's friend. Yuri would never forget Yana's expression when she saw him covered in blood.

Chapter 45

Raskolnovitch awakened to the sound of someone knocking. He struggled to come to consciousness, gasping for breath as though rising from the depths of the sea. He was perspiring. His head ached. At first, he thought he was hung over, but what he was feeling was something unfamiliar, something he hadn't felt in a very long time: fear.

The knocking repeated. He got out of his bed and steadied himself. He looked at his clock. It was a quarter to eight. Rarely did anyone awaken him, and never this early. He put on his silk maroon robe and opened the door.

"Sorry to wake you, your excellency," said the butler, his head tilted down, "but there are men here from the Prosecutor's office demanding to search the house."

"Tell them I'm sleeping. They need to contact my attorney," Raskolnovitch said.

"I tried that, your excellency, but they have a warrant," said the butler.

Raskolnovitch pushed past the man and strode down the

hallway and stairs to the foyer. The front door was open. Two men in suits and four uniformed police officers faced three of Raskolnovitch's guards who blocked their way.

"What is the meaning of this?" Raskolnovitch demanded.

"We have a warrant to inspect this house," said one of the suits. "One of your employees, Kostya Kybalchich, is a suspect in the murder of the journalist Georgiy Goritsky." He reached over the shoulder of one of the guards to hand Raskolnovitch the warrant.

Raskolnovitch scanned the document, threw it on the floor, then stepped on it as if he were putting out a cigarette. Luckily, he had moved Toni in the night to his mansion outside Kyiv. Kostya was long gone, so there was nothing these cops would find. He nodded to his guards to let them pass. Then he marched back upstairs to his bedroom and grabbed the phone.

"Ministry of Internal Affairs," said a female voice. "Please hold."

His heart racing, he placed a nitroglycerine tablet under his tongue.

"Dobryi den," came the voice again. "How may I direct your call?"

"Minister Zakharchenko," Raskolnovitch said. "It's urgent. Tell him Viktor Raskolnovitch needs to speak with him immediately."

A moment later a male voice said, "Mr. Raskolnovitch. I'm afraid the minister is in an emergency meeting dealing with the riots in the Maidan. Is there anything I can do to assist you?"

"Listen," said Raskolnovitch. "You fucking get him on the phone this minute. This cannot wait."

"One moment, please," said the man.

A minute passed, then two. Raskolnovitch held the phone to his ear, counting his breaths.

"Viktor Ivanovitch, to what do I owe the pleasure of your

forcing me from an emergency meeting of the Council of Ministers so early in the morning?"

"Vitaliy Yuriyovych," Raskolnovitch spit into the phone. "Why are your men searching my house? What the fuck is going on? Did you authorize this?"

"Please, please, Viktor. I don't know anything about this. Let me..."

"They came with a warrant about the journalist who was found dead. They claim my bodyguard was involved. They invaded my home."

"Viktor, please. I understand. I'll fix this. Please, put the officer on the phone. You'll excuse me—I've been up for two days dealing with this rebellion and there are many things I've missed. But I'm glad you called. I was going to call you right after this Council meeting." He lowered his voice and Raskolnovitch wondered who might be listening. "The couple you were searching for are here in Kyiv. They arrived yesterday at a small airport. We had a red flag alert for them, but none of my men were there when they landed. I've sent their photos to the Berkut. The Berkut are out in force everywhere. I assure you, we'll find them very soon."

The group of policemen entered his bedroom. Raskolnovitch went up to one of the suits and handed him his phone. "Here, you shithead. Minister Zakharchenko would like to speak with you."

The police officer took the phone and listened. "Tak...tak... tak," he said. He turned to Raskolnovitch. "I'm afraid there's been some mistake, sir. Please excuse our intrusion." He nodded to his men and they left, staring at the extravagances around them on their way out.

"Thank you, Vitaliy Yuriyovych," Raskolnovitch said into the phone.

"Any time, even in the midst of a revolution," Zakharchenko said.

He threw his robe on the floor and got dressed without his customary shower.

Prokofiev knocked on his door and entered. "I heard what happened," he said. "What did the Minister say?"

"Claims to know nothing. I'm not too sure," said Raskolnovitch. "Minister Zakharchenko gets a cut from Mogilevich's whores. He wouldn't be too happy if we asked him to clamp down on the business. But he gave me some important news. Seems our Yid friends flew here from London. Zakharchenko sent their photos to all the Berkut. This is good news."

"Very good news," said Prokofiev. "The Berkut are flooding the streets. Tens of thousands of them. You can't walk a block downtown without seeing them. Either the Berkut will find the two of them or Bertrand will deliver them to us. We're getting close. But that still leaves Mogilevich. What do we do about him?"

"We wait. We get ready. We'll need some more muscle. Bring up some of the Chechens. Could be war," said Raskolnovitch.

"Mogilevich is putting a lot of pressure on us to be paid," Prokofiev said. "We owe him a lot. Should we just refuse?"

Raskolnovitch thought for a minute. "I have an idea. Better we give a clear message to Mogilevich that we know it was his gang that tried to hijack our shipment. Tell the Don's man, Lazovsky, to come here, alone, to pick up his money. Take him to the library and have our men disarm him, put him in cage and fly him to Hairatan, the scene of the crime. Let him find his own way home. I think they'll get the message."

He sighed. "But first things first. We need to find those kids."

Prokofiev nodded and started to leave when Raskolnovitch called out, "Dima, one more thing. Get hold of Zakharchenko. If you have trouble reaching him, tell whoever answers that you have a message from the president. Tell the minister we are offering a $25,000 reward for the capture of these fugitives. Have him send that message to every member of the Berkut along with their photos."

Chapter 46

After a long night catching up with Yana and Taras in a funky hotel just off the Maidan, Yuri woke up late to the smell of tear gas, like spoiled vinegar. He could hear crowds forming in the square a couple blocks away. In the lobby, they learned the news: at 4 a.m. the Berkut had cleared the square of the few hundred remaining protesters, beating them savagely with steel truncheons, leaving pools of blood amid the debris. Word spread mouth-to-mouth about the attack. Although there had been no TV coverage on the main channels, video of the "Saturday night massacre" spread on smaller local stations and on Facebook.

Throughout the morning, hundreds of thousands of people began to mass on the Maidan, Kyiv's Independence Square. It was snowing and the mood was as icy as the weather. Yuri watched what had been a joyous celebration just twenty-four hours earlier turn into a grim and determined confrontation.

Yuri, Dora, Yana and Taras sat in the InterContinental's restaurant a few blocks from the Maidan waiting for Dora's TV friend Pavlo to show up. The two security guards sat at the next table. They had all slept poorly in the rundown hotel, but at least they had eluded the police and Raskolnovitch's men. Pavlo arrived a half hour late, brushing the snow off his quilted jacket. He had a full beard speckled in snow and deep lines across a wide forehead, as though weighted by heavy thoughts. His voice was deep and melodic and there was a twinkle in his eyes that warmed Yuri to him. Dora introduced everyone.

"Sorry I'm so late, but two of our cameramen were badly beaten last night. They're being treated at St. Michael's Monastery, which gave sanctuary to the protesters that were driven out of the Maidan last night. They've set up a makeshift hospital there. It's an amazing scene. You should see it. The monks are feeding everyone and providing blankets and shelter. The Berkut tried to break through the gates and arrest everyone, but the monks wouldn't let them in. They're true heroes." Pavlo blew warm air into his cupped hands.

They talked about the bid for a national television license. Pavlo explained how important it was. All of the other channels were owned by oligarchs. Pavlo represented a few dozen independent local broadcasters which had banded together to apply for this first-of-its-kind national license. "There can be no real democracy if the oligarchs monopolize the airwaves," he told them. "Even less if Raskolnovitch can front for the president to get his own personal channel. It was too great a power to allow." He said he had full trust in Dora but apologized that he could not accept help from another oligarch, even one who was a friend of hers.

This, more than anything, gave Yuri confidence in him. He explained how they had come into such vast sums. The irony of using Raskolnovitch's money to compete with him was not lost on anyone. Yuri had planned to offer a loan, but he understood why Pavlo couldn't allow himself to be obligated to any oligarch. "But what if I gave you the money as a grant, no strings attached? I'll run it through some western foundation." In the end, he agreed to put two hundred million euros into an escrow account that Pavlo could draw on as needed. He'd have Richard McEwan set it up at Berenberg Bank.

"I want to give all this money away while I can," explained Yuri. "It's a noose around our necks."

A former director of live television programs, Pavlo smiled but, otherwise, he seemed unfazed. "In Ukraine, one must be a stoic to survive. It's not every day I'm offered two hundred million euros with no strings attached, but who knows what will happen tomorrow," he said. "There are no rules anymore. When thieves run the government, the people are free to do whatever they like. I appreciate your trust, Yuri. I promise to use these funds for the good of the people."

When they got up to leave, Yuri turned to Taras. "We should do something for St. Michael's, don't you think? Would you mind taking them a donation?" he asked, before writing out a check for a hundred thousand euros.

"You'll be sure to go to heaven, Yuri," said Taras.

"Thank Raskolnovitch," said Yuri. There were hugs all around, then they left through the hotel lobby and into the swirling snow and biting cold outside.

By the time they got to the Maidan, Yuri guessed that the crowd had swelled to perhaps a million people, larger than any of the mass rallies during the Orange Revolution ten years before. The church bells at St. Michael's had been ringing incessantly throughout the night, calling on people to come to the Maidan, the first time it had done so since 1240, when Kyiv was surrounded by Mongol hordes. Taras led them along the edge of the square towards Bankova Street to meet some of the Ultras he had paid who gathered before buses and concrete barricades that barred the way to the presidential Headquarters.

The crowd roared as one. "They give us corruption! We give them revolution! Re-vo-lu-ti-on, re-vo-lu-ti-on!" they chanted, a million fists pumping the air. Freshly on edge, Yuri watched with concern a score of Ultras battling the police who massed in great force behind shields like a medieval army of black knights. He heard the "pop pop pop" of tear gas and stun grenades and still the protesters surged forward with him. A shout rose from behind them. They turned as the crowd parted to allow a large snow removal tractor to move forward and push its way through the barricades erected by the police. Yuri cheered with the crowd. But in the next moment, behind a barrage of explosions, the full force of the Berkut was loosed upon the protesters.

Swinging indiscriminately, the riot police attacked everyone in their path, men, women, children. Yuri, Yana, Dora, Taras and their two guards were caught in the mad rush to get ahead of the charging police force. They heard shots ring out as snipers on the rooftops fired into the melee. Bodies fell limp in the street, but no one could stop to tend or recover them. Screams mixed with the sounds of sirens and explosions and the rat-a-tap-tap of rifle fire as people tried to escape only to be beaten by the savage attack of the Berkut. "We've got to get out of here," Yuri yelled to Dora and Yana. In the midst of this blood bath, a policeman grabbed Yuri's arm from behind and pushed him to the ground, but Yuri's security guards pulled him off. Yuri scrambled to his feet to see Yana trying to run away. Another Berkut officer clubbed her with his baton and she fell like a rock.

"Yana!" he shouted, but Yana was being dragged away by four police and dozens more Berkut now massed between them, making it impossible to get to her. He tried to anyway, but Taras and the security guards pulled him back and Dora grabbed him close.

"Yana!" he screamed, but the cacophony of chaos around him made it impossible to hear even his own voice.

Chapter 47

"Viktor Ivanovitch? It's Zakharchenko. We have found the Yavlinsky girl, the sister," said the Minister.

"Wonderful. What about the boy and his girlfriend?" replied Raskolnovitch.

"Not yet, but it will be very soon, I'm sure," Zakharchenko said. "Once the word spreads that the honorable policemen who arrested her has received your reward, there will be no hiding for them."

"Good, very good," said Raskolnovitch. "I'll immediately send half the reward to the good officers. No, no, forget that. I'll send all of it. Another twenty-five thousand is pittance. Where is the girl being held?"

"In City Clinical Hospital #18 on Bibikovsky. The cops who found her are guarding the room. She suffered a concussion and a fractured skull yesterday, but she is fine. What do you want us to do with her?" Raskolnovitch smiled. She will suffer much more than she has, he thought.

"I'll send my men around to get her and pay the guards their reward. We'll take very good care of her here, I assure you. Please let your officers know we are coming," said Raskolnovitch.

When he hung up, he felt his whole body unwind. He remembered the day and the moment he was released from the gulag. It was as if he could fly. He had wandered deliriously around a shabby Siberian town in the frigid cold without a worry, drunk with freedom. Now, he poured himself a large glass of cognac to celebrate, then called to Dima to come up to his room. But his mind veered off to thoughts of Toni. He chastised himself for this. The look on her face after the gunshots taunted him, threatened to ruin his moment.

He would get justice the *Vory* way, he thought. He tapped the tattooed star on his left shoulder and drank greedily from the cognac. "I am *Vory*," he said to himself out loud.

No more patsy. No more being made a fool of. He would get his money back and these kids would pay for every kopek. And he would fuck that kike Mogilevich. He downed another gulp of cognac and felt it go to his head. He was back in charge. Let his enemies beware.

Prokofiev entered. "Dima, my friend," said Raskolnovitch. He went to Prokofiev and embraced him in a bear hug. "We've got Yavlinsky's sister. Zakharchenko just called. We can bring her here this morning. Now we shall see what the boy loves more, my money or his sister."

He could hear Toni's voice in his head: "Viktor, you don't need all that money. You have enough to buy that castle in France. We could be happy there." He took another drink to obliterate her.

"Dima, I want you to prepare a room for our guest. You remember the videotape Kostya made with all those Taliban beheadings and tortures? Maybe the sister will like watching TV when she arrives. Might put her in a good mood for conversation," Raskolnovitch said.

Prokofiev smiled. "Congratulations, Viktor. You played it right," he said. "We'll get back our money now. By the way, our friend Lazovsky is on his way back from Uzbekistan, I've discovered. It seems he didn't like his accommodations. Once our funds are restored, we can regroup, maybe sit down with Don Semion and make peace, or not. This whole thing with those kids has made us look weak."

"But our luck has changed," said Raskolnovitch. "I can feel it."

Two hours later, Dima called to say the girl was in a basement room. Raskolnovitch could feel the blood pounding in his head. He took the last sip of cognac in the decanter and headed to the elevator. One of his guards, standing at attention before a metal door to the boiler room, saluted and then opened the barrier for him. She was bound to a wooden chair. Her head was bandaged and her mouth was taped shut. On the screen a prisoner in an orange jumpsuit was being burned alive in a cage. Raskolnovitch signaled to the guard to turn it off. Yana's eyes were seared with fear.

He bent down and spoke into her ear. "The elusive Miss Yavlinsky. At last we meet. I believe your brother has something of mine." When he touched her bandage, she screamed, but the gag muffled the sound.

"I suppose you realize this is not a game. It's time to stop playing."

On a small table next to her lay her purse. Raskolnovitch pulled out her cell phone. He bent down so his face was just inches from hers.

"Miss Yavlinsky, this can be as short or as long as you wish. The guard who brought you here fought with me in Afghanistan. He has no formal education, but he is an expert at one thing, skinning people alive. Believe me, it's not as simple as you might think. He's like surgeon. But maybe you don't want to see him work. Maybe you'll do what I ask."

Yana nodded. She had begun to cry.

"I'll take the gag off now," he said. "You will call your brother and tell him you're my guest. Tell him to do what I say. Yes?"

She nodded again and he pulled the tape from her mouth.

"It's in speed dial?" he asked.

"Yes, under Yuri." Her voice shook.

He scrolled down, clicked on the name, and held the phone next to her mouth.

Yuri answered on the first ring.

"Yana?" he asked.

"Yes, it's me," she cried.

"Where are you?" he asked.

"I'm with Viktor Raskolnovitch."

Before Yuri could answer, Raskolnovitch took the phone.

"Hello, Mr. Yavlinsky, I think you have something that belongs to me and I have someone that may belong to you. Maybe we make a trade. Yes?"

"Whatever you say, just don't hurt her. She can't help you. Only I can. I'll give you back everything as soon as you release her," Yuri said.

Raskolnovitch laughed. "Yes, of course. But not so simple. There is interest to pay on the loan. First, we do an exchange, Miss Yavlinsky for you. It's only fair. Yes? You get the papers to transfer ownership from the new companies back to me. Then you call me and we'll arrange to meet. No tricks. But hurry. I think your sister's not very happy here."

Yuri was expecting this. Palmer had warned him that returning the money would not be enough to satisfy Raskolnovitch. He would need to exact his revenge. His honor as a *Vory* demanded it. Yuri had already accepted his fate. There could be no other way out. He would do anything to save his sister, even surrender himself to torture and death. He tried to act bravely, but inside he felt like a three-year old little boy about to cry. How could he win against this man?

He stared at Dora and saw the terror in her eyes.

"OK," said Yuri. "You release Yana and take me in her place. Then I'll sign over ownership of the remaining funds to you. But if you hurt her, the deal's off."

"I'll take good care of her, like a mother," said Raskolnovitch and hung up.

Chapter 48

An icy wind howled outside. Yuri, Dora, Taras, and the two private security guards sat on blankets on the floor of St. Michael's Monastery among a thousand protesters who had sought refuge there. The room was heavy with the scent of incense.

"There has to be a way out!" Yuri said, talking out loud to himself. Dora opened her mouth as if to say something, then closed it again and took his hand. He shut his eyes and shook his head. His phone rang.

"Yuri, it's Palmer," said a British accented voice. "We managed to get all the papers you requested. I'm faxing them to the monastery, as you asked. I wish I could stop you from doing this; but it's your money and your life. I guess you realize he will torture you and—"

"What choice do I have? He's probably torturing Yana right now. I've made a horrible mistake and now I have to pay for it. I never should have done any of this. All I've accomplished is the death of people I loved and now Yana. My only hope for redemption is to save her."

"Stop playing the hero, Yuri," Palmer said. "That's what got you into this mess to begin with. Yuri, I've been there before. I know what you're going through. But dealing with him yourself is the most daft thing you could do, old man. You're out of your league. Let the professionals help you."

"The professionals gave us Putin and a fucked up Ukraine and oligarchs who run the country and kill anyone they want."

"Yuri, listen please, we can get the British, French and American embassies to intervene at the highest level.

Yuri laughed. "You think Raskolnovitch gives a shit what the US Embassy thinks?"

"He does! The last thing he wants is to have the Americans breathing down his neck. He's already under investigation there."

"I wish I believed you," said Yuri. "If Yana was one of their citizens, maybe, but she's Ukrainian. Besides, Ukraine has decided to go with Putin, not the West. And with all the chaos going on, I doubt there's anyone in the government who would pay any attention."

"Please, listen to reason," said Palmer.

Yuri thanked Palmer for faxing the documents and then hung up.

"He's right, you know," said one of his guards standing next to him, overhearing the conversation. He was a tall muscular man with a bald head, who spoke with a New Zealand accent. "I lost a buddy in Vietnam who tried to free a wounded soldier the VC had captured. It wasn't pretty what they did to him. You can't do this alone."

Yuri looked around him at all the militants who had taken refuge in the monastery. "Maybe so, but the embassies won't move fast enough. They've got their hands full with a revolution happening here," said Yuri. "But there may be another way." They all stared at him. "I'll insist we meet in a public place. Taras will bring as many of the Ultras as he can. They're not going to hurt anybody with so many witnesses."

Taras nodded vigorously. "How long would it take to gather them?" Yuri asked.

"Not long at all. They're mostly in here. I have other friends, too, who don't like this Raskolnovitch. Enemies of your enemy are your friends, you know."

"Good, Taras. Thank you. Let's do that," said Yuri. "But that doesn't change the fact that I'll have to trade places with Yana to free her from him."

The security guard pulled Yuri aside into a vaulted hallway. "Listen pal, I've been in worse situations before, not just in Nam. I shouldn't do this, but I can't stand by and let some asshole work out his sadistic fantasies on you." He unscrewed a pendant hanging from a necklace and dropped a capsule from it into Yuri's hand. "If they're gonna torture you, bite this. You'll be happy you had it." He stared hard into Yuri's eyes. Yuri shook his hand, then pulled him close to embrace him.

Just then a young monk with a shaved head who looked to be about fourteen walked up to them.

"Ah, Mr. Yavlinsky, I was on my way to find you. Thank you again for your contribution," he said, bowing. "I don't know what we would have done without it." He smiled, but Yuri remained stone-faced. "These documents just came into our business office for you," the monk added, handing him a large manila envelope. Yuri scanned the documents and thanked him.

Yuri felt Dora's hand on his shoulder and turned to face her. "You can't do this," she said. Her face was wet with tears. Wrapping his arms about her, he could feel her shaking.

"What choice do I have? I got Yana into this mess and I have to get her out," he said.

"You can't give up, Yuri."

A thought suddenly appeared in Yuri's head. He straightened. His eyes widened. "Can you call your Uncle Morris? I need to talk to him about the Russian mafia."

Chapter 49

Viktor Raskolnovitch paced in the hallway outside the boiler room. He was thinking about the one time he was knocked out boxing. He had beaten a much older, more experienced boxer, one who was expected to have an easy time with the young upstart. But Raskolnovitch seemed able to take any amount of punishment his taller, stronger opponent could deliver. In the eighth round, Raskolnovitch landed a left hook that floored the man. As the boxer tried to get off the mat, the referee counted to ten, took Raskolnovitch's wrist, and raised it high above him in triumph. But in the next instant the downed boxer rose to his feet and sucker punched the young Raskolnovitch, who didn't wake up again until the crowd had left the arena.

He had worried ever since about being complacent in victory. There would always be someone waiting to take him down. For now, he held all the cards. The boy would do as he was ordered. He had no choice. But something bothered him. The sister was his trump card, but he despised himself for mistreating her. He had been raised never to hurt girls, and it was a cardinal rule among the *Vory* to respect their dignity. He tried not to think of

Toni. The girl in the room next to him, he told himself, had stolen from him and deserved to be punished. But he would get no satisfaction from torturing her. He'd get his just revenge when he had the boy.

The phone in his pocket rang, Yana's phone.

He answered on the fourth ring. "Pry' vit," he said. "It's early. You must be in a hurry to see your sister. It's never good to rush. Maybe we talk later."

"No good. It's now or I give away all your money," said Yuri.

Raskolnovitch laughed. "OK, OK. You have the papers?"

"Yes, everything is ready."

"Good. I will send a car to pick you up," Raskolnovitch said.

"No, no. That's impossible. It has to be someplace public," Yuri told him. "I need to see you free Yana, unharmed, before I surrender myself to you."

"You watch too many movies," said Raskolnovitch. "In real life, it's much simpler. Just a business transaction."

"Look. It would be easy for me to put a match to these papers and tell you to go fuck yourself. Maybe I don't have the courage to go through with this exchange. So, listen carefully—either we do this in some neutral public space, like Russians and Americans do when they exchange spies over a bridge, or I burn these papers right now."

"OK, OK. No tricks. What do you propose?" Raskolnovitch asked.

"How about we meet below the suspension bridge, the Bridge of Love, in Mariinsky Park. There's a large open meadow. No one will disturb us there, but we'll be in the open. We'll meet in the center. You come from the north and I from the south. Bring Yana."

Raskolnovitch laughed again. "By all means. What time?"

"In one hour, at noon," Yuri suggested.

"That's good. I'll bring Yana. We make a trade, you for her.

I'm not sure it's a fair trade, though. She's much prettier, but maybe cries too much."

"Just make sure she's not hurt. When I see she's free and OK, I'll sign the transfer of ownership papers and then you can do with me what you want," said Yuri.

"It will be my pleasure," said Raskolnovitch and hung up.

Chapter 50

He was condemned, sentenced to death by torture. A flock of crows scattered from the snow-covered courtyard as he walked back inside the monastery. Raskolnovitch's voice echoed in his head. He was nauseated with fear. He looked up at the vaulted ceiling, covered with mosaics. and slumped to the floor, alone. The cold made his teeth chatter. He hugged himself as best he could. The sweet smell of incense and the religious icons that surrounded him begged him to pray, but he didn't know how. He had no faith to sustain him, only his pathetic stubbornness.

Dora came into the hallway and sat next to him.

"We should never have come back to Kyiv," he whispered to her.

"You came to rescue your sister," she reminded him. She placed her hand on his knee.

"But it was pure hubris, Dora. Everything was for ego." He took his hands away from his face. His eyes were a vision of terror and despair. "All it did was get dad and Bubbie killed and put Yana's life in danger."

"Stop it! Yuri," said Dora. "You only did what you thought

was right. I'm very proud of you. You're the bravest person I've ever known. You did it for all of us."

She stood up and pulled him to his feet. "Come back inside. We don't have much time for this. We've got to plan our next moves."

In the hall, Taras stood talking to a group of Ultras. Looking around the room at the protesters, some badly injured, Yuri saw how others had acted courageously to oppose a corrupt regime, but they did it together. What made him think he could take down Raskolnovitch by himself? he asked himself. It was always this way, he mused. He was always a minority of one. But underneath his go-it-alone manner was a certain arrogance, he realized. He was feeling immobilized by his loneliness.

As if reading his mind, Taras turned to him and said, "See, Yuri. You are not alone."

Yuri looked in the eyes of each of the Ultras in turn. Only through them might he find redemption. "Thank you," he said. "Let's meet at Mariinsky Park in front of the football stadium at a quarter to twelve. Raskolnovitch has agreed to meet in the grove by the suspension bridge."

"We'll be there," said Taras.

What had felt infinitely empty inside him began to fill with a new resolve. All night he had ruminated on his failures, on his naivete and his carelessness. He mistook his obstinacy for courage. Now he was trapped. The game was over. He had nothing more to lose. His only purpose now was to save Yana and protect Dora.

Then his phone rang. "Hello, Rabbi?"

Chapter 51

At precisely 12 noon, Raskolnovitch, Dima Prokofiev, and a dozen guards in black running outfits, knit caps, and matching parkas stepped out of the woods onto the north side of the glen in Mariinksy Park. The guards all had Kalashnikovs strapped on their backs. The wind had disappeared, but a steady snow had blanketed the field with a half foot of white powder.

Across the meadow, a young man, unarmed, holding a manila envelope, stepped out of the woods by himself. He took a few steps towards Raskolnovitch and stopped. "Where's Yana?" he yelled.

So, this is the yid who thinks he can fuck me? thought Raskolnovitch. *He's so young, so arrogant.* Raskolnovitch wanted to fight him with his fists, pummel him, get this over with. But there was a voice that wondered whether he was too old to win against such a younger opponent, which made him even angrier. How could such a nobody threaten him at all?

Raskolnovitch yelled back, "She's here," pointing behind him. "Where are the documents?"

Yuri held up the manila envelope. "First Yana, then the papers."

"No, first you sign the papers, then we make the trade," Raskolnovitch hollered.

"No, the deal was you release Yana and then I sign and give myself over to you," Yuri said.

Raskolnovitch made a signal to his men, who lifted their Kalashnikovs and took aim at Yuri. Then two more guards appeared with Yana between them.

Yuri could see Yana was still bandaged, and her mouth was taped closed, but she was OK. Dora stepped out of the woods to stand next to him. Across the meadow, Taras's army of young Ultras, dressed in their team's colors, followed her. There were perhaps fifty of them, carrying baseball bats and metal pipes. Yuri's two security guards were among them. They all stopped in a line behind Dora and Yuri.

"Let her go," yelled Yuri through the muffling snow. The strength of his voice empowered him.

Nothing happened. The snow began to build on their heads and shoulders.

At the sight of Yana, Yuri felt the fear lift from him. Nothing could stop him now. It was an almost out-of-body experience. Raskolnovitch in the flesh was not as frightening as he imagined. The guns around him were intimidating but they made Raskolnovitch appear smaller. Yuri started to slowly walk towards him with the Ultras right behind. Something much bigger than him propelled him forward, a will even greater than his own. He felt like his life was about to end. But at that moment of surrender, Yuri had found its meaning.

. . .

With this mob advancing on him, Raskolnovitch felt his heart start to race out of control. He reached into his coat pocket and placed a nitroglycerine tablet under his tongue and another between his cheek and gum. He wiped the snow from his face. The Ultras moved in slow steps towards him as if to a drumbeat. When they were about twenty yards from him, Raskolnovitch turned towards his guards and shouted to them to prepare to fire. Still Yuri and the Ultras came on. When they were ten yards away, Raskolnovitch yelled "fire."

But nothing happened. His guards froze. The Ultras stopped where they were. Coming from the east, he saw another group of armed men appear in the meadow, their rifles pointed at his guards. There were perhaps two dozen of them coming forward at a jog. Raskolnovitch recognized Nikolai Lazovsky, Mogilevich's man at their head. Next to him was a tall man wearing a yarmulke. In a minute they were as close to Raskolnovitch as the Ultras. No one moved. A mourning dove sang.

"Fire," Raskolnovitch shouted again. Still nothing happened. "Fire!" he repeated. Raising an automatic pistol in his hand and aiming, he screamed with all his might. It felt like his heart cracked. One of his guards, a young Chechen man, threw his Kalashnikov down into the snow. Two others released Yana while the rest of his men retreated, walking backwards to their cars. Dima helped Raskolnovitch to his feet and led him away, his hand on his chest.

Part Three

Chapter 52

Dima fished the nitroglycerine tablets from Raskolnovitch's inside pocket and pushed them into Raskolnovitch's mouth. Raskolnovitch was seated on the back seat of the Maybach with the door open and his feet still on the ground, his face as white as the snow that fell heavily around them. A guard lifted his legs into place and shut the door. Dima went around the other side and sat next to him.

"Get me to the closest hospital, fast," Raskolnovitch managed to whisper to Dima.

He felt like his chest was folding heavily in on itself. It was hard to breathe. He knew what was happening, felt the crushing pressure that threatened to cut off his air. The last time was less than a year ago and he had been warned that another attack would be his last.

The Maybach took off in a fury of spinning wheels. A line of SUVs with his guards followed, swerving in the snow. More snow was falling, and it was hard to see the road ahead. Dima was already on the phone calling Dr. Korenz, Raskolnovitch's cardiologist.

"Tell him my heart is beating wildly and I feel a heavy pressure on my chest," he told Dima. Each of his words required a special effort, a gathering of strength. He wasn't sure he could end his sentence.

"And he's sweating," added Prokofiev, "even though it's freezing cold."

The anger that had ignited Raskolnovitch's coronary eruption did not subside, however. There remained an acetylene torch of rage at this brash young couple he vowed to destroy. And there was this other armed group that had come to their rescue. He was sure he had seen Lazovsky among them waving an automatic pistol before Raskolnovitch's chest seemed to crack in two. He had more questions than answers, but it was hard to think as the car lurched from side to side hurtling to the hospital.

By the time they pulled up to the emergency entrance, the color had begun to come back to his face. He put his hand around Dima's wrist.

"Dima, my friend, it's war now," he whispered. "We have to kill these bastards. All of them, the boy, the girlfriend and the little brat. That was Lazovsky at the head of that gang. Mogilevich is behind the whole thing." Prokofiev tried to calm him, to little avail. Medics lifted him from the car, placed him on a gurney and wheeled him into the hospital.

Three hours later he was released, shuffling out on his own feet. Dr. Korenz explained that, technically, he didn't have a heart attack, but it was debatable. "You were lucky this time," said the doctor, a short man with a large mop of red hair, "but the next time, not so much."

Prokofiev had summoned the helicopter to the hospital, and they flew to the mansion on the outskirts of the city, with Raskolnovitch sitting quietly in the back. The snow had stopped and the wind had died down as they landed in a vortex of white. The gold cupolas reflected the last of the afternoon light. An unearthly stillness descended as the rotors stopped. Raskolnovitch's butler was waiting with a wheelchair at the foot of the stairs, but Raskolnovitch walked past him without a glance.

Inside, Raskolnovitch made it unsteadily to the library followed by Prokofiev and several of his guards. "Where's Kostya?" he asked.

"He's in hiding, as you requested," said Prokofiev.

"Get him back here. We need to hold a war council. It's no time to be without him. We're going to need all the firepower we can muster."

Raskolnovitch knew he shouldn't let himself get so upset, but he was the only one who could mobilize his forces. He hated that Jewish punk who had humiliated him for the second time, stealing his money and then forcing him to retreat in front of his men.

Damn that prick, he said to himself. *And damn my own guards for failing to fire and letting the girl get away. Someone's going to pay.*

A servant came in and lit a fire in the walk-in fireplace. In a moment the dry logs roared to life. Prokofiev and Raskolnovitch sat in high-backed upholstered chairs and warmed themselves.

"Viktor, you need to stay calm. The doctor said you'll kill yourself, if you don't," Prokofiev offered. Raskolnovitch reached for a decanter of brandy, then put it back. He badly wanted a cigarette. He sat back in his chair and took several deep breaths.

"It looks likely," he said, "that Mogilevich has been behind this whole scheme from the beginning. How he got this boy involved is a mystery, but that explains why he was never able to catch him. And now he wants us to pay him for that?" he asked. "Bertrand thinks the girl, Osatinskaya, came up with this plan and the boy just got greedy. But however it started, we know for sure now that the Yavlinsky kid and Don Semion are working together."

Prokofiev leaned forward staring into the fire. "We're going to need a lot of cash. We don't have the manpower to stand up to the mob on our own. They've got their fingers in everything. Who can help us?" he asked.

"The *Vory* hates this Jewish mafia, but it will cost a lot to get them to fight. Our *krysha* will back us, I think. It's going to be harder to get our hands on those kids now that the Don is protecting them, but Bertrand believes he can deliver them to us," said Raskolnovitch.

"We're going to have to sell off some of our assets for all this," said Prokofiev. "Until we can recover those Panama funds, we don't have a lot of liquidity. The 25 million we put as a down payment for the Drake Hotel deal is now frozen, but we can sell some of the other New York condos we bought."

Raskolnovitch nodded but was not paying much attention, his mind wandering to Bertrand and Toni. "I spoke with Bertrand this morning," he said. "He hasn't reached the boy yet, but he's got a message in to his British handlers and expects to contact him today."

Prokofiev started to speak again, but Raskolnovitch stood up and cut him off. "Dima, get Kostya here. Sell those damn New York condos, if you think we need to, and call Minister Zakharchenko. Tell him we are upping the reward for the two Yavlinskys and Osatinskaya to $50,000 each, plus another fifty for himself. Explain that we had to release the little sister, but we want them all captured, and tell him that this time it's dead or alive." His only motive now was revenge.

With that he walked out of the library and puffed up the wide sloping stairway to the guest room where Toni was being held. A guard sitting on a stool outside her door stood at attention and saluted him as he approached. Raskolnovitch hesitated for a minute while he caught his breath and then knocked before entering. Toni was seated in a divan by a large bay window that looked out over the racetrack, wearing the same grey silk outfit she had on when he had last seen her. She remained seated as he approached.

"Are your accommodations adequate?" he asked.

"They'll do under the circumstances," she said. She studied him closely. "You look horrible, Viktor. What's happened?"

He wished he could tell her everything. She could comfort him as no one else could. But he was still caught in a vice between a longing for vengeance and a wish to surrender to her. She had never looked more beautiful to him. Where before she was an ornament for his desires, at this moment he could think only of taking her by force.

Toni was alarmed by his appearance, worried that he had been drinking. She didn't know what to expect or how to act. She had never seen him so vulnerable. She had spent most of the time locked in here convincing herself that she hated him. But seeing him now like this, like a frightened little boy, made her pause, even after all that he had done to her in bringing her here and keeping her captive against her will, terrorizing her and pretending to kill her. All her life she had gone for rough, abusive men. It was a weakness she vowed not to repeat. She could probably take him down, if she needed to. It had been a few years since she got her black belt in Taekwando, but she knew how to disable a man, even a former boxer. Her survival instincts, however, told her to try and connect with him.

He sat on the bed across from her. "I had some trouble with my heart. Nothing serious," Raskolnovitch said. "And how are you?"

"Better. I can hear in one ear now. But tell me, Viktor, why have you brought me here?"

He wondered how much to tell her. "It is only for a short while, I hope. I met with Bertrand. We worked out a deal," he said.

"Bertrand's a bastard. You shouldn't trust him," she interrupted.

Raskolnovitch looked taken aback, and he smiled. "But he is trying to gain your freedom."

She laughed out loud. "Bertrand only does what's best for him. He's my boss, yes; but I hate him. What's he want for me?"

"He's offered an exchange. I release you and agree to testify against Gavi, and he'll get me immunity from prosecution."

She raised her eyebrows in disbelief. "Oh yes, and one more thing," he added. "He said you were going to Paris to argue for immunity, but the prosecutors didn't feel my testimony would add much to the conversations you so cleverly recorded. So, I agreed to hand over the videotapes I made of Monsieur Gavi on my yacht."

Toni smiled and shook her head. "You surprise me sometimes, Viktor. For a crooked oligarch, you can be very naïve. The prosecutors never said any such thing. They would love to have you testify. I was going to Paris to ask for that, but Bertrand opposed me, told the prosecutors there was no chance that you would turn. He tried to stop me from leaving, but I refused his orders. He probably wants those sex tapes to blackmail Gavi."

Raskolnovitch's face softened. Toni thought he might believe her, appreciate her brutal honesty, let himself trust her. But still, she knew he would remember she had lied to him so many times.

"I have many reasons to hate you, Toni," he said.

"And I you," said Toni.

"Why? I never betrayed you and I didn't shoot you, either. Why would you hate me?" he asked.

"Because you turned me down."

He stood to leave. She stood next to him, taller than him. He pulled her next to him, their faces almost touching. She allowed him to do it. He looked into her eyes, and she could smell his oddly sweet breath. Then he turned and walked out.

Chapter 53

The train lurched forward with an iron jolt, throwing Taras off the ladder and splaying him onto the floor of their four-bed sleeper car at Yuri's feet. Taras'scomic fall released the pressure that had been building in them all day, provoking convulsions of laughter that wouldn't stop. Tara's tried to scramble up, and with another lurch from the train fell flat again.

Yuri caught his breath and said, "Taras, if this revolutionary thing doesn't work out, you may have a career in the Kyiv circus."

Yana held up her hand, "Please st...st...stop," she stuttered, "I'll p..p..pee in my pants." This only made matters worse. Rounds of laughter finally subsided when the conductor asked to see their tickets.

They had managed to get the last two sleeper compartments just ten minutes before the train left Kyiv. They would arrive at the Odessa-Holovna station at 5:10 am the next day, intending to stay and regroup with Dora's cousin Leon Kaminsky and confer with Uncle Morris. They invited Taras, who had become an inseparable part of their family, to join them.

Yuri had hardly been able to get Yana to say a word since the

307

standoff at Mariinsky Park. She found it difficult to describe what had happened to her, except to reassure them that she had not been physically abused. Yet Yuri could tell from her tensed body and wary face that her release had not relieved the frozen state of terror that gripped her, first from the Berkut and then from Raskolnovitch. It was Taras who got her to talk and eventually to laugh, beguiling her with stories of the Ultras' heroic attacks against the riot police. Yuri could see she was impressed by his bravery. She had seen him, baseball bat in hand, marching in Mariinsky Park next to Dora. But knowing his sister so well, he could imagine that it was some outsider quality about Taras, a rebelliousness, and a certain vulnerability that ultimately drew her to him.

For Yuri, after Mariinsky Park, the poison amulet he now wore around his neck had become a talisman of his new self. He was liberated from his former self like a chrysalis. Whatever doubts he had before were discarded like so much old skin. There was no pride in this transformation, no hubris, only a singular focus on getting revenge and taking down this corrupt parasite.

He thought back to the last moments of that confrontation: Dora running forward in the face of armed men to take Yana by the hand away from them, even as Raskolnovitch gave the order to fire, Taras and the Ultras armed with baseball bats standing shoulder to shoulder with him, and the miraculous appearance of that second group of soldiers forcing Raskolnovitch's guards to stand down and retreat. He had seen Uncle Morris with them, but he disappeared as soon as Raskolnovitch left. And he remembered feeling above the fray, as if in a dream state where nothing could hurt him, and how quiet and beautiful it all was in the muffled snow.

The moment when it was all over, when he and Dora threw their arms around Yana, Yuri had the realization that he not only could face death, but he could also kill. He'd look back at that moment as a dividing line, as the starting gun in a real war with Raskolnovitch. Everything until then had the feeling of an elaborate game. This was sterner stuff. There could be no turning back now.

Settled into their separate berths, Dora called her cousin Leon Kaminsky on her encrypted phone to tell him they were on their way. They spoke for just a few minutes in Ukrainian, but her excitement was obvious. When she hung up, she exclaimed, "Uncle Morris is there." She had tried to reach him after Mariinsky Park, she explained, but was told Morris was on a retreat in Syria, or so they said.

She turned to Taras and Yana. "Morris is a rabbi," she explained, "but nothing like what you'd expect. He used to work for the CIA. He's my mom's baby brother. He babysat me when he was a teenager. I had a huge crush on him as I grew up. He's movie star gorgeous. People mistake him for George Clooney. When my family emigrated from the Soviet Union to Israel in 1991, Uncle Morris stayed behind to help Jewish scientists and other refuseniks escape. I think that's when he started working with the CIA."

"Is he really a rabbi?" asked Taras.

Dora laughed. "Sort of. I mean he's ordained, or whatever it's called; but he's not attached to any synagogue right now. He's also a Zen Buddhist, a Yogi, a vegan, a Vipassana meditation instructor, and a practitioner of a whole bunch of esoteric martial arts. Oh, and he speaks about eight languages. He's also had his share of beautiful girlfriends, but never married. He's hard to resist."

"Sounds like you're crushed out on your uncle," said Yana.

"I'll always be," said Dora. "When I was in high school, he went missing for two years. Later, we learned he had been imprisoned and tortured in Istanbul by the Turkish Mukhabarat. I used to pin photographs of him on my wall and wrote letters to him every day in my journal, which I never showed him. He was the one who inspired me to get into the anti-corruption business—he told me how money laundering worked. He really helped us in London. And it seems he saved our lives in the park. No one knows more about fighting corrupt oligarchs than Uncle Mo."

At 4:30 a.m. the conductor knocked with authority on their door to wake them. They had all slept poorly but were excited to be anywhere other than Kyiv. The train creaked into the Odessa-Holovna station and came to a slow-motion stop. Yuri looked up and down the platform for any trouble, but all seemed clear. Trotting towards them, arms waving, came Leon Kaminsky, Dora's cousin. After hugs and an introduction to Taras and Yana, Kaminsky asked to help with their luggage. Yuri held his hands open. "This is all we've got," he said.

"Well, at least you've got a nice suit," said the tailor.

"I've hardly taken it off since you fitted me," said Yuri.

"Where's Uncle Mo?" asked Dora.

"He's home, doing his daily yoga and meditation," replied Leon, "but the rabbi's very excited to see you."

They walked through the empty train station under a three-story art deco glass dome and through an arched entrance into a city just waking from its slumbers. Leon's badly dented vintage grey Volga was parked in front. They all crammed in. His flat was in the old Jewish section of town in an eighteenth-century apartment building on a wide street lined with chestnut trees, four storeys above a McDonald's.

Entering the apartment, Yuri felt a strange sense of déjà vu. There was something about the faded wallpaper, the dark mahogany furniture, and the walls of family photos that made him feel nostalgic. Among the photos, Leon pointed out ones that were of Yana and Yuri's family, ones of their mother and their aunts and uncles. "This one is of your great-grandmother," he said, pointing to a six-year old girl posing on a white pony. When they came to Bubbie's photo, Yana began to cry. Yuri held her tightly until her sobs subsided.

"I'm confused," said Yuri. "How did you get photos of our family? And why are they here?"

Leon Kaminsky took a deep breath, then looked in turn at Yana, Yuri and Dora before speaking. "Yuri, when you and Dora came to see me, I recognized your family name. After reading about the killings at your apartment, I did some research. I was planning to tell Dora what I learned when all hell broke loose and we had to escape. I wanted to tell her that I had arranged for Yuri's great-grandmother, Bubbie, to be buried in the plot he bought next to his mother's in Odessa." He paused to let the information sink in.

"Yuri was too young to remember his grandmother," he continued. "She died when he was still a baby. His great-grandmother, Bubbie, moved in with him after that. And, Dora, you knew your grandmother when you were growing up in Lviv. She lived in the same apartment building; but you never met your great-grandmother, your mother's grandmother, since she was then living in Odessa. What I'm trying to tell you is that you both had the same great-grandmother. That makes you second cousins."

Dora heard these words but couldn't quite make out their meaning. Yuri felt the same cognitive dissonance. Yana, looking confused, spoke first. "So that makes me Dora's second cousin?" Leon nodded.

"Oh my God," said Dora. She and Yuri looked at each other in bewilderment. There were so many more questions than answers. Had they committed some moral sin?"

"Does this mean that we can't have babies?" asked Yuri.

Leon smiled. "I looked that up. The danger's extremely slight, about a half of one percent greater chance of an inherited disability compared to unrelated couples. You lovebirds have nothing to worry about. Fate has somehow brought you together."

Dora's expression crumbled into a look of grief and despair. "So, Bubbie was my great-grandmother, too? And now she's dead and I never knew her?" The tentacles of their fate wrapped itself around them.

Yuri took Dora's hand. "So, I'm your second cousin," he said.

"And I'm your first," said a deeper voice behind them. Uncle Morris had entered quietly from the bedroom. He was barefoot, dressed in black yoga pants, a black yarmulke atop his salt and pepper hair. He held open his arms and Dora melted into him like a baby.

"Why didn't you tell me this when we met?" Yuri asked.

"There was too much else going on, as I recall," said Morris. "Everything in its time."

He led them back to the wall of photographs and explained who each of them was. One of these pictures, faded and torn, was of a large man with fierce dark eyes and a walrus mustache who looked in the photo about the same age as Yuri and Dora, seated with a bolt action Mossin-Nagant carbine across his lap.

"This was your Great Uncle Kurt, Bubbie's brother," Morris explained. He was a hero of the Jewish underground that resisted the Nazi invasion in Lviv and then in Kyiv. He and his partisans were betrayed by Stalin, specifically by a rival band of *Vory* that had been released from the gulags to fight with the Communists. They were arrested and taken to the killing fields of Babi Yar, forced to strip, and with 35,000 other Jews, machine gunned to death. The shooting never stopped for two days."

He looked at Dora and Yuri. "History works in mysterious ways. Each ending is a new beginning. Sometimes justice takes generations. But shall we all visit the grave that started this meshuggah?"

Chapter 54

Seated around Raskolnovitch at a mahogany table in his office, its walls covered in the original green silk wallpaper that once adorned Catherine the Great's bedroom, were Dmitry Prokofiev, Kostya Kybalchich, Raskolnovitch's security chief, and the two Israeli black ops experts, Harry Beinfeld and Chaim Kurtz. An amber crystal decanter of a 1953 Hine 250 Cognac sat untouched on the table. Raskolnovitch had not slept well the night before and he was in a foul mood.

Only once before had he called a war council. Then, as now, there had been masses of young protesters flooding the Maidan in a popular uprising against the president in the "Orange Revolution" of 2004. Even though his *krysha* had been overthrown back then, Raskolnovitch had managed to consolidate his power over the lucrative drug trade and secured a tobacco monopoly in a bloody turf war that, by some accounts, left over two hundred people dead. Ten years ago, he faced a half dozen gangs and criminal syndicates who were still fighting over the spoils of a newly independent Ukraine. But this time, instead of several weaker competitors, his enemies were the head of the worldwide Russian mafia and a boy zookeeper.

"Have you seen this shit?" asked Raskolnovitch, throwing down an eight-page full-color newspaper insert in the *Kyiv Post*, headlined "How the Tobacco King Pays No Taxes." With graphs and photocopies of bank and tax records, the report outlined how hundreds of millions of dollars were deposited in offshore shell companies like Advanced Holdings International and Global Opportunities Fund and then moved around like the proverbial shell game to dozens of other companies in order to hide the funds from the tax authorities. The article detailed deposits of over a billion dollars alongside tax returns showing zero payments.

"This is scandalous," he shouted. "How am I supposed to fight off the mafia while this prick keeps attacking me? It could only have been the Yavlinsky boy. He stole all those records when he robbed us." No one answered.

"We're under attack from several directions at once," Raskolnovitch began. "I don't like war, but we have no choice except to fight back. It's worse than ten years ago. The French are after us, the police are searching for Kostya, the Yavlinsky kid is growing bolder and that fucking kike, Mogilevich, is moving on our drug trade." He looked at the two Israelis and held up his hand as if to apologize. "Let's hear your ideas," he said.

"One advantage we have, that we didn't have ten years ago, is the president is our *krysha*," noted Dima. "We should have him press Zakharchenko to clamp down on prostitution, which Don Semion controls."

Raskolnovitch exploded. "Damn it, Dima. We've already discussed that. Our real advantage last time was firepower. We were more willing to kill than they were. We need to get General Dostum to send us some of his best fighters, like he did before. It will be expensive, but we've got to protect ourselves whatever it takes."

Prokofiev, unfazed, spoke up again. "Viktor Ivanovich, how are we going to pay for that? We have an acute liquidity crisis. We're holding plenty of rubles, but Dostum insists on US dollars upfront."

"Well, turn them into dollars like we always do," Raskolnovitch snapped.

"It's not so easy anymore," continued Prokofiev. "The way we've usually done that was to use 'mirror trades,' but the authorities have caught on to that trick."

"Mirror trades? How's that work?" asked Harry Beinfeld.

"It's pretty simple," said Prokofiev. "We take two or three million dollars' worth of rubles at a time to the Moscow branch of Deutsche Bank, which Putin effectively controls, and buy blue chip stocks like Gazprom. Shortly after, we have one of our people, preferably a non-Russian, sell exactly the same number of securities at Deutsche Bank in London for dollars. It used to be an easy way to change rubles into dollars, but they're watching for that now. It's just too risky."

"I don't give a fuck how risky it is! Do it anyway!" Raskolnovitch said.

Chaim Kurtz leaned forward and spoke next in a heavy Israeli accent. "Viktor Ivanovich is right. Do whatever is necessary to get dollars. But we need to be more strategic. We're thinking defense when what we need is to figure out how to hurt Mogilevich. Even if you could stop the sex trade, it would just be an irritant to him. We need to think bigger."

They all leaned closer. "His biggest asset is a piece of all the natural gas that Russia ships to Ukraine. Dmytro Firtash is Putin's middleman, one of Mogilevich's lieutenants. A percentage of every drop of gas that comes into or through

Ukraine gets siphoned off by Firtash to be shared with Putin and Mogilevich. It's the glue that holds together the marriage of the state and the mafia. The last thing Mogilevich wants is to piss off Putin."

"So how do we attack that?" asked Kostya.

Kurtz's partner, Harry Beinfeld, answered. "Firtash's son is getting Bar Mitzvah'd in a month. Anyone who's anyone in the Russian mafia will be there, including Mogilevich. If we plan it right, we should be able to kidnap the boy. We've had a lot of experience doing that."

The room grew quiet. Raskolnovitch smiled, "I like it. I like it a lot."

They continued meeting for another hour, reviewing all the steps they'd need to make war with the mob. The idea of kidnapping the Firtash boy remained their highest priority. Raskolnovitch worried what Putin might do and how it might affect his own relationship with his *krysha*, but he believed the Russian president respected power more than anything and would force Mogilevich to back off. The realization that Firtash was Jewish like Mogilevich surprised Raskolnovitch, but it shouldn't have, he thought. He'd teach these kikes a lesson.

Feeling much relieved, he walked upstairs to the locked bedroom where Toni was being kept. There had been no word from the French in the last day and a half, but Bertrand assured him that the Elysée would go along with their proposal. Raskolnovitch tapped on the door.

"Entrez-vous," came Toni's lilting French voice.

He entered. She was dressed in a sheer full-length negligee, sitting at a vanity combing her hair. She did not look up from the mirror. Although she was his prisoner, she knew the power she held over him.

"How are you, my dear?" he said in his kindest voice.

"Good," she answered, not looking at him, "for a woman who's been shot at and abused."

He smiled. "It won't be long, I hope. Bertrand said it would take a couple days to get an answer."

"Viktor, Bertrand won't help you. I understand why you might trust him more than me right now, but it's a mistake. You could get a much better deal letting me be your advocate. They need my testimony as much as yours. I could get you immunity and maybe even a promise of citizenship in return for turning state's witness."

"Why would you do that?" he asked.

"It's a simple business proposition, Mr. Raskolnovitch, something you should understand. My freedom in exchange for my help." .

"Is that the only reason?" asked Raskolnovitch.

She paused, halfway between honesty and manipulation. "Maybe it's pity. Maybe it's a desire to save you from yourself. Or maybe I still like the idea of living in that castle with a rich man I can easily control."

"Are you suggesting I let you go?" he asked.

"As you wish. I'm telling you I could get you a deal. I'm not sure Bertrand can. You could escape all the shit you've gotten yourself into, buy that chateau you wanted. We could make a go of it," she said, surprised to hear herself say that.

"My dear Antoinette," he responded. "You're forgetting that you're my only leverage. If I let you go, I have nothing to bargain with."

Toni stood and walked up to Raskolnovitch. "Don't be a fool, Viktor. If Bertrand is stupid enough to tell them you've kidnapped me, you'll never get a deal. They have strict rules against paying ransom. I can help you. I think deep down you know you can trust me."

She could see the doubt in his eyes, saw him wavering before he pulled back, turned and walked out the door. The sound of the key turning was left hanging in the air.

Chapter 55

"God, full of mercy, Who dwells above, give rest on the wings of the Divine Presence, amongst the holy, pure and glorious who shine like the sky, to the soul of Esther, daughter of Miriam, mother of Yana and Yuri; and to the soul of Naomi, our Bubbie, daughter of Belle, grandmother of Evelyn and Morris, great-grandmother of Yana, Yuri and Dora, whom charity was offered in the memory of her soul. Therefore, the Merciful One will protect her soul forever, and will merge her soul with eternal life. The Everlasting is their heritage, and they shall rest peacefully at their lying place, and let us say: Amen." recited Uncle Morris.

Uncle Morris stood in prayer for a minute, then set a small stone onto each of the two graves which were marked by simple marble tombstones in a corner of Odessa's Third Jewish Cemetery; both the first, cemetery established in the 1770's, and the second, a hundred years later, having been destroyed. The cemetery was well cared for with rows of tall leafy trees. Some of the graves had been abandoned and were overgrown, but others displayed photos of the deceased, Soviet style, and there were some statues and elaborate tombstones, all marked with a Jewish Star of David.

Yana was inconsolable, her body racked by sobs. Taras put his arm around her and she leaned against him. Uncle Morris came up on the other side and whispered to her to speak to her mother, father and Bubbie in her mind.

"They will hear you," he whispered.

After a few minutes her breathing slowed, and she placed a small stone onto each grave.

It was Dora's turn. She stepped forward holding her stones tightly in a fist, looked at Cousin Leon as if for permission, and wiped away her tears. She reached for Morris's hand, closed her eyes, and tried to pray. She had never actually prayed before and she didn't know how to go about it. She didn't believe in God, but she couldn't make sense of the unexplainable coincidences of the past weeks. She didn't believe in free will, either, but knew she could not escape her role in this mysterious web. How could she have become so involved with Yuri, a stranger, who had turned out to be her second cousin? How did she end up here before her great-grandmother's grave when she never even knew of her existence before?

She thought she had been crying for her dead great-grandmother whom she had never met, but whose murder had been inexorably connected to her own choices and actions. But she realized her tears were for herself and her fears for the unknown and possibly unknowable forces that had entrapped her. Had she somehow sinned by falling in love with Yuri? She wanted to protect him and Yana, especially Yana, who was the only innocent player in this drama. She opened her eyes and stared up at the sky. There was no voice from God, no burning bush, and yet she felt a new determination to move forward. She lightly tossed her stones.

Yuri stepped forward feeling like his heart would burst,

trying not to cry, afraid if he did, he would never stop. He had buried his mother here with the money he got for his passport. He had managed not to cry then, though her death had devastated him. She was the one light he had, the only one he could depend on. When she died, he felt his future died with her. Now he felt that she was somehow here, watching them. Her burial marked the beginning of the mad odyssey that had brought them all full circle back here, but he could make no sense of it.

As he stood silently before Bubbie's grave, he knew it was his fault she died. If he hadn't withdrawn the three thousand euros in Cyprus none of this would have happened—not Bubbie, not his stepfather, not Yana's capture, none of it. He had overreached. It was pure chutzpah, simple greed. He begged his mother for forgiveness. He had never known Bubbie's real name before, Naomi, or that his great-great-grandmother was called Belle. This, too, felt like a moral sin. He would redeem himself, he swore on his mother's grave, by killing the monster that murdered Bubbie. Saying this to himself, though, he knew that would not be enough. An eye for an eye, okay; but redemption would require some higher good that made these blood sacrifices worthwhile. He could not just eliminate this one Raskolnovitch. The fight was for the very soul of Ukraine.

Uncle Morris, Rabbi Weissgold—he changed his name from Osatinskaya—saw the anger in Yuri's face and seemed to have read his thoughts. "We'll find a way," he spoke.

Yuri looked in his eyes and said, "We'll need your help, rabbi." Morris nodded. Then Yuri turned back, mouthed a prayer asking for forgiveness and set his stones onto the graves.

Dora, Taras, Yana, Morris and Leon came forward and the six of them stood holding hands in silence. Rabbi Weissgold recited the opening line of the Kaddish, the Jewish prayer for the dead: "Yitgadal v'yitkadash sh'mei raba. Glorified and sanctified be God's great name throughout the world which He has created according to His will."

As they walked out of the cemetery, Uncle Morris excused himself and walked over to a man and a woman holding hands by a large tombstone.

"Hi, Lev," Morris said to them. "I'm glad we could meet here. Thank you."

"Rabbi, good to see you again," answered the man with a welcoming smile. "It's my pleasure. I come here often." He was dressed in a dark overcoat with short cropped grey hair and had a round puffy face. He shook Morris's hand. "Rabbi, my wife, Svetlana Parnas." The man turned to the young blonde next to him. "This is an old friend, Rabbi Weissgold." Morris shook her hand. "The rabbi and I worked together in the final days of the Soviet Union helping refuseniks to get out. He's one of the most dangerous men I've ever met," he said. "Especially for beautiful women."

"It seems you and I share that honor," said Morris, nodding to the young Ms. Parnas. Congratulations." He looked to the large tombstone. "Your parents?" he asked.

"No, my grandparents," replied Lev.

Morris bent down, took a small stone, said a blessing in Hebrew and placed it on the grave.

"What brings you here, rabbi?"

"My niece Dora and her cousin Yuri Yavlinsky. His mother and their great-grandmother, my grandmother, are buried there," said Morris, pointing back from where they came.

"Yavlinsky. I suppose that's why you wanted to talk. I just heard a crazy story about a Yavlinsky. Is he from Kyiv?" he asked, looking back at Morris's relatives.

"What did you hear?" asked Rabbi Morris.

"It's complicated. I don't know all the details, but the story goes that some young kid, this Yavlinsky guy, stole a billion dollars from Raskolnovitch, and the Bratva got hired to find him. It's really *meshuggah*; let me tell you. In any case, the Don's red-hot mad. I heard it from him myself. There was some armed standoff between Raskolnovitch and this Yavlinsky boy in the park and Lazovsky heard about it and brought a small army to stop it. Can you imagine?" He bent over laughing. Morris smiled to himself.

"Sounds like war," said Morris.

"Yeah. The whole country's going mad, I tell you," said Lev.

Morris thought for a moment. "You know Lev, Yavlinsky and I might be able to help you. It seems we might be on the same side again, like the old days. Can you arrange a meeting for me with Mogilevich? Might be worth something to him."

Lev Parnas looked over to the young man. "Perhaps. Firtash's son is getting Bar Mitzvah'd soon. All the *alte kaker* Jewish oligarchs will be there, Firtash, of course, Abramov, Fridman, Mikhelson, Rabinovich, Abramovich, Kolomoysky and the Don himself. Let me talk with Igor. Fruman's the one who's close to Firtash. I'm staying at his wife's hotel, the Otrada. I'll ask Igor to arrange something."

Uncle Morris glanced skywards and whispered to himself, "*toda le CHa Elohim.*" "Thank you, God."

Chapter 56

"Count me out! I won't be any part of this," exclaimed Dora, pushing her chair back from the dining table. Her cousin Leon looked up at her with surprise as he poured tea from a silver samovar.

"Can we please discuss this rationally?" replied Uncle Morris.

"No, we can't fucking discuss this rationally. These guys are Nazis, actual Nazis. Look at their logo, just like a swastika. Their red and black flag was Bandera's flag. 'Glory to Ukraine and Glory to the Heroes,' they shout. What don't you understand? These are the guys who made a pact with Hitler during the war," yelled Dora.

Taras turned to face her. "Yeah, they're also some of the guys who saved Yana's life," he retorted. "They risked their lives for us. Many of my friends in the Ultras are joining the Bandera Brigade and Svaboda because they're the most militant nationalists. Bandera is an historic symbol of Ukrainian nationalism for them, against Russia, not against Jews. Fuck, there're even some Jews in Svaboda."

"Oh, great! Let's invite them over for tea on the anniversary of Babi Yar," said Dora. "Oh, but I forgot. They think the Russians were the ones who machine gunned 34,000 Jews, don't they?"

Yuri had been pacing around the room. Now he sat down between Dora and Taras. "Why are we even discussing this?" he asked.

"Because Uncle Morris thinks we should team up with them," answered Dora. "He said we need some muscle."

"We already have," Taras shot back. "We've given them money to protect us and no one could have asked more of them. We're on the same side. We both want the government to fall."

"And be replaced by what?" Dora asked. "A fascist dictatorship under Andriy Mroz and the Bandera Brigade?"

Uncle Morris blew on his teacup to cool it down and placed it back on its saucer. "Listen, Dora. I understand your feelings, I really do," he said. He looked at each of them in turn seated at the table. "Let's not quibble. There may be some exceptions, but for the sake of this argument, we can all agree that Bandera and Svaboda are largely fascist."

No one objected. Morris continued. "I've spent my entire life fighting for freedom and in every case I've had to work with people that I despised. I know Mroz. He's a politician and a would-be revolutionary, more than a Nazi. But even if he were a real Nazi, we'd need to work with him. Our goal is to defeat Raskolnovitch, which means bringing down this corrupt regime. For better or for worse, the Bandera Brigade is the core of the shock troops in this revolution."

"The enemy of our enemy is our friend," said Taras.

"Exactly," said Morris. "All those brave people who've camped out in the Maidan in this miserable cold for the past month won't win without some of these angry young rightist men who are willing to fight for independence. You want to end corruption in this country? You're going to have to prepare for a real war. The Russians won't allow Crimea or the Donbas, with its oil and its steel mills, to fall to the West. This is the historic heart of the Russian empire, of the Russian Orthodox Church, of the Rus. They'll invade or they'll arm Russian-speaking partisans to fight for them."

Yuri spoke up. He had been very quiet since they got to Leon's apartment and learned he and Dora were cousins. He hardly said a word after visiting the graves of his mother and Bubbie. "I've been thinking a lot about this," he said. They all turned to hear him. "Ever since we faced Raskolnovitch's armed guards, I've dreamed of using our money to build a volunteer army that could defend Ukraine. The majority of people want the regime to fall. We can have a million people demonstrate peacefully in the Maidan, but as long as the Berkut has all the guns, we won't succeed."

Morris smiled. "Bravo, Yuri. You couldn't be more right," he said. "If we can support even a small volunteer army, it would make the Russians think twice before invading and occupying all of Ukraine. If we succeed in overthrowing this regime, any new government will require time to consolidate power and field a modern army to defend its borders. NATO won't do it."

He paused and took a careful breath. "I'll share something with you," he said. "I've been trying to get the CIA to arm the Bandera Brigade for all the reasons you've just laid out. But I failed. They're too afraid the Russians would use that to discredit this popular revolution. They'll claim it's all being manipulated by George Soros and the Americans. But Yuri, you have the funds to do this. We don't need sophisticated anti-tank missiles or counter-radar systems, not yet anyway. But a few hundred hunting rifles could make all the difference at this stage, enough at least to defend the protesters on the Maidan and show the

Russians the kind of popular resistance they'd face if they invaded."

Silence filled the space between them as the gravity of their decisions weighed on them all. Dora had sensed it would come to this. She had changed since escaping from Leon's Kyiv apartment. The idealism that had inspired her campus activism and even her previous work with prosecutors had tempered into something harder, edgier, more determined. She would do whatever it took to save Yuri, with force if necessary. The fear she had carried ever since her brother's death was gone, cut from her that day on the Maidan when she watched helplessly as the Berkut dragged Yana by the hair. She could not avoid her way to safety. She'd have to fight.

"I'm not against using violence to stop much greater violence," she insisted. "I just don't want to ally ourselves with proto-fascists."

"What choice do we have?" Taras asked.

"Not much," Yuri answered. "These ultra-nationalists are the only ones willing to meet force with force."

Morris spoke up again. "The man I talked to at the cemetery, Lev Parnas, is a business partner of Igor Fruman, who's connected to the oligarch Firtash and the Russian mafia. In this case, the mafia are also the 'enemy of our enemy.' They have their own reasons for opposing Raskolnovitch. They're the ones who came to your rescue in Mariinsky Park. I'm trying to arrange a meeting with Firtash and maybe some of the Jewish oligarchs who oppose this regime. They all attend the same synagogue in Kyiv, the Brodsky Choral Synagogue. Firtash's son is getting Bar Mitzvah'd there soon, and I'm hoping we can all go. They could be very helpful."

Yuri tapped his lips with his finger. His eyes brightened. He thought out loud. "So, anything we can do to encourage a war between the Russian mob and Raskolnovitch will help us. If we set fire to one of his tobacco warehouses, he'd assume it was Mogilevich."

"Not a bad idea," said Morris.

"Uncle Morris, I trust you," said Dora. "You've been in a dozen situations like this. Tell me, though, if we partner with the mafia and the neo-Nazis and the oligarchs, how do we create a democratic Ukraine after we've won? It's not just Raskolnovitch we're after. We want to end all the corruption,"

Morris smiled. "Ah, my wise and hopeful niece. That's always the hard part. It will take time. But the people here, especially the young ones, have risen up before—against the Russians in 1991, in the Orange Revolution ten years ago and now again in this so-called 'Revolution of Dignity.' It might be a lifetime struggle, but I'm certain we'll win. The money you and Yuri have expropriated can help build strong democratic political parties, trade unions, a free press and anti-corruption NGOs like the one you started."

"So, what's the next step?" Yuri asked Uncle Morris. He appeared calm, but Dora knew his heart and his mind were racing ahead.

"We each will have a job to do," Morris said. "Taras, you will go to Kyiv to meet with Mroz. I know an arms dealer in Croatia who can deliver whatever he needs to him."

"I'm going, too," interjected Yana, "with Taras." She put her arms around him and they kissed.

Dora worried Yana was too young, too innocent for this role. "It will be too dangerous for you," said Dora. "The Berkut have your photo and there's a $50,000 reward for your capture."

"I don't give a fuck anymore," said Yana. "They can kiss my fucking ass. I'm staying with Taras." No one objected.

"We'll all need disguises," said Uncle Morris. "Those rewards for your capture are a serious incentive for the Berkut. But if we're careful, we'll be all right."

"What about you, Dora?" Yana asked. "What are you going to do?"

Dora put her elbows on the table and clasped her hands together. "Actually, I've been cooking up something that could be important. I spoke with our lawyer in Panama, Felix Rodriguez, at Mossack Fonseca. He told me that there's a lot of pressure on him to reveal the names and accounts of the shell companies we created. He's thinking of quitting over it, but I begged him to stay on for a while. He's sitting on some explosive information about corruption in the world. I'm thinking of going back to Panama to see if I can convince him to share some of that with me. It could undermine the president and Raskolnovitch both, plus a lot of other people who hide their money in these offshore accounts."

She and Yuri locked eyes. It seemed like they didn't need words anymore. "That's good," Yuri said. "Better Panama than the Maidan for you. And me, Uncle Mo?"

"You and I are going to synagogue."

"Synagogue?" asked Yuri.

Chapter 57

Morris and Yuri stood by the Sholem Aleichem statue across from the Brodsky Choral Synagogue, honoring the Yiddish playwright whose stories inspired the musical *Fiddler on the Roof.* Snow had accumulated on the outstretched hat the statue held above its head and on the head as well. The flurries had eased up, and dozens of families were entering through the yellow archway of the temple on Shota Rustaveli Street for Sabbath morning services. The sounds of explosions and the occasional rifle shot still echoed from the Maidan a mile away, shattering the silence of the early morning.

"Yuri, have you ever been here before?" asked Uncle Morris.

"My mother used to bring me for the high holidays when I was little, after my dad died. I didn't understand anything, but I loved the chanting and the music. They let me sit in the back on the floor and draw. That's when I taught myself how to do caricatures. Mom sometimes went through periods when we lit candles and said sabbath prayers at home, but I never had a formal education," said Yuri.

"Did you get Bar Mitzvah'd?"

"No. I wish I had. A few of my friends did. But I learned about the history, mostly just through osmosis: Moses leading the Jews out of slavery, Judah Maccabee, the suicides at Masada, the pogroms and the concentration camps. I guess that makes me Jewish."

"Ah, the sacred suffering," said Morris. "It is what defines us to this day."

"Were you a good Jewish boy from the start?" Yuri asked.

Morris smiled. "My family was strictly secular. They made fun of observant Jews. I guess I got into the religion as an act of rebellion. I was enchanted by the rituals and the mystery of it all, especially the Kabbalah. I loved its calling to repair the world. Through the rabbi here, I got involved with the refusenik community and helped smuggle Jews out of the Soviet Union to Israel."

"Do you still believe?" Yuri asked.

Morris laughed. "Some of it, I guess. These days I get more of my worldview from Buddhism and the Vedas than from the Torah. But don't tell anyone I said that. Being a rabbi, however, gives me considerable advantages and has saved my life several times."

"Does it get you girls?" joked Yuri.

"You'd be surprised," said Morris.

A man in a wide brimmed black hat and frock coat, with a long thin beard that came halfway down his chest, walked toward them. Morris's face lit up.

"Rabbi, what a delight to see you again!" Morris wrapped his arms around the man. "This is my cousin Yuri Yavlinsky. Yuri, meet Moshe Azman, the Chief Rabbi of Ukraine, the man I was just talking about. Moshe is the one who got me into all my trouble."

Yuri and the rabbi shook hands.

"What brings you here, Morris? Not to pray, I presume," Azman said.

"I wanted Yuri to hear you sing," he said. "Moshe should have been a cantor, not a rabbi," said Morris. "We're here to meet Dmytro Firtash."

"You should know better than to do business in the temple," Rabbi Azman remarked. "But with you, I know it's always God's work, even with the mafia. I'll leave my office open. It'll be more private in there." Embracing Morris again, and shaking hands with Yuri, he said, "It's show time. See you inside."

"Nice man," observed Yuri.

"Yeah, but don't ever cross him. He spent a number of years with the Israeli Defense Forces in Lebanon and learned a thing or two," said Morris.

"Tell me, cousin, what do we hope to accomplish here?" asked Yuri.

Morris patted the snow off his jacket. "In Ukraine the oligarchs control everything: the TV stations, the large factories, the banks and the gas and oil. The mafia gets a cut from most of that for their protection, let us say. Firtash, the man we hope to meet, is a close associate of Mogilevich, the Godfather of the Russian mafia. For some reason, Mogilevich is at war with your nemesis Raskolnovitch."

"So, the enemy of your enemy is our friend?" Yuri asked.

"Precisely. These Jews pray to the same God but they each have their own turf. You want to enter this club, you'll need to make friends with one faction or another. Right now, we seem to have a friend in Firtash. Maybe we can find out from him what Mogilevich has against Raskolnovitch."

They crossed the street by the Bessaraby kosher market and walked under the yellow arches of the Romanesque Revival-style synagogue, built like a classical basilica, constructed by the sugar magnate Lazar Brodsky at the turn of the century. Morris opened a blue velvet bag he carried and took out a white silk tallis, kissed each corner of its braided fringes and wrapped it around his shoulders. An elderly man greeted Yuri with a smile and handed him a yarmulke and tallis to wear.

About a third of the pews were filled with men quietly davening, chanting prayers, swaying back and forth, side to side and frantically bowing. The women were segregated in the balconies above. When Rabbi Azman mounted the pulpit, the chorus of prayers quieted. Raising his hands, everyone stood as he led them in the most sacred prayer in Judaism, the Shema.

Shema yisraekl, Adonai loheinu, Adonai echad.
Hear O Israel, the Lord our God, the Lord is one.

Baruch shem kavod malchuto l'olam va-ed.
Blessed is the name of his glorious Kingdom forever and ever.

Yuri was surprised that he remembered the words and recalled his mother telling him that every Jew needed to learn them so they could recite the prayer at the moment of their death.

After the prayers, the rabbi turned to face the eastern wall, where the holy arc of the covenant lay framed by black marble pillars and a gold façade. After bowing several times, he pulled open a red velvet curtain revealing a dozen Torah scrolls embellished with silver and gold ornaments, pulled one out, and held it over his head. The congregation chanted in Hebrew as a procession formed, carrying the Torah around the great hall of the synagogue. The rabbi handed the silver covered scroll to a man with tousled grey hair and a stubble of a beard who held it in his arms like a baby.

"That's Ihor Kolomoysky," Morris whispered to Yuri. "He's

the head of the United Jewish Community and another oligarch we should talk to while we're here."

"The guy walking with him, isn't he the comedian, Zelensky, who plays the president in Servant of the People?" asked Yuri.

Morris watched as the procession passed them. "I think it is. Kolomoysky owns the 1+1 TV Channel where the series plays," said Morris.

"I'd like to meet him, too, if we can. I've got an idea for them," said Yuri.

Someone tapped Morris on the shoulder. The two of them turned to see two scruffy looking men. They shook hands and Morris introduced Yuri. Igor Fruman looked the part of a gangster: unshaven, with grey hair combed back, botoxed forehead, long sideburns and a permanent scowl. Lev Parnas had a pudgy round face and heavy eyebrows. When the congregation stood again, Morris signaled for them to follow him and walked them all back into Rabbi Azman's office and shut the door.

A minute later Dmytro Firtash walked in. Handshakes all around. Parnas and Fruman bowed, then left without a word when Firtash nodded towards the door.

"Tweedledum and Tweedledee," Firtash murmured to himself, shaking his head. A tall, well-dressed man with a trim grey beard and heavy brown eyes, he had the perpetually bored look of a man with too much money. He turned his attention to Yuri. "Young man, I wanted to thank you personally. You did me a great favor," he said with a thin smile. "I've never trusted Viktor Raskolnovitch. I think he's an anti-Semite. Frankly, I never understood why our beloved president relies on him like he does. You exposed him for the idiot he is. You made him look like a fool. If the story is to be believed, you are either the bravest or the luckiest person on Earth."

Before Yuri could answer, Firtash turned to Morris. "Rabbi, I've heard some wild stories about you from the rebbe. I didn't know the righteous could have so much fun. He credits you with saving the life of my uncle, a mathematical genius. So, I guess I owe you, too."

Morris smiled. "Thank you. I remember your uncle. We had permission to send this one elderly woman, a widow of some trade union official, to Israel. We dressed your uncle in black mourning clothes with a veil and flew him to Tel Aviv. It wasn't always so easy."

"So, tell me, gentlemen. What can I do for you?" Firtash asked.

Morris opened his mouth to speak, but Yuri spoke first. "I want to take Raskolnovitch down. He murdered my great-grand-mother and my step-dad. He threatened to torture my sister and he's poisoning our country with drugs. I want to join forces with anyone who's ready to fight him," he said.

Firtash smiled. "You're not the only one, Mr. Yavlinsky. He made a big mistake humiliating Mogilevich. Don Semion doesn't take well to being humiliated." He turned to Rabbi Morris. "That's why his men joined you in the park that day. Mogilevich realized how weak Raskolnovitch was. Believe me, it's only a matter of time before he is taken down, as you say."

These words reverberated in Yuri's mind. If any force could cut Raskolnovitch down to size it was the Russian mob. *What else could we do to encourage that?*

He looked at Rabbi Morris as he spoke. "Rabbi Weissgold could arrange for a representative of Mr. Mogilevich to meet with General Dostum in Kabul," said Yuri. "He's the other half of Raskolnovitch's export business. The general is known for switching sides, all sides, the Russians, the Taliban, the Americans. Maybe the time will come when it would be in his interests to switch business partners."

Firtash smiled. "Dostum's a real charmer. He raped and tortured his political opponent in the election campaign, you may have seen. Likes to run a tank over prisoners and churn them into dust. With friends like that, who needs enemies?" He paused, thinking. "I will get back to you on that."

Yuri could see that Firtash was about to leave. "I'd like to thank Mogilevich personally," said Yuri. "He saved my life. Can you arrange that? I may have some information that could be useful to him."

Firtash stood and held out his hand. "Let me invite you to my son's Bar Mitzvah. Mogilevich will be there. You can meet him then. Give Lev and Igor your contacts. It's good to meet you both," he said, and left.

"That was good," said Morris. "He respects you. It's just what you want. And by the way, how did you know that I could arrange something with Dostum and what's the information you have?"

"I don't know yet," said Yuri.

Chapter 58

As they were leaving the synagogue, a gruff voice called from behind them, "Don't listen to Firtash. He's Putin's man."

Yuri stopped short. He and Rabbi Morris turned to see a heavyset man with a mane of curly silver hair and beard, with pink cheeks and wire rim glasses. He was laughing as he followed them down the steps. Yuri thought he looked like Father Christmas. They stopped at the bottom of the stairs.

"Hi, I'm Ihor Kolomoysky," said the man, holding out his hand, "but my friends all call me Banya."

"I'm Rabbi Weissgold and this is Yuri Yavlinsky," replied Morris.

"You're the young man I keep hearing about," said Kolomoysky. "Word spreads quickly around here. 'Yuri and Goliath,' they say." He laughed again. "I hear you made Raskolnovitch look like a schnook." He laughed at his own little joke. "I'm glad we met," continued Kolomoysky. Pointing to a short, ordinary looking man standing behind him, he asked, "You recognize him? He's the president in *Servant of the People*. It's about a high school teacher who makes a viral video ranting against corruption and gets elected president. It's very funny."

The young actor put out his hand, "Volodymyr Zelensky."

"Hi, Morris Weissgold."

"I'm Yuri Yavlinsky. *Servant of the People* is the only program I watch. I was hoping to meet you, both of you. I have a crazy idea I'd like to share with you."

"How about we all get something to eat next door at the King David," said Kolomoysky. "It's closed for Shabat, but I had some food brought in. There's a lot to talk about."

They walked around to the back entrance of the restaurant, which was owned by the synagogue. Outside of the area around the Maidan, the city seemed eerily normal, as if the roars from the protests were just a distant football game in a nearby stadium on a snowy Saturday morning. As they walked, a dozen bodyguards hovered close by. Kolomoysky had a key and let them in. They sat alone at a table with a gold tablecloth in a large dining room dominated by a wall-sized photograph of Jerusalem. There was a lavish spread of delicatessen foods on silver platters: smoked salmon, gefilte fish, bagels, cream cheese, white fish and a dozen desserts.

"So, Banya, why the nickname?" Uncle Morris asked. "After the lion in the Russian cartoon? Or after Banya Krik, the famous Jewish gangster in Babel's *Tales of Odessa?*"

"A little of both, I think," Kolomoysky said. "Fussy like the lion but a little ruthless like Banya Krik." He waited a moment for them to laugh. "I understand why you wanted to see Firtash," he continued. "The Bretva has it in for Raskolnovitch. It's a personal thing with Mogilevich, and Firtash does whatever the Don wants. But, believe me, it's only temporary. The mafia wants to get rid of Raskolnovitch but not his *krysha*. They take their orders from Moscow. But they'll regret that someday."

A platter of salmon was passed around. Yuri was awed by the

food, the most opulent spread of Jewish-centered delicacies he had ever beheld. A waiter poured them champagne and coffee. Kolomoysky put down his fork and continued.

"We saw what happened to the Jewish big shots in Russia. Guzinsky owned NTV, the most popular news channel, but Putin chased him out of the country. Khodorkovsky was the richest man in Russia, but when he spoke out about corruption Putin threw him in jail and seized Yukos Oil. And then there was Berezovsky, who owned the first television channel, and you saw what happened to him. They say it was a suicide, but I don't think so," said Kolomoysky.

"It will be a disaster, if Russia invades Ukraine, not just for Jews," said Morris.

"You're right. I tried to convince Firtash and some of the other *machers* to support the protesters and withdraw their support from the president, but most of them want to hedge their bets," said Kolomoysky.

"It's too late for that," said Yuri. "We need to start building a volunteer army right away with training and arms."

Kolomoysky's face lit up. He stood and raised his champagne glass. "To Yuri, the Goliath slayer," he offered and everyone said "L'Chaim."

"I'll join you," said Kolomoysky. "Some of the political parties have been meeting secretly to plan for an interim government should the president get overthrown. Things can't go on like this much longer. I've been asked to take over as the governor of Dnipropatrovsk Oblast. I plan to raise a militia to defend us with my own funds. The Russians are already organizing and arming Russian-speaking anti-government partisans in the East."

"I'll match you dollar for dollar," said Yuri. We're meeting with Mroz and will offer to train and equip some of his followers. The government's gonna collapse. We need to be ready"

Kolomoysky spoke again. "The government's paralyzed. All

their sources of financing are drying up. They're hemorrhaging money as the banks shift funds overseas. The demonstrators have stayed on the square through months of freezing cold and constant attacks by the Berkut. They aren't going anywhere." He paused and then added, "But Mroz? He's an out and out Nazi. He'll try to take over the state and make himself dictator."

"It's a risk, but Bandera and Svaboda are the ones willing to fight. As soon as possible, we'll need to deploy the regular Ukrainian Army. But in the short term, we need Mroz's troops," said Yuri.

"What kind of arms are you talking about?" asked Kolomoysky.

Yuri nodded to Morris to answer. "Hunting rifles for now. It'll be enough to train them and defend themselves and also keep Putin from claiming it's all a Western invasion. But once the fighting starts, they'll need everything."

Kolomoysky smiled. "The rebbe told me you had some, shall we say, connections, rabbi. Can we get TOW missiles or Javelins?"

"Not yet. Obama's a very cautious man. But we'll see how things develop. The important thing is to get some training and a semblance of command and control," Morris said.

Kolomoysky cut into a large cheesecake and passed it around. "I'm very happy we met," he said. He turned to Yuri, "Was this volunteer army the crazy idea you wanted to speak with me about?"

Yuri took a sip of champagne and looked at everyone in turn. "No, it's about him," he said, pointing across the table at Zelensky. "I never miss an episode of *Servant of the People*. The way you speak about politicians and corruption in this country has struck a nerve. I saw a poll that said you were the most popular person in Ukraine, by far. It's getting harder for people to separate television from reality. I think television personalities could become popular politicians. They know how to use media. My crazy idea is that you should become the real president."

Zelensky's expression never changed. He looked at Yuri and said, "The thought has crossed my mind. It would be very expensive."

"I'll pay whatever it costs," said Yuri.

"But Volodya is Jewish," said Kolomoysky. "This country has had a deplorable history persecuting Jews."

"Precisely why people in the new Ukraine will vote for him, to prove that they aren't anti-Semitic," said Yuri.

"Let us pray you are right," said Kolomoysky.

Chapter 59

From inside her locked bedroom, Toni looked at the blue sky and the thoroughbreds waiting impassively for their turn on the dirt track behind Raskolnovitch's mansion. The blustery wind of the previous days had died down but there was still frost on the edges of the bay window. The ringing in her ear had subsided, but her anger at Raskolnovitch had not. It wasn't just that he had imprisoned her or had come close to shooting her. She understood his feelings of betrayal. She had trapped him, lied to him about everything. But the real reason she was mad was because he wouldn't accept the bigger truth: that she wanted only to save him from himself.

And there he appeared in a tweed riding outfit and brown leather boots looking every bit the alpha dog. He swung onto his saddle with effortless grace. It was hard to believe that just a few days before his heart issues had left him white and drawn. His trainer opened the metal gate to the racetrack, and he trotted inside. She watched with envy as he led the chestnut stallion into a canter. Horse and mount appeared as one as they glided around the track. Then, to her surprise, she saw Kostya and Arnaud

Bertrand come around the corner in a golf cart. They got out and stood by the gate as Raskolnovitch approached at a gallop. He sped by them, then pulled on the reins, turned his horse around, and sauntered up to them at a trot.

Raskolnovitch didn't dismount. Bertrand, wearing a dark overcoat and a black fedora, looked up at him. She peered at them, wishing she had her phone with her to videotape the encounter so she could try to lip read what they said. Bertrand gesticulated with his hands and Raskolnovitch seemed pleased, nodding his head several times. She never considered that Bertrand would help free her. He was probably happy to leave her where she was so he could maneuver without her and get whatever credit came out of this affair. But, undoubtedly, Paris was asking what had happened to her. Would he tell them the truth, that she had been kidnapped? That would take everything out of his hands and expose him for his own incompetence. But what would he say?

Raskolnovitch leaned over to shake Bertrand's hand, then turned his steed around and led it into a gallop as Bertrand and Kostya returned in the cart to the front of the mansion. She stopped watching, sat on a recliner, and pondered what had just transpired below her window. She was still thinking of all the possibilities when there was a knock at her door.

"Entrez-vous," she spoke.

A key turned and Raskolnovitch entered.

"Well, my dear. Good news. You are free to go. Bertrand has arranged for all the charges to be dropped in return for my testimony and any documentation and tapes I might have. There is no need to detain you any longer."

"That's too bad. I was enjoying myself here. The service is a little slow, but the food is exquisite."

Raskolnovitch bent his head. "I'm really sorry I had to do this to you, Toni, but I think you can understand my disappointment. You lied to me, about everything."

"Not everything."

"We shall see. You can do as you wish now. To be honest, my main reason for letting you go was to learn whether your affections were real. You'll excuse me, if I'm reluctant to take you at your word. It's gotten me in serious trouble and, to be frank, has broken my heart. I meant everything I said to you. We'll see what song you'll sing when you're free."

"I meant all that I said, as well," she answered. "I've forgiven you for threatening me and holding me against my will. I understand how badly I deceived you. It was my job. It was an act. I wasn't expecting it to turn into something else, something real. You have every reason to hate me."

"So, what will you do now?" he asked.

"Exactly as I had planned to do before you kidnapped me. I'll go to Paris and argue they should grant you full immunity in return for your testimony and not prejudice your request for citizenship. If we each play our part, we could try to turn this fairy tale into something real."

She could tell he wanted to believe her. He even edged slightly toward her, as if he had a desire to pull her close and kiss her.

"But Bertrand has done what he promised," he said. "There's nothing more you need to do. You owe him your freedom."

Toni laughed. "Monsieur Bertrand was the one who tried to stop me from going to Paris to argue for you. Believe me, any deal he made wasn't done to win my freedom. That would be his last concern. I'm very doubtful he succeeded as he told you. Have you seen anything in writing? Did he say whether you will be deposed in Paris or here? Can your lawyer accompany you?"

"He didn't say," Raskolnovitch. answered "He said they had

an agreement in principle, and he'd have it in writing in a few days."

"Sounds fishy to me," said Toni. "The Elysée has never trusted Bertrand. I doubt they'd make any kind of a deal without speaking with me. I'm the only one who can verify the recordings I gave them. I'll go to Paris as I had planned to meet with the prosecutors and see what I can do to convince them they need your testimony."

Now it was her turn to edge slightly closer. "They don't give a shit about you, Viktor. It's Gavi they want, and you alone can put him away. But you'll need to testify, fully and honestly. Then we can see about us."

Chapter 60

Dora was startled by the vibration and then ringing of her phone, lost as she was in her head, grappling with a million questions as her taxi approached the exit for Boryspil Airport.

"Dora, it's Arnaud Bertrand," said a familiar French accent. "Are you somewhere we can talk privately?"

"I'm in a taxi headed to the airport." She looked at the driver in the rearview mirror. "I think it's OK." The driver seemed to be lost in his own thoughts. "What's up?" She recalled the last time Bertrand had called her, warning her to leave her cell phone and run from her cousin Leon's apartment. The memory sparked a surge of adrenaline.

"I assume you're still in Kyiv. I keep in daily touch with Palmer, but I try not to call unless it's something urgent. Where are you headed?"

"I'd rather not say over the phone," she replied.

"Yes, I understand. But something's come up and I need to talk with you, face-to-face. How about I come to the airport and accompany you to the gate? We don't want a repeat of what happened to Yuri and his sister. The police all have your photos and are looking to get that $50,000 reward that's been offered for your capture. You'll be much safer under my diplomatic protection."

He had saved her life before. She would trust him with it again, if she needed to. "Of course," she answered. "You might have trouble recognizing me, though. I'll be near the Lufthansa ticket counter, international flights. I've got short black hair now and glasses and I'm wearing a plain grey ski jacket."

"Very well. One more thing, please don't let Palmer or anyone know I'm meeting you. I'm afraid I'm breaking a few laws by sharing some secrets I learned, but your security is more important to me than anything."

A half hour later, Bertrand strode into the departure area. Tall and dignified, he looked every bit the diplomat. Dora recognized him immediately and waved him over to her.

They hugged like family. "How are you, Dora? I heard all about the confrontation at Mariinsky Park. Sounded harrowing. I'm glad you got out safely. How is Yuri?" He looked around. "He's not with you?"

"No, he's meeting with some people connected to the gang that saved us in Mariinsky park," said Dora. "I'm headed to Panama to arrange some things with our lawyer. I'll just be gone a couple days."

Bertrand clapped his hands in delight. "This is truly amazing, one of those impossible synchronistic things that make you wonder who's writing this script. I can hardly believe it." He paused, breathing in deeply through his nose. "I came here specifically to ask if you would consider going to Panama."

They laughed at the seeming coincidence, but then his expression turned serious. "Look, what I'm about to tell you is strictly between us. The Americans have intercepted some emails from Raskolnovitch. It's all very hush-hush, some new technology they've developed to break the toughest encryption. In any case, I'd lose my job if Palmer or anyone discovered I leaked this to you."

Dora frowned. She was afraid to hear what was coming next.

"Raskolnovitch's putting enormous pressure on Mossack Fonseca. He's claiming the funds for the offshore shell companies you created are his and he's threatening the owners of the firm with more than just lawsuits, if they don't freeze your accounts. The bank manager who helped Yuri has disappeared. We fear for his life." He held Dora by her shoulders and stared with exaggerated intensity at her. "I don't know how much longer you can hide these assets."

"What can we do? Transfer the funds to new offshore accounts?" Dora asked.

"I'm afraid it's not so simple this time. As you know from your own work exposing corruption, the only certain way to hide assets is to hold ownership in bearer bonds. Then there's no paper trail whatsoever. It's inconvenient and dangerous, but it works. Whoever holds the bonds owns them, just like cash. The challenge is keeping them secure. But I think I have a solution," he said. "You can keep them in our safe at the French Embassy. There's no safer place on Earth."

Dora was confused. She understood what he was suggesting. She knew all about bearer bonds and why oligarchs often turned to them to keep the authorities from tracing their assets. But something about this didn't add up, though she couldn't say what. In the end, she agreed to do what he advised. Still, she was left with a lingering sense of unease, as if walking on ice.

On the long flight to Panama City she was unable to sleep. Separating from Yuri and Uncle Morris already left her feeling unanchored, but seeing Bertrand brought back all her old fears.

She knew she was over her head. It was only a matter of time, she thought, before their luck would run out.

Twenty-four hours after leaving frosty Kyiv, she was in the air-conditioned foyer of Mossack Fonseca. Her attorney, Felix Rodriguez, came out to greet her and then led her to his office. She sat in the same chair where they first met. How totally her world had changed in just these few weeks, she reflected. Rodriguez wore the same wire rim glasses, had the same short curly black hair, the same blue shirt rolled up to his elbows. But he looked like he had aged ten years. There were bags under his eyes and creases on his brow that weren't there before.

Over the course of these weeks they had gotten to know each other well through long and frequent phone calls. He had a fairly good idea of what she was going through, of her battles with Raskolnovitch. He had become a trusted part of their team. He often complained about the dark money he was protecting. Working for Yuri and Dora offered him a bit of redemption.

"Felix, it's so good to see you again," said Dora. "How've you been?" She knew the question was rhetorical. She could see the toll this job had taken on him.

"I'm surviving, barely," he added. He seemed very nervous. Taking a notepad, he wrote, *there could be ears in these walls. Let's go out.*

They left together, never saying a word, and exited into the noise and heat of the city. He led her across the street and into a parking garage to a beige Lexus sedan.

"I think we'll be free in here," he said, letting out his breath. "It's gotten insane around the office. I never realized how corrupt the world has become. It's depressing and now the pressure on me is almost more than I can bear."

"It's our fault. We never should have gotten you into this shit," Dora said.

"No, no. You're the only light in this dark tunnel," said

Rodriguez. "You opened my eyes, let me see that we could do something about this crazy corruption. Without you and Yuri, I would've spent my whole life abetting the worst crimes in the world."

"But I've put your life in danger. I just heard about Mr. Michaels, the HSBC bank manager. Is it true?" she asked.

Rodriguez shut his eyes for a moment. "Yes, I'm afraid it is. I could be next."

Dora reached over and grabbed his hand. "Please no. You must protect yourself. Get out of here while you can. Give them whatever they want."

Rodriguez forced a smile. "I was never meant to be a hero, Dora. Frankly, I've been a coward my whole life. But this is bigger than either of us, much bigger than even you realize. I've made my decision to be a whistleblower, fully aware of the consequences. After all that I've discovered, I can't turn back. He handed her a memory stick. "I've tried to give this to some of the biggest newspapers in the world and they all turned it down. I thought you could help me."

"What's in it?" she asked.

"Everything," said Rodriguez. "Eleven million files. Two hundred countries."

Dora felt a lump forming in her throat. The almost weightless thumb drive was heavier in its way than anything she had ever held before. Mossack Fonseca was the impenetrable black hole for corruption investigators worldwide. This tiny object was the Holy Grail.

"Why are you risking this?" asked Dora.

"I don't want to live in a world where eight billionaires own as much as the poorest half of the world's population. Maybe this can do something."

"Have you read all these files?" asked Dora.

Rodriguez laughed. "It would take ten lifetimes. But I read

enough to know this is bigger than Wikileaks or Snowden or anything that's come before." He was practically shaking. "I've got documents that show how King Salman of Saudi Arabia hides billions of dollars. The prime minister of Iceland hides money here to avoid paying taxes. Bashar Al Assad, Prime Minister Sharif of Pakistan, David Cameron's father—the list goes on and on. Vladimir Putin's best friend, Sergey Roldugin, a simple cellist, somehow deposits a billion dollars with us through a series of opaque offshore shell companies. Putin himself laundered another billion through the Bank of Rossiya. His Swiss lawyers hired Mossack Fonseca. We ran it through RCB of Cyprus, then an offshore company called Sandalwood, then, one called Ozon and another Igora. Putin used some of this money to buy a winter resort where his daughter got married. It would be impossible to trace these funds if we didn't have these documents."

Dora felt her mouth open in amazement. Rodriguez took a deep breath and continued.

"Your friend Raskolnovitch used to employ us. You'll undoubtedly find those transactions interesting. Just in the past few weeks, the president of Ukraine has been funneling billions and billions of dollars out of the country to shell companies all over the world. It's called 'state capture.' Criminals and oligarchs have taken control of the major institutions of the state for their own wealth and power.

He couldn't stop. "There are terrorists like Carlos Quintero, Carlos the Jackal, and narco-terrorists like La Reina Del Sur, Spanish royals and sports stars like Lionel Massi and Americans, too. You know that *Apprentice* guy on TV, Trump? He's in here over three thousand times. There are documents on this drive that show how Newland International Properties helped the Trump Ocean Club right here in Panama City become a virtual money laundering ATM for the Russian Mafia and drug cartels. I could go on and on."

Dora felt a mixture of excitement and fear as she imagined the explosive effect these data files could have in countries all over the world. Everything she had ever done in her life seemed to lead to this one moment.

"What can I do?" she asked.

"Find me a news outlet that has the courage to publish this," he said.

She thought for a few moments. "I know just the person: Bastian Obermayer. He knows more about shell companies than just about anyone. He's employed by Suddeutshe Zeitung in Munich. We've worked together for years. He'll do it and once it's out there, every paper in the world will have to report on it."

"Can you call him?" he asked.

"I know he'll insist on talking directly with you. But whatever you tell him, don't say anything that can reveal your identity. Just tell him you have some data files from Mossack Fonseca and would he be interested. Once he sees some of them, he'll jump all over it. Just say you're John Doe."

She opened her phone and in a second summoned up his number. "Here's my phone. It's fully encrypted. It can't be traced to me." She handed it to him.

They looked at each other, hardly able to breathe.

Rodriguez pressed call. On the fourth ring, he hung up. Sweat formed above his lip. After a few deep breaths, he made eye contact with Dora and called again. This time someone answered right away.

"Danke schön, Obermayer here."

Chapter 61

"You look good, Mr. President," shouted Raskolnovitch above the noise of the rotors. "And you, too, Paul," he said, shaking hands with his *krysha*'s political advisor. He handed them each a set of Bose headsets which allowed them to speak normally to each other and then lifted off into the sky like gods.

"How was China?" asked Raskolnovitch.

"I gained seven pounds in three days," said the president, patting his belly. "I'll need to see your tailor again," he said, turning to Manafort.

It always amused Raskolnovitch how much Manafort had groomed his *krysha* in his own image: same suits, same fake tan, same haircut. But it worked. He had transformed this ex-felon from his frumpy gangster image into a more competent looking executive, someone you could trust to get things done. The ubiquitous American-style political ads Manafort produced portrayed him as strong, optimistic, and kind. It was the ultimate makeover.

The president looked down at the tiny cars obediently driving along the highway in single file. "Thank you for picking me up, Viktor. I couldn't stand the thought of confronting all those journalists shouting at me. They're hyenas. 'How many people were killed yesterday? Did you order the attack on Bankova Street? Do you still have confidence in Zakherchenko?' Will this Euromaidan shit ever end?"

"Will it?" asked Raskolnovitch.

"It will," answered Manafort. "We just have to wait them out."

Raskolnovitch was doubtful. Manafort's advice felt naïve and out of touch. The Russians were going for broke and Raskolnovitch feared it would not end well for the president or for him.

"Paul, I've tried it your way," said the president. "But the protesters have been sleeping out in this fucking cold and snow for a month now. Bortnikov keeps pressuring me to use live ammunition. He thinks only a big killing will force them to leave. Zakherchenko's keeping the pressure on the protesters, but Moscow insists we need to do more. They're threatening to send in their own sharpshooters."

They flew over vast fields of hay stacked for winter feed that spread to the horizon. From the air it was easy to see why Ukraine was called the breadbasket of Europe. The land now lay vanquished under a sea of white.

"They're beginning to move troops to the border, I hear," added Raskolnovitch.

"Yes," frowned the president, the veins in his face growing more pronounced. "These *siloviki* know how to apply pressure. They're infiltrating hundreds of soldiers masquerading as partisans into Crimea. The Orange Revolution is starting to look like it was a picnic, compared to this."

"It was different last time," Raskolnovitch said. "Ten years ago, we could still compromise with our opponents. This time there doesn't seem to be an easy off ramp for us or them."

The motor seemed to stutter for a second, then continued.

Raskolnovitch pitched the helicopter towards Kyiv off to the west.

"They won't be satisfied unless we sign the Association Agreement and side with Europe," Manafort remarked.

"But Putin won't allow that," the president said. "He'll send his troops across the border knowing NATO wouldn't dare risk a ground war so far from home. NATO will impose sanctions, but that will be the extent of it. Russia has much more to lose here than the West does."

"I doubt Putin will do something so overt right before Sochi," said Manafort. "The Olympics are the ultimate symbol of his power and prestige."

"So, what's your next move?" Raskolnovitch asked the president.

"We try to stall Bortnikov as much as we can and hope time and Mother Nature wear down these rioters," answered the president.

So, he's bought into Manafort's strategy after all, Raskolnovitch thought. *He doesn't have the stomach for a real fight.*

On the horizon, as they approached the capital, the farm-lands, fenced in geometric order, were about to give way to the vertical shapes of an uneven urban landscape. Looming in front of them, lay the sprawling square known as the Maidan now occupied by a ragtag army in full siege.

"Shall we take a look?" asked Raskolnovitch, steering the Sikorsky low over the steel and concrete city towards the golden domes of St. Michael's and St. Andrew's. Snow, swirling around the protesters, blanketed pavements and streets. There were scores of tents and makeshift plastic shelters and bonfires scattered throughout the crowd with mostly young men and women, many in helmets, trying to keep warm. Raskolnovitch estimated there were around fifty thousand protesters, with at least ten thousand uniformed riot police and Berkut blocking the protesters from reaching the main government buildings.

The sight of so many people in the square braving freezing temperatures felt menacing to all three men. Their conversation stopped. Raskolnovitch circled the Sikorsky several times above the crowd, then headed towards the president's mansion on the outskirts of Kyiv.

"I'll admit it's an impressive crowd, but they'll eventually lose heart," said Manafort. "In the meantime, though, it's going to hurt our credit and investments."

The president turned towards him. "You know, Paul, having lost power once before, I learned nothing lasts forever. It can be a big mistake to wait too long to hedge one's bet. I'm beginning to move some assets, even some state funds, to offshore accounts, just in case the need should arise. I'm using Mossack Fonseca in Panama, as Viktor advised me."

Raskolnovitch said nothing. He didn't want to talk with his *krysha* about the trouble he was having with the firm. It would make him look weak. He changed the subject.

"I suppose you heard that I'm having a little trouble with Mogilevich," said Raskolnovitch.

"Stories do get around," said the president. "Firtash visited me last week. He never does anything without Don Semion's explicit approval. He told me he'd like to support me in the next election. I understood that to mean he wanted to replace you as my favored son. He and I have never been very close, as you know."

"Firtash and the Jews have never been your friend," Raskolnovitch noted.

"Depends. Mogilevich leaves me alone so long as I leave him alone. But none of these other Jews can deliver the kinds of votes and money that Firtash brings. He reminded me that he owns seven television stations, as if I didn't know. But you have nothing to worry about, Viktor—no one can replace you."

That he would say such a thing worried Raskolnovitch more than if he hadn't. The two of them had each been loyal to each other ever since the president was governor of Donetsk Oblast through his first term and later, when he lost in the Orange Revolution. It was always a marriage of convenience, though. With the pressure growing on the president from the protests, Putin and the EU, how convenient would it still be if Mogilevich pressed to get rid of him?

"But be careful," the president continued. "Mogilevich is out to get you. Firtash let slip that the Don's man, Lazovsky, met with General Dostum in Kabul. They might just be sending you a message, but they could mean business."

Raskolnovitch sneered. "Dostum would grind him under his tank treads before he'd turn on me, a technique he's famous for. He might be a monster but he's a loyal monster."

"Still, I would be careful. That's all I'm saying," said the president.

As if on cue, Raskolnovitch's cell phone rang in his earphones. It was his security chief, Kostya. One of their tobacco warehouses was on fire, the one just two miles down the road from the president's house. Raskolnovitch looked to his left and saw the flames in the distance.

"It seems you are right, Mr. President. I must be more careful. That fire up ahead is one of my warehouses. If it's a message they are sending me, I've got it. It will be war."

Chapter 62

"Da?"

"Viktor? Hi, it's Toni. I'm back in Kyiv. I'd like to speak with you. Are you free today?"

"Perhaps. How was Paris?"

"Paris is always Paris. It was wonderful. I love Paris in the snow," Toni said.

"The snow has stopped here," he said. "I was thinking of going hunting. Would you want to join me?"

"Not for hunting. You probably can guess that I'm on Bambi's side of the argument," she said.

"But you're a smoker," he answered.

"I didn't realize smokers all hunt. In any case, I don't anymore and I've stopped eating meat," she said.

"Where are you?" he asked.

"At the airport."

"I'll have a car bring you here. We can walk and talk, maybe snowshoe. Is all right?" he asked.

"Will I be safe?"

"That depends. Will I be recorded?" he asked.

"Let's declare a ceasefire. You won't imprison me, and I won't lie to you," she said.

"*O chen khah rah show*, very good, he said.

An hour and a half later a black town car arrived at his mansion. Raskolnovitch greeted her at the top of the stairs.

Opening his arms to the endless white expanse around them, he said, "Is beautiful, yes?"

"Like a fairy tale," she answered.

She felt at peace with herself and safe with him. They rode in an ATV on the narrow road behind the horse barn and into the forest where they had ridden before. The air was still. There was not a sound, not a leaf moving. Snow like diamond dust cloaked the land. They said nothing to break the silence. To speak in this vast stillness was a profanity. They parked where the road turned into a trail lined on either side by the white barked trunks of a birch grove. When he turned off the motor, the silence was deafening.

After several minutes, she turned to him. "How are you, Viktor? You look good."

He smiled. "I'm happy. Soon my troubles will be solved, God willing."

That morning Bertrand had assured him their plan was working. The girl was coming to the embassy the next morning bearing bonds like a sacrificial lamb. Soon he would be made whole again.

"And you, my dear. You are as ravishing as ever. Paris was good for you."

"It was. Like seeing an old friend. So many stories to recall. I went to the Marmatton to see the Petro Bevsta exhibit you funded. It's extraordinary. It inspired me to get seriously into my painting. Thank you," she said.

They were quiet again, neither of them sure how to proceed. She could see that Raskolnovitch was surprised she came back but remained hesitant to trust her. He sensed a lightness in her presence, despite himself, an ease he experienced with no one else. She brought out the best in him, she knew. But how much of his desire for her came from the challenge of winning her, she wondered? Men were like that, she understood. Did he fear that if he were to have her, that magic would disappear?

He reached in back and took out two pairs of red snowshoes that weighed almost nothing.

"Have you done this before?" he asked.

"When I was a child, but they were very different back then," she said.

"These are easier," he said.

They walked side by side in slow motion in the dazzling whiteness like ex-lovers with no direction back to each other. Toni knew her attraction to him was not rational, but she could not help herself from wanting to save him from himself. Everyone she consulted in Paris had warned her not to return. She insisted on giving him one last chance at redemption. If only he would trust her. In any case, her goal, above all else, remained to get him to testify against the former French president.

"Why did you come back here?" he asked.

"I'm not sure," she said. "It was folly for me to fall in love with you. That was a fantasy. It probably never could have worked. But I care about you, crazy as that might seem. I wanted to offer you a way out. You are too good a man to waste your life doing bad things and worrying what you might lose. Testifying against Gavi could be your ticket to freedom. I wanted to give you one last chance. I owe you that."

"Toni, you should have been a nun saving souls like Mother Teresa. But you're a spy, not a nun; and I'm a gangster, not a saint," he said.

"People can change," she said.

Raskolnovitch didn't respond. A shower of snow fell on their heads. They looked up to see two squirrels running along the branches. They continued walking one step at a time, lifting and pressing their weight against the forgiving snow. A single gray cloud cast a shadow across them before surrendering again to the sun.

"Are you still counting on Bertrand to help you?" she asked.

He smiled. "We'll see. He says he has everything under control."

"You asked why I came back here," she said. "Partly it was to warn you that Bertrand is lying to you. He hasn't contacted anyone at the Foreign Ministry or the Prosecutor's office about you. I checked. In fact, they were concerned that he wasn't responding to their requests. I don't know what he's up to, but he lies when he tells you he has an agreement."

Raskolnovitch stopped and faced her. "He says he has a deal. I need only produce the tape I made of Gavi cavorting with three prostitutes. I have it on my yacht which will be in Sebastopol tomorrow. I'm hosting an important meeting there tomorrow. I believe Bertrand will be able to complete the deal by then. It's in his own interests," he said.

This last remark struck alarm bells in Toni. Was it a slip of the tongue? She stored it in her mind to process later. Then she responded, "But there is no deal, Viktor. Believe me. I'm certain. Did he show you anything in writing—something like this?" She reached in her purse and pulled out an official looking folder and handed it to him. He peeled off his gloves and read it. The first page was in French but there was a translation on the next and succeeding pages.

In bold capitals across the top it read, RE VIKTOR RASKOLNOVITCH AGREEMENT TO WAIVE CRIMINAL CHARGES IN RETURN FOR TESTIMONY

Date

2014 14 November 00:00 (Thursday) P878719-0562_b

Original Classification

Secret Unclassified

Handling Restrictions

Sensitive —N/A or Blank—

Executive Order

R9 Helsmann, A A , Gavi, Jacque Text on digital fsx

Tags

Ukraine – European Union –Russia—UK Drug Enforcement
—Council of

USA—ENRG—Gavi—XTMinisters. Antoinette Schwab—
—CSCE Ministers—Pierre Brossolett Immunity—Wire tap—
Interpol 37563-LMF-16. Tax—PAL tape evidence.

From To

    Prosecutor General Assize Ct Ambassador Ukraine

    GD External Security

"This is a cable from the prosecutor in the Gavi case to the
General Directorate of External Security and the French
Embassy concerning a proffer of immunity to you in exchange for
your full, complete and truthful testimony including any physical
evidence concerning the guilt or innocence of Jacques Gavi,"
Toni told him. "This is what happens when there is a real deal.
Bertrand has nothing like this. But here it is. You can accept that
and be done with this. But you will have to cooperate fully."

"And deliver the tape, too?" he asked.

"Yes, of course," she said.

"Everyone wants the tape," he said. "You, Bertrand, even my

krysha. He wants it for leverage over Gavi. He thinks without the tape, Gavi won't get convicted. When this Euromaidan crisis escalates, Putin will need Gavi's support for Russia."

"Is the tape really that embarrassing? If Gavi is seen acting like a porn star having great sex with three women, the French public will love him all the more," she joked.

Raskolnovitch laughed out loud. "You're right. But when he asks the girls to beat him and barks like a dog? Believe me, my dear Antoinette, your Monsieur Gavi will not want anyone to see this tape."

They stopped by a wooden bridge that crossed a mountain stream. Sounds of gurgling water under a thin layer of ice broke the silence around them. On the opposite side of the creek was a vertical rock wall. Where a waterfall once cascaded, there was now a wall of icicles glittering like diamonds in the direct sun.

"*Eblouissant!*" exclaimed Toni. "Dazzling."

Raskolnovitch was quiet. After a minute he said, "I don't know about these bureaucratic things, this paperwork. Bertrand has another day to come through with everything I need. My problems are much bigger than this whole affair with Gavi. You won't be able to help me with those, but maybe Bertrand can. We'll see."

She couldn't imagine what he had promised him. Bertrand had no deal with the prosecution. That much was certain. There were rumors in Paris that he was under some kind of investigations over gambling debts and false expense reports. She couldn't see any way he could be useful to Raskolnovitch.

"Will you testify?" she asked, "and provide the tape?"

He didn't answer. She was wasting her time, she realized. She sensed he was flirting with the idea of living with her, starting a new life in France. But it was all a pipedream. He was in deep to his eyebrows in Ukraine with the president, the mafia, and this sordid entanglement with the young couple who ripped him off.

She was deluding herself that she could redeem him, one more bad boy she hoped would give it all up for her. She should have listened to her therapist.

"Tell me, Viktor, what's going to happen here? The demonstrations are getting bigger and more violent. Where's it all going to end?"

"The president's been listening to his American advisor, Manafort, who insisted the demonstrators would tire of this game. But three months and it's only getting bigger. Now, I think, he'll have to listen to the Russians. That will mean a bloodbath. I don't see any other way," he said.

"And then what?" she asked.

He shrugged. "Who knows. A revolution, probably, and then the Russians will take over again. It won't be pretty."

"And you? What will happen with you?" she asked.

Chapter 63

The road to the abandoned military airfield had more potholes than asphalt. Uncle Morris was in the front seat of the SUV next to the driver. Yuri, Yana and Taras were in the rear. Yuri glanced at his watch and realized that Dora was about to land in Kyiv and deliver the bearer bonds to the French Embassy. The driver kept apologizing as one after the other of them hit their heads on the roof. It was hard to see ahead in the dark and the freezing rain or to hear each other above the drumming of sleet and hail. Finally, they arrived at a rusted chain link fence through which they could make out an aluminum Quonset hut that once housed a squadron of jet fighters. A car parked beside it flashed its headlights twice.

Three armed security guards met them by the front of the hanger and escorted them inside. Seated at a table lit by kerosene lamps and surrounded by a half dozen aides dressed in camouflage outfits, Dmytro Mroz stood as they entered.

"It's like being inside a metal drum here," Yana said at the top of her voice.

"You get used to it," said Mroz.

He served them all tea from a large samovar that sat on the floor of the cavernous hangar.

"It's a good place. You chose well," Mroz said. "There are no enemy forces near here that we know of and it's close enough to Kyiv. Thank you."

"But it's cold as snot," Taras joked.

Yuri looked at his watch, then spoke up. "The plane we promised should arrive here in ten minutes. It's a much bigger shipment than we first agreed. We think the situation is coming to a head and it will be vital to get supplies out immediately if the Russians invade."

"They've already invaded," Mroz said. "Fifty Russian Special Forces took over the parliament in Crimea yesterday. They've taken off their insignias, but no one is fooled by these little green men. They've also stormed many of the administrative buildings in the Donbas and are arming and funding their so-called Donetsk and Luhansk People's Republic."

"They've got heavy equipment pouring across the border," Morris interjected, "some tanks, Grads and the newer BM30 Smerch multiple rocket launchers. There's no time to lose. We can only supply small arms at this point, but if you can bloody enough of these green men and separatist militia, they might hesitate before they venture too far west. It was the body bags coming back from Afghanistan that finally turned Russians against the war. Meanwhile, we need to gain time for the Ukraine Army to deploy."

"That won't happen until the regime falls," said one of Mroz's deputies. "The president has invited Putin to intervene."

"A real patriot," said Yuri. "But how much longer do you think the regime can last?"

"Days," said Mroz. "Zakharchenko signed a decree to authorize the use of live ammunition against protesters. They've used some already, but once there's a real bloodbath, we think they'll quickly lose whatever support they still maintain."

Something about the way he said that felt ominous, Yuri thought, but he said, "Then we must be prepared."

The sound of a plane motor stopped their talk. They all looked up, as if eyes could hear. A moment later, they rushed outside. The runway was illuminated with headlights from a half dozen cars and pickups. The sound of the plane grew louder above the noise of the pelting rain. Yuri looked at his watch. It would be on time to the minute. Finally, they could see its lights.

"I hope that runway is better than the road we just drove on," remarked Taras.

Out of the pitch black sky a four-engine C-130 Hercules roared its approach, landing smoothly and coming to a stop just a few meters from them. With the engines still running, the rear cargo flap opened and a few minutes later a Jeep eased down the ramp, turned and drove right up to them. Inside was a middle-aged man with a stubble of a beard dressed in civilian clothes. Morris walked up to him.

"Boris."

"Rabbi, it's so good to see you again," he said in German-accented English and saluted. Afraid I can't stay for tea. But help us unload this so I can get airborne quickly. I get nervous on the ground."

Morris introduced Yuri and Mroz. The security guards took up positions around the plane while everyone else helped unload six more Jeeps and dozens of crates. As instructed, Mroz had brought a forklift and within fifteen minutes the plane was emptied of its cargo. Boris waved to them from the opening of the hold which closed like a turtle's tail behind him and the turbo prop soon rumbled down the runway and lifted into the night sky.

"What've we got?" asked Mroz, excited as a kid at Christmas.

Morris looked over each container. "Here are your hunting rifles, which you can distribute right away, and here," he patted a wooden crate, "are a few sniper rifles. There are hundreds of grenade launchers, howitzers, and automatic rifles, mostly Czech, but we can't release them just yet, not until the Russians are seen as the aggressor. In the meantime, these arms will be well guarded here. Also, there's enough ammunition to fight a small war. You've only got a few hundred men right now, but there's enough gear and ammo for five thousand. Bigger items like Javelin anti-tank missiles and counter battery radar will have to come from NATO or the CIA. We're not quite there yet."

Yuri spoke up. "It's probably too late to stop Russia from taking over Crimea. The streets are already being patrolled by Cossack mercenaries and the Russian Fleet is based there. But we should be able to mount a defense of the Donbas. The oligarch, Kolomoysky, and I are each putting up ten million dollars to start with. He's funding the Azov and Dnipro battalions and we're both offering $10,000 bounties for the capture of any separatist leaders or Russian soldiers."

He turned to Morris, who laid out detailed plans for recruitment and training of volunteers and establishing a clear command and control structure. Mroz listened carefully. "When do we start?" he asked.

"Right away," answered Yuri. "But it's important that we not be the first to attack. You won't have to wait long, though, I'm afraid."

"We'll be ready," Mroz said.

Yuri felt good about Mroz, despite all the disturbing words he'd heard about his neo-Nazi leanings. Bandera volunteers had proved their courage on the Maidan and they were prepared to sacrifice themselves in defense of the country. There was no one else to draw on. NATO would not intervene and even the CIA was holding back, Morris told him. But he worried he hadn't heard from Dora. She should have landed by now and gone directly to the French Embassy, despite the late hour. Phone connectivity regrettably was non-existent out here. He wondered if he should have stayed back to accompany her and let Morris handle Mroz. But there really was nothing to worry about, he told himself. Dora could take care of herself.

Chapter 64

Dora had not closed her eyes once on the long flight from Panama City to Frankfort and Kyiv, afraid if she fell asleep someone might steal the attaché case she held in her lap. It might have been safer, she realized, to simply put it in the storage bin above her seat, but she would not let it out of her hands. She wished she hadn't had to check the Taser gun she bought for $800 at a store in Panama City that sold home security systems. The latest law enforcement model, the X26P Taser, could deliver 50,000 volts of energy, immediately disabling its victim. That was comforting.

It was an odd feeling to be carrying a billion dollars in shares payable to the "bearer." She had lied on the custom form she filled out when she marked the box that said she was not carrying more than ten thousand dollars. In truth, she was carrying a hundred thousand times that.

The Uber ride from the Kyiv airport felt as long as the flight from Panama. She couldn't wait to get inside the French Embassy and hand the certificates over to Bertrand for safekeeping. But despite the jetlag and fatigue, Dora felt a humbling sense of awe at the scale of what she had accomplished. Her journalist friend, Bastian Obermayer, had already contacted Marina Walker Guevara at the International Consortium of Investigative Journalists, who would go on to pull together a few hundred reporters to research the millions of documents from Mossack Fonseca. It was a far greater expose of corruption around the world than any of her colleagues had ever dreamed possible.

Before she left Panama City, she sent documents to the online newspaper *Ukrayinska Pravda* in Kyiv that proved the president was siphoning billions of dollars from the Treasury and spiriting them to shell companies he had set up in his name. Exposing that might just be the last straw that would break the back of the regime.

When, finally, she heard the locking mechanism in the door to the Embassy close with a definitive click behind her, she let out a long exhalation of relief. It was 10 p.m. and the Embassy hallways were nearly deserted, as a French National Gendarme in white patent leather boots and white belt and holster escorted her to the Consulate on the second floor and Bertrand's office. Seated behind a large Tricolor flag and a framed photograph of the French president, Bertrand leapt to his feet and embraced her when she entered. She was surprised by this exaggerated show of affection, so different from his usual formality.

"How wonderful to see you," he exclaimed. "You have the bearer bonds, I assume. No trouble along the way?"

"No," said Dora, "but I was terrified the whole time."

"Well, now you can relax. They're as safe as the Banque de France. May I see them?"

She handed him the attaché case. "There's a combination lock, 2175."

He opened it and took out a handful of papers which he glanced at, put back in their case, and placed it on the floor by his feet.

"As long as you remain in Kyiv, you may come here at any

time to retrieve them. We should meet again with Mr. Yavlinsky at the earliest opportunity to go over everything. How about the two of you meet me at my apartment the day after tomorrow?"

Dora nodded, "Sure."

At that moment there was a persistent knocking of the door and a tall, beautiful brunette, clearly agitated, walked into the room and announced, "Arnaud, we must speak."

He rose from his chair to protest. There was a look of terror on Bertrand's face. "I'm afraid I'm in a meeting, but we'll be through in a few minutes."

The woman glanced back and forth between Bertrand and Dora and then smiled.

"You must be Dora Osatinskaya," she said, extending her hand. "I'm Antoinette Schwab. I was the one who alerted Monsieur Bertrand when I learned that Raskolnovitch had located you through your cell phone."

Dora stood to shake her hand. "I've wanted to meet you and thank you for what you did. You saved my life."

"It appears I may have to save it again," said Toni, glaring at Bertrand.

Dora looked puzzled.

"What lies have you told her, Arnaud? Raskolnovitch told me he had a plan with you. What are you scheming?" said Toni.

"Get out of here this minute!" Bertrand shouted, but Toni only smiled.

"What has he told you, Dora?" she asked. "Did you know he's been meeting with Raskolnovitch, making some kind of deal with him? I saw him there. I was a prisoner in Raskolnovitch's mansion. He almost killed me when he discovered it was me who alerted you and saved you and your cousin."

Dora realized with a jolt that this was the spy inside Raskolnovitch's operation, the woman who saved her and her cousin's lives when the men in balaklavas came to kill them.

Toni turned to face Bertrand. "It's over for you, Bertrand. The Elysée knows all about this now. I've told them everything. But it appears they were already on to you and your gambling debts and all the false expense reports. It's over. *C'est fini.*"

Bertrand grabbed the attaché case and tried to push past her out the door, but Toni blocked the way. Seeing this, Dora latched on to the case with both hands and pulled it from him. Bertrand turned to get it back, drawing a small silver pistol from his jacket, but Toni brought him to his knees with a swift kick.

Dora heard a frantic pounding on the door and three uniformed National Gendarmes entered holding pistols attached by cords to their white holsters.

"Monsieur Consul General, on orders of the Prosecutor General of the Assize Court, you are being charged with criminal fraud. We are to detain you here tonight before sending you back to Paris tomorrow for a preliminary examination before a *juge d'instruction.* You will have the right to an attorney. Please accompany us now."

Chapter 65

Two hundred elite Spetsnaz sailors toting Kalashnikovs, wearing red berets and camouflage outfits, patrolled a half mile *cordon sanitaire* around the 80-meter tri-deck superyacht anchored alongside the Black Sea Fleet in Sevastopol, Crimea. The sky was a cauldron of black storm clouds. On the third deck, in a dark cherry wood paneled living room, seated before a warm fire, Toni and Raskolnovitch were finishing the final dessert of a twelve course meal prepared by his much-touted chef.

"I've never eaten so much or so well in my life," Toni admitted. "What are these tiny berries?"

"I've forgotten the name. They only grow in this one Himalayan village in Tibet, I'm told," Raskolnovitch said.

They had been eating for almost three hours, talking about Paris, the art world and what each of them might do in the future. Toni yawned. "I could use a nap," she said.

Raskolnovitch looked at his watch. "That would be perfect. I had planned to give you a tour of the boat after dinner, but I'm afraid we've run out of time. The president is due here in fifteen minutes and the other guests should arrive soon after. I would love to introduce you to them, but their presence in Crimea is a state secret. Once they've gone, though, I would love to show you around before we fly back to Kyiv.

"Why did you bring me here?" asked Toni. "Did Bertrand let you down?"

Raskolnovitch shook his head. "Probably you are right about him. I have tried to reach him all day. It doesn't matter. I've given up this dream of living in France. No, I brought you here to show you the boat and," he paused, collecting himself, "to say goodbye. I'm afraid I'll have to leave Ukraine for a while until things settle down."

They looked at each other in silence. Toni was not used to seeing him look so defeated. She was filled with a jumble of emotions from sympathy to loathing. He was not the person she hoped he'd be. She should have known better. Being a spy was like being a method actor. It had been easy to convince herself that she cared for him and easy to seduce a man when you're a beautiful woman. And yet, there was something about him, his alpha dog confidence, his manly grace, that had genuinely attracted her. There were moments when she felt guilty for betraying him. But people rarely change.

"Where will you go?" she asked.

He didn't know.

"What about your house and the Faberge Eggs?"

"I've already shipped all the art and valuables off for safe-keeping," he said.

"So, the revolution is coming soon, you think?"

"That or a civil war, I'm afraid." He shrugged. "In either case, I need to hedge my bets. You probably saw the reports that the president is sending his money out of the country. I need to be prudent. This will all blow over in time and then we'll see."

She studied him. He seemed weakened. When she didn't say

anything, he added, "Maybe you and I will meet again in different circumstances."

He looked at his watch again, stood, and pointed to a door almost hidden in a wall. "That's the door to my bedroom. Feel free to take a nap there, but please excuse a bachelor's drawings. And Toni, don't try to wander. There are guards posted everywhere."

"Do you plan to imprison me once again, this time here on your pleasure boat?" she asked.

"Not at all," he said. "I'll not be long, I expect. These are very busy men. As soon as the meeting is finished, we can leave after a quick tour."

The men came in one at a time, faces somber, leaving their security guards outside the large revolving dining room which had been swept for bugs by an Alpha Group counter-intelligence team. The president and Paul Manafort arrived first and stood in a corner with Raskolnovitch. The president appeared nervous and Raskolnovitch wondered if he might be drunk.

"Viktor Ivanovich," the president started, "this war of yours with Mogilevich has got to stop. This is no time for personal vendettas. Bortnikov told me Putin himself wanted it to end."

"Of course, but make sure Don Semion gets the message, too. He needs to back off," Raskolnovitch said.

"And what about this French thing? The girl you're dating and the Gavi case?" the president asked.

"It's over, completely over. They offered me immunity if I testified against him. But, of course, I refused," Raskolnovitch said.

"Viktor Ivanovich," said Manafort. "It's good that you refused. You should know that Putin is betting heavily on Gavi. You say you have a video that could compromise him?"

"Yes, it's upstairs in my safe. I don't need it anymore."

"Excellent," said Manafort. "When this meeting ends, please get it to us. We could use it to keep Monsieur Gavi on our side."

The door to the dining room opened and Rinat Akhmetov walked in. A bland-looking man with beady eyes and pinched nose, Akhmetov had been an enforcer for Akhat Bragin, the Godfather of the Donetsk Clan, but reportedly was behind the bombing outside his football club that killed Bragin and six of his bodyguards. Somehow Akhmetov inherited Bragin's assets and became one of the richest oligarchs in Ukraine. It was Akhmetov who started the president on his political career, appointing him Governor of Donetsk Oblast, and later hired Paul Manafort to run his campaign for the Presidency.

Next to come in was Dmytro Firtash, stylishly dressed in a dark blue suit and silver tie that matched the color of his well-coiffed hair. Everyone understood him to be representing Mogilevich. He was followed by Oleg Deripaska, the largest aluminum producer in the world and an oligarch with close ties to the Izmailovsky Syndicate, another Russian organized crime group. Close behind them came two Russians, Alexander Bortnikov, Putin's spymaster, and Yevgeny Prigozhin, known as Putin's chef, but an oligarch in his own right who took on much of the Kremlin's dirty work abroad. Bortnikov took his seat at the head of a large mahogany table and the others sat on either side of him.

"Comrades, it's good we are all here," Bortnikov began. "Thank you, Viktor Ivanovich. This is a difficult moment and we must all work together. It is time we put aside our differences." He looked first at Firtash and then Raskolnovitch. "Tomorrow, we can expect some conclusion to the fascist riots that have been taking place in the capital for too long. These provocations require a stronger hand. No longer will rubber bullets suffice."

Addressing the president, Bortnikov went on, "You have asked for our assistance and we'll give it to you. Two days ago, the

Russian Parliament approved the use of military force in Ukraine. Already, here in Crimea, we have effectively taken over the Rada and control all key administrative facilities. We are conducting large scale training exercises on the border and have massed sufficient troops to deter any Western interference. But we hope to avoid a direct invasion in order to limit the reaction by the West. President Putin is determined not to mar the finale of the Sochi Olympics next week."

Prigozhin spoke next, waving his finger in the air, commanding authority. "From a propaganda perspective, there will be no images of Russian soldiers. Resistance to the fascist coup will come from local armed separatists." Nodding to Akhmetov, he added, "Thank you, Rinat Leonidovych. Your generous support for these partisan brigades in Donetsk is a model that I trust others of you will follow."

"You're welcome," said Akhmetov.

Bortnikov, who was drinking copious amounts of water, spoke again. "President Putin likes to quote that Canadian hockey star. What's his name? Gretsky. 'Play to where the puck is going to be.' Whatever happens tomorrow on the Maidan, we can expect punitive sanctions from Europe and the United States to follow immediately." He put down his glass.

"Everything must be done to limit these sanctions," said Bortnikov. "We have developed detailed plans which we expect you to help us carry out. The goal is to cause as much division in the West as possible."

He turned to Raskolnovitch. "Viktor Ivanovitch, we understand you have some influence with the former French President Gavi. He is an important and respected voice for a rapprochement with Russia. He might be persuaded to oppose sanctions. Do what you can to encourage him."

Raskolnovitch blanched. He was so tired of these political schemes. And he disliked this guy Bortnikov, a pushy bully he'd like to take out with an uppercut to his glass jaw. He was tired of all of them, so corrupt, so full of themselves.

Prigozhin, waving his finger again, elaborated, "We are lavishly funding populist and nationalist parties in France, Germany, Italy, Poland, Hungary and elsewhere. Also, separatist movements in Great Britain and Spain. Our intelligence agencies believe there is a growing wave of anti-establishment anger in the Western democracies, which we can exploit, especially through the Internet. We've had great success with this strategy in Georgia, but we are about to go all in here with a massive disinformation campaign that will be run out of the Internet Research Agency in St. Petersburg, which I head, and the GRU's Main Center for Special Technology."

Raskolnovitch had a sinking feeling that all this bravado was nothing but a prelude to a looming disaster. He had trouble concentrating. He wished he could be back in his stateroom with Toni. His mind wandered to all the preparations he had made to safeguard his wealth. Whatever fate these men had in mind for the protesters, no one, not even his *krysha*, believed things could return to normal.

Oleg Deripaska spoke up. "This is all good, but we need to engage the mainstream political parties, as well." He turned to Manafort. "Paul, I've been paying you ten million dollars a year to build political support for Putin's policies in the U.S. and Europe. Tell them what you told me your former partner, Roger Stone, said." He turned back to Bortnikov. "Stone's convinced Donald Trump to run for president and he thinks he can get Paul hired to run his campaign."

They all looked at Manafort, who managed a salesman's grin. "Roger Stone and I have been involved in a number of presidential campaigns over the last thirty years," Manafort said. "But we think the next election will be different. Americans don't want another politician. They want someone strong enough who can take down the political establishment. I think Trump's the perfect candidate. He's his own man, a celebrity, and he's rich enough that he won't have to bow down to special interests."

"You must have a direct line to our president," Prigozhin said. "Putin said almost the exact same thing to me the other day, that a TV personality could be elected president in America."

"Even if he can't win, he will create divisions in the country that we can exploit," Akhmetov added.

"Maybe he'll be able to pay us back all the money we've loaned him," Firtash joked, provoking general laughter from the other oligarchs. They had all laundered money through Trump's properties and golf courses.

"Is it true that Don Semion bought a whole floor of Trump Tower when Trump's casinos went bankrupt?" Deripaska asked Firtash.

Firtash smiled.

Not to be outdone, Prigozhin added, "Trump's compromised in more ways than one. I've seen a tape our counter-intelligence department has passed around of him performing perverse acts with prostitutes in a Moscow hotel a couple years ago. He appears to like to watch girls piss on themselves. For the life of me, I don't get it."

On the deck above them, Toni Schwab scanned the walls of Raskolnovitch's bedroom with a Schonstedt Magnetic Locator wand until she heard the telltale ping of a metal safe hidden behind one of the Kama Sutra paintings of a man on his back sexually engaged with five women. She laughed to herself.

Finding a way to open the panel took a while, but she finally found a soft spot on the breasts of another woman depicted in a different panel that, when she pressed it, released a three-by-three foot section that covered a steel safe.

One of the newer digital models, it would be hard to crack, she knew. But anticipating that, she had brought with her a fingerprint kit. Lightly dusting the ten digit key code with a magnetic applicator, she ran a battery powered UV lamp over it which revealed blue florescent prints on three of the keys. It could be three numbers or four, if one were repeated, perhaps ten thousand different combinations. She might only have three chances before an automatic locking system would shut the device down.

She looked at her watch. Twenty-three minutes had passed since Raskolnovitch had left. She felt sweat bead on her forehead. God knows what he would do if he caught her. She tried the first three digits of his phone number. No luck. Then, holding her breath, she tried his birthdate, 1124, and, miraculously, there came the sweet whirling sound of tumblers falling into place. She opened the door. Inside were bundles of cash in dollars, rubles, hryvnias and euros and dozens of DVD's in plastic cases. She shuffled through them. There were names of various politicians she recognized and then the one she was searching for marked "Gavi."

She closed the safe and the wood panel on the wall, then left him a quick note with lipstick on the mirror above his bed that said simply, "We must all hedge our bets." Then she slipped the tape into a waterproof bag she carried in her purse and walked out to the hot tub deck. Behind the Plexiglas wall with his back turned to her was a Spetsnaz sailor in camouflage looking out from the helipad. She tiptoed towards him, but the wood covering squeaked and he turned to face her not three feet away.

"Excuse me," she said with her most coquettish smile, "Could you give me a hand?" As she turned back to the bedroom, she dropped her bag. When the sailor bent down to get it, she pivoted in one motion and kneed him hard. He hit the ground and she kicked him on the side of his head, knocking him out.

On the wharf there were a dozen or more sailors in red berets smoking and laughing. For a moment, time seemed to stop, as she scanned the scene below her. Then, without hesitation, she launched herself over the side, falling three stories into the black water below. She held her hands against her body, diving as deep as she could. A few of the sailors turned at the sound but paid no attention and thirty seconds later she made her way under the wooden docks and escaped into the early evening night.

Chapter 66

"We were incredibly naïve," Dora told them, walking along the tree lined path to the Babi Yar memorial. She was tired but eager to join the fray again. The snow had mostly melted from the grass, leaving patches of white here and there. Crows cawed nearby.

"Very," Yuri replied. "But we had every reason to trust Bertrand."

Dora agreed, "He saved my life and without him you and Yana would never have gotten out of Prague alive."

"I worked with the French DGS on their investigation and no one ever warned me about him," Uncle Morris said. "Well, all's well that ends well. The bonds are safely hidden in Leon's tailor shop for now."

There was much to catch up on. It was the first time the three of them had been together since Dora came back from Panama.

"What did you think when that woman came in yelling at Bertrand?" asked Yuri.

"I had no idea what was going on until she realized who I was and introduced herself. I still had no reason to suspect Bertrand. But when he grabbed the attaché case and tried to run, it all made sense in an instant," Dora said. "Afterwards, she and I talked till two in the morning. I learned a lot about Raskolnovitch and Toni, too. Her grandparents on her mother's side were French partisans, fighting with the resistance in the Jura mountains. They were executed by the Nazis just a week before the war ended. Her father served in the French Foreign Legion in Algeria and was quite conservative, apparently. Toni was an artist, pretty apolitical, studying to be an actor when she was recruited by the DGS because of her extraordinary language abilities. She still considers herself an actor. I think Toni and I will remain good friends."

She glanced at Uncle Morris and thought what a handsome couple he and Toni would make, two gonzo spies. She wondered when they'd have a chance to meet. Yuri took her hand. She turned to him. "You'd like her, Yuri. She's beautiful and incredibly brave."

"I'd love to," said Yuri. "She sounds a lot like you." Dora squeezed his hand.

Yuri told her about their meeting with Mroz and the arms shipment. Then they walked silently.

"You're unusually quiet today, Uncle Mo," said Dora. "What are you thinking about?"

"I was thinking about the 34,000 Jews that were machine gunned to death here in 1941 and a line from Yevtushenko's poem about Babi Yar where he says,"

I'm every old man executed here,
As I am every child murdered here.

"Humans are capable of such hatred," Dora mused out loud. She reflected on their own hatred of Raskolnovitch and thought of something Toni had told her. "It is always better to understand your enemy, to see the world as they see it, rather than judge them." But how? she asked herself, as she walked atop this hallowed earth.

Chapter 67

The neon lights startled Viktor when he entered the gym from the dark corridor in the basement of his mansion. It had been months, he realized, since he had worked out down here. He threw his bathrobe over one of the elliptical machines and put on a pair of red boxing gloves, wrapping the Velcro bands tightly around his wrists. A speed punching bag hanging in one corner beckoned him. As he approached in his bare feet, he felt the rage begin to rise, but kept it steady, under control. Striking the bag with the side of one fist after another, he felt old muscle memories reawaken as the staccato sounds of fist against leather accelerated to a rhythmic crescendo. One, two, three, one, two, three.

Images of Toni riding a horse, skating at Davos, dining on the boat flashed through his mind. A slideshow of betrayal. He replayed the memory of seeing her note in lipstick on the mirror above his bed, mocking him. With each return of the bag, his rage grew. He felt the strength returning to his arms. He would get his revenge.

The easy rat-tat-tat of the speed bag could not contain his simmering fury. He turned to the heavy bag behind him and began to pummel it with relentless blows, denting it with all his might. He cursed out loud, driving himself further and further until his body gave out and he crumbled to the floor gasping for breath. He would get his revenge.

An hour later, after sauna and breakfast, Raskolnovitch entered the library, now empty of Faberge Eggs and artifacts, and signaled for his guests to remain seated. His anger at Toni and at Yuri and Dora had not subsided. Seated in upholstered chairs around a polished cherry wood coffee table were Kostya, his chief of security, Dima Prokofiev, and the two Israeli operatives, Harry Beinfeld and Chaim Kurtz.

"Do we have a plan?" Raskolnovitch asked without introduction.

Chaim Kurtz, the tall redhead, said, "Our original plan is probably too risky, too many variables we can't control. But we've discovered something that could be a game changer."

"What can't you control? I liked the plan. The Firtash boy would be just the bargaining chip we need, and it would embarrass the Don."

Kurtz nodded, but he continued in the same tone. "For starters, Firtash has six or eight bodyguards with him at all times. With Mogilevich and at least six other oligarchs expected, we anticipate more than thirty armed security guards will be there. The boy will be riding in an armor-plated town car with his family. There'll be a security car fore and aft of it. They'll park two blocks from the synagogue and walk from there—they won't want to be seen riding on the Sabbath. The guards will be on their highest alert during that walk. Once they get into the synagogue, it will be very difficult to get the boy alone."

"What about at the reception?"

"We looked into abducting him in the kitchen. There's an exit to an alley behind the synagogue. They blocked it off during the rehearsal and we expect they will for the service and reception. They had a guard posted at the kitchen door, as well. We can anticipate that Mogilevich will have redundant security on top of whatever Firtash provides."

"What about a diversion, an explosion outside or something?"

Harry Beinfeld, the short bald partner, spoke up, "The bodyguards' immediate reaction will always be to surround the family. We've tried to think of every angle, but with so much security, there aren't any good options. With assassinations or bombings there are always possibilities, but with kidnapping there are few."

Kurtz held up his hand. "We could brainstorm this all day, but there's a much better opportunity that's presented itself, that you will like, Mr. Raskolnovitch. We've managed to intercept calls to Firtash's cell phone. One of them was from a rabbi, a Morris Weissgold, apparently a relative of the Yavlinsky boy and Ms. Osatinskaya. We think he's the same Morris Weissgold who was exposed on WikiLeaks as a CIA contractor in Iraq. He was calling Firtash to arrange a meeting with Mogilevich at the synagogue, which confirms that Don Semion is planning to be there, as we hoped. Firtash invited him to the reception after the service. But more importantly, this rabbi's bringing Yavlinsky and Osatinskaya with him."

The room was quiet for a minute as Raskolnovitch absorbed the import of this information. Kurtz continued, "Instead of kidnapping the bar mitzvah kid, we can grab the two you've been looking for, and it would be much easier."

"How?" asked Raskolnovitch, leaning forward on his seat.

"We get hold of a police car and four uniforms and grab the boy and girl off the street in front of the synagogue," said Kurtz. "We use some of your *Vory* friends. We can't do that with the Firtash boy because the bodyguards would use force, if necessary, to prevent that. They'd insist on seeing a warrant or whatever. They'd never allow them to take Firtash's son into custody. But these two shmucks? Nobody's going to stop the police from taking them away. And the beauty of this is that none of the other guests or their bodyguards will have their cars to follow them."

"And this rabbi?" asked Kostya.

Kurtz smiled, holding up a silver pen. "This can shoot a dart three meters through layers of clothing and disable someone in seconds. We could take out their security guards as well."

"Sounds like we've got a plan, gentlemen," Raskolnovitch said.

As the meeting broke up, Kostya pulled Raskolnovitch aside. "Boss, these yids are afraid of doing anything inside the damn synagogue. Believe me. I scoped it out with them during the rehearsal. The place is practically unguarded at night. I could get in there on Friday and place plastic explosives inside the ark where they stash all their silver scrolls. We could attach a trigger to one of them and when they lift it out at the start of the service, the whole synagogue would come down. You could kill Mogilevich, Yavlinsky, Osatinskaya and a half dozen Jewish oligarchs in one swoop. And we could plant evidence to make it look like those Bandera Brigade guys did it."

Raskolnovitch smiled, patted Kostya on his shoulder. *What a elegant idea. Fuck these damn Jews*, he thought.

Chapter 68

Yuri, Dora and Uncle Morris walked briskly towards the synagogue, their two guards trailing discreetly fifty feet behind them. There were many others on the street heading for the Saturday morning Shabat service on a day when the weather had warmed enough to melt some of the snow off the trees. It was comforting to be among so many people walking peacefully.

Dora was feeling ambivalent about this meeting with Mogilevich. With allies like Mroz and the head of the Russian mafia, who'd be their friends? "Tell me again why we're meeting with these mobsters," she asked. Morris slowed, facing her. "Our goal is to take down this Raskolnovitch character. Nothing's changed. For the moment, at least, the mob's on our side. Yuri was smart to ask for their help in Mariinsky Park. It saved your lives. Maybe there are ways we can help each other put Raskolnovitch out of business."

Dora was exasperated. "How does this change anything? The corruption doesn't stop. It just goes to Mogilevich instead of Raskolnovitch. He'll just take over the business."

"You're right in a way," said Morris. "In the short term

anyway. But Raskolnovitch is out to kill you and you'll need more power than you have to stop him. There's a much bigger game going on, as well. If we can bring down Raskolnovitch, the president's main financial backer, we weaken the whole system of oligarchical rule. It's not just Raskolnovitch anymore. It's part of the revolution to turn Ukraine towards the West, away from Russia, and create a democratic state with the rule of law."

Dora looked at him dubiously. They continued to argue with each other as the synagogue came into view. Yuri, Dora and Morris walked past the Besarabsky Market, shuttered for Sabbath, and came up to the front of the synagogue where Rabbi Azman was greeting congregants as they came in.

"Moishe," exclaimed Azman, opening his arms to hug Uncle Morris.

"Rebbe," said Morris.

"And Mr. Yavlinsky. It's good to see you again," said the rabbi.

As Yuri turned to introduce Dora, he noticed a white van parked across the street and a man holding a large telephoto lens leaning out of the driver's side window. He assumed it was the routine surveillance that documented meetings of mafia dons, like so many movies he had seen.

But suddenly, Uncle Morris grabbed his chest and slumped to the ground as he was about to speak. Yuri saw their security guards go down, as well.

A moment later there was the sound of a siren. A police car, white with yellow and blue stripes, came careening around the corner with its lights flashing and screeched to a halt before the crowd of people surrounding Rabbi Azman. Four policemen leapt from their car guns drawn. "Dora Osatinskaya?" said one to Dora. She nodded, then was grabbed on either side by a policeman and shoved into the back seat. The two others took Yuri by the arms and, pushing his head down, threw him in the back with her. He wanted to fight back but felt himself overpowered. A policeman pressed in on either side of them and shut the rear doors while their two partners sat in front. It all took less than ten seconds before they sped away, sirens blaring.

"Where are you taking us?" asked Yuri. Looking back, he saw people crowded around Morris and the two guards who lay prone on the ground. It was all happening too fast. How could he protect Dora?

None of the policemen said anything. A few blocks from the synagogue, they turned the sirens off.

At first Dora assumed these were police hoping to score the $50,000 reward offered for each of them. "We can pay you twice the reward money, if you release us," she said, something she had rehearsed in her mind when she imagined this moment coming. But none of the cops reacted at all. Then she wondered about the long hair that hung over the shirt collars of two of the men. They just didn't look or act like police, she thought. "You're not cops, are you?" she asked.

The man seated next to her by the door slapped her hard with his left hand. Yuri reached across her, trying to hit him; but the cop next to him grabbed his arm and held a knife against his throat.

"No more funny stuff," he said. Dora's face stung. She was terrified but glad to see Yuri surrender and sit back when the man put the knife away.

The driver of the car had his arm draped across the top of the front seat. There was a gold ring on his forefinger with an engraved skull inside a square, a design Dora recognized from a paper she wrote in law school about the *Vory*. It signified that the man had been convicted of robbery. She had noticed a similar *Vory* ring on Raskolnovitch in photos she studied in the prosecutor's office with a symbol for killing a policeman, considered a badge of some honor in the gulag.

These were no police. She reached into her right coat pocket and felt the metal handle of the Taser she bought in Panama City. She would remember the feeling, the cold lethality of it, for the rest of her life. She made eye contact with Yuri for a second, then she pulled out the gun, jammed it into the back of the driver's neck and pulled the trigger. He screamed and slumped over the steering wheel. The recoil sent her back against the seat as the car careened, crashed headlong into a semi-trailer, spun around three times, and smashed against a statue of Taras Shevchenko. The front of the car was pulverized, the two fake cops in the front seat unconscious, if alive. Above the sounds of the explosion, the driver's scream, and scraping of metal against metal, Dora could hear her heart pounding. The shattered glass cut the four of them in back, but, except for some blood, they were largely unhurt. The men next to Yuri and Dora pushed open their doors and fled on foot.

Chapter 69

"Yuri, it's Yana. Sorry to wake you. I know it's late, but the Trade Union Building, our headquarters, is on fire."

"We'll come right over," he said. Yuri picked up his watch on the bedside table. It was 3 a.m. He didn't know how they might help, but Yana was sounding desperate and he needed to support her, if nothing else. Dora sat up next to him.

"I'll go," said Yuri. "You go back to sleep. You just flew back to back red-eyes to and from Panama. You've got to get some rest." He knew she had to be emotionally spent after yesterday morning's kidnapping and car crash and the altercation with Bertrand at the French Embassy. But she insisted on joining him.

There was a knock on their door. Morris was there, already up and dressed, having overheard the conversation from the adjoining room. They were staying at some cheap hotel two blocks from the Maidan. The lobby downstairs had a Keurig coffee maker and the three of them, Dora, Yuri and Rabbi Morris, took turns ravenously fueling themselves with as much caffeine as they could stomach. They were too tired to talk. Walking outside, a bitter wind assaulted them. The sky was black. From a couple blocks away on the Maidan, they could hear a drum circle rhythmically beating as if it were the collective pulse of the revolution. Fires burning in oil drums illuminated the square. Everywhere he saw tents and makeshift shelters constructed with plastic sheeting.

The fire at the Trade Union building was already extinguished by the time they arrived, but the smoke and smell hung in the frigid air. Yuri approached a group of medics in white helmets who were sharing cigarettes around a fire pit, raising his fist in the ritual salute. "Hi. We came when we heard about the fire," said Yuri. "What happened?"

A young girl in blond pigtails said she didn't know how it started. "Snipers shot and killed several of us who were fighting it. They tried to disperse us, but we held. They're crazy if they think they can defeat this army of the people," she declared. Yuri could see in her face a resolve that could not be shaken by any force.

Arriving at the smoldering building, they looked for Yana and Taras amid the chaos of the ground floor hospital that had become a scene of carnage. Limp bodies were rushed in on stretchers and lined up on the blood soaked floor as medics frantically fought to save the living. They found Yana holding a bag with a saline solution over a patient lying on the concrete floor. Her face was smeared from sweat and tears. She looked like she hadn't slept in days.

"At least twenty died here last night," she told him. She seemed to be pleading with him. Yuri wanted to console her, but this was not the time or place for that.

"The hardest thing is knowing when someone has died and should not be resuscitated," she said. "I never thought I would be the one to pull the sheet over the heads of such beautiful young men." She began to cry again but was interrupted by the shouts of the growing crowds gathered outside: "Glory to Ukraine,

Death to Our Enemies." After the fire, the mood of the protesters had darkened.

Taras came up beside them depositing another stretcher with a wounded protester. Volunteer medics quickly took over. "Word on the street is it was Russian-trained Alpha Group sharpshooters who set fire to the building, and 1500 Russian airborne soldiers and 400 marines are deployed under the direction of the SBU," said Taras, referring to Ukraine's Security Service. He said the Interior Minister, Zakharchenko, went on television after midnight to announce that they had begun arming the Berkut with lethal combat weapons. Yana added, "I spoke with some BBC journalist who said that the president had sacked the head of the armed forces and that the Deputy Chief of Staff resigned to protest the use of the army."

"It's time to put an end to all this," Taras told Uncle Morris, who was standing next to him. Everyone understood the curtain had risen on the final act. They were ready to give their lives for the revolution. Taras and Yana were inconsolable.

Looking at the pools of blood on the concrete floor, Yuri thought about his great-grandmother and step-dad and the blood in his apartment. Their deaths and the ones on the Maidan were one and the same. It was all one war. He wanted revenge. But, did he? No, it was no longer just revenge, he told himself. That wasn't enough. He wanted victory. The regime of wealth and corruption had to end, here, this very day on the Maidan.

For Dora the sight of such wasted lives made her angry enough to kill. She had perhaps already done so yesterday when she fired her Taser into a man's skull. She felt no guilt about that, nor about the guns they were supplying to the Bandera Brigade. It was all self-defense. She thought of a paper she once wrote extolling Gandhi and non-violence. It might have worked in

India back then, she thought. Now the killing of unarmed protesters left them little alternative but to meet force with force.

"Where are our guns?" she asked Taras.

"They're coming. I saw some of Mroz's self-defense forces heading for the Hotel Ukraina, the Kozatsky Hotel, and the Zhortnevyi Palace with some of the 7.62 mm shotguns and sniper rifles we gave them," Taras told her.

It frightened her to think that Ukrainian citizens could do this to each other. How much more might they do? She could see with her own eyes the brutality that humans were capable of. But she was equally moved by the heroism of the doctors, nurses, and volunteers. She watched as Yuri spoke with the wounded and saw the strength he brought them and felt her heart open to him.

With the first light of day, Dora stepped outside and saw volunteers hanging canvas screens on the sides of the building emblazed with the words "Glory to Ukraine, Glory to the Heroes." Suddenly, the shouting and chaos quieted inside the makeshift hospital. The doctors, their blue smocks covered in blood, stood for a moment of silence, crossing themselves as pall bearers carried out some of the coffins. An Orthodox priest, swinging incense, led them in prayer.

As the chants of the volunteers and the wounded rose around her, Dora felt as if she were being carried away by angels. It was a feeling of purification, of an absolute love unlike anything she had ever experienced before. She was ready to die for this cause, she realized, or to kill.

A procession formed behind the priests as they left the hospital. It was early morning, but there were already tens of thousands of people gathered outside. Yuri signaled for Dora and Morris to follow him behind the caskets which snaked their way through the crowd gathered on the Maidan. As the pallbearers passed through the throngs of protesters, old women wept, and everyone began singing the national anthem. The bells of Saint Michael's Monastery pealed in the distance.

Yuri choked up. The protest city had become a living organism. There was little talk anymore; people just looked into each other's eyes. They had all passed beyond their fears.

Yuri felt this day would be decisive. The Bandera Brigade had called for a "peaceful offensive" aimed at the parliament for 8:30 a.m., throwing down the gauntlet. University student organizations and trade unions had joined the call and now an unending river of people began a silent, dignified march to the Verkhovna Rada. Either the government would give way or there would be a bloodbath. Surrounded as he was by so many peaceful demonstrators, the anger and despair he felt at the hospital in the Trade Union building began to give way to feelings of optimism and shared humanity. Women walked with baby strollers, whole families marched hand-in-hand.

He put his arms around Dora's shoulders and whispered, "I love you, Dora."

Surging forward on a wave of humanity, Yuri felt a power that had eluded him his entire life. Growing up under Soviet rule and then in a society, nominally independent, but thoroughly corrupted by oligarchs, he had learned to survive without hope or opportunity. His only escape was cleaning up elephant shit at the zoo and drawing cartoons in the middle of the night in a room he shared with his great-grandmother. But at this moment, surrounded by tens of thousands of citizens like him, Yuri felt his dignity restored. No wonder that people were calling this the Revolution of Dignity. The power he felt now he shared equally with all the men, women and children around him. It was like shedding an old skin.

"I just don't understand humanity," said Dora, as if reading his thoughts. "Here we are among ordinary people risking their lives to have a voice in their government. All they want is to get rid of the criminals who have taken over the state. And there," she said, pointing to a line of Berkut armored like Darth Vader, "what is it they're fighting for—more corruption?"

"They're paid to fight, like the *titushki*, who get released from jail and paid $25 a day to beat us," said Yuri.

"I get the *titushki*, but I don't understand how the Berkut can do this," said Dora.

"They've been told that without them there would be anarchy. They've learned to fear freedom and democracy and they're well paid. There aren't other jobs for them," said Yuri.

He looked at her intently. "You know, Dora, when I first met you all I could see were those violet eyes. I was a little intimidated by you, to be honest. But now I really see you, all of you. You're the strongest, bravest woman I've ever known. You brought me out of the shadows and gave me back my life. If anything happens to me here, know that I fulfilled my greatest ambition, to love and be loved."

Dora looked at him without words. Tears streamed down her face.

As they reached the line of last defense, Yuri saw a formation of Berkut officers stand their ground and take aim at the oncoming marchers; suddenly, they were met with volleys of shotgun blasts. Two young men fell just in front of them. Yuri pulled Dora to the ground and shielded her under him. Everywhere there was screaming. Morris yelled for them to run back out of range. What had been an orderly and peaceful demonstration instantly turned into a chaotic retreat.

They slowed to watch the shock troops of the Bandera Brigade in a mad fury overturn several personnel transport trucks blockading the building of the Central Officers Club, breaking through police lines and flanking the Berkut. From Shovkovychna Street the police, armed with Fort-500T shotguns, fought back with a barrage of stun grenades.

Now the full force of the state was thrown at the protesters. "We need to get out of here," Morris shouted. As Yuri, Dora and Morris retreated along with thousands of demonstrators towards Khryschatyk, the main shopping street of Kyiv, snipers fired from rooftops, picking off individual protesters. Braving continuous gunshots and explosions, young men holding makeshift shields rushed to retrieve the bodies, only to be killed themselves. Morris stopped to help someone pull his injured friend to safety, dragging him along the ground by his feet. Two volunteer medics came up and took the young man on a stretcher to the hospital in the Trade Union Building.

"They're shooting people randomly like animals," shouted Yuri above the constant sound of explosions and firearms."

Dora. just shook her head. While they waited for Morris to catch up with them, they could see protesters regrouping behind barricades of dump trucks positioned to block the marchers from getting to the parliament, but the momentum was with the police who pressed forward in a last determined assault to clear the square and end the rebellion, crushing the protestors, Yuri and Dora among them.

Chapter 70

Morris came running up to them breathing hard, holding his phone. "Let's go," he said, "I just heard from Taras that the president's Party of Regions headquarters on Lypska Street is burning. There's not much we can do here right now. Let's join Taras and Yana there."

"Good—I don't like being so separated from them," said Dora.

When they arrived at the scene, there was black smoke billowing from the drive-in entrance to an interior courtyard and firemen in orange suits with oxygen tanks strapped to their backs were dragging fire hoses through the front door. Smoldering papers and pamphlets littered the grounds.

They found Taras and Yana standing with a group of onlookers. Yuri came over to them and whispered something to Taras. Suddenly, the two of them bolted past the firemen and into the burning building. Uncle Morris held Yana and Dora back. Inside the air was dense with smoke. Yuri led the way up a set of stairs by the courtyard. He could hardly see anything. They rushed up three more flights to the top floor.

"Where we going?" shouted Taras, coughing. Their voices

seemed muffled. They could hear walls collapsing nearby and the sounds of sirens and gunshots outside, and felt the heat rising steadily, but it was as if they were in a bubble. "I think the director's office will probably be up here," shouted Yuri. "I have a feeling we'll find something."

The heat under their feet was getting intense. They passed by a dozen solid oak doors in ascending importance, it seemed, 'senior this and vice that,' until finding a set of large double doors marked 'Director.' The office was locked. Taras tried kicking it in, to no effect. Yuri stepped back and lunged at it with his shoulder. He felt some give. "Let's do it together," he yelled above the crackling sounds of fire and small explosions. They hit it as one and the doors sprang open.

There was a large wood-paneled suite filled with expensive leather furniture. A second door with the director's name on it was unlocked. They rushed in. File drawers were left open and papers strewn on the floor. A large safe was also open. Yuri bent down and looked inside it. In the back was a black leather bound ledger that had either been overlooked or left behind. Yuri opened it. "Statement of Accounts," it said on the first page. It looked important. They had no time left. Already, thick black smoke was pouring into the office from the hallway and the floor threatened to ignite below their feet. It was getting hard to breathe.

"Let's get out of here," Taras screamed. Yuri shut the ledger, grabbed some files off the desk, and bolted for the door. It was dark as pitch and the heat was singing their hair. They rushed back the way they came, blindly running down three flights of stairs, past firemen in orange suits and gas masks. They emerged finally into the fresh air, gasping for breath, their faces blackened by smoke, unharmed.

Dora threw her arms around Yuri and pressed her mouth to his. "I was so scared," she said. He could see she had been crying.

"I don't want to lose you, Yuri. I can't live without you. You're my life now." He kissed her again, pressing her to him. "I won't leave you again. I promise."

They stepped back from each other. "You won't believe what we found," he told her.

He handed Dora an armful of files they had taken from the director's desk and the black ledger."

She opened the ledger and skimmed through it. "These appear to be accounts of payments by the Party of Regions to various politicians and contractors," Dora said. "I think these are records of bribes. And, look at all these payments to that creep Paul Manafort, millions of dollars. This ledger is dynamite!"

Morris turned to Dora. "Who do you know who can make sense of all this and get it out to the media?"

"Serhiy Leshchenko. I just saw him over there. He's a member of parliament but also a really good journalist."

They found him standing among a crowd watching the fire and pulled him aside, thrusting the files and ledger into his hands with a quick, breathless explanation.

"Dora, this is fucking amazing," Leshchenko said as he looked down the ledger. "This is the evidence we need to put these fuck-heads in jail. You should get a Pulitzer for this and another one for your expose of how the president is sending the nation's money to his own secret offshore accounts."

"Taras and Yuri get all the credit for this one," she said.

They decided to return to the Maidan where protesters were gathering for a final defense. All around them, the sound of gunfire increased as the Berkut drove the protesters back towards the square. There were thousands of people crowding in the street. Yuri recalled the Jews who were herded towards the Babi Yar killing fields. Suddenly they heard the sharp popping sound of a machine gun, a weapon that hadn't been used up to now, an ominous development that prompted both police and protesters to run back to their positions. "Whose side is that?" asked Dora.

"Not ours," said Morris. They hurried back towards the Maidan. As they ran along Instytutska Street, they saw the Berkut and the "titushki," thousands of mercenary thugs released from jails and armed by the police, start savagely beating demonstrators. Over the next ten minutes, as they watched from what they hoped was a safe distance, they saw water cannons, tear gas and stun grenades thrown in a frenzy at the protesters, several of whom began to fall from sniper fire.

"But police were also being killed," said an American journalist retreating beside them. "I saw several riot police go down. At least ten of them had been shot by snipers firing from the seventh and eleventh floors of the Hotel Ukraina."

"Those are ours," Morris whispered to Taras. "I know their sound."

"Makes sense. Bandera controls those buildings," Taras said.

But something was horribly wrong, Yuri realized. Other shots from the eleventh floor of the Ukraina were striking protesters, and not just the police. With the shooting intensifying, they took shelter behind a garbage bin with a dozen others. Yuri saw several unarmed demonstrators cut down just meters from them. He couldn't believe what he was seeing.

"Oh, fuck! They're killing our own people," cried out Taras. "It's a false flag operation. They want a massacre."

Before Yuri could stop him, Taras bolted towards the Ukraina. "They can't do this," he yelled. He held up a white handkerchief above his head. "Glory to Ukraine! Hold your fire." Yuri stood up to run after him, heard a deafening roar of rifle fire and explosions, and then, as if the world had turned silent, saw a single shot hit Taras in the chest. He fell spread eagle onto the snow. Yuri rushed after him, grabbing a metal shield from one of the slain protesters. When he got to Taras, a pool of fresh blood had spread beneath him. Yuri turned him over. Taras tried to sit up but blood was gurgling from his mouth. He smiled at Yuri, then shut his eyes and fell to the ground.

Yuri looked back helplessly at his friends. Morris and Dora held Yana, but she broke away and ran to Taras. Crouching behind the shield that Yuri held, she cradled Taras's head against her breasts and cried as if she would never stop .Yuri was in utter despair. He felt responsible. He had to stop this before Dora or Yana got killed. Still holding the shield to protect them, he dragged Taras by one foot, leaving a red scar across the snow, back to the garbage bin. He crouched helplessly as Morris and Dora tried to comfort Yana. Then Morris stood without protection, put his yarmulke on and recited the Shema.

Shema yisraekl, Adonai loheinu, Adonai echad.

Hear O Israel, the Lord our God, the Lord is one.

Seizing the shield again, Yuri stood up and began to walk steadily towards the Ukraina. Dora went to stop him, but Morris tackled her and held her behind the garbage bin. "You promised you wouldn't leave me!" she cried after him. He heard her, but nothing could stop him. There were shots hitting the ground around Yuri and a few that struck the shield, but he continued walking in a straight line towards the Ukraina Hotel. Miraculously, he got to the entrance, which was guarded by Bandera volunteers armed with the Kalashnikov-based hunting rifles he had procured for them.

"I need to see Mroz," he demanded.

The guard looked past him, and he heard a voice say, "It's OK."

Turning, he saw Andriy Mroz standing with six bodyguards in camouflage uniforms with Bandera Brigade insignias.

Yuri stepped up to him. "You killed Taras!" he yelled, white with anger.

Mroz shrugged. "I don't know what you mean."

"The weapons we gave you are for fighting the Russians, not our heroes!" Yuri cried.

"I'm sorry. I, too, have lost friends," said Mroz. "But I swear to you, it wasn't us."

"It must stop now. Or everything stops. Understand? "Do you understand?"

Mroz nodded but said nothing, then walked back into the hotel. Yuri turned and, holding the shield behind him, returned to his family.

They had located a stretcher and were lifting Taras onto it when they saw Yuri coming. Dora threw her arms around him sobbing, while he held her tight, then held Yana.

"Was it a false flag operation?" he asked Morris.

"It could be or it could be the Russians making it look like a false flag. There's no way to know now," said Morris.

"Is it worth it?" Dora whispered. "All the lives we lost?"

He looked over her shoulder into Morris's eyes.

"Is it worth it?" he repeated.

Morris looked at each of them. "We are fighting for Taras now," he said, pausing for a moment. "And for Ukraine. Glory to the heroes."

Chapter 71

They bore Taras's body in silence to St. Michael's, where several initiates took the stretcher and its grim burden to the morgue that had been set up in the rear of the monastery. Yuri wanted to return to the battle but waited, after Yana refused to leave the body of her lover. "He proposed to me this morning," she told them. "Got down on his knees on that blood sticky floor at the Trade Union hospital and told me he wanted to be with me the rest of his life." It took her a minute before she could go on. "I guess he *was* with me for the rest of his life. We were going to get married as soon as this shit was over. We wanted a ceremony right here at St. Michael's.

Yuri felt hollowed out inside. Yana's fiancé was dead before she was even 19. She seemed so much older than that. He could see she had found a meaning in life that had escaped her growing up. She had lost her lover, but his cause was hers now, too.

By the time the four of them got back to the Maidan, it was dark, and the protesters appeared to be making their last stand against the armed might of the security forces. Yuri scanned the scene. They were encircled on all sides. Then there was a roar from the east side of the square as a police armored personnel carrier drove through the barricades, crashing into the crowds. It was met by dozens of Molotov cocktails setting it on fire.

Yuri noticed that the Berkut, the police, and the *titushki* had taken over the October Palace and a footbridge, giving them control of the heights above the square. They were trapped, he realized. He watched helplessly as the police lobbed Molotov cocktails, setting the tent city on fire.

Fire was everywhere. There were constant explosions throughout the square. But no one left. Yuri grabbed a megaphone from the stage and ran towards the burning tents.

"The fire is our shield!" he shouted. "Throw tires, create a wall of smoke!"

As if they had been waiting for instructions, people began throwing the tires that were on the barricades on the flaming tents, sending up a curtain of heavy black smoke. The winds were in their favor, blowing the smoke up towards the footbridge, driving the police back. Soon the protesters surged against them. With the police ceding the high ground once, an uneasy stalemate again took hold. Both sides paused to take a breath.

From the stage, leaders of parliamentary opposition parties announced, "a small victory," that they had reached an agreement with the president for a truce and for elections to be held in December, nine months away. But the protesters reacted with fury, screaming at the politicians for even meeting with him. They wanted him out, now.

Yuri recognized Volodymyr Parasiuk, the commander of Maidan's self-defense forces, who grabbed the microphone from one of the politicians, and shouted to the angry crowd, "Glory to Ukraine! Glory to the heroes!" The demonstrators roared back. "If the president doesn't resign by 10 a.m. tomorrow, I swear we will go on an armed offensive," Parasiuk declared. "My compatriot was shot down! He had a wife and a baby. And our leaders shake hands with these murderers! Shame on them!"

"Resign! Resign!" chanted the crowd.

Thousands of cell phones recorded everything. Television crews from dozens of countries filmed every battle, broadcasting graphic footage of the fights, injuries and death, and resolve of the protesters. Yuri and Dora were standing close to a tent for the international media when word began to spread that Zakharchenko, the hated interior minister, and the chief prosecutor had fled Kyiv with their families. Dmytro Firtash had also evacuated his wife and children to Vienna, one of the reporters told Yuri. And there were rumors that 17 members of the Party of Regions had quit, leaving the president without a majority in the parliament.

"They will crumble," said a voice behind Yuri. He turned to see a smiling Kolomoysky, looking ever like Father Christmas, with

Volodymyr Zelensky, the comedian who played the president on TV. Kolomoysky held open his arms and embraced Yuri and Morris and shook hands with Yana and Dora.

"So, you're the hero of the Bar Mitzvah, I understand," Kolomoysky said to Dora. The story of her taser gun attack after the failed kidnapping had filtered back to the congregants. He turned to Yuri. "I think your Mr. Raskolnovitch and his president will not be around much longer. The regime is beginning to fall apart. The massacre on Institutska has galvanized the West. The foreign ministers of Germany, France, and Poland are negotiating with the opposition and the president along with the foreign minister of Russia."

"We were there on Institutska," said Yuri. "Our best friend was shot dead there. Do you think it could have been a black flag operation?"

"We will never know. It will be like the Kennedy assassination. But whoever was behind it, it is an indelible tragedy," said Kolomoysky.

"The West must do something to stop this," said Yuri.

"They are. They are," Kolomoysky told him.

Indeed, Yuri noticed a change in the atmosphere of the crowd after the latest speeches, as if the barometric pressure had suddenly dropped. The fighting had ebbed after the riot police retreated from the footbridge and the October Palace. And the political agreement, although roundly rejected by the protesters, showed that the government was beginning to make concessions. From the stage a female rock star led everyone in the national anthem.

"Yuri, I have been meeting with the opposition parties. They're forming an interim government and have asked me to be the Governor in Dnipropetrovsk. They want to know what role you want," said Kolomoysky.

Yuri laughed. "Let me think about that," he said. He found it so ironic that he, a former janitor of animal cages, would be offered a high position. He was an oligarch now, wasn't he? But Taras had not died so that bad oligarchs would be traded for good ones. The system of corruption would have to change after so much sacrifice.

A group of young teenagers, recognizing Zelensky, came up to them. A girl of sixteen said, "We want you to be president, not just on television." The others applauded.

"Maybe when you can vote," Zelensky answered. They did not ask for his autograph, not at this time, not on such sacred ground.

When they left, Kolomoysky said to Yuri, "We'll speak again tomorrow."

Uncle Morris, Yuri, Yana and Dora then walked up

Hrushevskoho towards the parliament to see what the security forces were doing.

"Oh, my God, look," said Dora. "They're moving out."

Ahead of them, thousands of black-clad warriors were retreating, personnel carriers, buses and police trucks were turning around and heading away from the square. Yana, over-whelmed, began to cry. Dora took Yuri's hand. "It's happening," she said.

They dashed back to the Maidan, where they saw that all eyes were on the Main Clock Tower, 24 meters high, whose 7x4 meter screen was showing the news. It was a solemn moment. The announcer reported that the foreign ministers of France, Germany, and Poland had negotiated an "Agreement on the Settlement of the Political Crisis in Ukraine," calling for elections in one month, the return of all security forces to their barracks, and the restoration of the 2004 Constitution, which was one of the protesters' key demands. The Russian Foreign Minister, Vladimir Lukin, had refused to sign on to the agreement. Yuri could barely breathe as the screen switched to live coverage from the floor of parliament. The Speaker read a resolution to remove the president from office. As the ballots were recorded, a roar began that grew louder and louder until the final vote, 328 to 0.

People all around them wept with joy, applauded, broke into dance, hugged strangers, and prayed. It was over. "Glory to Ukraine. Glory to the Heroes!" they shouted once again. Morris held Yana, who was sobbing into his parka. "Glory to Taras," he whispered to her.

Dora and Yuri kissed, cheeks wet with tears. "I love you Dora," he said.

Dora stared into his eyes, "I see you, Yuri Yavlinsky. I believe in you and I love you, too," she said.

Chapter 72

An eclectic group of mourners gathered at dawn in the small cemetery behind St. Michael's monastery. Mixed among Taras's relatives, dressed in black, and the priests and initiates, in their black habits and black hoods, were a dozen Ultras in their bright team colors. The skies were dark and gray. An acrid smell of smoke still lingered from the fires of the night before. Only at the end of the service, when the priests chanted the Trisagion Hymn, could Yana see the first rays of sun strike the golden domes.

Yuri and Dora held Yana between them. There were no tears left for her to relieve her grief. She felt dry as ash. She had wanted to speak, to honor Taras's courage and proclaim her love for him, but she felt any words she could say would be just breaths in the wind. "Glory to Ukraine. Glory to the Heroes," she mouthed in silence. She would go on, she told herself. Taras's spirit would live inside her.

When the burial ended, Yana joined Yuri as he gathered the Ultras in a group off to the side and asked them to join him in a final operation. Taras would have approved.

. . .

Viktor Raskolnovitch sat on the floor of his library, alone. A bottle of cognac lay half empty next to him. The glass display cases that once held the second greatest collection of Faberge Eggs in the world were bare. Books were strewn about the floor. There was no one to light the logs in the cavernous fireplace. He was looking down at a letter crumbled in his left hand when Dima Prokofiev walked in without knocking.

"I'm leaving," Prokofiev announced, standing over him. "I'm taking the family to Montenegro. We were lucky to get the last seats on the plane. It seems that even in the 'new Ukraine' bribes still work."

Raskolnovitch looked up at him. He wanted to protest, but there was no fight left in him. He felt maudlin, a feeling that was new to him. He thought he saw scorn in Dima's face. He opened his mouth but couldn't decide what to say.

Prokofiev broke the silence. "Viktor Ivanovich," he said, nodding his head respectfully, then turned on his heels and left.

Raskolnovitch uncrumpled the letter and read it again. It informed him that the bank that held the mortgage on his mansion and his helicopter had been sold and the new owner was demanding immediate payment of the outstanding loans. He crushed the letter again, got up, and threw it into the cold fireplace. *Where are all the servants?* he asked himself, even though he knew the answer. He wanted someone to light a fire.

He opened the twelve-foot high oak doors and wandered down the hallway, bottle in hand, his footsteps echoing behind him, each room he passed littered with odds and ends. His staff had abandoned him and grabbed what they could on their way out. What paintings he had not previously packed and shipped abroad were gone, leaving behind the faded outlines of their shapes. In one of the rooms the glass prisms were missing from a 17th Century chandelier. He slumped to the floor.

He half expected Toni to walk in. He could not now conjure

up the anger he had felt after discovering her lipsticked message on the yacht. She had defeated him, yet a part of him admired her for it. He was never good at love. He was glad he had not killed her. *Beautiful women and Faberge Eggs should be handled with great care.*

His mind abruptly turned to his mother. She had cried when he enlisted and then had gone to the Air Force recruitment center to implore them not to accept him. The last time he saw her, she dragged him to church and forced him to pray with her. He was devastated when she died and the Air Force wouldn't allow him to go home for her funeral.

She would judge him a failure. He was everything she despised in this world, with his greed, his debauchery, his mistreatment of women. Toni was his path to redemption, and he had failed to take it. He deserved his fate. He always felt that suicide was for losers, but it was a way out of his misery. He pictured himself flying as high as he could go in his helicopter before crashing it in an empty field. It was a comforting thought, but it would be the ultimate act of faithlessness that a son could commit.

He remembered his first wife who deserted him and his second who wanted only his money and Toni who had so easily made a fool of him. He felt his heart racing and reached in his pocket for his pills. *Where were they?*

For some odd reason his mind flashed back to riding the children's merry-go-round in the little park behind his Soviet-era apartment complex, which he spun faster and faster, frightening the other kids. He was the neighborhood bully even back then. But now he felt the world accelerating around him and he feared its centrifugal force. He flashed on his friend, Grisha, and how he had held him in a headlock and punched his nose till the blood poured out like a faucet. *Where are those damn pills?*

He stood up, wobbly, and wandered through the eerily empty

mansion imagining the ghosts of centuries past. *Surely, the security guards would still be on duty.* He lumbered down the great stairway and then another to the basement and through the long narrow hallway with the exposed heating ducts, past the gym, and came to a stop by the nerve center of his elaborate security system. It was a small room, its walls covered with dozens of TV monitors. The door was open, the room vacant. The monitors displayed empty scenes of inactivity—except for one.

Coming across the outer perimeter on the south side, across the fairway on the eighteenth hole of the golf course, was a group of young men in their team jerseys holding rifles and baseball bats, running towards the house. At their head, he recognized the "boy," the Jew Yavlinsky, who appeared to be shouting something to them. Next to him, holding a Kalashnikov, was a taller man wearing a yarmulke.

The acid taste of panic rose in his throat. He reached in his pocket, again searching for his pills. His heart was racing out of control. He tore open the gun cabinet, but it had been stripped bare. On the monitor he could see the attackers closing in on the mansion.

He ran back through the basement hallway, tripped on some cables, got up, and sprinted up the servants' stairs that led to the kitchen. Food was strewn on the floor and the cabinets were emptied. He pushed open the screen door to the side porch and, wheezing and out of breath, walked briskly past the statue of Lybid towards the airplane hangar and the helicopter parked outside. He could hear the attackers yelling as they approached the front stairs.

Raskolnovitch was drenched in sweat. His heart was pounding irregularly. He had trouble getting into the cockpit but finally managed to struggle into the pilot's seat.

The key was not in the ignition as it should be. He frantically rifled the glove compartment and then found it on the floor. He put on his helmet, made sure his throttle was closed, turned on the master switch, flicked on the battery, held the primer for five seconds, and then pushed the starter. With a whirl, the engine came to life. As it warmed, he saw the Yavlinsky kid and his gang come running across the asphalt towards him. As the helicopter lifted off the ground, he saw one of them fire a hunting rifle at him and miss.

Raskolnovitch flew vertically up into the gray sky. He glanced at his altimeter, deciding to go higher than he had ever flown before, higher than his perilous flights over the Hindu Kush where the air was too thin for the rotors to operate. His heart hurt as if it were being crushed in a vice and ripped apart. The forest below him receded ever further. He thought of his mother and began to cry.

At that very moment, a phone rang in his head-set. It was his *krysha*. Raskolnovitch listened, then leveled off, and put the copter into a slow descent, coming in to land on a manicured expanse of lawn. In minutes the former President of Ukraine climbed into the cockpit. .

"It's time to go," said Raskolnovitch, and he lifted off the ground.

Chapter 73

Yuri walked out of the Politeknichnyi Instyutut metro on the first warm day of spring into the bright light of Pushkin Park. Most of the snow had melted and some of the trees were beginning to leaf out. He smiled when he noticed a clump of pink and blue crocuses along the path. Seasons change. The endless brutal winter was surrendering its hold over Kyiv. As he walked, cardinals serenaded him with songs of love. Yet he felt vaguely apprehensive. You never knew what to expect when you return to such an important place in your life.

After three minutes, he came to the entrance. There were a dozen families, mostly women with children, standing in line for tickets. Everyone looked happy. He bought a ticket and walked in. Passing the pond with the pink flamingos and the great brown pelicans, he headed towards the primates. The petting zoo was filled with the sounds of laughing children. He watched a toddler chase a baby goat, and he walked by a mother reaching across a fence to feed a cracker to a bison. A man holding a baby on his shoulders tried to attract the attention of a two-humped camel lounging in the dirt. The animals looked healthier than when he left and there seemed to be more of them.

The male gorilla was sleeping with his head resting on his folded arms, as if he had fallen asleep at his desk. But swinging towards Yuri on hanging ropes came Lucy, the baby. She clattered along the chain link fence to him and stuck her little hand out through it.

"My you've grown since I left," said Yuri. "I brought you a treat."

He pulled a banana from his jacket and handed it to her. She knew just what to do, plopping herself on the dirt and peeling it. As she took her first bite, she looked up at Yuri. He could swear she was smiling.

Yuri turned and began walking towards the elephant house, past the lions, and the striped tigers. His heart began to beat faster when he approached the brown bears. There were still three of them in the cage, as before. He wondered whether he might be able to track where the female cub was taken and reunite them. But the bears looked well fed, better than he had ever seen them. They were eating and paid him no attention.

Ahead of him was the cinder block elephant house. There was no sign of Danylo outside. The yard was empty. Yuri had worried that the old bull might have died, and he braced himself for the loss. He walked in back and found the door unlocked and quietly let himself in the paddock. There was a shaft of light coming from a high window that lit a rectangle on the empty floor. His heart sank. But as his eyes adjusted, he saw a baby elephant facing away from him, swinging its tail behind it. Then in the corner, he saw Danylo and the old bull saw him.

Raising his trunk in greeting, Danylo lumbered towards him and laid his trunk on Yuri's shoulder.

"It's good to see you, old man. I see you have a new friend."

Yuri closed his eyes and took in all that had happened since they parted: the many people killed, the love he had found, the change in his fortunes. Everything about his life had transformed. He thought about Bubbie and Taras, his step-dad, the confrontation in Mariinsky Park, the escape from Prague, the synagogue kidnapping and the battles on the Maidan. He petted Danylo's trunk. "We're gonna be all right," he said.

Just then, someone shouted, "Don't get so close to the elephants."

Yuri whirled around and saw Mykola holding an iron rake in his hand.

"Gotcha, didn't I?" said Mykola. "I thought you were dead, Yuri. The police were searching for you and your sister after the killings in your apartment." He paused a moment. "I'm sorry about all that. I know how much you loved your Bubbie."

They embraced. Danylo swung his trunk back and forth.

"I'm fine. I'm good," Yuri said. "It's a very long story. Maybe we can go for a beer after work. I'm glad you're working here again."

"Yeah, some anonymous philanthropist gave a bunch of money to save the zoo and hire us all back. I kept hoping you'd be hired back, too. Things are better now. I got paid for all the back paychecks we missed. You're probably owed some, too."

Yuri held out a long cardboard oval tube. "Here, this is for you. I'd like you to have it."

Inside, tightly rolled, was the drawing that Yuri had worked on for four years, now expertly restored.

"I'd promised to show it to you someday, and I just thought this was a good time to pass it on. You can see that it isn't finished."

Mykola unrolled it in amazement and started laughing the moment he realized who was depicted and what they were doing.

"Oh, my God. Is that Putin and Hillary Clinton? And

Marilyn Monroe?" he exclaimed, peering at each of the tiny drawings. He looked up. "But you have to finish this.".

Yuri smiled. "No, I'm done with it. It was a different life. I may draw again, but I really need to find some different subjects. It's yours. Enjoy it."

With that, he said he needed to see the director before the boss left, and the two men made plans to meet after that.

Yuri walked back past the elephant house again, inhaling the pungent smell of dung that was so familiar to him and up the steps of the red brick administration building to the director's office. The door was open. Yuri tapped lightly on it and entered. The chandelier was missing virtually all of its prisms now. There were open boxes on the desk and the director was filling them with framed photographs hanging on the wall. Yuri noticed that the men shown shaking the director's hand or standing next to him were all politicians from the Party of Regions, the former president's party. He had forgotten that Evgeny Khrytor was a deputy in the Rada.

"Yuri, so good to see you. I wondered what had happened to you after all that fuss in the news. How are you?" He didn't offer to shake his hand.

"I'm good. I'm getting married," he said.

"That's wonderful. Things are much better here, than when you left. You can have your old job back, if you want."

Yuri smiled but said nothing.

"Well, as you can see," said the director, "I'm clearing out. It's time for someone else to take this job."

"I'm sorry for you," said Yuri.

"Everything's so political now," said the director, not stopping at his task. "What can I do for you?"

Yuri reached into his inside jacket pocket and pulled out a yellow envelope. Inside on government letterhead was a formal letter signed by Oleksadr Turchynov, Acting Prime Minister of the Interim Government of Ukraine.

"By order of the Interim Council of Ministers, as authorized by the Parliament on February 23, 2014, I hereby appoint Yuri Yavlinsky to be the director of the Kyiv Zoo with all the authority residing therein, effective immediately."

The big man's hands shook as he read the directive and reread it. Handing it back to Yuri, he said, "Good luck."

"I'll need all I can," said Yuri. Then he reached his hand out and they shook for the last time.

About the Author

My passion is for human freedom. I became interested in the role of media and social change as a political activist. For the past forty years my colleagues and I have been involved in establishing independent media in more than 100 countries. I founded Internews, a global non-profit organization, to do this work.

We have seen firsthand the power of information to change peoples' lives. Sometimes it's watching residents of a refugee camp get information in their native language from a radio station we helped set up with a staff we trained. It's protecting journalists in closed states. It's covering intimate public health issues like HIV/AIDS with expertise and compassion. It's assisting a devastated community following an earthquake or humanitarian disaster with vital information that saves lives. Empowering local voices all over the world.

* * *

David Hoffman is the author of seven books and has been a contributor to *The New York Times*, *The Washington Post*, *Foreign Affairs Magazine*, *The Wall Street Journal*, *USA Today* and other publications. He founded Internews in 1982. He won an Emmy Award for the Capital-to-Capital series on ABC and was the first recipient of the European Commission Humanitarian Award for human rights broadcasting. He led Internews' project to support the establishment of the first independent news agency, television stations and tv network following Ukraine's independence in 1991.

Made in the USA
Las Vegas, NV
09 March 2023

68741513R00256